Lucy Diamond

The Best Days of Our Lives

QUERCUS

First published in Great Britain in 2023 by

QUERCUS

Quercus Editions Ltd
Carmelite House
50 Victoria Embankment
London EC4Y 0DZ

An Hachette UK company

A CIP catalogue record for this book is available
from the British Library

HB ISBN 978 1 52942 038 8
TPB ISBN 978 1 52942 040 1

10 9 8 7 6 5 4 3 2 1

Typeset by CC Book Production
Printed and bound in Great Britain by Clays Ltd, Elcograf S.p.A.

The Best Days
of Our Lives

Prologue

Everything could change so much in a year. Twelve months ago today, on her thirty-fourth birthday, Leni had woken up to the sound of Adam clattering around in the kitchen of their Ealing flat, making her a surprise breakfast. Things weren't perfect between them, sure – they were rowing on and off, both stressing about whether or not their final round of IVF would work – but he'd put in the effort with poached eggs, coffee and orange juice at least. He'd even gone out to the garden in his boxers to snip a couple of white shrub roses to slot into a glass of water, their velvety perfumed heads nodding from the tray as he re-entered the bedroom with a cheery 'Happy birthday!' He was trying, in other words – they both were – and as she saw him there in the doorway, giving it his best shot in the role of loving husband, she thought, *Okay, we can do this. We're going to be all right.*

A year on, and she was starting the day in a different bedroom, in a smaller, cheaper flat all alone, unless you included her ginger rescue cat, Hamish. So far his sum contribution to festivities had been a dead mouse on the kitchen floor that morning, a gift she could have done without. 'I appreciate the effort, Haymo,' she said, picking up the stiff little corpse with a piece of kitchen roll, feeling a pang for its delicate pink feet. 'But, you know, sometimes less is more, mate, do you hear me?'

She pushed open the back door; mid-May and it was unseasonably warm. A cabbage-white butterfly fluttered in jerky zigzags across the garden and the sight of its papery wings beating felt like an encouragement. Keep going, she reminded herself, the sunshine falling benevolent and golden against her bare legs. Keep flying. Her family were coming to celebrate with her today, and they would fill the place with laughter and chat; they would eat and drink and reminisce. The comforting weight of familiarity and belonging would settle upon her, the layers of so many other birthdays and good times from years gone by. Here you are. These are your people. They've got your back, remember?

'This is where it all turns around,' she pep-talked herself, heading for the shower. 'Life begins at thirty-five.' And who knew, by this time next year, she could be madly in love with a handsome prince, radiant with a surprise pregnancy ('It was meant to be!') and looking forward to a whole new wonderful chapter. There was a happy-ever-after out there somewhere, Leni was certain of it.

'Ta-dah! Have you got any candles, Len?'

It was a few hours later and Alice was in the kitchen holding a plate where she'd arranged the mini brownies into a chocolate rockery. They looked about as dry and hard as real rocks, Leni thought, glancing round from where she was carving the roast chicken. *I'll bring cake, obviously!* Alice had said during the week, because she was the best baker in the family and prided herself on her birthday bakes. Last year, for example, she'd appeared with an incredible chocolate and hazelnut meringue creation, and the year before, the most heavenly devil's food cake with a praline topping. The vision of her sister, apron on, whipping up some new chocolatey masterpiece for her had sparked a little match inside Leni, the small act of love a welcome light in the darkness. But then Alice had arrived with a plastic box of supermarket-branded brownies and excuses about being *just so insanely busy at work*, and the bright flickering flame inside her had promptly been snuffed out.

It didn't matter, she told herself. There were more important things than cake. Anyway – silver lining – at least Alice hadn't brought Noah with her. Apparently he'd come down with another of his migraines; it was uncanny how they always struck whenever he had to do something on Alice's behalf.

'Cake candles? No, sorry,' she replied, dismembering the bronzed chicken legs. When she and Adam split up, he'd stayed on in the Ealing flat and she'd been the one to move out, which meant that all of the vaguely useless detritus you accumulated through years of marriage – spare batteries and cake candles and Sellotape – had stayed put in the bottom kitchen drawer of their old place. For Leni to have packed and taken any of it would have seemed petty, but now, as a consequence, she kept being reminded of all that she'd once had and then lost.

'Uh-oh,' came Molly's voice from across the room. *A*

compact through-plan living space, the estate agent had called it, when Leni was trailing around west London looking at the scant few one-bedroom flats affordable on a divorced teacher's budget. Translated, this meant the kitchen had a sofa and telly at one end, which was where Will, her brother, was currently sitting with his giggling, hair-flicking girlfriend, Molly. It was the first time Leni had met her – Will seemed to operate a revolving-door policy with his love life – but the couple were apparently at the surgically attached stage. Molly had been perched on Will's lap since they arrived, while he looked permanently dazed with lust. 'Is that a *chicken*?' the hair-flicker asked now in a slightly too loud whisper. 'Babe, you did tell your sister I was vegetarian, didn't you?'

Leni's jaw clenched, her hand tightening on the knife because no, obviously Will hadn't told her anything of the sort. 'There are plenty of vegetables,' she said brightly without turning round. It was the voice she used with her class of nine-year-olds – cheery but firm. *We're not going to make a silly fuss about this, are we?* She tried to catch Alice's eye – the two of them had form when it came to post-match analyses of Will's girlfriends, and she could already imagine her sister's wicked, wide-eyed 'Is that a *chicken*?' impression, complete with all the mannerisms – but Alice was preoccupied, peering into cupboards. 'How about some icing sugar?' she was asking. 'Edible glitter?'

The doorbell rang at that moment, thankfully, and Leni escaped the room, head jangling, feeling as if everything was out of kilter today, as if she couldn't quite align herself with the happy mood of togetherness previously envisaged. It had only been a few months since her divorce and she still felt so depleted and fragile; she wasn't sure she could remember how to behave like the person they expected her to be any more. Was she acting too uptight? Should she try harder to care about the edible glitter situation? Yesterday's strange encounter flashed back into her head — the man who'd done a double take on hearing her name. *Coincidence!* he'd said, blinking and staring at her in an unnervingly intent way. *I used to know a Leni McKenzie.*

Yeah, tell me about it, she thought to herself now. *I wish she'd hurry up and come back.*

'Happy birthday, darling! So sorry we're late. Traffic was appalling and then it took us forever to find a parking space. But here we are at last!'

Here they were indeed, nearly two hours late — Leni's mum, Belinda, and her partner, Ray. Wearing a yellow silk shirt with lots of necklaces, Belinda had brought cellophane-wrapped peonies that rustled against Leni's back as she enfolded her in a perfumed hug. Despite everything, Leni sank gratefully into her mum's warmth, already looking forward to telling her about yesterday's unexpected twist. *You'll never guess who turned up at work!* she imagined herself saying, anticipating the way her mum's eyes would flick open a little wider, the laugh that would bubble up in her throat. Belinda loved surprises.

That could wait though; right now her mum was disentangling herself, necklaces jingling, with the air of a woman who wanted to get on with the day. 'Any word from your dad? Is he joining us?' she asked, giving Leni a beady look.

5

'Nope, nothing.' Leni hugged Ray, who, as usual, was wearing a long-sleeved T-shirt with some obscure band name on the front, plus jeans. Years ago, he'd worked in the music industry, getting himself into all kinds of trouble in the process. He'd left the business and retrained as a landscape architect, but still dressed as if he were on his way to a gig. These days he got his kicks through more acceptable hazardous activities: hang-gliding and snowboarding – sometimes even persuading Belinda to join him, much to Leni and Alice's hilarity. (Belinda trussed up in a bungee harness was an image that Leni still returned to if ever she needed cheering up; she would prob-ably still be cackling about her mother's expression of deep discomfort on her deathbed.)

'I invited him but I'm assuming he's forgotten,' she went on, deliberately airy so as to prevent any actual feelings slipping out. Her dad, honestly: there was a therapist's case study in human form if ever you needed one. You'd think after all these years, with one new wife after another briefly appearing as bit parts in the Tony McKenzie show, the rest of the family would be immune to his abominable disregard for them, but the lapses still stung. *Do you think you have daddy issues?* Adam had once asked her and she'd laughed her head off, before pretending to frown. 'Daddy ... Wait, I'm sure I've heard that word somewhere before. Remind me what it means again?'

'Not even a text?' Belinda looked exasperated as they went through to join the others. There was an immediate clatter as Hamish took one look at Ray and scuttled through the cat flap, ears back. Having been brought to the animal shelter as an underweight stray, he took against some men on sight.

'No,' she confirmed curtly, and the edge in her voice must have cut through to Alice, mid glitter-mission, because her sister promptly darted her a quick sidelong glance and came to the rescue.

'Mum! Ray! We were starting to think you'd been abducted,' she said. Crossing the room to hug them both, she touched Leni's arm in passing to let her know she was taking this one on. 'Shall I dish up the veg, Len?'

'Oh darling, you've already cooked!' Belinda cried, seeing the chicken on the side, the pans of vegetables bubbling on the hob. 'I thought I was going to do that for you?'

'Well, yeah, so did I, two hours ago, Mum,' Leni said, hoping she sounded jokey rather than plain old annoyed. Belinda was the most generous person in the world with her offers but you couldn't always guarantee them actually coming good on the day. *Plan B for Belinda!* she and Alice often said to one another. 'I thought I should get on with it.'

'On your birthday, though – oh, now I feel awful!' Belinda said, putting a hand up to her face.

A year ago, Leni might have assured her that it didn't matter, but do you know what? Today, it was starting to feel as if it did. It mattered that she'd heard Molly murmur pityingly to Will, 'She's thirty-five and still single? In this poky flat? I think I'd rather kill myself,' when they thought Leni couldn't hear. The crap brownies mattered, as did her dad's disinterest. Any minute now, Belinda would announce news of her latest friend to become a grandmother and Leni wouldn't be able to stop herself from screaming. Watch out, everyone, if the carving knife was in her hand at the time. That yellow silk shirt of her mum's would need some specialist attention at the dry-cleaners for starters.

Deep breaths, she ordered herself. Calm, kind thoughts. 'Who wants a drink?' she asked, opening the fridge to pull out a misted green bottle of Prosecco. The soft pop of the cork, the first cold mouthful could not come soon enough, she reflected darkly. She registered a momentary ache as she remembered previous birthdays where Adam had stepped up as entertainment manager, splashing out on champagne. He'd cook something flamboyant and showy that always drew admiration and compliments, mix cocktails (the more outrageous the better), and make everyone laugh, charming the room like the charisma-bomb he was. Although being married to a charisma-bomb had its downsides too, of course. You could quickly tire of having random women hanging on your husband's every word, for instance. She certainly didn't miss finding their phone numbers stuffed in his pocket, the paranoia that snaked in whenever he was unexpectedly late home. Also, while she was on the subject, show-off cooking was all well and good, but if Adam had bothered to check in with her first, she'd have chosen good old roast chicken every time.

But that was in the past now, she reminded herself. He had a new partner's family to dazzle these days, didn't he? Besides, that handsome prince who was due to appear in Leni's life any day now would not only be an absolute ace in the kitchen, he'd be modest about it too. Charming without being an egomaniac. Imagine!

'Anyone for fizz?' she said brightly.

'Bubbles!' cried Molly as if she were five. 'Yes, please!'

'Lovely,' added Belinda, bustling over to tend to the abandoned chicken. 'Let me get on with this while you pour.'

'Is everyone having a glass?' Leni asked, counting out flutes. Ray didn't drink these days, but Will, Molly and Belinda all replied yes. Alice, meanwhile, was at the sink, filling a tumbler with water.

'I'm fine with this, thanks,' she said, her long chestnut hair falling in front of her face, perhaps so that she didn't have to meet Leni's eye.

'Oh.' Leni's hand suddenly felt clammy on the bottle, her stomach turning over as her mind leapt ahead. The moment of solidarity she'd just felt with her sister seemed to blister, vanishing in the next second. Was Alice saying . . . ? Did this mean . . . ? The air seized in Leni's lungs as she tried to catch her breath. Alice was wearing pale blue cropped chino-type trousers with a black silky short-sleeved blouse, and Leni found herself peering covertly at her sister's body, wondering if her belly looked a bit rounder than usual, if her loose top was in fact hiding something.

Oh God. She didn't think she could bear it if Alice was having a baby. She might actually drop dead with envy and bitterness, after everything that had happened. She would cover up, of course, put on a good show – *oh wow! Exciting!* – because she knew all the right things to say by now. She'd be the best aunty-to-be ever too – she'd buy the cute little outfits and remember to check in after Alice's scans, conjuring up expressions of delight and wonder, clapping a hand to her heart, and then she'd go home and weep into her sofa, bilious with jealousy.

Leni popped the cork from the bottleneck, but no longer felt so steady on her feet while such unsisterly thoughts were pushing to the forefront of her mind. Was Alice seriously going to have a baby with that idiot Noah? Back in the day, the two sisters had entertained a long-running narrative that they'd marry a prince and a baron and live in neighbouring castles. Prince Antonio, Leni had christened her imaginary future husband at the time, although he'd also been Prince Brad, Prince Keanu and Prince Idris in later conversations, depending on who she was into. 'And Baron . . . Darren,' Alice had quipped, only for the name to stick throughout the years that followed. Couldn't Alice hang out a *bit* longer for the dashing, castle-owning Baron Darren of her dreams, instead of settling for good-looking but shallow Noah?

Belinda, sawing at the chicken breast, did not seem to notice the unspoken frisson between her daughters. Leni was surprised she hadn't pounced upon Alice's uncharacteristic booze refusal with a hopeful gleam in her eye. She had knitted a small white baby hat when Leni and Adam started IVF, and crocheted a little yellow jacket second time around. Then their last attempt had come to nothing, and her woollen production line ground to a halt, along with their optimism. Maybe Alice could give their mother what she wanted, because Leni had failed and failed again.

Come on. Keep it together. Happy families, remember. Glad for an excuse to hide her face, she crouched at the cupboard to retrieve her nicest plates – the set that Adam had bought

10

her for Christmas three years ago, crackle-effect porcelain in turquoise, plum and emerald shades – but her fingers were trembling. Perhaps the glass of Prosecco she'd just thrown back in a single, despairing gulp had affected her coordination, or maybe her hands were a bit sweaty, but as she stood up, then attempted to squeeze around Ray, draining the peas at the sink, she lurched sideways and somehow lost her grip on the stack of plates, which went crashing to the floor.

'Oh God!' she wailed as they smashed into pieces. 'Oh *no.*'

It was only *crockery*, she scolded herself later on when the six of them were finally squeezed around the small table for lunch, the food dished out on to the four plain white plates she had bought for everyday use, plus a couple of plastic camping plates she'd unearthed to make up the numbers. Worse things could and did happen. She might be able to glue the pieces back together, she thought, drinking more wine and trying valiantly to engage with the conversation. Trying to smile. But in the moment after they'd fallen from her grasp, smashing into so many bright broken shards on her kitchen floor, she had sunk to her knees beside them and burst into tears – for the plates, for her marriage, for her whole life.

When so many things were broken, how on earth did you go about sticking them back together again?

Chapter One

Years earlier, when Alice was eight years old, she'd had flute lessons at primary school for a while. Three of them from her class were taught in a group – her, Joe McPhee and Becky Braithwaite – but for some reason, the teacher, Mrs Janson, singled out Alice for a new nickname every week. 'Shorty,' Mrs Janson called her, probably because she was smaller than Joe and Becky; a summer baby yet to catch her peers up in height. 'Titch.' Alice tried to laugh along each time but couldn't ignore the uneasy feeling at the bottom of her tummy. It was confusing. Thus far in life, grown-ups had been mostly kind to her. In fact, until now, she'd go as far as to say that grown-ups had been pretty firm about not calling other people names. So how come this lady was allowed to? Had Alice done something wrong?

Her sister Leni was in the last year of primary school at this point. Year 6 pupils were given extra responsibilities – collecting class registers, running errands and delivering cups of tea or coffee to school visitors. 'Life skills,' the head-teacher called it, but everyone knew it was free skivvying. By coincidence, Leni was on duty this particular day, and appeared in the music room, carefully balancing a cup of coffee on a tray, just as Mrs Janson was saying, 'Oh dear, never mind, Joe,' after he'd mangled an easy scale. 'Let's see if the dwarf can manage it.'

Up until this moment, Alice had been smiling with excitement to see her sister, but when Mrs Janson's words filtered through to her – *the dwarf?!* – she was immediately consumed by a massive wave of embarrassment. She swung her gaze away, but not before she saw Leni's eyebrows shoot up in surprise. Heat flared in Alice's cheeks as she raised the flute to her lips, unable to concentrate until she'd heard the clink of the coffee cup being set down, then the soft closing of the door as Leni left.

'Does she always talk to you like that?' Leni asked that evening. The two girls were in their shared bedroom, with Leni sprawled out on her bed, admiring her non-bitten fingernails. Their mum, Belinda, had said that if Leni could stop biting her nails for a whole month, she would buy her a pot of nail varnish as a reward. There were still ten days to go but Leni, confident of success, was already in a delicious dilemma about which shade to choose, having pretty much committed to memory the entire range of options at the big Boots in town.

'Who?'

'That horrible flute teacher, calling you a dwarf. How mean!'

Alice, on the bed across the room with a comic, twiddled one of her bunches around her finger and said nothing for a moment. She'd managed to put the mortifying scene out of her head but now it leaped up once more: her teacher's sharp voice and cold blue eyes, the awkward giggles from Joe and Becky, the conviction that Alice must be a bad person who deserved the name-calling. 'I dunno,' she mumbled.

'Does Mum know she's nasty to you?' her sister persisted, chin pointy, eyes fierce; a face that said *Don't try and fob me off with a lie now.*

Alice shook her head. Belinda had a short fuse and, in hindsight, good reason to be irritable, when things had been chaotic at home for as long as Alice could remember: that horrible year after Will was born, for starters, when he was in and out of hospital with bronchiolitis and breathing difficulties, with Alice and Leni both having to stay with Janet-next-door when he was really poorly. Then their dad had moved out, initially with talk about a new job a long way away but then not reappearing for seemingly months on end. Belinda had started to say, 'Look, I don't *know*, all right?' in answer to questions about when he'd be back, with enough exasperation that even a small person could sense there might be an issue.

'No,' Alice replied, then glared at her sister with sudden suspicion. 'Don't *you* tell her,' she said, not wanting to be at the centre of any drama. Somehow it would end up being Alice's fault, she knew already. 'You won't, will you?'

Leni was back to admiring her stubby but unbitten nails. 'I'm thinking Mauve Shimmer,' she announced, wiggling her fingers with anticipation. 'Or maybe Coral Kisses. Oh, how am I going to decide?'

A week later, and it was time for another flute lesson. The door opened as usual halfway through, for the arrival of a

Year 6 pupil bearing a coffee for Mrs Janson – but to Alice's surprise, it was Leni again. This was unexpected, as was the strange expression on her sister's face: a sort of gleeful triumph, her mouth twitching in a way that made Alice think she was trying to suppress a laugh.

Minutes later, with Mrs Janson midway through her coffee, Alice realised why. 'Ugh,' spluttered the teacher, only to choke and fish about in her mouth with a look of abject horror.

'What *is* that?' cried Becky Braithwaite, eyes goggling at the small white crescent plucked from her teacher's mouth. 'Is that a *fingernail*, Miss?'

Mrs Janson looked completely ashen. 'Excuse me a minute,' she said, grabbing the cup and fleeing the room.

It turned out there were *ten* small, jagged fingernails in the coffee, bitten quickly off and added to the drink en route to the music room. '*And* a bit of spit too,' Leni said carelessly that afternoon once they were back home. 'Helena McKenzie, what on earth were you *thinking*?' Belinda had exploded, pink in the cheeks, having been called away from work to learn of this crime. 'Well, you can forget that nail varnish now, young lady. And you can forget about going round to Victoria's party at the weekend too. Fingernails in a teacher's coffee, indeed. You're in so much trouble, I can hardly even *look* at you right now!'

Leni was sanguine about the punishments – 'Vicky's already said she'll rearrange the party for when I can come, I don't care,' she told her sister with a lofty shrug – but Alice knew that the withdrawal of nail varnish rights was an absolute stinger.

The first chance she got, dragging around town with her

mum and Will some weekends later, Alice seized the opportunity to sidle back to the make-up shelves while Belinda dithered over nit shampoo brands then queued up to ask the pharmacist about cough medicine. Mauve Shimmer – straight up her right coat sleeve. Coral Kisses – straight up her left. Her heart thudded like a jackhammer as they eventually departed the shop. By then, she'd managed to secrete the two small bottles in the depths of her duffel coat pockets, all the while expecting the accusatory 'Oi!' of a security guard to boom after her. None came. She'd done it. *You see off my mean flute teacher for me, I'll shoplift nail varnish for you*, she thought, picturing the look of delight that she knew would dawn across Leni's face when Alice revealed her stolen booty. It seemed a pretty good deal, frankly.

And totally worth it, too, for my brilliant, loyal sister, she typed now, reading back through the words of her story once more before pressing *Post* and sitting back with a small sigh. It was a Sunday evening in December, five and a half months after the accident, and Alice was hunched in bed with her laptop, its screen casting blue light on to her face while a belligerent wind outside rattled the window in its frame. The memorial page was her online sanctuary, a place to which she returned frequently with updates or photos, and she loved scrolling through other people's fondly remembered stories. It was a comfort to retreat into nostalgia when real life kept tripping her up with horrible surprises. Tomorrow, for instance, she would almost certainly be called in for a little chat with her boss, following the debacle with Nicholas Pearce on Friday evening and ...

Don't, she ordered herself before any bad thoughts could take root. *Don't think about that.* She refreshed the screen instead, where comments were already appearing beneath her new post.

She was the best, wasn't she? RIP.

Love this story, Alice. Can totally imagine her doing this. Hope you're okay.

Oh Leni, we all miss you so much.

'I'm sorry, Alice,' said Rupert the next day, after he had, as expected, requested a quick word with her in his office. The grim set to his mouth signalled that the quick word would not be about a pay rise nor her fantastic work. (It probably wouldn't even be quick, Alice registered with an inner groan.) 'But the phone call from Nicholas Pearce was the final straw. I'm afraid this conversation will be minuted as a verbal warning about your misconduct. This can never happen again, do you understand?'

Leni had once confided in Alice that whenever people said fatuous things like 'Do you understand?' or 'Are you listening to me?' her instinct was to reply in the negative, if only to annoy them even more. Sitting in her boss's office now, facetiousness didn't seem a great option to Alice though. 'What, so you're saying you're taking his side over mine?' she asked, trying to choke back the *Are you fucking kidding me?* boiling within her. 'Even though he thought it was fair game to fondle my leg in a bar, and then follow me to the bus stop? When I'd made it clear that was not appropriate?'

Rupert was a successful, charming man, used to being

adored by clients and staff alike. He liked to boast that he'd dreamed up his award-winning marketing and communications agency on the back of a fag packet, but that was yet another example of his own-brand spin; Alice knew for a fact he'd relied heavily on family wealth and some very well-connected friends in the early days. Whatever – it sounded good, and she of all people understood the sheen that a slick of marketing gloss could bring. Except when it turned out that Rupert was *all* gloss, and slippery as hell with it. 'And you think him behaving that way is okay, do you?' she burst out.

'Of *course* it's not okay,' he replied, dark eyebrows sliding together. He tapped a silver pen on the desk for good measure and the tinny noise was so irritating, Alice felt like snatching it off him. Maybe even whacking him over the head with it for good measure. 'But by the sound of it, you completely overreacted. Swearing at him in a bar—'

'His hand was halfway up my thigh!'

'And pushing him in the street like some kind of oik—'

'I was scared for my own *safety*!'

'You're lucky he's not pressing charges for assault, you know. Very lucky.'

'Lucky?' Alice's voice rose almost to a screech. She'd plunge that silver pen into his eyeball in a minute. 'I didn't *assault* him. Jesus! I wish I bloody *had* assaulted him, and he'd have had it coming to him too, the dirty old pervert, I—'

'Alice—'

'And you're disciplining *me*, like this is somehow *my* fault? When I was just trying to do my *job*?'

'ALICE.' He was thundering now and she broke off, clutching

her hands together in the vain hope she might stop them from shaking. How she wished her fingernail assassin sister could burst into the room and come to her rescue. Even appear as a ghostly apparition just to frighten the bejeezus out of him. No such luck. 'That's not the only problem, though, is it?' Rupert went on. 'I might have been prepared to overlook this whole disgraceful business were it not for the fact that you've not been yourself for some months now. Many months.'

Alice hung her head. Here we go. 'It's not like I haven't had good reason,' she muttered, face blazing. *Sure, drag me into it*, she imagined Leni drawling, one eyebrow raised sardonically. *Get that excuse on his table, see if that shuts him up for a minute. There must be some perks to having a dead sister, right?*

'Absolutely,' he said, his tone softening a fraction. Not enough to change tack though. 'We're all aware that you've had a very difficult time. However.'

Oh Christ. She did not want to listen to the 'However'. She was still reeling from his dismissal of her defence just now, furious that he didn't seem able to understand how awful the encounter had been. She and Nicholas Pearce were in the bar together, supposedly to go through a few final details of the contract he was poised to sign with the agency, only for her to feel sinking dismay when she realised his actual agenda. Rupert didn't get it because he'd never had to deal with such a situation, presumably; he'd always been respected, valued for his work, taken at face value. Did he really not see that it was different for women?

'I have caught up on all the days I missed,' she said halt-ingly, wanting to pre-empt whatever criticism was coming next. 'I have worked so hard on the Red Lobster campaign; Edie and I smashed it at the presentation last week. Yes, I've had a difficult time, but I'm turning a corner now, I'm on the way up again.'

She crossed her fingers under the desk because saying she was on the way up was a massive exaggeration but, you know, marketing. She could gild a lily with the best of them.

'The thing is though, Alice,' he went on, 'this has come after months of poor time-keeping, unreliability, outbursts in meetings. And we've all been very patient with you but there comes a point when enough is enough. I'm wondering if perhaps you should take a bit more time off. Possibly look into some anger management sessions.'

Alice swallowed hard. The clock on the wall seemed to be ticking particularly loudly all of a sudden. Her skin felt sticky, her throat dry; her breath was shallow in her lungs as if she was on the verge of a panic attack. *Alice, you're, like, mentally unhinged*, Noah had shouted the day he finished with her. He'd actually put his hands up in the air as if she were a wild animal, saying he couldn't cope with the drama any more, he was sick of it. Now here was her boss intimating pretty much the same thing. *We've all been very patient with you*, as if the whole office had been bitching about her. They could sod off too, she thought in a new explosion of fury.

'Do you know what,' she said, the words spilling out of her before she even knew what they might be, 'I quit.' She got to her feet, sweat prickling in the small of her back despite it being December and Rupert ever-stingy about the office heating setting. 'I don't want to work here any more.'

'Alice—' He was doing that weary, patronising sigh that her dad sometimes used to adopt, as if she was a silly little girl. This alone was enough to make her double down on her impulse decision.

'I've got some holiday left and it's Christmas coming up,' she said. 'I'm not staying where I don't feel valued. Shove your anger management sessions – and find someone else to do your shit job while you're at it.' And then she was storming out of there, only stopping to grab her bag and coat, barging past her wide-eyed colleagues, some of whom called after her in concern – *Alice, are you okay?*

Erupting into the freezing Soho street, she half expected buildings to be collapsing around her, fires to be blazing in cars, the ground shifting beneath her feet, because that was how it felt: as if the world was ending. Leni, Noah, now her job . . . all of those solid structures in her life, everything she'd treasured six months ago, had crumbled to rubble. She put her arms around herself for a brief moment, tried to banish forever the image of Rupert's supercilious face, and stumbled blindly along the street, unsure where she was going or even what she might do next. 'Fuck,' she said aloud and then, for good measure, yelled at the top of her voice. 'FUCK!'

Chapter Two

'You know, I think you might have been all right if you hadn't said the "shit job" bit,' Lou ventured that evening, a mixture of side-eye and sympathy.

'You could probably still go back if you sent a grovelling email,' Celeste added. The three of them were squeezed around a corner table in the Queen and Compass, Alice's local pub, and she was starting to wish she'd suggested a different venue, seeing as the house band were in tonight and their set list was resolutely festive. They'd already murdered Mariah Carey's 'All I Want for Christmas', and were now trying to persuade the clientele to join in with a headbanging cover of 'Last Christmas'. 'This is a really bad time of year to lose your job, for one thing.'

These were Alice's two best friends and she was grateful to them for dropping everything in order to come out with her in commiseration, but if they thought for a minute she was regretful or about to beg for her old job back, they had completely missed the point. 'It's not gonna happen,' she said. 'Me grovelling or going back. And it's January in a few weeks anyway – I thought that was meant to be the perfect time for a new start. That's what all the adverts say.'

'True,' Lou conceded. 'Have you got anything in mind?'

'Well, first up: getting absolutely hammered,' Alice replied, raising her glass in the air with a bravado she didn't quite feel. Lou had bought them all Christmas-themed cocktails in an attempt to bolster spirits, and Alice's so-called Jingle Juice Punch had come complete with a candy-cane-striped straw plus a liberal helping of cranberries. The lead singer of the band gave a drawn-out, many-syllabled flourish to the word 'special' just then, complete with an enthusiastic drum roll from the drummer to end the song, and Alice joined in with the half-hearted applause. 'Cheers.'

She slugged back her drink, catching a tiny private look exchanged between her friends as she set the glass down. 'In the meantime,' Celeste said in a bright voice, 'we've been thinking. We know you've had a shit time of it this year, but how about us making some plans together for the next one, to keep us all going? Only I've had a few ideas – like organising some nights out? Booking in a weekend away?'

'And I was wondering about us starting a fitness challenge together,' Lou said, ignoring the look of horror that appeared immediately on Alice's face. 'Like – every month, we try a different activity. Kick-boxing or climbing or—'

'There's a women's cycling group in Hackney I keep hearing about,' Celeste put in.

'Yeah! Or go old-school and join a netball club. It could be fun! What do you think, Alice?'

What did Alice think? She thought the word 'fun' was

doing a lot of heavy lifting in that sentence, for one thing. And while she knew her friends were trying to gee her up, she'd have preferred to spend longer on the 'weekend away' option rather than the dismal image of sporting a polyester netball bib on a rainy winter's evening. 'Mmm, maybe,' she said unconvincingly, then pretended she needed the loo so that she could escape before anyone pinned her down with actual arrangements.

Inside the safety of a toilet cubicle, she leaned against the wall, the alcohol racing hectically through her bloodstream. The situation didn't seem quite real yet; it felt like a fever-dream, her storming out of the ReImagine office building, the door closing behind her. What had she done? 'You've lost it, Alice,' she remembered Noah saying, the words still smarting a full two months after they'd split up. 'You're, like, mentally unhinged. This is doing my head in, I don't want to be with you any more.'

Gorgeous, sexy, utterly shallow Noah, who'd moved in with her, holidayed with her, with whom she'd idly discussed a future, babies, commitment, before the world spun off its axis and everything went dark. Had he ever meant a word of it? Because he'd been so spectacularly shit when Leni died and Alice broke into a million tiny pieces; he could hardly scramble out of the relationship quick enough. *I could have told you he was no Baron Darren*, she'd imagined Leni intoning, while her friends had similar comments to make. 'Absolute wanker,' they chorused as one, swooping in with wine and Marks and Spencer trifle, plus a side helping of venom. 'You're better off without him. Forget him!'

To be fair to Noah, she *had* kind of lost the plot back then. If Alice had seen a woman at the side of a busy street on a dark evening, yelling incoherently, before stumbling into the road and almost getting herself killed amidst a blare of horns, the word 'unhinged' might have come to her own lips. What was more, if she'd been the one driving the car forced to swerve around a drunk woman falling into the path of traffic, she would definitely have called the police and reported this dangerous behaviour – for the woman's own safety. But at the time, Alice hadn't been thinking in rational terms. She'd been so overcome by rage, she'd felt compelled to stand at that particular spot in Shepherd's Bush, shouting her sister's name so that it would be heard, it would be known. So that nobody would forget her. 'What about planting a tree instead, love, have you thought about that?' the tired-looking police-woman asked, as Alice was bundled into the back of the cop car. 'That's what most people do and it's a lot less dramatic, on the whole.'

I'm wondering if perhaps you should take a bit more time off. Possibly look into some anger management sessions, she heard Rupert say again, and an unwanted image came to her: of her standing in the shadowy driveway of a house, an egg in her hand – and then a man appearing out of the darkness, striding towards her. *Don't you ever come here again*, he'd warned, his angular face half lit by the streetlights, his body taut like a boxer, everything about him a threat. She hadn't cared a bit though, because yeah, she was angry. You bet she bloody was.

There was a loud knock just then and she reoriented herself

with a start: pub toilet, the faint sounds of a grungy 'Santa Baby' cover drifting under the door. 'Alice? Are you all right in there?' she heard.

Lou, come to get her. No doubt they'd been fretting at the table following her departure. *Is she okay? Should we check on her, do you think?* Her friends, doing their best to haul her up from rock bottom with their plans and solidarity. *Exercise is good for mental health, isn't it?* they'd have said, cooking up schemes beforehand of how they could help her.

Then Alice remembered the way Lou and Celeste had glanced at one another when they thought she wasn't looking, and wondered if they, like Noah, thought she was unhinged, but were too nice to say so. Oh God. She'd already lost so much this year. She couldn't lose them on top of everything else.

'I'll be right there,' she called back, doing her best to sound cheery. *Come on, Alice,* she ordered herself, with a flashback to how she'd sat at the funeral, hands twisted in her lap, tears streaming down her face, vowing *I'll live for both of us from now on, Leni. I promise you I will.*

Yeah, right, she imagined Leni saying drily now, giving her a ghostly nudge. *And you sitting in the pub bogs feeling sorry for yourself is your idea of living for us both, is it? Sheesh! Don't bother on my account, will you?*

She pulled a face at the idea of her big sister bossing her around from beyond the grave, but all the same, she had a point. *That's my girl,* said Leni minutes later as she got to her feet and returned to her friends. *Up and at 'em, Alice!*

★

26

A subdued Christmas passed, the first without Leni, and Alice hunkered down with her mum and Ray at the old family home in Oxford. Together they limped through the days, propped up by plentiful carbohydrates, back-to-back old films and too much alcohol, plus Ray's insistence on dragging them out for regular walks as if they were dogs, like it or not. The year was almost over, Alice consoled herself as she returned to London with a Tupperware box of mince pies and the dazzled feeling of having been indoors for too long. Once home, she gamely put on a party dress for New Year's Eve and knocked back cocktails with her friends, trying to ignore the empty feeling inside. Next year would be better. It had to be.

January began and she fixed up some temporary work so as to keep the wolf from the mortgage payments, before returning once more to her mum's house with a stressful task looming: that of helping to sort through Leni's belongings that had been stowed up in the loft. Belinda had decided to sell up and move on, and they could put off this onerous challenge no longer.

Alice forced herself to take a calming yogic breath as her mum hauled down the concertina loft ladder first thing. It was only *stuff*, after all, she thought. Tonight, once they'd got through this, they would drink a toast to Leni and no doubt both cry a bit, but there would be a new layer of relief bedding down in the background too, because the dreaded task would be behind them by then. *It's going to be a tough day but think of the closure*, Celeste had texted that morning. Lou, meanwhile, had sent details of a Park Run on Saturday, which Alice was pretending not to have seen. That was for Future Alice to deal with, she decided, climbing the cold metal steps.

'All right?' came her mother's voice as Alice reached the top and crawled on to the dusty loft carpet. Unsurprisingly, Belinda was anxious about injury or worse befalling another member of the family. Between the time it had taken Alice to leave her flat that morning and reach Oxford approximately an hour and forty-five minutes later, Belinda had sent seven texts, including travel updates, weather updates, advice about pulling over for a break if she felt tired, plus the unhelpful worry that Alice hadn't checked her tyres lately. 'I'd be more likely to die trying to read your flipping texts on the motorway than any weather-related problem,' Alice had grumbled on arrival, but hugged her nonetheless.

Shuffling bent-backed to the pile of boxes and bin bags in the centre of the attic space, she wished for the hundredth time that her mum hadn't chosen now as the time to pack up and move house. Look at any bereavement leaflet or website, and the advice was stark: avoid making big decisions within the first year. Admittedly, Alice could hardly talk, seeing as she'd split up with Noah and impulsively quit her job, but Belinda had comprehensively outdone her. First, she'd taken early retirement from her social work job, and now she was overhauling the family home to put it on the market, which meant a bulk-buy order of magnolia paint plus countless trips to the dump. The plan was for her and Ray to buy a house in the countryside to run as a bed and breakfast, but Alice couldn't help having a few misgivings. Surely that was

28

far too many life changes in quick succession, on top of the loss of a daughter?

'I just want to keep busy,' Belinda said mutinously whenever Alice tried to persuade her to slow down. 'Being in this house makes me sad, Alice. Every single day, I'm reminded of what I've lost. And I can't keep living like that. For my own sanity, my own peace, I need a fresh start.'

Fair enough. Leni's death had thrown everything up in the air; it was like stepping into a new room and being unable to turn back. Their family had altered forever, the great chasm of loss rupturing their lives. Will had left the country, relinquishing himself to a non-stop hedonistic lifestyle. Tony was feathering the nest for family number two, and Belinda was a paint-speckled whirlwind of decluttering. They'd all pin-balled away from one another, Alice thought ruefully, her breath drifting in puffs on the freezing air like small ghosts as she picked up the first box. She wondered if they'd ever find their way back.

After Leni died, Tony had borrowed a transit van to drive down to her Ealing flat to clear out her belongings. Will had helped, the two of them returning with bin bags of clothing, and boxes of hastily packed possessions, plus Leni's cat Hamish, hissing and spitting from inside a borrowed cat carrier. Hamish had initially stayed with Belinda and Ray, but when they began redecorating last autumn, he became stressed at this further upheaval and took to peeing everywhere. With Noah's fur allergy ruling out Alice taking him in, and Will already far away in Thailand, everyone had hoped Tony and his partner Jackie might rehome the poor creature. Only ten years older than Alice, Jackie was something impressive in the financial world and owned a fabulous architect-designed barn conversion with a big garden, perfect for a cat – or so you'd think. But apparently she'd refused point-blank to take him. 'Probably too worried about getting fur on her designer clothes,' Belinda had snarked to Alice at the time.

Hamish might have gone but Leni's other belongings remained, and Alice worked steadily to pass them down to Belinda, box by box, bag by bag. She felt proprietorial about the contents – determined to sort everything as Leni would have wanted her to – as well as kind of curious too. Back on Leni's birthday, the two sisters had fallen out and, for one reason or another – a week-long hen do abroad for Leni during the May half-term, the fortnight's holiday taken by Alice and Noah in early June, general busyness – they had never seen each other again. It had haunted Alice ever since that she'd missed out on the last six weeks of her sister's life. Might there be some clues to that time within these boxes and bags?

'Any secrets in here, Len?' she murmured aloud, hauling the biggest box of all along the old carpet. 'What am I going to find out, hey?'

The box was heavy and she banged it clumsily against the top of the ladder, apologising under her breath in the next minute. After Leni and Adam had split up, Alice had helped Leni move into her new flat, lugging these same possessions into and then out of the van they'd hired, both of them determinedly cheerful. 'Oi, mind the heirlooms,' Leni had said whenever Alice took a speed bump too quickly. If Leni was watching her now, she'd be tutting and moaning about her precious 'heirlooms', Alice knew it. The thought made her smile, just a little bit. 'Yeah, yeah, all right,' she told her. 'I'm doing my best, okay?'

Down below, Belinda had carried everything through to Will's old bedroom. It had once been Alice's room, decades ago, but she'd moved in to share with Leni when their new brother came along, and she had only a few dim memories of this being her space: waking up with a nosebleed one morning, the shock of scarlet blood across the pillow; the toadstool-shaped nightlight she'd had that shone a soft pink glow through the darkness; her dad's weight at the end of the bed as he told her stories when he got in from work. Since then, the room had been home to model train tracks, toy dinosaurs and a glow-in-the-dark solar system dangling from the ceiling, all the way through to posters of pouting pin-up models and a strong smell of cheap spray deodorant and hair gel. These days, it housed Belinda's overflow wardrobe, Ray's surfboards, and a fold-up exercise bike that still had the instructions taped to the saddle, bought presumably in a short-lived flush of self-improvement. Also, as of this morning, the full collection of Leni's belongings. Alice knelt beside her mum, feeling a quickening grip of dread take hold inside her. They were doing this. *Here goes.*

'Shall we start with the clothes?' Belinda suggested, untying the handles of a bin bag. 'Might be more straightforward.' Then she stopped, a nervous look flitting across her face, still clutching the top of the bag. She was wearing mascara and sparkly gold eyeshadow, as well as a traffic-stopping pink lip-stick, but all of a sudden it was as if she'd shrivelled beneath her armour. 'Okay. We're going to get a blast of Leni's perfume, I bet, just as soon as I open this properly, and it'll probably set us both off. So brace yourself, all right? This will be tough.'

Alice nodded, steeling herself. 'Rip off that plaster, Mum.'

Belinda was right about the unmistakable fragrance rising from the clothes. The scent of her sister's favourite woody perfume practically cracked Alice's heart in two. For a moment it was as if Leni was present in the room with them, about to tell a joke or funny story. Both Alice and Belinda made laugh–cry sounds as they absorbed the shock, then, after a deep breath, they settled into a routine, distributing the bag's contents between three piles: Keep, Charity Shop, Chuck. Leni had always been tiny, two sizes slimmer than Alice at the time of her death, and so there were few clothes that Alice could fit into, which simplified what to keep. Plus, aside from all of her primary-school-teacher work clothes, Leni had hung on to a lot of her former art-student wardrobe; a style all of her own. Fake-fur jackets, plasticky-looking trousers, a healthy selection of neon items, a lot of tartan and at least seven skinny black polo-neck jumpers. Into the charity-shop mountain they went.

Glancing over at her mum, she saw Belinda delve into one of the bags with a little cry, then retrieve some woollen baby clothes – a pale lemon jacket with round buttons, a tiny white hat. Alice felt a lump in her throat as Belinda pressed them wordlessly against her cheek, pain etched across her

32

features. Clothes for a baby that wasn't to be. 'Are you okay?' she asked, reaching over to put a hand on her mum's arm. Stupid question.

Belinda exhaled, lowering the jacket and hat from her face although she didn't let go of them immediately. 'I'm okay,' she replied with a watery smile. 'Let's keep going.'

Having eventually worked through the clothes, Alice took some photos of them. Then, while her mum went to make a phone call, she added them to the online memorial page she'd set up for Leni. *These are bringing back some memories today . . .* she typed beneath the images. *I'd love to see any photos you might have of Leni wearing her wackier outfits. Please share! One of the things I miss is arranging to meet her for a drink, arriving before her (always) and looking out for her, wondering what she would turn up in! PS This particular collection will be heading to the Oxford charity shops soon, but shout if you spot something you'd like as a memento.*

What next? With her mum still out of the room, she reached for a carrier bag stuffed with papers, wondering if it contained something that would help in her quest for answers. Taking a deep breath, she tipped the contents on the floor, lightly sorting through them with her fingertips. Letters, loose photographs, birthday cards, a folder marked 'Lesson Plans' . . . Then her heart accelerated at the sight of a small pocket diary with a soft grey cover and the year stamped in gold foil in the top corner. Leni's *diary* – jackpot. What might she find inside?

Chapter Three

Before Alice had a chance to open the diary, she heard her mum's returning footsteps and instinct told her to stuff the little book into the back pocket of her jeans. Guilt pounded through her along with a shot of adrenalin as Belinda reappeared and Alice picked up a couple of old utility bills and pretended to be checking the dates. 'These have been paid, I'll start a recycling pile,' she announced, fakely efficient. She wasn't even sure why she'd hidden the diary like that; she just knew she wanted it to be her own private discovery, something of her sister's that she could pore over in peace without her mum's involvement. Was that bad? Was it mean of her not to share?

'This looks a bit more complicated than clothes,' Belinda commented, kneeling down on the other side of the papers with an apprehensive expression. She pounced on a pencil drawing amidst the paperwork. 'Oh, look! A drawing of the cat. She was so creative, wasn't she?'

Her eyes were faraway, and Alice experienced a jealous little stab inside at the adoring expression on her face. Mums weren't supposed to have favourites, of course, but Alice had long suspected that Leni was Belinda's number-one daughter, the golden girl, while Alice had always struggled to keep up. Back when she'd been seven or eight, she'd kept getting nosebleeds, but the family doctor had dismissed the problem, telling Belinda, 'It's psychological, in my opinion. Attention-seeking', as if Alice was so desperate to catch her mother's eye that she could produce blood at will, like some kind of witch.

'Yes,' she agreed now, wondering what it said about her when, even after her sister's death, she still felt a twinge of envy at any praise sent in Leni's direction. She touched her nose surreptitiously, half expecting it to start gushing blood again. Was she horrifically insecure or merely needy? And why hadn't she grown out of feeling this way?

Belinda put the drawing to one side and picked up a notebook, flicking through its pages uncertainly. 'She said we shouldn't hang on to everything,' she commented, then pulled herself up short. 'I mean ...'

She had turned a strange shade of puce, Alice noticed, but perhaps that was from the emotion. 'I talk to her,' Belinda blurted out in the next moment, fiddling with the binding of the notebook. 'I talk to Leni.'

'So do I,' Alice replied, with feeling. 'All the time. Every day.' Often quite exasperatedly, admittedly – *Why didn't you get that bloody bike sorted out? How could you have been so stupid?* – but frequently she would come across something during the day – a snippet of tabloid gossip about an old soap star they'd both fancied, or a new series of a TV drama they'd been equally mad about – and she'd want to share it with her sister. 'I nearly messaged her only this morning. It must be a muscle-memory thing.'

'No, but ...' Belinda hesitated. She seemed embarrassed for some reason. Confessional, even. 'I mean, I *really* talk to her. And she replies.'

'Mum, it's fine to talk to her. I think it would be weirder if you didn't. Whatever helps, right?' Alice picked up a sheaf of old Christmas cards and put them in a pile to be recycled. 'I have spent entire evenings rereading stupid text conversations I had with Leni and laughing till I cried. The therapist I spoke to said that was healthy, part of processing what happened. We're just working through stuff, that's all. And talking is better than ...' Now it was her turn to stumble gruffly over her words. 'You know, being angry and behaving like an idiot.'

Belinda reached over and squeezed her hand. 'Don't be hard on yourself. You loved her, that's all. And she loves you.'

The use of the present tense was jarring but Alice decided not to comment. Maybe this was a coping mechanism, a means of keeping Leni alive, she reasoned. And if it helped, where was the harm?

She picked up a large brown envelope, oddly light, and peeped inside to find a handful of peacock feathers, still somehow sellotaped to a piece of bamboo. 'Oh my God,' she said, as a hundred memories tumbled dizzily into her mind. 'Mum, look!'

Belinda put a hand on her heart, eyes damp. 'The Flying Beauties,' she said, with a noise that could equally have been a sob or a laugh.

'Flying Beauties forever,' Alice replied, emotions in tumult.

She felt as if she'd been flung back in time as she touched the frondy edges of the feathers. 'Oh gosh, Mum, I can't believe it.'

'It was that summer Will was born, wasn't it?' Belinda said.

Yes, it was the summer Will was born. Alice and Leni had been packed off to stay with their maternal grandparents in Dorset, so that their parents could have some respite during the school holidays. The two girls always shared a bunk bed there and spent ages one day playing birds and jumping off the top bunk on to a pile of duvets and pillows beneath, flapping their arms and trying to fly.

'I think I really did fly a *bit* just then. Did you see?' eight-year-old Leni would say each time she collapsed into the soft squish of bedding. 'I'm definitely getting better at it.'

Soon, bunk beds were not their only take-off point. They leaped from the tops of walls and from their grandparents' stairs. They jumped from some of the big rocks down at the beach too, their bare feet curling around the hard ridges until, with a bend of the knees and a yell of 'Lift off!' they would take flight for a split second of exhilaration before the inevitable sandy landing.

Then came the thrilling moment of discovering Grandma's battered old peacock-feather fan when poking around her bedroom one day. 'Wings!' cried Leni, her face lighting up. 'This could make the prettiest wings in the world!'

Grandma was a kind-hearted sort who recognised a passion in a small girl, and knew to take it seriously. 'What a good idea!' she said when Leni went to her, brandishing the fan, and asked if they could please cut it up to make wings please please please. Grandma carefully snipped the feathers free from their bindings, then taped them to chopped-down bamboo sticks, requisitioned from Grandad's shed.

'Now, no funny business with these, my beauties,' she warned, handing over a pair of 'wings' to Alice then a pair to Leni. 'Your mum will have my guts for garters if any bones are broken, okay?'

Alice could remember even now the updraught of air that came through the trembling, vibrant feathers with their beautiful, mysterious-looking 'eyes' at the end; how convinced she had been that, if she just tried hard enough, she'd soon be soaring off the ground.

'We're *flying* beauties now,' Leni cried, swishing and swooshing with such gusto that the pages of Grandad's newspaper, perched on the kitchen table, lifted and fell with a flutter, as if they too were possessed with the exuberance of new-found flight.

'We're the flying beauties!' Alice, nearly six, had echoed, in thrall as ever to her sister's leadership.

The Flying Beauties became their favourite game that summer. Their peacock-feather wings were too precious to take on the beach or out along the coastal path, Grandma decreed, but they were permitted around the garden and throughout the house, and the long, sunny afternoons rang with cries of 'I'm flying!' and 'Flying Beauties forever!', soft thumps of landing and whoops of delight. It had felt so glorious, so free after an intense period at home where Mum or Dad – often both of them – kept dashing away to the hospital, looking strained. Not listening properly whenever Alice or Leni tried to tell them interesting things about school. Arguing in low voices – not always that low, actually – when they thought the girls were asleep. Here at Grandma's, the two of them were the centre of the world; they were showered with love. They were the Flying Beauties. Who could ask for more?

It had continued as a shared thread between the sisters from then on. As teenagers, Leni made them both matching T-shirts one Christmas with the logo FLYING BEAUTIES FOREVER! painted above an elegant silhouette of a peacock feather. The following year, Alice was browsing a vintage jewellery stall in the covered market when she came across a bangle with a stone that shimmered iridescent green and blue, and knew instantly that Leni would get the reference. Sometimes when drunk or merely sentimental, they'd end up clinking glasses and chorusing, 'Flying Beauties forever,' like an incantation, and the connection between them would be forged all over again, shining and true, as sure as a bird in flight.

She had no idea what had happened to her peacock-feather 'wings' made so many summers ago, but somehow or other, careless, erratic Leni had managed to hang on to one of hers for all this time. Here it was, as vivid as ever, despite the prolonged thrashing about it had suffered in the name of attempted launches. Alice touched a fingertip to the delicate feather ends then pressed it to her face. 'Thank you for my heirloom, Leni,' she said under her breath, unwilling to set it down again for fear that it might dematerialise before her eyes. But it was real, a dusty weight in her hand, battered yet still shimmering. A talisman sent to help Alice through today?

★

After lunch, Alice was relieved when one of her mum's neighbours popped round to ask a favour. She wasted no time in heading back upstairs alone to open the diary, with a jolt of anticipation. The little book was laid out with a week per double page, plus a box marked 'Notes' in the bottom right-hand corner. The size meant it was for arrangements rather than any confessional outpourings, but the mere sight of her sister's neat handwriting charting term dates and weekend plans was oddly comforting. She flipped to mid-August and saw 'Alice's birthday' written with a heart penned beside the words, and couldn't immediately drag her eyes away from that small symbol of love. It was only the sight of the emptiness around it in the diary, blank pages she hadn't lived long enough to fill, that gave Alice an ache inside.

She leafed back slowly to Leni's birthday, the last time she'd seen her sister, squirming as she did whenever she thought about that day. Everything had gone wrong – Belinda arriving late, Tony forgetting completely, the plates smashing – and of course Alice and Leni had had that horrible argument. *Everyone here 12 o'c!* Leni had written and Alice cringed at that jaunty exclamation mark when it had not turned out to be an exclamation-mark kind of day.

Moving on, some of the entries afterwards were obvious – the hen do break to Valencia during half-term, dinner with her friend Francesca 7 p.m., for instance – while others were more cryptic. *T 7.30 p.m.!!!* baffled her – who was 'T'? she wondered, until she realised that the same entry, minus the exclamation marks, appeared every Tuesday evening throughout June and into July. A recurring appointment, but

40

what for? Did 'T' stand for 'therapist', maybe? she wondered, biting her lip. Leni hadn't exactly been happy the last time Alice had seen her. She continued turning the pages, noticing *Josh 8 p.m.* had been written in on a Friday in early June and a couple more times in the weeks that followed, on a Saturday morning and a Tuesday evening. She frowned, unable to place a Josh in her sister's life. Was he a new friend? A *date*?

Her fingers shook as she reached the last week in June when Leni had died. The accident had been on a Thursday evening, and Alice's heart almost stopped when she saw written there, on that fateful day, *A!! 8 p.m.* Did 'A' stand for Alice? she mused, putting a hand to her chest and feeling her heart thud beneath the skin. Leni had tried ringing her that night, after all, but Alice hadn't answered. She felt sick with the idea that Leni might have been cycling over to hers, maybe with some kind of peace offering in mind, only to be killed before she even got there. Was this something else to feel guilty about?

'Another tea?' Belinda called up the stairs at that moment, making Alice jump.

'Please!' she called back, still staring at her sister's cryptic note. Maybe the 'A' her sister had written didn't stand for Alice at all, but 'Adam', her ex-husband, she reasoned – although would Leni really have put in exclamation marks after his initial, when the two of them had parted on such bad terms? Then she noticed an address had been jotted in the 'Notes' section at the bottom right of the page: 62 Cherry Grove, W12. A Shepherd's Bush postcode, she registered, feeling her skin prickle. Leni had been killed in Shepherd's Bush. Was

41

Cherry Grove where she'd been heading that night? And who was the mysterious 'A' she was going to meet there?

Someone must know, she figured, as the handwritten words refused to divulge their secrets. She could ask Leni's friends, maybe see if one of them lived on Cherry Grove or knew who did. Putting down the diary, she typed the road name into her phone, staring at it on the map, then zoomed in to the street numbers. 62 was larger than the adjoining buildings and as she zoomed in even closer, a link appeared: Cherry House. Clicking on it took her to the web page of a community centre with listings for a Brownies group, pensioner breakfasts, toddler mornings, infant ballet classes ... *Hire this space!* read a banner along the bottom of the screen. Maybe someone – the mysterious 'A'? – had booked the venue for a birthday party? A supper club? She'd be able to find out, she was sure, and was struck in the next moment by how important it felt to her to unravel this mystery, to discover everything about the last weeks of Leni's life she'd missed out on.

Returning the diary to her back pocket, she abandoned the paperwork for the time being and opened a nearby box instead. She unpacked various novels and cookery books, stacking them in wobbling towers on the carpet. Then she stopped, her breath catching in her throat as she peeled away a newspaper wrapping, to discover Leni's gorgeous, colourful plates inside, the plates she'd dropped so spectacularly on her birthday last year.

Lifting them carefully out, she wondered why Will – if it had been him who'd put them in the box – hadn't simply dumped the whole stack in the bin. Perhaps he'd recognised them from that day, too, and felt the same guilt that she did on seeing them again. The plates were nearly all either cracked or chipped or, in some cases, broken into sharp, glinting pieces, but Leni had kept them, presumably wanting to fix them at some point, or perhaps because they had been given to her by Adam, and it would have pained her to lose them entirely.

Gently she ran her finger along one of the broken pieces, a lavender colour with a pearlescent lustre. She remembered an article she'd read online about a Japanese tradition of repairing broken pots, highlighting their fractures and scars with golden glue to make the object more beautiful than ever; shattered but mended. Would she ever feel shattered but mended? Maybe painstakingly repairing Leni's crockery would patch her up a little bit, she thought, carefully rewrapping the broken plates and setting them aside. It was definitely worth a go.

Okay. Good progress. Was that everything sorted out from this particular box? She peered inside to see that the only thing left was a magazine. No, a brochure, she realised, lifting it out and reading the words *Your Family With Our Help* below a picture of a woman holding a tiny baby to her chest. The IVF clinic, she guessed, until she saw, in smaller lettering, the words *Specialist International Adoption Agency* and nearly dropped the thing. What the hell? Leni and Adam had not been able to get pregnant, despite their best attempts, but Alice wasn't aware that they'd considered adopting. Why hadn't Leni told her?

She heard footsteps coming up the stairs just then and instinctively stuffed the brochure into an empty bag. Her mum had been so upset when Leni's IVF failed each time, Alice didn't want to raise the spectre of another possible grandchild she'd been denied. Also, she didn't think she could bear it, if this was something Belinda knew about and she didn't. She returned to the paperwork, trying to look busy as her mum re-entered the room.

'Sorry about that,' Belinda said, carrying a tray of tea things. 'I've brought cake too, to keep us going.' She set the tray down on a dusty weights bench. 'Flapjack? Swiss roll? Bit of both?'

'Flapjack, please,' Alice said, picking up a scrap of paper with a name and phone number scrawled on it, then putting it down again uncertainly, before doing the same with a letter from someone she'd never heard of. What was she supposed to do with them? There were so many tiny jigsaw pieces to a life, she thought, suddenly overwhelmed.

'Everything all right?' her mum asked, turning with a mug of tea and a flapjack on a plate. 'Other than the obvious?'

'It's just ...' Alice broke off, gesturing to the papers in front of her. 'I don't know what's important and what's not. There's a letter here from someone called Cathie – no idea. A phone number of someone called Graham – no idea. And I don't – oh!'

Belinda's hand must have wobbled or maybe the mug was too full, because in the next moment, hot tea went splashing everywhere. 'Oh dear,' she said, setting down the mug and snatching up the sodden papers. 'I didn't scald you, did I? Sorry, I'm so clumsy.'

'I'm fine, Mum, don't worry,' Alice said, but her mum seemed really stressed, an expression of what could only be described as anguish on her face. 'It doesn't matter, I'm sure,' she called after her as Belinda hurried out of the room, saying something about getting kitchen roll and that she'd be back in a minute.

Alice watched her go, frowning. Maybe Belinda's emotions were getting to her, because in Alice's eyes, that had seemed a massive overreaction. She hadn't seen her looking so panicked since ... well, since that weird moment on Leni's birthday, come to think of it. Biting into the soft, buttery flapjack, Alice took herself back to that afternoon: how she'd gone out into the garden after lunch, only to find her mum and Leni deep in private conversation, voices low. She'd forgotten until now that, right before they noticed her there, Belinda's face had become stricken. Frightened, almost. What had Leni said to her to make her look like that?

The flapjack was sticking to her gums; its sweetness suddenly made her feel nauseous. Today had already prompted so many unsettling questions about her sister, she wasn't sure if she could cope with any more mysteries. Did she even want to know Leni's secrets?

Belinda returned, pink in the face, with two squares of kitchen roll, still clucking about how clumsy she was. Alice couldn't stop herself. 'Mum – do you remember, back on Leni's birthday, you two were having a chat outside in the garden at one point, and I walked out and interrupted you,' she blurted out. 'I was just wondering, what were you talking about? Only—'

'Nothing,' Belinda said quickly, before Alice had even finished the sentence. 'I mean – I can't remember. We talked about lots of things.'

'Yes, but ...' Alice saw it again in her head: the shaken

expression on her mum's face. Real alarm in her eyes, mirroring the alarm she'd seen two minutes ago. 'You looked really rattled. Did she upset you? I'm not being nosey, but . . .' She *was* being nosey, obviously, but whatever. 'If you want to talk about . . . anything, then . . .'

'Honestly, darling, I'm not sure what you mean,' Belinda said. 'You know what my memory's like!' She flashed Alice a smile that wasn't wholly convincing. 'Shall we crack on? Where are we up to?'

'Sure,' said Alice. But for the rest of the afternoon, she couldn't help glancing sidelong at her now and then. She didn't want to accuse her mum of lying, but it was clear that she knew exactly the moment Alice was referencing, only, for whatever reason, didn't want to discuss it. Had her mum and sister kept a secret from her, Alice wondered, her frown deepening. What did Belinda know that Alice didn't?

Chapter Four

Leni McKenzie memorial page

*Leni and I went to Glastonbury one summer and, slightly worse
for wear, we tried to blag our way into the backstage VIP area. Leni
gave the security guys on the gate a very convincing story that we
were backing singers for Elvis Costello, and all was going pretty
well, I thought, until one of the security team, clearly not buying it
for a second, asked us to give him a song. God knows why, but Leni
launched straight into 'When the Red, Red Robin' at the top of her
voice, shimmying and bopping like there was no tomorrow, with me
joining in a beat or two behind. The security guy burst out laughing,
as did everyone else around him – including a couple of guys from
the Kaiser Chiefs who had just arrived and proceeded to JOIN IN.
Needless to say, we failed in our mission, but I think everyone who
heard the performance enjoyed it in a so-bad-it's-good way.*

Leni, you were such fun to be with. I'll miss you forever. Love, Suze

'Hey! You! Flip-flop guy!'

Will didn't pay any attention to the shouts at first because there were always people shouting on Chaweng beach – noisy games of frisbee or beach tennis, as well as calls from the other sales people as they trudged along the hot sand, announcing they had sarongs to sell, goggles, bat and ball sets, fresh fruit. Flip-flops too, sometimes. On this particular day, his head was buzzing with a combination of dazzling sun and too much weed the previous evening, plus a bad night's sleep, and he was trying to zone out all unnecessary noise. It was taking a lot of his energy to conjure up the big smiles and charm he was currently displaying to the pasty-white couple spread out on two beach towels, in the hope of flogging them some crap sunglasses.

'I've got homage Armani, Dior, Pilot, Ray-Bans,' he said, crouching down to set out the cellophane-wrapped glasses before them. His golden rule: get enough stuff out and on to their space until it was impossible for them to ignore you. Also, say the word 'homage' really quick at the start of the list of designer names and hope that they didn't know what it meant or assumed it was merely another cool brand. You're not just a pretty face, he'd sometimes say to himself in the small bathroom mirror of his flat. Sometimes he'd even point his index fingers at his tanned reflection in a gameshow-host sort of way. *You da man.*

'I like the ones you're wearing,' the woman said to him now, in a tone flirty enough that her boyfriend shot her a peeved look. The two of them were English, which was always a good way in; he'd already flattered the bloke by asking him about the football back home, even though Will had access

Especially as it was mid-afternoon now and he was yet to sell a single sodding thing so far today. 'Do you mind? I'm in the middle of—'

But the woman on the towel had already put the sunglasses back down and reached over to pick up her book. 'I'll give them a miss, thanks,' she said, with a new, chilly edge to her voice.

'Yeah, we're all right for sunglasses, cheers, mate,' her boyfriend said, rolling over on to his front and shutting his eyes as if the matter was closed.

'Wise move,' the red-haired woman told them. Even the way she was standing was aggressive, Will thought crossly: chin jutting, chest forward, legs planted in the sand as if braced for imminent combat.

He ignored her. 'Well, thanks anyway,' he said to the couple, leaning down to pick up the unwanted sunglasses littering their towels. The blood rushed to his head and weariness overtook him, coupled with a strong surge of pissed-off-ness. He was sick of these whining tourists. What did they expect when they bought something from a beach seller – that they would get a guarantee and printed receipt? In their dreams. The Scottish woman, meanwhile, was still griping on, however hard he tried to block her out.

'I mean, I guessed they were knock-off from the price, but come on, the strap broke that same night, the first time I'd actually worn them,' she complained shrilly. 'The first bloody time! It's all just landfill, the shite you're selling, isn't it? Absolute rubbish. Aren't you ashamed of yourself?'

He stuffed the final pairs of sunglasses into his bag, heaved it on his shoulder and strode past her without replying. The sun slammed down on him with dizzying intensity, and he felt dehydrated and empty; he hadn't been able to face breakfast first thing but now he regretted not trying harder to force something into his stomach. *Aren't you ashamed of yourself?* Yes, he was, more than she would ever know, but not about anything as trivial as a pair of effing flip-flops.

'*Hey!*'

Oh great, now she was following him across the sand. This was the last thing he wanted, a beach-wide public scene with her loudly berating him, as well as his stock. If she kept this up much longer, he could kiss goodbye to customers on this patch, that was for sure. Did he even have the energy to try again somewhere else though? He should have guessed that today would turn out to be difficult, having woken up that morning to find a message from Alice: *Did Leni ever mention a place called Cherry House to you? I think she was going there the day she died.* Will had flinched because he had been trying very hard not to think about the day Leni died. Or anything to do with home, for that matter.

He whirled around. 'What do you want?'

She was right there at his shoulder, her forehead a bit sweaty where she'd matched him stride for stride. The sun shone into her face and she put up a hand to shield her eyes. 'What do you *think* I want? I already told you. A refund and an apology is the least you owe me, for starters.'

What a buzzkill this woman was. And she was on *holiday*, for heaven's sake. Did she not have better things to do with her time? He heaved a sigh. Might as well get this over with.

'Okay,' he said flatly. 'I'm sorry your shoe broke.' Then he shrugged. 'As for a refund ... do you have the item in question with you?'

'Do I have ... ?' Incredulity spread across her face. 'Are you kidding me?' She made a show of patting herself down as if checking for pockets. Given that she was practically naked apart from the bikini, this was actually quite enjoyable, although Will did his best to maintain neutrality. 'No, funnily enough, I'm not carrying around a broken *flip-flop* on the off-chance of seeing you again,' she went on scathingly and he jerked his gaze back up to her face. 'But I'm hardly gonna lie about that, am I?'

He gave another shrug, as if to question her honesty. How should he know? Then he said, somewhat sanctimoniously, 'I'm afraid I can't issue you a refund without evidence,' which had her rolling her eyes. *Yeah, well, up yours, Ginger,* he thought. *You started this.* 'There are some very dodgy people around here,' he went on for good measure. 'I'd love to believe you, but ...'

She snorted with derision. 'Oh *please*. Spare me,' she said. 'The only dodgy person around here is you, you total chancer. God! What a cheek. Like I'd keep a useless, broken shoe, my arse. It went straight in the bin, obviously. Where the rest of your tat ought to be shoved.'

He assumed a bland, polite expression which he hoped she would find deeply irritating. 'Sorry. Nothing I can do, then. Company rules, you see,' he said, even though they both knew very well that there was no company and there were no rules. 'Very nice to meet you, anyway. Enjoy your holiday!'

He loved saying that. *Enjoy your holiday!* – one, because it was ever so slightly patronising, and two, because it underlined the fact that he was not a holidaymaker like the rest of them, he had climbed above that lowly position to acquire new status as a local. Someone who lived and worked here on Koh Samui, paradise island. Admittedly, he didn't love the fact that he heard her say, loud and clear, 'Bellend,' in response as he walked away, but whatever. Who cared? He never had to see her again, after all. She'd be getting on a plane home in a matter of days, and good riddance to her, frankly.

Having walked a safe distance away, he risked a glance over his shoulder to see that, yes, good, she was currently stomping off in the opposite direction, shoulders tight, bottom wiggling with indignation. Farewell forever, he thought, before scanning the horizon for suitable mugs who might want to buy a pair of knock-off sunglasses. Please, for the love of God, let there be someone gullible enough soon.

Aha. His gaze landed on two lads with white torsos and legs that showed they were newly arrived. Even better, one was lying on an Arsenal beach towel, the other West Ham. Jackpot. 'Afternoon, fellas,' he began, arriving beside them. 'Cor, bit of a result for West Ham at the weekend, wasn't it?' Cue a friendly grin that said, *I'm one of you, boys.* Then he plunged a hand into his bag and pulled out the fake Dior, fake Prada, fake Balenciaga, holding them up like cards in a magic trick. 'I've got some cracking gear here, if you're interested?'

Later that day, over in Oxford, Belinda was sitting in the driver's seat of her car, engine off, down at the quiet end of the

54

Park and Ride car park. A small white knitted baby hat sat in her lap – she had taken to using it as a phone case since discovering it in Leni's possessions the week before last – and her phone was pressed to her ear because the connection with Apolline was often a bit on the iffy side. She had wondered previously if Apolline was even in the UK, as she claimed, but it seemed rude to ask, as if she was accusing the other woman of lying. Mind you, the hotline was expensive enough that she might as well have been in Australia or some other faraway place, but what price could you put on your own daughter's words from the other side? These calls were worth every penny.

'I see,' she said now as Apolline described at length how at peace Leni said she was, how she wanted for nothing. She often said this sort of thing, but Belinda never minded because it was so soothing to hear. Sometimes she closed her eyes in rapture as if listening to a beautiful symphony on the radio rather than a woman's slow, breathy voice. She had been so anxious the first time they had connected that Leni might not even want to speak to her. 'Is she ... angry with me?' she had asked tremulously, almost unable to speak with relief when Apolline assured her no. *Thank God. Oh, thank God*, she had thought, tears careering down her face. It had been such a weight off her mind.

A car manoeuvred into the parking space next to hers and a man got out, slamming his door unnecessarily hard and making Belinda jump. This wasn't the optimum place for a phone call to commune with one's deceased daughter, but you could sit here for up to an hour without having to buy a ticket, which was rare in Oxford. Plus she was sick of Ray making little comments about her phone calls at home. This was the alternative: telling him she was running an errand (you wouldn't believe how many trips to the dump she'd had to invent) and then parking up here, dialling with breathless urgency to reconnect.

It wasn't always possible to hear from Leni. According to Apolline, newly liberated souls (as she termed them) were unpredictable, temperamental entities; they could be hard to pin down for communication purposes. 'Sounds like Leni,' Belinda had remarked wryly on hearing this. Sometimes Apolline was able to channel other spirits who had interesting things to say, often words of wisdom for her. Her dad had once appeared, offering his thoughts on her boiler, of all things (which was so typical of him, Belinda had felt the most enormous lump in her throat). At other times, Apolline herself was the one to advise her and listen to her problems. It had been Apolline, actually, who'd floated the idea of moving house. 'Free yourself from the past,' she'd said, and the phrase had cemented itself into Belinda's mind with such certainty that the suggestion turned quickly from mere syllables in the air into physical actions, a plan set in motion.

When Belinda first broached the subject of a house move with Ray, explaining that she needed to free herself from the past, he'd agreed and said he understood, only for her to then make the mistake of admitting that the idea – and those exact words, for that matter – had come from Apolline. She'd told him this because she wanted to impress on him how wise Apolline was, how sensitive to Belinda's feelings, but found herself wishing, almost immediately, that she'd kept quiet. Another time, she'd know better. Ray had made it clear from the start that he was dubious about the whole idea of a clairvoyant hotline ('There are a lot of scams out there, that's all I'm saying'), but he became so scathing during this particular discussion that they ended up having a blazing row, culminating with her bursting into tears and not speaking to him for the rest of the day. 'Apolline? I bet that's not even her name. A tenner says she's really called Pauline,' he scoffed.

Since then they'd made up but he'd remained resistant to accepting Apolline as the pillar of support she had become in Belinda's life. 'What about talking to a counsellor instead?' he suggested a few times. 'You can get free ones on the NHS, you know. Maybe mention it to the GP next time you have an appointment?'

She didn't want to take up NHS resources though, not when Apolline offered her something that no health service ever could: the voice of her daughter reassuring her that she was okay. Well – obviously Leni was not really okay, seeing as she was still dead, but according to Apolline, she had accepted this new state of affairs and was in no pain or distress. Even better, the minefield conversation the two of them had had back on Leni's birthday had never been resurrected. Did this mean her daughter had gone to her grave without knowing the full story? Oh gosh, she hoped so. When Belinda had spotted that bit of paper with Graham's number on it in Leni's belongings the other week, her heart had nearly stopped. Why had Graham given Leni his number? What had he *told* her? Thank goodness she'd had the presence of mind to whisk the paper away from Alice so swiftly.

The nicest thing about these conversations was that Leni seemed far more loving in death than she had been in real life. Way more affectionate! Having Apolline pass on 'She adores you and says you are her rock' was incredibly gratifying, especially when you compared it to the way Leni had lost it on her last birthday, wailing amidst a sea of broken crockery, shouting, *What is wrong with this bloody family? Why are we so shit?* (The scene, needless to say, had cut Belinda to the quick. Having worked all her life in social care, she knew that theirs had been a good family compared to some she'd had to look after. There wasn't anything fundamentally wrong with the McKenzies. Was there?)

'The spirits are telling me that they've sent people to help your other children,' Apolline said now in her soft, sweet voice.

'Oh! That's kind. Who?' Belinda asked in reply. Alice had looked so pale and drawn the other week, but she'd started a new temporary job now at least, which would keep her busy. As for Will, although he talked a good talk on the phone, Belinda couldn't help but wonder if he was telling her everything.

'People who will show them a path through the darkness,' came Apolline's cryptic response. She could be a little *too* mysterious at times, Belinda thought. It was the one frustrating aspect of these phone calls. If only her guide could be slightly more exact, give a touch more detail – dates, names, places, that sort of thing – Belinda would really appreciate it. But then again, it probably wasn't very zen to badger the spirits for specifics, was it? To whip out her diary and demand extra. And she didn't want to annoy Apolline.

She jumped again as a woman in a mustard-yellow coat got

out of the neighbouring car and started yelling across the car park to the door-slamming man that he'd left his phone on the seat, and wouldn't he need it to buy the ticket? Belinda blinked away a rush of exasperation – couldn't a person take an important call in peace any more? She'd deliberately parked at this end of the car park because it was hardly ever used! – before tuning back in to Apolline, who was urging Belinda to pay attention to her dreams this week, as she would be sent an important message.

'What sort of message?' she asked, stroking the neat stitches of the white knitted hat. The hope that had gone into those stitches! The grandmotherly love! She tried not to think about the baby that should have been wearing it, had life turned out differently, but it was hard to banish the rosy-cheeked cherub of her imagination. The grandchild that had never quite appeared.

'A symbol to interpret, a sign of change,' Apolline told her with typical opacity and Belinda sighed in the torment of anticipation.

A symbol to interpret in dream, she jotted in her notebook so that she wouldn't forget. With regret, she saw that her time was nearly up. In two minutes she would have to end the call and leave the car park before she was issued with a fine for overstaying. 'I've got to go,' she said unhappily, already feeling an ache at the thought of saying goodbye once more. With Apolline her only remaining link to Leni, it always wrenched her heart to break the connection. 'Please tell her I love her, won't you? Always have, always will.'

'She knows that, Belinda,' Apolline assured her. 'She knows it deep in her soul, and the knowledge comforts her.'

59

A sob burst from Belinda's throat because, at the end of the day, this was all she'd ever wanted. 'Thank you,' she managed to say before the timer on her phone gave a warning beep. 'Thank you, Apolline. I'll talk to you soon.'

She draped her arms over the top of the steering wheel and rested her head there for a few moments, tears sinking into her coat sleeves as the usual wave of emotion rolled through her like a breaker on to shore. Until last year, the worst thing ever to happen to Belinda was Tony leaving her and the children high and dry. But you could get over a failed marriage in time; you could rebuild yourself, fall in love again. How did you ever get over losing your own child?

She became aware of a light tapping at the window and jerked out of her position, startled to see the woman in the mustard coat standing there, mouthing ARE YOU OKAY?

Belinda nodded weakly, gave her a thumbs up and then started the engine and shoved the gearstick into reverse. Her would-be Good Samaritan gave an audible yelp and had to leap out of the way to avoid a potential foot crushing, but Belinda didn't stop. Back to the grindstone of the house-clearing and painting; she had approximately one million small jobs to complete before the first of their estate agent appointments tomorrow. But Leni loved her, and that was enough for now. Certainly, enough to see her safely home and through Ray's suspicious glances and the rest of the day. Until the next phone call and the next assurances, anyway.

Chapter Five

Leni McKenzie memorial page

My favourite Leni story was when we were both in a club one night and she persuaded a couple of blokes she could read palms. Before we knew it, there was a massive queue of people lined up with their hands out, wanting theirs done! Was it true about her looking at the palm of one particularly hot guy and telling him that his luck was in that night, especially when it came to a woman with long brown hair and a black dress? 'Wow — coincidence!' she said, looking down at herself and pantomiming surprise. Well, he ended up coming back to our flat, so judge for yourself!

God, I miss you, Leni. RIP you beautiful woman.

Francesca

'Here we are,' Alice slurred, slotting her door key into the lock. The crop-haired man was standing very close behind her and a warning bell rang in her head momentarily: *you don't know him, you're completely hammered, this could be a really bad idea.*

But she ignored it – she just wanted a bit of fun for a change, all right? – and asked, 'You coming in, then?'

'Sure,' the man said. She couldn't remember his name, was that terrible? Had he even told her? She couldn't recall how they'd got talking in the first place, come to think of it. She'd met up with one of Leni's friends, Francesca, in a pub near St Paul's because Francesca worked around there too, and then when she left – too early – Alice didn't feel like going straight home. He'd caught her eye across the room and the next thing she knew, he was sidling over with his smile and chat, buying them more drinks and then . . . Well, to cut a long story short, here she was letting him into her flat, and here they were kissing in the hall before she'd even had a chance to put the light on.

He was a good kisser, the man with no name; sexy and passionate, his hands expertly peeling off her clothes, the two of them laughing together as they staggered into her living room. 'You are so hot,' he said thickly into her ear, pausing to retrieve a condom from his pocket (a bad sign, surely, she registered distantly) but then they were kissing again, standing in the middle of the room, and she felt shivery all over from wanting him. He didn't know Sad Alice, he had no idea about Mad Alice – and how bloody lovely that was, how utterly refreshing, she thought, to meet someone who wasn't aware of the massive airport trolley of baggage she'd been carting around with her for the last six months. He thought she was hot, and that was all he needed to know right now. That was enough.

As for her, she was so pissed she couldn't remember anything he'd told her about himself, but he was considerate enough to check, *Is this okay?* a couple of times, at least, before he pushed her roughly over the table in the living room and rammed into her from behind. The force was enough to send a pile of paperwork – Leni's paperwork, yet to be fully dealt with – cascading to the floor and Alice cringed, feeling disrespectful. *Well, that's just charming,* she imagined Leni deadpanning in her head. *Don't let me stand in the way of your animal passion, you hussy.* Alice sent up a mental apology to her sister, but a minute or two later it was over anyway and he'd collapsed on top of her, his body fever-hot against hers, his breath juddering into her hair. Human contact, she thought wistfully, before he withdrew and fiddled about getting the condom off.

'You all right?' he asked afterwards when she remained there motionless. 'Sorry about the—' He bent down to gather the scattered papers, and she yanked up her knickers and helped him.

'Whoa – adoption certificate?' he exclaimed in the next moment. 'Who's Hamish, your kid?'

She shook her head weakly. 'No. A cat. My sister's cat.' She jabbed at the paper. 'See that, where it says "West London Animal Shelter"? Bit of a clue for you there. They don't tend to give out kids as well. Not unless you pay extra.'

He didn't respond to her sarcasm, putting the pile of papers back in a neat stack on the table. 'Oh, right,' was all he said. Then an awkward silence fell, where neither of them quite knew what to do. She thought about offering him a drink but couldn't be bothered. *Go away now, please.*

'Well,' she said brightly, in the end. 'Nice to meet you, er—'

'Darren,' he said. 'It's Darren.'

She almost laughed. Baron Darren? Had Leni pulled some heavenly strings to send along her handsome husband-to-be? 'Delighted to meet you,' she said, mouth twitching. 'Tell me, do you have a castle, Darren?'

'A what?'

'Never mind.' Of course he didn't. 'Well . . . thanks?' she said, gesturing rudely to the door.

'Bye, then,' he said, taking the hint and going.

She sank into the sofa as she heard the door close behind him. 'That was unexpected,' she said into the emptiness, still feeling a bit giggly about the whole business. Not-a-Baron Darren . . . well, there were worse ways to spend an evening.

Not that she'd intended any kind of passion when she'd left work to meet Francesca earlier. Francesca and Leni had become friends when they did their postgraduate teaching course together and she'd got in touch after Alice's Facebook post about Leni's clothes, to ask if she could have a rust-coloured jumper of hers that she'd always loved. Sorting through her sister's possessions, Alice had found a book of Francesca's too, and so they'd met up for the handover and a chat. Half-Italian with a cloud of dark curls and a sweet round face, Francesca was warm and bubbly, hugging Alice and then pressing the jumper to her face and saying she'd think of Leni every time she wore it.

'Francesca, does this address mean anything to you?' Alice remembered to ask. She had brought Leni's little grey diary with her and held it open between them, pointing out the note from Leni's final week. 'Only I'm trying to fill in the blanks of what Leni was up to, when she was alive. We'd fallen out, you see, and I feel as if I missed out on that whole time.' Her voice shook, not least because she hadn't got very far with her investigations. Will hadn't replied to the message she'd sent but that wasn't a surprise, he never wanted to talk about Leni. Nor had she got any further with the other mysteries thrown up by the diary: where Leni was going on Tuesday nights (*T 7.30,* regular as clockwork), who 'A' was that Leni had gone to meet on the day of her death, the identity of 'Josh'...

Francesca shook her head blankly. 'No idea, sorry,' she said. 'But I can ask around.' The smile left her face. 'I feel bad too for not seeing more of her last summer. I was so caught up in the kids; Greta was only six months then, I wasn't getting out much at all. The last time I saw her ...' She leafed back through the pages of Leni's diary until she came to one with her name on. 'Yes − dinner at our favourite Chinese place, that's right. If I'd known then that I wouldn't see her again ...' Her eyes filled with sudden tears; she looked distraught. 'God. I have the horrible feeling I just talked about the kids, baby stuff, you know. Me, me, me. Because Leni was such a good listener, wasn't she? I wish I could have ...' She put the diary gently back down on the table, her mouth buckling with sadness. 'I should have listened more to her while I had the chance.'

Alice nodded. 'Same.' She tried again. 'How about this guy − Josh, 8 p.m.?' she asked, finding the page. 'She met him a couple of other times too. Was she dating, do you think? Oh, and did she ever talk to you about trying for adoption?'

But Francesca couldn't answer any of her questions, grimacing apologetically and blaming 'baby brain', and before long saying she should go home to help her husband with bedtime. As well as the swirl of confusion inside her head, Alice had also felt a pang for her sister that so many of her friends seemed to have babies and children, when she hadn't been able to. It must have chipped away at her a little whenever there was a happy announcement made, or the detailing of domestic arrangements, knowing that she had to keep up a smile of feigned delight or understanding each time.

As the other woman got up, putting on her coat and saying how lovely it had been to catch up, it was all Alice could do not to grab her hand and force her to stay, begging her for more memories and stories. But then they were hugging goodbye and Francesca was gone. Was it any wonder Alice had ordered herself another drink to blot out her dismay at this non-starter? Was it any wonder that when the crop-haired man – not-Baron Darren – approached her, she was all too willing to be sweet-talked and distracted?

Standing in the middle of an upmarket babywear shop the following day, surrounded by overpriced prams with stupid names, Tony McKenzie could feel his irritation levels rise past 'Bit Annoyed', exceed 'Pretty Fed Up Now' and continue on, all the way up to 'For the Love of God, Get Me Out of Here Before I Lose My Mind'. Lullabies tinkled from the speakers overhead; you had to pity the poor bastards working in here, having 'Row, Row, Row Your Boat' on a loop. Give it another few minutes and he'd be smashing the music player with his own bare hands. Besides, if the lullabies were meant to soothe the customers' offspring, it wasn't working. One small girl in a padded turquoise coat was yelling on the floor, face puce, in the midst of a full-blown tantrum. Tony was this close to doing the same, to be honest. Christ, this was awful. This was so bloody awful.

He would be sixty next year, astonishingly. Every time the thought crossed his mind, it landed with a thud of shock. In his head, he was still mid-thirties, king of the castle, but in a real-life twist, not only was he nearly sixty, he was also about to become a dad again for the fourth time. Would the baby make him feel even older, or would he experience a new surge of life as a consequence? He hoped fervently for the latter, needless to say. He'd always been a handsome man, tall and lean with thick hair and twinkly blue eyes, and he'd traded on his looks shamelessly, talking his way in and out of all sorts of shenanigans. These days, his hair was starting to thin and he was having to put brightening drops in his eyes, and, perhaps most alarming of all, women had started looking straight through him, as if his charisma had exceeded its sell-by date.

It made it even worse, being here with so many young couples, excitement shining out of their faces. He had a creeping dread that, any minute now, somebody would assume he was a grandad, not a father-to-be, and he'd be forced to storm out of the place in a massive huff. Actually, that wouldn't be so bad, he conceded; he could recover from the ordeal with a large coffee downstairs, let Jackie take care of all the decision-making alone.

'Which one do you think, then, Tony?' she asked at that moment and he blinked, aware that he had totally zoned out of the store assistant's pram-versus-buggy patter for the last few minutes. Possibly longer. Hours, days could have trickled by for all he knew.

'Um,' he said blankly, staring around in the hope that, subconsciously, he somehow might have gleaned enough information to form an opinion on this, the biggest purchase of the trip. But no. His mind hummed like an empty fridge. 'Well ... what do *you* think?' he hedged in the end.

She narrowed her eyes at him and he knew she had seen right through him. A highly successful company director, Jackie was as sharp as a gleaming new tomato knife, and often about as cutting, too. Would she be kind and overlook his lapse in concentration though, or mercilessly hang him out to dry? 'In terms of what Fern here was saying about considering a single-to-double,' she replied, eyes boring into his, 'would you be for or against?'

Shit. What the hell was she talking about? He chanced his arm. 'Er ... for?'

She burst out laughing – which was better, at least, than a sharp dig in the ribs. *'Really?'* She shook her head. 'You have no idea what I mean, do you?'

He glanced down at the carpet which was printed, rather nauseatingly, with a repeating pattern of storks carrying nappy-slung cherubs. 'No,' he confessed. 'Must admit, I drifted off a bit towards the end there.'

'Time for your afternoon nap, is it?' Jackie teased, which annoyed him because he wasn't *that* old, for goodness' sake. Even if he did often enjoy a quiet forty winks around this time of day, if work was on the slow side. 'Okay, well, for your information, a single-to-double pushchair is one that can be adapted for when you have your next baby.'

'Your *next* baby?' he spluttered. 'What, you mean—?'

'*I* don't want another baby after this one,' she said. (Thank heavens.) 'But you apparently do, if you want us to consider that kind of kit.'

The assistant was smirking. Jackie apparently found this hilarious too. He gave them both a tired smile. 'Okay, ha ha, very good.' Time to remind them he knew a thing or two about vehicles. 'So. We need good suspension. Comfort for the baby. Decent tyres. A model that can be folded up and down quickly, preferably one-handed. If there's a removable car-seat element – all the better,' he reeled off briskly. Then he paused, enjoying their startled expressions – expressions which said, *Oh, okay, maybe he does know what he's talking about after all. Maybe we should stop patronising him now.* 'We'll have one like that, please,' he summed up to the assistant. 'My girlfriend can choose the colour. What?' he added, as Jackie pulled a face. 'Look, I have done this before, remember. Three times over. I'm not a complete novice, whatever you think.'

Jackie exchanged glances with the assistant. 'That's me told,' she said. And then, perhaps resentful of Tony's reference to his other children (it was the only area of their lives in which he could pull rank, the only thing he had done already that she hadn't), she added, 'Okay, he's bored, let's cut to the chase, then. We'll take the Cosy Kanga all-terrain travel system in the navy, please. With the matching changing bag.'

A thrilled light flashed through the assistant's eyes (shit, it must have been a very expensive choice) then she bowed her head subserviently. 'Of course. Excellent,' she replied, adding to the list she was compiling on an electronic tablet.

Tony leaned over so that his mouth was in the warm space of Jackie's neck. 'You are so sexy when you bark out orders like that,' he murmured into her skin.

Jackie yanked her head around to give him a withering look. She was statuesque and well-groomed – glossy brown hair, French-manicured nails, perfect make-up – and Tony knew that her friends privately (some not so privately) wondered what she was doing with him, a car salesman in his late fifties who'd already been around the block a few times. To be fair, sometimes he wondered the same. The two of them had met at a race day at Newbury – she was there because she loved horses, he was there because he loved a day out betting with his mates. She was great fun, he made her laugh, they'd had a bit to drink and really hit it off. Things progressed from there, although faster than either of them had anticipated, what with the accidental pregnancy. 'Looks like you're moving in with me,' she'd said at the time, 'seeing as I don't fancy living in your gaff, no offence.' Before he knew it, he was waking up every day in her very expensive barn conversion, all moody lighting and gleaming surfaces, enjoying the monsoon shower, the designer farmhouse kitchen with underfloor heating, the remote-controlled security gates that made him feel like a celebrity every time he approached. There were worse places to find yourself, he'd figured.

'In your dreams, mate,' she said from the side of her mouth now. '"Sexy" will be a distant memory for you, if you don't pull your finger out and take more of an interest in our baby's future, do you hear me?'

'I *am* interested in our—' he began protesting, only for her to raise an eyebrow and keep talking over the top of him.

'Good, because that means all the boring shit too. Like shopping for the right gear.' She lavished another smile on the assistant before asking, 'What next, then, Fern? Things for the bathroom, is it?' She elbowed Tony in a friendlier manner. 'Come on, indulge me. I'm only doing this once and it's a big deal for me.'

'I know. Sorry. And it's a big deal for me, too,' he replied, which was true at least. He had worked out that Jackie and he must have conceived pretty much the day that Leni had died, and the realisation had come with an enormous weight of conflicting emotions that he was still struggling to come to terms with. Was this some kind of redemption? A second chance to get fatherhood right?

Alice had been scathing when he had – admittedly foolishly – mentioned the timing of the conception. 'One in, one out, is that what you're saying?' she'd asked angrily. 'Dad. Please tell me you are not suggesting this baby will compensate in any way for Leni dying. This is not a like-for-like replacement situation here, do you hear me?'

Oh, he heard her all right, loud and clear. The whole of the east London café where he'd taken her for lunch had probably heard her too, because there seemed to be one heck of a lot of angry vegans giving him dirty looks after that. As for telling Will over a video call there was a new half-sibling on the way, that hadn't been exactly cheering either; his son looking very much as if he was grimacing with revulsion. Tony tried to console himself later that the screen *had* been pixelated due to wi-fi issues, but it was a tough sell.

Both conversations had left him disconcerted. No parent wanted to feel waves of contempt from their own children. 'Give them time, they're still cut up about their sister,' Jackie had said, which was decent of her, when both Alice and Will had snubbed her attempts to sympathise at the funeral. 'They'll love their little half-sister or -brother once they meet them. Come on – with our combination of genes? Who wouldn't?'

Over in a different area of the store, they now had to choose between pastel-coloured infant bathtubs, and giant sponges, and soft little hooded towels with cute animal ears. He and Belinda hadn't bothered with any of this sort of paraphernalia when Leni was born – they hadn't been able to afford a cot for six months; they'd had her in bed with them the whole time. Why did every single life experience get turned into one massive shopping expedition? *Duh . . . it's called capitalism, Tone,* he heard Leni say sarcastically in his head and had to hide a smile. She and Alice had gone through a stage in their teens when they both called him 'Tony' or 'Tone' because . . . well, he wasn't entirely sure. He hoped it was merely teenage affectation, their efforts to be cool, rather than the pair of them making a point about him not earning the name 'Dad' any more. (*Was* that what they'd meant?)

'Lilac or aquamarine?' Jackie was asking, a changing mat in each hand.

Uncaring, he pointed at the blue one. Then, trying to show willing, he grabbed a yellow plastic duck. 'Ah – here's an essential,' he said, and in the next moment was hurtled right back to the tiny flat he and Belinda had bought just off the Cowley Road – their starter home. There he was, young and dashing, kneeling at the side of the bath with his shirtsleeves rolled up, one arm around baby Leni's back as she sat there, a similar duck bobbing in the water before her. 'Duck!' she had said, her very first word, and he and Belinda had stared at each other, eyes wide. Their baby was a genius! The cleverest baby ever! 'I thought she was about to throw it at me for a moment,' he remembered quipping. 'I took "Duck!" as an instruction,' and they'd both laughed, and it had felt such a moment of togetherness for the three of them. Such joy. He couldn't quite believe he would be doing all of that again.

'Panda or fox?' Jackie asked, thrusting two hooded towels under his nose. 'Aren't they sweet? Should we get both, do you think?'

'Panda,' he replied. 'Adorable.'

For all his avowed wisdom at having done this before, for all the shocked delight that had rushed through him when Jackie broke the news, it was becoming impossible to ignore the doubts simultaneously doubling and mutating inside him like a virus, now that they were here, buying stuff, making it real. And it wasn't as if they'd planned things this way. In fact, Alice's first response on hearing about the pregnancy back in November had been a scornful laugh. 'Oh dear. A mistake, I take it?'

Thank you, Alice. Astute as ever.

He picked up a packet of white flannels, remembering the harrowing days and nights in the parent and baby intensive care unit when Will had been in and out of hospital throughout his first year. He was too tiny and weak to be bathed like ordinary babies, so they'd sponged him down with warm wet flannels, section by section, whenever he needed to be washed. Tony's back had ached as he leaned over the unit, carefully cleaning the creases in his son's small neck, his face, his bottom, and the memory made him feel sad that he could have cared for Will with such tender love and devotion then, only for the connection between them to break like a cheap necklace chain, for the links to drop away.

Blinking, he returned to the pastel surroundings of the store and reached for Jackie's hand, forcing himself to pay attention to what Fern was saying. He *would* get it right for this baby, he vowed, squeezing his girlfriend's fingers when she glanced over at him in surprise. (His *partner's* fingers, he reminded himself in the next moment, because Jackie had complained previously that whenever he called her his girlfriend, it made her feel as if they were fifteen.)

If you're going to do something, do it properly, his own dad had been fond of saying. No cutting corners or shortcuts. Sure, he was usually referring to DIY jobs – cleaning and repairing surfaces before slapping on a new coat of paint, that sort of thing – but his words came back to Tony now. If he was so set on being a good father this time around, maybe he should get in some practice beforehand, try again with his other children. Make an effort, if they'd let him. It wasn't too late to offer some fatherly love where it was needed, surely? A bit of friendly advice and encouragement.

Three months and counting, he calculated as they selected

a white baby bath and a massive sponge in the shape of a whale and a set of toiletries in lavender-coloured bottles. Three months to roll up his sleeves and make an effort. He might have been the one to leave the family back in the day, but what if he could reunite them all? Bring them back together? He'd prove that he was a good person, a good father, and he'd start by doing his best to repair the fractures and fault lines within family number one. He could do this for the McKenzies, couldn't he?

Chapter Six

Dad created group 'McKenzies Together'
  Dad added you
  Dad is typing . . .
  Will frowned down at his phone, both at the unexpected
sight of his father's name appearing there in his messages – this
in itself a rarity – and the fact that he had apparently started a
new family group chat called McKenzies Together, consisting,
astonishingly, of Will, Alice and both parents. 'Seriously?' he
muttered in disbelief. You had to laugh, honestly. Did his dad
have any idea that there was a word 'irony' in existence? Since
when had Tony McKenzie ever felt a shred of togetherness
with the rest of them? Maybe the imminent arrival of child
number four had prompted a late-onset midlife crisis (another
one). Or maybe he'd been caught up in a sentimental moment,
and would go on to delete the group in later regret.
  His dad was apparently still typing and Will turned his
phone over on the table, not wanting to wait for the message. He would read it some other time, he decided. He
certainly wouldn't expend any energy hoping that this was

a sea change in his father, because he'd been there, worn the disappointment too many times. *You know Dad left because you were such a nightmare when you were born, don't you?* Leni had once said to him in a vile teenage mood. She'd muttered an apology later but he'd only been eight, and that sort of thing stuck with you. He shook his head, as if trying to dislodge the memory from his mind before it could totally harsh his mellow.

Exist in the moment, he reminded himself, and right now he was sitting at a rickety wooden table in his favourite rustic beach bar, a cold bottle of Singha in front of him. He also had a perfect view of the sea, which was starting to turn flamingo pink with bronze highlights as the sun descended steadily towards it. With half an hour to kill before he met Juno, a friend who happened to sell the best grass on Koh Samui, he planned to sit here, exhale slowly and watch the waves rush in and out again, as the sky filled with deepening colours. Breathe out the stress of the last few days, which had not exactly been the best of his life. For one thing, he hadn't sold as many sunglasses as he'd hoped, and he was wondering if he'd lost his edge. He'd certainly lost his motivation to get out there every day, pandering to holidaymakers as they said no to him and no again. It hadn't bothered him at first because work had been such a small element of his life compared to the parties, the scene, the casual friendships and even-more-casual sex, but the fewer items he sold, the less money he had, and the less money he had, the more he found himself obsessing over it. Meanwhile, the boxes of souvenirs, bought with such optimism back when he'd decided to just not go home, to try and make a living here, were still piled up in his flat, reminding him of his shortcomings.

He frowned again, taking a long cool glug of the beer, the alcohol sinking soothingly through his system. He was just a bit flat, that was all, he told himself. He'd be back in his groove within a few days, for sure. Absolutely.

A group of young people were heading out for a sunset paddleboard trip, he noticed, watching them stride across the sand together in their boardshorts and swimsuits, along with a guy lugging down a wheeled rack of boards. In the next moment, he felt a pang for his old sixth-form mates back home and missed feeling part of something bigger. Missed being among people who got him.

'Oh my *God*,' he heard then, followed by swift footsteps and a loud rubbery slap as a broken black flip-flop was slammed down on the table in front of him. And there was the red-haired Scottish woman again, looking insufferably pleased with herself. '*Voilà*,' she said, as if she'd just performed a magic trick, then held out her hand. 'My refund, please.'

So much for this being a relaxing half hour gazing at the waves. He stared in disbelief from the shoe up to the woman's triumphant face. Seriously? he thought. What was wrong with people? 'Wow,' he said sarcastically, feeling very much like hurling the flip-flop into the sand at their feet. 'You must feel so vindicated. For what, a few quid? Well done. Great.'

If anything, she seemed disappointed that he wasn't about to engage in combat, her big moment ruined as he dug into his pocket for his wallet, then dumped some money on the table without another word. *There. You won. Happy now?* his expression said, with a hefty side order of disdain.

'Thank you,' she said, stuffing the cash into a zip-up money belt around her waist. No blue bikini tonight, she was wearing denim shorts and a pale pink off-the-shoulder top with floaty sleeves. She picked up the shoe somewhat self-consciously. 'No hard feelings,' she added when he didn't respond.

He gave a snort. 'Getting that flip-flop out of the bin and carrying it around with you was clearly so worth it,' he commented without looking at her. 'I'm thrilled for you.'

She left without another word, and he drained the rest of his beer in a single exasperated gulp, feeling as if the peace he'd enjoyed at the start of the bottle had now deserted him. Just to top everything off, a message came through from Juno: she'd been waylaid, sorry, hon, could they rearrange? *Love you,* she signed off and he felt nauseous all of a sudden, sick of people he barely knew bandying that phrase around as if it was a mere pleasantry. And calling him 'hon' like they were old friends rather than two relative strangers who'd got stoned together a few times at beach parties. *You don't know me,* he felt like replying. Nobody knew him – that was the point.

He stared bleakly out at the idyllic beach scene before him, noticing the coral tones of the sky as the sun slid ever lower, the silhouetted palm trees, their leaves like dark feathers. The paddleboarders were out on the water, drifting serenely through the sunset colours. It was the sort of paradise image you'd see on postcards in the souvenir shops, but all he could think about was his small, empty flat awaiting him a few streets away. Now that he'd been denied the prospect of being able to smoke a numbing spliff to take the edge off his day, he couldn't face returning to its quiet, to the accusing sight of all those boxes full of stuff he was yet to sell. If he hadn't necked the rest of his beer so quickly, he could have lingered over it for another half an hour, but he couldn't really afford to buy a second one in this pricey tourist bar. Damn it. Now what?

His phone vibrated with the arrival of his dad's inaugural group chat message.

Dad: *Hi all. Losing Leni has made me realise we only have a limited number of days together – and I want to make them count. We're still Leni's family members, aren't we – can we try to support one another through this difficult time? I know I haven't been good at this in the past but I want to do better. Maybe talking to each other here might help?*

Will rolled his eyes. 'Oh my God,' he muttered under his breath. Had the old man lost the plot? There was more.

Yes, I'm starting a new family with Jackie but you guys are still so important to me. You're family number one – the originals! Can we coalesce around our grief and offer mutual support? I'm here if so. Love Tony/Dad x

Jesus. Whatever had possessed Tony McKenzie to start pontificating about family matters in this vein, like he had any right? Why did he think anyone needed *his* support at this precise moment in time? He was no dad to Will – he never had been. It wasn't until his mum started seeing Ray that Will had realised just what having a father figure in your life really meant. Ray had taken him rock-climbing and paddleboarding with a bunch of his ageing but surprisingly cool mates; he'd helped Will find his apprenticeship and driven him to Swindon for the interview. He'd traipsed round rental properties with him, dealt with a dodgy landlord when Will felt too intimidated ... Where had his real dad been all this time? Not there, anyway.

He put the phone down and cradled his head in his hands as a sudden wave of melancholy washed through him. It was all closing in around him: his own uselessness, his dwindling funds, the shadow of real life back home looming larger at the corner of his eye with every passing day.

Can I ask you a favour, Will? he heard Leni ask in his head, words which had tormented him since the bombshell of her death, and he swallowed hard, conscious of all the guilt and regret he'd been pushing down this whole time, aware that it could come rearing back up any second to consume him again. Don't think about that, he ordered himself fiercely. Do not go there.

There was a soft throat-clearing behind him and then a new bottle of Singha was set down on the table, like a mirage, its neck frosted with condensation. He looked round and saw the Scottish woman there again, looking sheepish this time. A slight, dark-haired woman with a nose ring stood behind her, arms folded in a meaningful sort of way. 'Sorry,' the Scottish woman said, sounding and looking astonishingly meek compared with earlier. 'My friend has been very clear that I acted like a total dick just now. Have a beer with my apologies.'

Will glanced from the Scottish woman to her friend but this didn't seem to be a wind-up.

'You looked a wee bit down in the dumps, if you don't mind me saying,' added the dark-haired friend. 'Isla here's terrible for grinding men into despair. Don't worry, I've put her in her place on your behalf.'

Not a wind-up. Not a trick. He had a lump in his throat at this startling turn of events. At the beer he'd wished for having manifested before him so unexpectedly. 'Thank you,' he croaked. And then, because they were still hovering and he noticed they had their own drinks in hand, he rallied himself. Made an effort to resurrect the last dregs of his charisma. Maybe this was the distraction he needed to see him through this lonely evening. 'Would you like to join me?'

Chapter Seven

Leni McKenzie memorial page

One of my favourite memories of Leni is back when we were ten years old, and went to a Brownie camp together. An older girl from a different Brownie pack kept picking on Alice, Leni's sister, and obviously Leni was determined to get her back for it. But how? We were all out in the woods for various activities and games when Leni became very thoughtful, and I guessed she was hatching a plan. That evening, she told the most blood-curdling ghost story about a forest monster made of branches and owls' beaks who loved to eat little girls ... and you could always tell who it was going to kill that night because they'd find three sticks beneath their pillow. Later, a great scream went up when we went back to our beds because, you guessed it, the bully had just discovered three sticks under her pillow and was crying so much, her parents had to be called to take her home. As an adult now, I hope the girl wasn't traumatised for too long but as a kid, I just thought it was the funniest thing ever!
  Danielle

★

Like her brother, Alice had been taken aback to see the messages from their dad in the new so-called McKenzies Together chat group. *WTF???* she messaged Will with several eye-rolling emojis. *Is this some kind of joke?*

He'll get bored of it soon, he'd replied. *Let's ignore him and hopefully he'll go away.* Belinda similarly didn't sound in any great hurry to fall in with her ex-husband's new idea. 'That old leopard will never change his spots,' she said dismissively when Alice mentioned the subject on the phone. 'He was probably drunk and maudlin when he wrote that. Take no notice, it won't mean anything.'

So far, none of them had replied to Tony's initial message and Alice felt paralysed by indecision. On one hand, wasn't this what she'd always wanted – for her dad to reach out with fatherly concern? But then again, after all the times he'd let them down, choosing other women over his 'first family', as he put it, forgetting important events in their lives . . . wasn't it already too late? The other day at work, a girl had been regaling the office with how her dad had grilled her boyfriend on meeting him for the first time. 'How much are you earning?' the dad wanted to know, gimlet-eyed. 'What car are you driving? So what makes you think you're good enough for my daughter?' *It was so embarrassing!* she'd cried, clapping her hands to her face as the office erupted in laughter, but all Alice could feel was a twist of envy that her dad had never bothered to meet *her* boyfriends over the years, let alone pepper them with questions to see if they made the grade.

It was complicated, she thought, emerging from Shepherd's Bush tube station on Saturday morning. Life was far too bloody complicated. Although maybe today she'd be able to resolve one of the mysteries that had floated into her consciousness following the discovery of Leni's diary. She paused to check the map on her phone, then headed off along the green. *Cherry Grove, here I come.*

The road was a fast-moving river of traffic, the pavement almost as full, with people hurrying along in their winter coats and scarves: parents holding hands with dawdling children, clusters of track-suited youths with huge white trainers and loud voices, tired-faced women in headscarves lugging bags of shopping. Food smells drifted out from the takeaways — fried chicken, doughnuts, curry spices — and Alice's stomach flipped over with a rush of nausea to be back here, so near the place where her sister had died. She hadn't returned to this part of London since the dark nights of the previous autumn when she'd caused such a scene she'd ended up in the back of a police car. She pushed the memory away, striding determinedly on.

Alice hadn't been able to get very far finding out more about Cherry House. She'd called the number on the website a couple of times and emailed to ask if they had any details about who'd booked the venue for the June day when Leni had (possibly) been heading there, but she'd had no response. *A!! 8 p.m.* was all that was written in her diary that day, and Alice had combed through her sister's social media friends and contacts for people whose names began with 'A', only to draw a blank each time. *Adam, sorry for the random question, but I don't suppose you had made arrangements to meet Leni on the day she died?* she'd messaged her former brother-in-law, but he'd replied in the negative too. If only Leni's phone was available to pore over, it would have been so much easier to piece together her last movements, but that wasn't an option either. The phone had bounced out into the road when Leni was hit by the car, only to be found much later, run over by another vehicle and completely destroyed.

Maybe it wasn't a person she was going to meet. Turning off the main road on to Cherry Grove, Alice remembered the adoption brochure she'd found at the bottom of one of Leni's boxes. Could 'A' stand for 'adoption group'? Aerobics class? Amateur dramatics club? She bit her lip uncertainly. Surely Leni wouldn't have added two exclamation marks if she was going to an aerobics class?

She was getting nearer. 84, 82, 80, she counted, walking past the houses. She could see a red-brick building ahead, different to the Victorian terraced houses she was currently passing, and quickened her step. There it was. She imagined a receptionist behind a desk, tapping away at a keyboard, pot plants set around her. Soft music playing. The receptionist would be calm, helpful. 'You've been trying to call? So sorry, we've had connection issues,' she'd say apologetically. 'But you want some information on a date last June? Of course, let me see ...' And then she'd click a few keys, perhaps squint at the screen a little (the receptionist in her imagination had been meaning to book an optician's appointment) before her face cleared. 'Ah, yes. Of course,' she'd say. And then ...

Alice broke out of her reverie as she arrived at the hall, only to be greeted in the doorway by three little girls in Brownie uniforms. CHERRY GROVE BROWNIES BRING AND BUY SALE, read a hand-painted sign behind them.

'It's 50p to come in,' the tallest Brownie told her, shaking a biscuit tin that jangled with coins.

'Ah,' said Alice. 'Actually, I just wanted to—' There was a woman in a bright pink hair wrap sitting beyond the Brownies, presumably stationed to help out if need be, and Alice looked over the girls' heads, trying to catch her attention. 'Excuse me!' Unfortunately the woman seemed glued to something on her phone and didn't raise her head. 'Could I talk to that lady there, please?' Alice asked the girls.

'That costs 50p as well,' giggled the smallest Brownie, who had red curly hair and a riot of freckles.

'Florence! No, it doesn't!' scolded the middle Brownie crossly. She also had red hair but it was tamed into two neat plaits. Sisters? Alice wondered, remembering with a pang the message someone had left on Leni's memorial page, about the two of them at Brownie camp with Leni coming to her rescue once again. 'She's only six, she shouldn't even *be* here, but Mum said—'

'We've got lots of nice stalls,' the tallest Brownie wheedled, elbowing the other two. Clearly she was the entrepreneur of the group. 'There are clothes and baby things and cakes. I made some of the cakes,' she added, like that might be the clincher.

Browbeaten, Alice got out her purse. 'Fine. 50p,' she said, putting it into the tin, telling herself it would be money well spent if she came away with any answers.

Having finally been allowed over the threshold, it was clear there was no receptionist, so Alice approached the woman in the pink hair wrap. 'Hi. Do you work here?'

The woman had humorous brown eyes and a dimple in her left cheek. 'Me? No! I'm just helping out. Keeping an eye on these monkeys,' she said, raising her gaze from her phone screen.

'Ah, okay. Is there anyone here who might be able to help with a question about booking the hall, do you know?' Alice tried next. 'A booking from last year, I mean; I don't want to make one myself.'

The woman looked blank. 'Sorry, I've got no idea. You could ask Brown Owl, I suppose? I think she's on the tombola. Tall lady. Fluffy blonde hair.' She put her hand up in a confidential manner. 'Been channelling Stalin all morning but don't tell her I said that.'

Recounting this story to her friends Lou and Celeste the following day, Alice was greeted with gales of laughter at this point. 'Intrigue at the Brownies' Bring and Buy Sale,' Lou gurgled. 'This story is taking us to some wild places, Alice.'

'Please tell me the Stalinesque Brown Owl was worth your 50p,' Celeste added, panting slightly. The three of them were jogging very slowly around Victoria Park with the promise of lunch at a dumpling place afterwards; a compromise from Lou's original Park Run suggestion that Alice had vetoed as too ambitious. It had been raining all night and the ground was pocked with puddles reflecting the grey sky, while over on the sodden grass, blackbirds pecked industriously for worms.

'Brown Owl was singularly unhelpful,' she replied, clutching her side where she was getting a stitch. 'I'd even say she got quite arsey with me for interrupting her very important tombola work.' She spoke the words lightly to disguise how deflated she'd felt, standing there in the packed hall, full of excited girls and their parents, stalls laden with second-hand children's books, Brownie-made arts and crafts ('Come and get your home-made pencil cases!') and various bits of pre-loved baby equipment.

'Bummer,' said Lou. 'How frustrating.'

'Yeah. I found a noticeboard with a couple of numbers and a different email address, so I've sent off an enquiry about the date, which is a start. Oh, and the other thing . . .' They swerved to one side to make way for a group of mums wielding buggies with gigantic all-terrain wheels. 'Well, it wasn't an entirely wasted trip.'

She'd been about to leave, she told them, when her eye was caught by a stall selling home-made cushions with appliquéd felt designs – a red house, a blue rabbit, an orange cat – and the latter had reminded her of Hamish, Leni's old cat, and of finding his adoption certificate the other night, after her encounter with sexy Darren. (No, she hadn't told her friends about sexy Darren. Would they make a fuss about her drinking alone and taking home random men for casual sex? You bet. Did she need that in her life? Definitely not.)

'So on my way home, I thought I'd see if I could find out what had happened to Hamish. You know, in the hope he'd been adopted by a lovely new family,' she went on, dodging to avoid a runaway toddler in a red puffa jacket who was bearing down on a nervous pigeon.

Alice still felt bad for not being able to take Hamish in

when he'd needed rehoming, little knowing that Noah and his fur allergy would be moving out of her flat anyway mere months later. Sitting there on the swaying overground train, she'd looked up the Oxford cats' home where her mum had eventually left him and her heart sank with sorrow to see that he was still there, glowering from the web page, no doubt having put off every prospective cat-seeker with his slit-eyed unfriendliness. Oh, Hamish. You deserved better than this, she thought disconsolately. Unless . . .

An idea had struck her like a ray of sunshine beaming through thick cloud and she'd sat up a little straighter. She had space now in her life for a pet to love, didn't she? Her sister's pet . . . what if she was the one to give him his forever home? It would be something really good she could do for him – and for Leni too. Surely this was meant to be? (*Of course it's meant to be!* she imagined Leni crying in frustration at her slow-wittedness. *Just get on the ruddy phone already, will you?*)

The idea had taken hold all the way home and she found herself dialling the number of the rescue centre as soon as she got in her front door, before she'd even taken off her coat. The woman who answered didn't soft-soap Alice about what she might be letting herself in for. 'We tried him with one family before Christmas but his fur started falling out – with stress, we think – and then there were a couple of biting incidents which meant they changed their minds about having him.' She also seemed dubious about someone from London adopting a cat from them – 'We like to do home visits, you see, to make sure you have a suitable place for our animals' – but when Alice explained the situation, only just managing not to cry, and promised she would do everything she could to make him feel loved and safe, the woman softened.

'Bless you, darling,' she said. 'Leave it with me and I'll see what I can do.'

'Oh my God!' cried Lou on hearing this. They were passing a group of lads having a kickabout and the cheer that went up as one of them scored sounded as if they too approved of the story. 'So what happens now?'

'I've had to send them photos of the flat and garden to prove I can give him a safe new home,' Alice replied, panting with the exertion of trying to jog *and* talk. 'And I've filled in an application form and sent that off too. Now I just have to wait.' She was too out of breath to tell them how, unlocking the back door to the garden to take pictures, she'd been ashamed to realise that it was the first time she'd been out there in months. But as she tidied up a little, appreciating the waxy white snowdrops gleaming in the small flowerbed and remembering how the honeysuckle always smelled so beautiful in summertime, she had felt the first faint glimmerings of hope. *This could be a nice space for Hamish, and for her too,* she thought. It might be midwinter now, but on warm days, the garden became a real suntrap; he could stretch out on the cobbles and catch some rays while she perched on the deckchair with a good book. She would fit a cat flap so that he could come and go as he pleased. And on cold evenings, they could curl up together, cosy and warm. Forget all those clichés about spinsters and their moggies, she was up for it.

'Well, fingers – and paws – crossed,' Celeste said. 'I'm totally here for this love story.'

'Me too,' said Alice. If she could bring Hamish back into the McKenzie fold, it would feel like a connection across the void, a shining new link minted with her sister, spanning then to now. *Darren picking up the adoption paper, the ginger cat cushion at the Brownie fair . . . maybe a pattern was emerging,* she thought hopefully. Was this Leni's way of leaving her a breadcrumb trail showing her how to get through this, how to live?

Chapter Eight

Leni McKenzie memorial page

I met Leni at uni and some of my funniest memories ever are from when we shared a flat in Wavertree. One hot June day, we were trying and failing to revise for our second-year exams when an ice cream van trundled along the street. I don't know how, but Leni talked the ice cream man into letting us help him because we needed 'work experience for our careers'. 'Have a break, I'll make you a coffee,' she told him. 'We'll serve your customers.' He must have been mad — or maybe he just hated the job — but anyway he agreed and we both ended up in the van for over an hour, serving terrible ice creams to the Wavertree kids. Much more fun than revision!

I still think of Leni and smile every time I hear an ice cream van. I think I probably always will.

Maxine

Ray pulled on the handbrake and they sat motionless for a moment, staring at the house in front of them. 'Well,' he

93

said unnecessarily. 'And wow. Bloody hell. Here we are, your ladyship.'

Here they were indeed. Outside a double-fronted Cotswold stone farmhouse, way out in the sticks, with a crescent-shaped gravel drive and planters either side of the door. Belinda gulped. Despite the weeks they'd spent clearing out and painting, all the trips to and from the storage centre and the dump, she hadn't quite believed in what they were doing. Now, belatedly, the magnitude of their plans was hitting home and the reality seemed ... well, pretty daunting. 'Are you sure we can afford this?' she asked eventually, her voice a croak.

'With the money from my flat, and what we'll hopefully get from your house, plus a fair wind behind us, just about,' he replied, reaching over and patting her leg. 'Don't be fooled by first appearances, by the way. When I booked the appointment, the estate agent himself warned me that it would need a hell of a lot of TLC to make it habitable for us, let alone any paying guests.' He nudged her across the handbrake when she didn't reply. 'You do still want this, don't you?'

She tried to say yes but the word wouldn't fall easily from her tongue. They had talked endlessly about their shared pipe dream of running a B. & B.: creating a beautiful, comfortable haven for a stream of interesting guests. Ray was keen to offer bespoke experiences to the guests – quad-biking and falconry and kayaking; he had all sorts of ideas. Now that they were here though, presented with a version of that dream in actual bricks and mortar, she felt paralysed with uncertainty. *Did* she want to do this? Had she ever wanted this, or had it been a suggestion that she'd seized upon, clung to as a way out?

Her own hesitation made her feel such an idiot after all the work they'd done together to reach this point, not to mention all the couples who had already come traipsing round their spotless house flicking glances into every corner. It was as if she'd been joining in a game all along, a lovely distracting game of make-believe that she hadn't quite expected to turn into anything more.

'Yes,' she managed to say at last, but there was a quaver in her voice that he must have heard too. 'But . . .' It was so quiet here. Only the sound of the birds, and the wind in the trees. The nearest neighbours were a few minutes' walk away and the centre of the village half a mile. She had lived in her home for three decades and her entire life was centred on that street, that postcode. All her friends were nearby, she had her routines, her favourite shops and pubs, walks on Port Meadow . . . 'It's just . . . I feel a bit weird,' she confessed.

She looked at the house again, this time taking in more of the details. There was a beautiful stone portico around the doorway, its roof carved in the shape of a seashell; a stained-glass fanlight above the white-painted door; two twisting red-brick chimneys on the roof. First impressions – it was undeniably beautiful, however crumbly the inside might turn out to be. A hundred times fancier than anywhere she'd ever lived before. The driveway, for starters – imagine never having to parallel park on her narrow street any more. Sometimes you could be tootling around for ten minutes or more, looking for a space to squeeze into. And yet, according to Ray's calculations, that daily irritation could be removed. Oxford house prices were insane, but even so, she was astonished to realise that her small three-bedroom terraced house had gone up in value enough over the years for them to even consider a place like this.

'You *are* allowed to be happy again,' Ray reminded her gently and she flashed him a grateful smile.

'I know,' she said, pulling herself together. 'I'm just being silly. Come on, let's go and look around.'

She'd met Ray soon after Will had left for university, nine years ago. The noisy, busy family home now an echoing empty nest, she hadn't known what to do with herself. 'You're free, lucky you,' sighed her sister Carolyn, who'd had children much later than Belinda, and was still stuck in the routine of swimming lessons and gym kit and pet hamsters that either escaped or died. Friends whose houses were now similarly depleted all seemed to be booking themselves holidays and relishing the independence that came with having newly dispatched their offspring. 'It's our time now!' was the gleeful catchphrase among them.

Belinda, meanwhile, had gone through something of a crisis of confidence. After twenty-plus years, certain of her place as a mum at the centre of her family, it was unsettling to find herself relegated to a lower priority in her children's lives. No longer needed in the same way, no longer the lynchpin keeping them all together. She still had work, sure, but coming home to a cold, dark house each night felt so dispiriting, she sometimes felt very much like turning round and going straight back out again. And it was all very well for her friends to gallivant about, but most of them were settled in couples, which made the whole experience easier and more fun to navigate. Who did Belinda have to gallivant with? Were the best days of her life already over?

In the end, it had been a friend, Kath, who rescued her from total stagnation by throwing a wild house party for her fiftieth and inviting everyone she knew. And this happened to include Ray, an old mate of Kath's husband from the days when they'd both been roadies together. That night, Ray had made Belinda laugh again for what felt like the first time in weeks, with some of his tall stories about life on the road. He was funny, charming and unconventional, and although he had a pretty wild hinterland – addiction demons, and a marriage and family life that he'd destroyed (his words) due to his own selfish behaviour – he was twelve years clean at that point and great company.

Sod's law, of course, Will dropped out of university after a single term – 'Just full of snobby arseholes from private schools' – and so he was home again anyway, but by then she and Ray were an item, and she had a new spring in her step. Belinda had previously led something of a conventional life – she'd married young, and then had the dual responsibilities of children and work to keep her busy – but Ray brought an extra spice to her life, opened her eyes to new thrills that the world had to offer. He took her to festivals (and seemed to know *everyone* backstage), they travelled around India together – he even taught her how to surf one summer in Cornwall.

So *this* is living, she kept finding herself thinking, fizzing with reinvention.

Almost a decade later, here they were, planning to throw in their lots together in the name of a whole new joint adventure. Maybe even based around this very house they'd parked in front of – if it didn't fall down before then, obviously. She eyed it with new wariness. It wouldn't fall down, would it? There were so many accidents that could happen at any moment. Maybe they'd be better off with a new-build after all?

Before she could suggest this to Ray, the estate agent pulled up beside them in a smart racing-green Mini and hopped out, a whirl of energy, brandishing keys and a rather dog-eared brochure. According to Ray's intel, the house had been on the market for eight months already, long enough for the estate agent to have honed his spiel about 'potential' and 'transformation' plus a hastily mumbled – and ominous – warning about not touching any of the wiring: *it's probably safe but best not to chance it.* Oh heavens, thought Belinda, who'd always been a dreamy toucher of things, the sort of person who'd trail her fingertips absent-mindedly along walls and surfaces without even knowing she was doing so. 'Let's hope we get out of here alive,' Ray said, taking Belinda's hand as they crossed the threshold. 'You don't need *all* your limbs, do you?'

Inside, the house smelled of damp and neglect, there were cobwebs in the corners, dust everywhere, and interesting-looking mould creeping up the wall of the downstairs loo. Bare wires sprouted alarmingly from ceilings and occasionally from what once had been light switches on the walls. Faded wallpaper bubbled and peeled around the living-room hearth, a withered brown sprig of holly lay forlornly on the mantelpiece, a relic from a Christmas long before, while the carpet throughout had seen better days. The kitchen looked about twenty years out of date, and without needing to touch anything (no thanks) Belinda knew that every surface would be coated with a disgusting sticky film. Meanwhile, outside, the garden was positively jungly, with long grass invading what was left of the flowerbeds, bindweed strangling elderly rose bushes and the flagstones of the patio covered in moss.

'Well, it's a mess, all right,' Ray said cheerfully as they stood there on the grimy old patio. As someone who'd had his name down on the local allotment list for almost three years, Belinda knew he would already be thinking about vegetable plots and a greenhouse and a proper lawn with stripes. 'But there's definitely potential. This must have been the most glorious house in its heyday, don't you think? Imagine the parties!' He whistled under his breath, shaking his head. Then, when she made no immediate reply, he prompted, 'What *do* you think?'

Above them, the milky white clouds parted and Belinda turned her face to the weak winter sun, grateful for its benevolent warmth. She could hear birds singing, the distant rumble of a tractor, a breeze soughing through the bare branches of the old cherry tree nearby. She thought again of the large quiet rooms they'd walked through; their generous sizes, the big windows with their views out on to the Oxfordshire countryside. Yes, the house was rundown, but it was gorgeous. Its walls whispered to her temptingly about all the good times it had seen, and her imagination obligingly filled in the gaps to conjure up colourful images of decadence and beauty.

They'd have to roll up their sleeves and work harder than ever before, but ...

Her stomach cramped as she thought again of the memories she would be leaving behind. Christmas dinners and birthday parties in the kitchen. All of those broken nights with babies, nursing them in the bedroom as the sun sent the first rays of pink morning light beneath the curtains. The walks to school. The trick-or-treating along the street. The washing machine forever rumbling through school uniform and PE kits and bedding ... *You know you're not meant to make any big life decisions in the first year after a bereavement,* she heard Alice chide again in her head, and bit her lip that she could have dismissed her daughter's advice so breezily. Might they be making a mistake after all?

'Bel?' prompted Ray, still looking at her expectantly. 'So I was thinking we could run the zip wire from the attic window down to the back wall there ... Maybe turn the garden into a mountain bike circuit ... Nope. You're not listening, are you?'

Something even more serious had occurred to her. What did Leni think of this place? And Apolline? Would she still be able to speak to Leni here? *She keeps mentioning a man,* Apolline had said the other day and Belinda's heart had almost stopped. *A name beginning with G, perhaps?*

'I ... I ...' she stuttered now, aware of Ray's eyes on her. The thing was, she felt unable to give a proper opinion without the soothing tones of Apolline steering her in one direction or another. How could she make such a massive decision without guidance? 'I think I'd like to speak to a ... a friend,' she stammered, unable to look him in the eye any more.

His sigh sounded very much like one of exasperation. 'Don't I count? I'm right here. Can't you talk to me? I won't even charge you a premium hotline rate.'

She flushed. 'Yes, but I need . . . I'm not sure . . .' She broke off because she couldn't bear the irritated stiffness of his body language, the resignation now on his face.

'You're talking about your psychic pal, I take it,' he said stonily and she hung her head. 'Bel – this has got to stop. This is holding you back, can't you see? She's not good for you. I dread to think how much money you've already wasted calling her.'

'It's *not* holding me back! And it's not a waste! How can you say that? She means everything to me!' Her voice was more passionate than she intended and the sound seemed to reverberate off the stone wall behind them.

'And that, right there, is the problem,' he replied, folding his arms. Ray was not the argumentative type, but today she had the feeling he was digging in mulishly for the long haul, that he was not about to back down. Well, so be it, she thought, hackles rising in self-defence. Because neither was she. 'These phone calls have become a problem,' he went on. 'You must know, deep down, that it's a scam. You must do. None of it is real. She's a charlatan, this woman, she's preying on your unhappiness. And at what price, eh?'

Belinda gasped as if he'd hit her. 'She is *not*! She's my friend! Our calls are the most precious thing in my life because through her I can talk to Leni again.' Her voice shook. 'How can I give that up? How?'

She was starting to feel hysterical, which was not helped

101

by Ray taking hold of her arms. 'Listen to me,' he said. 'Leni's gone. I know it's awful. I know it's the worst thing ever. But—'

'How are we doing, then?' Of course the estate agent had to pick that moment to walk out of the kitchen door towards them, his eager face drooping as soon as he realised he'd interrupted an emotional scene. 'Ah. Sorry. I'll ... I'll give you a few minutes,' he said, backing away immediately, hands raised.

'It's fine, you don't need to,' Belinda said heavily, wrenching herself from Ray's grasp. 'We don't want the house. It's a no.'

'We – wait. We haven't even talked about it yet,' Ray protested, but she was walking blindly past him by then, past the startled-looking estate agent too and back into the cold damp air of the house, feeling overwhelmed by everything. 'Bel!' he shouted after her, hurrying to catch her up. 'Wait!'

Chapter Nine

McKenzies Together group

Saturday
Hi all, hope everyone has nice plans for the weekend. Am attaching some of my favourite photos of Leni. I love the one with her gappy teeth! Take care of yourselves. Love Dad/Tony x 10.17

Sunday
Happy Sunday, everyone! What are you all up to? Anyone fancy a chat later? Love Dad/Tony x 15.43

Monday
How are you all doing? I've been reading up on grief and keep seeing that talking can really help – to a counsellor or a bereavement group. What do you think? Maybe we should all give that a go? 09.27
Will: *You first then, Dad 18.50*

'He was only nineteen; he'd barely started his life. Everything was ahead of him: falling in love, finishing university, travelling with friends, his first proper job ...' The blonde woman's voice wobbled. You could tell she was trying her hardest not to cry. *Christ*, thought Tony, shifting uncomfortably on his seat, wondering if it would be too obvious for him to make an excuse to leave the first chance he got.

'As far as I knew, he'd never even smoked a cigarette before, let alone tried drugs,' the blonde went on. 'And to think of him there, all alone, in his final few moments ...' Her shoulders heaved. 'The post-mortem said ...' She broke down and beside her, a young woman with short pink hair reached out and put a hand gently on her back as she sobbed. 'The post-mortem said his organs failed. He must have been in absolute agony.'

Tony bowed his head so that he didn't have to witness the woman's distress with his eyes as well as his ears. This was *horrific*. Pretty much on a par with having his fingernails ripped out one by one. Whatever had made him think that coming here, to the east Oxford bereavement support group, would be a good idea? Already he had sat through so much suffering, so many tragic tales of loss. It was deeply disturbing, being this close to raw grief and heartbreak. He thought longingly of the Champions League match taking place right now, wishing he could check the score on his phone. Not because he was totally callous – more as a temporary, necessary reprieve from the misery currently sweeping through this chilly village hall; so that he could be reminded that life went on at European football grounds and elsewhere, that other people were still happy and excited and enjoying themselves.

'You, going to a support group? Wow, that's ... good. That's really good, Tony,' Jackie had said in surprise when he announced his whereabouts for that evening. Admittedly, he'd surprised himself with the decision, but after days of silence on the group chat – you could practically see the tumble-weed rolling across the screen – he'd been so pleased to get a response from Will, even a sardonic, challenging one, he hadn't felt able to fudge the issue. Meanwhile Alice was yet to reply to any of his messages, and as for Belinda ...

He sighed to himself, remembering her expression when he'd seen her the other day: shock, guilt and finally dislike crossing her face within a single second. The whole thing had been discomfiting, frankly. He'd popped into town on his lunch break and was walking up the high street when he glimpsed her through the window of a café, sitting there on her phone. In the past he might have glanced across and kept on walking, but in the spirit of McKenzies Together, he knocked on the window instead and gave a friendly wave when she looked up. Sod it, he thought. They had once been married and the best of friends; they had children together. Whatever had gone wrong between them in the past, didn't he owe it to what was left of their family – and to Leni – to be civil and pleasant now?

She didn't seem to agree, shaking her head at him when he gestured that he would come in and then looking extremely fed up when he arrived beside her table. 'I'm on the *phone!*' she hissed, clutching her mobile protectively to her chest. 'Is it important?'

'Well ... no, I ...' His good intentions shrivelled away. 'I just thought I'd say hello, that's all.'

'Right. Hello,' she replied, pretty rudely, on reflection. Then she turned away, pressing the phone to her ear once more. 'Hi. Sorry about that,' he heard her say. 'Carry on.'

That might have been that, him sent packing and sloping back out again, but then he heard her asking in a low voice, 'Has Leni told you anything else?' which stopped him in his tracks. His heart thudded, his skin prickled; for a stupid, wild moment he found himself wondering if he'd been mistaken and Leni was actually still alive, before catching on to himself. *Idiot. You went to her funeral.* He must have misheard.

Something prevented him from walking any further though. He dropped down, pretending to retie his shoelace, ears on stalks to hear more. Belinda gave a little chuckle. 'Well, she *would* say that,' she said happily. 'One thing you should know about Leni, she loves to wind me up.'

A silver-haired woman on the table nearby shot Tony a disapproving look as if she'd seen right through him, crouching there with his fake shoelace problem. He got reluctantly to his feet, keen not to be confronted in case it alerted Belinda's attention. Could there be another Leni in her life? he mused on his way out. Unless he'd heard wrong and she'd said 'Penny' or 'Nelly' or some other similar-sounding name. It was possible, he supposed.

Anyway, he would keep on trying with Belinda and his children, he'd vowed – hence him being here at this bereavement group meeting, having a very uncomfortable time. When he'd suggested talking to a counsellor or group to the rest of the family, he'd intended his advice to be gratefully picked up by *them*, rather than thrown back at him, but never mind.

The blonde woman was now shuddering to a tearful halt, poor thing. Looking at her made Tony feel as if he in comparison was a weak imitation of a grieving parent, as if he hadn't loved his own daughter adequately, as if his heart wasn't big enough to contain the equivalent depths of feeling. Nor would he ever be able to unload his feelings like that to a room full of strangers with such unflinching honesty. It was as if she had peeled open the layers of her skin to reveal her heart, stuttering valiantly along, despite everything.

'Thank you for sharing, Ellen,' the group leader, Monica, said gently. Monica was tall and rather headmistress-like, nearing retirement age, with a kind but firm manner. Her bespectacled gaze roamed the circle of grievers and then – horror of horrors – stopped at Tony. 'Tony, is it? Would you like to say anything this evening?'

Tony swallowed, under pressure. 'Oh,' he mumbled, floundering for words as he stared down at the beige lino floor. 'Er ...'

'It's completely up to you,' Monica told him, pushing her glasses a little further up her nose. She had bobbed, greying hair and wore a smart navy skirt with a mustard blouse which was adorned by a big amethyst brooch. His mind wanted to lead him off on a tangent about brooches and how you never really saw people wearing them any more but he dragged himself reluctantly back to the room.

'Um. Not today,' he muttered, embarrassed. 'Thank you though.' He could feel everyone looking at him, wondering what his story might be, and his cheeks began heating up under their collective gaze. 'I'm ... I'm still coming to terms with ... the situation,' he said awkwardly after a moment, which earned him a few nods of understanding at least.

'That's fine. We're here when you feel like speaking – and for when you'd rather listen, too,' Monica said. Then she turned to the rotund man with a cast on his ankle who was perspiring under the light, even though it was a freezing January evening and most people still had their coats on. 'Gary? How are you this week? Do you want to talk to the group?'

Gary's mouth was trembling and he passed a hand over his face as if overcome, but then nodded and began. He was a newly widowed dad to three children and spoke eloquently of the guilt he felt at being the parent who'd survived, as well as the dread that he was letting down his sons and daughter on all counts.

Jesus, Tony thought, sinking lower in his seat. This got worse and worse. He was actually starting to feel tearful himself, listening to Gary berate himself for crying in front of his kids, for not knowing the right things to say to them, for feeling as if he was getting everything wrong, every day. Tony was not proud of the heady jag of relief that came when Monica said, a short while later, that they would have to finish now for the evening, but honestly, he wasn't sure he could sit there any longer and be part of this man's unhappiness. Thank heavens for that.

Monica was still talking: if anyone wanted to continue the conversation, they could move next door, to the Four Oaks pub, she told them. 'Although, remember, alcohol is not always your friend when you're fragile,' she added as some of the group got to their feet, looking more cheerful. 'Soft drinks *are* available and are, in my opinion, the advisable choice during difficult periods.'

Tony, meanwhile, could hardly make for the exit fast enough. But his swift getaway was snatched from his grasp when a young woman fell purposefully into step with him.

'I know it's hard, on your first time,' she said, zipping up her silver padded coat as she walked. It was the pink-haired woman – not much older than a girl, really; she had the youthful bloom of someone still in their twenties. 'I was the same, the first few weeks I was here. Didn't trust myself to speak in case I lost it. But it does make you feel better, if you can get stuff off your chest. Everyone's lovely, as I'm sure you noticed.'

He gave her a brief, tight-lipped smile, not really wanting to get into conversation. He didn't feel like admitting that the problem was not that he was worried he'd 'lose it', as she'd said, more that the evening had left him feeling emotionally unqualified from start to finish. He was a middle-aged, pretty old-fashioned bloke at the end of the day – pouring his heart out to strangers was not what he did. Besides, what if the others judged him for not having been much of a dad in the first place?

'Yes, they seemed nice enough,' he responded blandly, longing to be in the sanctuary of his car by now, 5 Live providing football updates, his hands on the wheel as he sped away from this place forever. 'I'd better go – I think my parking ticket's about to run out. Nice to meet you.'

She opened her mouth as if there was more to discuss, but he didn't give her the chance to say another word, calling

'Goodbye!' and striding quickly out into the street. Instantly, he felt like a wanker for doing so. She was young and only trying to be friendly, after all. Presumably while still dealing with her own bereavement on top of everything else.

God. How come when he tried to do something good he ended up making a prick of himself? Even the bit about the parking ticket was a lie. 'Sometimes I wonder if you're actually human,' his second wife Isabelle had shouted at him shortly before their marriage broke down irreparably. She was half Spanish and a dancer, and he'd been bewitched by her passion and tempestuousness, until both of those personality traits rebounded on him, and not in a good way. 'Do you *have* any feelings in there, or are you merely selfish bullshit through and through?'

He had reached his car by now and slunk into the driver's seat, exhaling with his eyes shut for a few moments. *No*, he told the Isabelle of his memory. *I am not entirely made of selfish bullshit.* Then, as if to prove it, he reached for his phone. 'Call Alice, please,' he requested, glad that Jackie wasn't there to tease him for it. *It's not a person, you don't have to be polite to your phone!* she hooted whenever she caught him out. Tony had been brought up to mind his P's and Q's ('McKenzies have manners!'), and privately thought barking orders at technology was the beginning of the end for civilisation.

'Hi Dad,' Alice said, sounding surprised. Perhaps a little suspicious. 'Are you okay?'

'Yeah. I just ...' He ducked his head away as he saw a couple of people from the group walking by – a couple whose severely disabled son had died at the age of two, seven years

110

earlier. *We're having another baby but we're both very scared*, the woman had said, eyes filming over with unshed tears. Tony blinked their faces away and forced himself to continue. 'Well, I just thought I'd ring for a chat.' Even to his own ears, his words sounded implausible. He tried to think when he'd last called her like this. Christmas, maybe?

He braced himself for a sarcastic reply – *Wow, I'm honoured* or something similar – but none came. If anything she sounded a bit flat. 'Okay,' she said uncertainly. 'So ... how are you?'

'I've had better evenings,' he replied. 'I took my own advice tonight and went to talk about my feelings at a bereavement support group,' he went on. 'Although ironically I didn't say a word. Sat there feeling depressed about everything. God knows why anyone thinks these things help. Everyone there was crying their eyes out. It was awful, Alice. Terrible. We must never take my advice seriously, ever again. I mean it. I know nothing.'

She laughed – politely, perhaps, but the sound lit a tiny flame inside him nonetheless. 'Oh dear.'

'Exactly. A spectacular own goal.' His thoughts flicked back to that evening's football – he still hadn't checked the scores – and then he had to hunt around his mind for something else to say because suddenly, already, it felt as if the conversation had lost momentum. 'How's work?' he said, cringing as he did so, because it felt like all those awkward weekend dad *How's school?* conversations he'd attempted back when the children were little and he'd moved out.

'Fine,' Alice mumbled, just as she and her siblings had always done to the *How's school* question. Then she must have changed her mind, because she added, 'Actually no, it's really boring and tedious. I'm temping at the moment, it's not great.'

'Oh,' he said, wrong-footed. The last he'd heard she'd been working for a glamorous-sounding marketing agency in London, and absolutely loved it. 'What happened to your other job? Fancied a change, or ... ?'

'Something like that,' she muttered in a way that didn't invite further discussion.

'Right,' he said, frowning. 'And how are you ... in yourself? I mean, with everything, you know ...' He grimaced, hating feeling so tongue-tied with his own daughter. At work, he could schmooze anyone into a sale, but when it came to actual sincerity, the right words seemed to slide out of reach.

'Well ... Not great, to be honest,' she said. 'But I've been sorting through some of Leni's things, which makes me feel closer to her, at least. Mum and I started a few weeks ago and I've taken the rest of her stuff back to my flat to finish.'

'That's good,' he said heartily, putting her on speakerphone and starting the car. 'There's something comforting about doing useful tasks like that; I remember me and your uncles sorting out Grandad's house after he died.' His parents had passed away one after the other, as neat and punctual in death as they had been in life, and he found himself back there momentarily, standing with his brothers in the living room of that small Kidlington semi, confronted by the accumulation of two lifetimes: the soft, faded armchairs, the prickly hearthside rug they'd wrestled on as boys, the yellowing paperbacks in the bookshelves constructed by his dad. 'It's not an easy job, I know. So please don't feel you have to do it alone. You've got me, remember, keen and eager to offer my services.'

There was a small pause and then she said, 'I'm finding it quite emotional, actually. I'm trying to do right by her – you know, make sure everything goes to a good home. Giving her stuff to her friends, which has been really nice, especially hearing their memories of her.' He heard her sigh. 'But it's made me realise there was a lot I didn't know about her, which makes me feel sad.'

He felt the weight of her grief compound his own mood. 'Same,' he said, his voice catching on the word. He drove past the pink-haired woman just then, walking with her head down, looking completely miserable, and felt a further wrench of guilt that he'd been so quick to shake her off. 'You always think there's more time, don't you? All the time in the world to tie up loose ends, say sorry, make amends. But ...'

'Mmm,' Alice said, with rather an edge to her voice. 'Anyway, talking of things going to a good home – or at least a new one,' she went on with determined-sounding brightness, 'I'm adopting her cat. Remember Hamish?'

'The ginger savage who scratched your brother's arm to pieces? Oh yeah. Yowled the entire van journey back up the M40.' The full meaning of her words belatedly sank in. 'So you're having him, are you?'

'That's what I said. Picking him up after work tomorrow. The start of a beautiful new relationship, I hope.'

'Oh, Ali, that's lovely. Really lovely. Leni would have been so chuffed. I felt bad that, you know, we didn't step up for him at the time, but ...'

'Mmm,' she said again, before he could launch into excuses. Another little cut, right there. 'How's Jackie?'

'Jackie's fine. We're starting antenatal classes next week,' he said. A black BMW was coming towards him and his fingers tightened automatically on the wheel. It had been a BMW that had knocked Leni down that night, and for a while he'd found himself obsessively calculating the driver's braking capacity, wondering darkly about the state of his tyre treads. He still detested BMWs and their drivers. 'Screw you,' he said under his breath, like he did whenever he saw one.

'Pardon?'

'Sorry – not you. Um. Yes, so antenatal classes, everything's getting real now. I'm a bit nervous, Ali, about going through it all again.'

'Going through it all again? What do you mean – whether you'll stay the course this time?'

He winced at her iciness and scrambled to clarify. 'I mean – the sleepless nights, the anxiety about every little rash and cough and whether or not they're still breathing . . .'

'Dad – you know Leni was desperate for a baby, don't you?' she interrupted angrily. '*Desperate*. She and Adam tried and tried and tried. She was even considering adoption at the end, I think. So for you to be moaning about feeling anxious, when you're so bloody lucky that you can apparently produce babies at the drop of a hat, without even trying—'

Oh God.

'– Then it's kind of bad taste, don't you think? But maybe that's part of the problem – that you *don't* think. Anyway, I'd better go. Thanks for ringing, okay? Bye.'

Phone disconnected, the automated voice told him through the speaker and he gave a groan of frustration before tooting a dawdling Volvo in front, out of sheer irritation. Damn it, he was trying, all right? He was doing his best. As for Leni being 'desperate' for a baby, that wasn't the sort of thing daughters talked to their dads about, was it? How was he supposed to know?

Except she might have confided in him, if he'd been there to listen, he reminded himself. If they'd had a decent father-daughter relationship to start with. And now she was gone and it was too late, and he was left feeling like a failure, neither liked nor trusted by any of his kids. Or even his ex-wife, he thought, remembering their strange exchange the other day. Then he felt like kicking himself for not having mentioned it to Alice while he had the chance. Although she'd prob-ably have torn a strip off him for that too: criticised him for eavesdropping, saying it was none of his business who Belinda spoke to or about.

Tony sighed again and thumped the steering wheel mis-erably, overwhelmed with self-recrimination. He had to do better for the new baby, he told himself. He could do it, couldn't he?

Chapter Ten

Alice: Dad rang me last night – really pissed me off tbh. Going on about sorting through Grandad's things after he died, like that's in any way the same as me sorting through Leni's stuff! So insensitive!!

Belinda: That man has absolutely no idea sometimes [angry-face emoji, dagger emoji]

Belinda: Also – is it too much for you? Don't feel you have to do everything yourself, darling [heart emoji]

Alice: It's fine, Mum. I want to do it, if that doesn't sound weird. Just got fed up with Dad making it about himself as usual. Talk later? Going out with the girls tonight but could ring you afterwards?

Belinda: Sounds good. Have fun! Love you [clinking-glasses emoji, heart emoji]

'So how's it working out with your new feline flatmate?' Lou asked, a forkful of chicken jalfrezi halfway to her mouth. 'I bet he's glad to be back in a home again, after the rescue centre.'

Alice pulled a face. 'You'd think so, wouldn't you?' she said drily. Was it too soon to admit that she was already wondering if she'd made a terrible mistake in adopting Hamish? So far he'd repeatedly peed in a corner of the bedroom despite his clean new litter tray, he'd sharpened his claws on the sofa (her only decent bit of furniture) and he'd turned his nose up at the food she set down, the bed she'd bought him, the love she kept trying to offer. It was Saturday evening now, two days since she'd gone to pick him up, and frankly she was relieved to be out with her friends in their favourite Hackney curry house rather than feeling bad about her inability to make Hamish happy. 'It's early days, I guess,' she added with a shrug.

'Yeah,' said Celeste. 'And if he doesn't buck his ideas up within a week or so, there are plenty of chicken shops around here that might take him off your hands. I'm kidding!' she cried as the others rounded on her with horrified looks. 'Although ...' She held up a piece of meat from her own curry and sniffed it dubiously. 'Maybe not. I've no idea what I'm eating here, after all.'

They laughed, and Alice felt a rush of gratitude that the two of them had insisted on her coming out tonight, with Celeste even driving over to give her a lift when she'd initially made an excuse about being too tired.

It turned out that chat, delicious curry and background sitar music was the holiday from real life she needed. Lou had surprised everyone with a cool new fringe ('Are you sure it's not too short?') and cracked them up with stories about her boyfriend's eccentric family. Meanwhile, Celeste, who worked as the events manager for a wine company, always had juicy anecdotes about badly behaved partygoers. Thank God for friends.

'And what else is happening with you, Alice?' Lou prompted during a conversational lull. 'Have you got any further with your investigations?'

'With Cherry House? Not really,' she replied. She'd had a dream last night that she was lost in a high-hedged maze, calling Leni's name, disoriented and alone. *Where are you?* she kept yelling. *I can't find you!* Her search for answers was proving similarly hopeless. 'I finally got through to the person who runs the bookings for the place, but there's no regular booking for Thursday nights at eight o'clock. Leni had put 8 p.m. in her diary,' she added, seeing their uncomprehending looks. 'And it was a Thursday when – you know.'

'Right,' said Celeste sympathetically, tearing off a piece of naan bread.

'A local junior orchestra book the space from 6.30 to 7.45 on Thursdays, apparently, and then there's a choir that meets at 8.30, but nothing in between. So I think the address must be a red herring, unless this "A" Leni wrote down was, like, a junior saxophonist called Albert or a soprano called Amaryllis, maybe.' She shrugged, disappointed that she didn't have more to report. That she seemed to have hit a brick wall in her investigations. *I can't find you!* she heard herself shout once more in her dream.

Lou and Celeste exchanged a look. 'Must be frustrating,' Lou said after a moment. 'But ...' She hesitated and Alice steeled herself for what might be coming. 'Maybe you could ... let it go? Sorry, I'm not being flippant,' she added hastily. 'I'm really, really not. I know how much you wished you could have been with her in those last few weeks, but ...'

She was floundering, so Celeste stepped in to help. 'But at the end of the day, you were thick as thieves for all of those months and years beforehand, right? So ...'

Alice stared down at her plate as Celeste left her sentence unfinished. They didn't get it. 'It matters to me,' she said quietly, flashing back to the argument they'd had on Leni's birthday, the last time she'd seen her sister alive. It transpired that Leni had read far more into Alice's refusal of a glass of fizz than she should have done, and later, when everyone else had gone home, she had lashed out, drunk and nasty with it.

'I don't think you and Noah should have a kid' was her opening salvo. By then, the sunny May day had sweated into a heavy, oppressive afternoon and Leni was fiddling about opening windows while Alice finished the washing-up.

'*What?*' Alice wasn't sure she'd heard correctly at first. She put the last wine glass in the drying rack and turned, looking around for a tea towel to dry her wet hands.

'You, not drinking earlier. Is that what it's about? *Let's have a baby!* Well, it's a bad idea for you two, that's all. If you ask my opinion.' Leni's chin was up in that defiant way she had, but usually Leni's defiance was aimed at other people, not Alice. It was horrible, Alice thought shakily, to find herself in the firing line. 'He's just another Tony McKenzie, can't you see? A man-child who won't stay with you. Don't saddle yourself with him *and* a kid, whatever you do.'

Alice felt as if she'd been slapped by her sister's presumptions, not least because they were all wrong. 'I wasn't asking your opinion,' she said in reply, wiping her hands on her trousers for want of anything else. Leni was not herself, sure, but Alice had done nothing to deserve this. She thought longingly of the street outside, the walk to the tube station and home. Get me out of here already. 'Right. Well, if that's everything, I—'

'Why aren't you being honest with me? Worried I might cry or something? Tell me the truth!'

'Stop being so paranoid! I'm not hiding anything,' Alice snapped, irritation rising. 'We're not trying for a baby. But even if we *were*, it wouldn't be up to you to grant me approval or police the whole thing, like you seem to think. Because it would be none of your goddamn business.' Sod off, she felt like saying as she walked stiffly over to pick up her bag. Why couldn't Alice and her boyfriend make their own decisions without consulting her? The truth was, yes, they had occasionally talked about babies, but only in that idle, dreamy way that couples did after a while. 'I've got a hangover, that's all,' she added. 'That's why I didn't want a drink today. So you can take your little paranoid theories and shove them.'

That might have been it, a quick stride to the front door and then across the threshold and out, but Leni hadn't finished yet. 'Yeah, whatever, I was only thinking of you,' she called down the hall. 'Because Noah's not good enough for you, Alice.'

'Well, I like him, all right?' Alice was unable to suppress her anger. Just because Leni was the older sister, it didn't give her the right to toss her opinions about like this. Not good enough for you, indeed. What about all the dodgy boyfriends Leni had had before she married Adam? 'I *love* him. We're happy together. Just because you're still moping around, doesn't mean I can't be happy!'

'When are you going to grow up though? What do you know about adult life? Nothing, because you're still acting like a teenager, passively letting stuff happen to you; you've never had the bottle to commit to anything. Lucky you! You get to be the younger sister who keeps screwing up while I'm—'

Alice was out of the house by then and didn't hear any more. What the hell? she raged to herself, all the way to the tube station. What the actual fuck?

Sorry, Leni had texted a few days later. *I didn't mean the things I said, I was drunk and horrible. Forgive me?*

But Alice had found it hard to move past the vicious words because she knew Leni *had* meant them at the time, that they clearly contained some knotty truth at their centre. She'd always basked in her sister's approval and love, but now ... now she didn't feel Leni had her back in quite the same way.

Sure, she eventually replied, but a coolness had set in by then. They had texted a few more times but hadn't seen one another again. How Alice wished she could have picked up that last phone call. Why, oh why had she listened to Noah when he said, 'Hurry up, babe, we're going to be late. Call her back some other time'?

It had plagued her ever since, wondering what Leni would have said. Was she lonely? Unhappy? In need of a friend? If Alice could have just answered her phone and said, 'I'm sorry too, let's not argue again, come out with us tonight,' Noah might have had a sulk – he had been saying for months that Leni took advantage of Alice's kind heart – but they would all still be alive, wouldn't they? Leni would be alive. Why had Alice been so selfish, so small-minded as to refuse her own sister that small act of charity?

'Most people find it easier to be angry rather than sad,' the policewoman had commented to Alice back in October, driving her home in the police car, after picking her up for 'making a public nuisance of herself' on the street. Despite the woman's stern manner, Alice could detect a certain gruff kindness too – the officer herself had lost her brother two years ago, it turned out, and she understood the pain. What was more, she was right. Sadness was bloody awful. It never went away! At least with anger you could burn off your feelings with an explosive blow-up now and then.

'Sorry,' Lou said now because obviously some of Alice's painful memories were showing on her face. 'I didn't mean – I wasn't saying—'

'I just want to know where she was going that night,' Alice said flatly, and tipped the rest of her beer down her throat. 'It feels important, like finding out might bring me closer to her.'

'We understand,' Celeste said, taking her hand and squeezing it. 'And if there's anything we can do …'

'Thanks,' Alice said, and then changed the subject, asking Lou about a work conference she'd been dreading. But as her friend launched into the story, she found it impossible to concentrate because her thoughts were sliding back down into the bad place again, remembering the coroner's inquest, how they'd seen the grainy CCTV images of Leni losing control of her bike and then the car ploughing straight into her.

Callum Ferguson, the driver was called: a stocky, grey-haired man in his late fifties, a plumber on his way home from fixing a leaking shower. He'd held a full clean driving licence for almost forty years, without so much as a speeding fine to show for himself. 'She came from out of nowhere,' he said, wringing his hands. 'There was nothing I could do.' He'd been exonerated, with the coroner saying Ferguson had been put in an impossible situation. The announcement of the conclusion had him breaking down in tears, putting big meaty hands up to his eyes, shoulders shaking.

Alice had watched, unmoved. Not good enough, she thought, anger stoking ever hotter in her inner furnace. This changed nothing – he'd still killed Leni with his massive, dangerous car. It was all his fault!

In hindsight, she was not proud of her behaviour over the weeks and months that followed, but it was as if she couldn't stop herself. She tracked down Callum Ferguson to a terraced house in Perivale, then made a point of going round there whenever possible and throwing an egg at the front window. Yes, it was petty. No, it didn't change anything. But God, it was satisfying to throw something hard and see it smash, to cause someone else pain for a change.

One night she turned up as usual though, only for a wiry young man to step out of the shadows and approach her before she could make her move. 'Throw another egg at my parents' house and you'll have me to deal with,' he said, his voice soft with menace.

'Your dad killed my sister,' was all Alice could say in response, trembling with heightened emotion. 'A fucking egg on his house is the last thing he should be worried about.'

He took another step towards her, jabbing a finger. 'Your *sister* has destroyed my *dad*,' he said and she could see it then, the flash of pain across his face, an agony she recognised. 'He's catatonic in there. Signed off work with depression. It's completely ruined his life. So think about that for a minute, will you? It wasn't his fault. The best driver in the world couldn't have done anything differently. *It wasn't his fault.*'

He was yelling at her by then, his face colouring below the yellow glow of the streetlight, and Alice's hand had tightened inadvertently around the egg she was holding ready, feeling it break stickily between her fingers. *He's lying, don't listen*, she told herself shakily, driving away afterwards. *We're the ones suffering, not them!* But his angry words rang in her head for days afterwards.

'Anyone fancy dessert?' Celeste said at that moment and Alice blinked, realising that she had been miles away. Somehow or other she'd finished her plate of food having barely tasted it.

'You all right, Alice?' asked Lou as if reading her mind. 'You went a bit quiet there.'

'I'm fine,' she said, then screwed up her face because she'd always been a terrible liar and she was remembering the egg crumpling within her palm, the slimy liquid dripping on the ground. 'Well – not really,' she admitted in the next breath. 'But . . . you know. Hanging on in there.'

She was aiming at jokey but it must have come out sounding downbeat because the two of them looked concerned and Lou promptly grabbed her hand across the table. 'Oh, lovely,' she said. 'It will stop feeling so painful one day.'

'We're right with you in the meantime,' said Celeste. 'Good times ahead.'

'And I bet that if Leni has any say in the matter, something really great is just around the corner for you,' Lou added. Alice's phone beeped with a notification a split second later and they all laughed. 'There it is now,' she said.

Smiling faintly, Alice glanced at her phone, only to almost hyperventilate with shock. 'Oh my God,' she said, staring at the screen and reading the message again. A little laugh escaped her throat. 'No way.'

'What? Is this the something great that Leni's sent your way?' Lou asked.

A thrill ricocheted through Alice. *Leni, was that really you?* she thought, half amused, half excited. 'You're never going to believe this,' she said.

Chapter Eleven

McKenzies Together group

Tuesday
How are we all doing? Everyone bearing up? Love Dad/Tony 12.23

Hurtling through the air, high above the treetops, Will felt a scream rip from his lungs as he plunged down the cable, adrenalin shooting wildly around his body as if he'd had a close encounter with death. Ironically, he couldn't remember when he'd last felt so alive. SMILE – YOU'RE IN PARADISE! read a sign at the end of the zip line, presumably for a photo-sale opportunity, but he didn't need any reminding because he was already smiling like a total idiot. 'Whoaaaa,' he exclaimed, arms and legs turning to jelly as he made it on to the landing jetty where a young Thai man stepped forward to unclip him.

'You like, huh? You scream?'

Will laughed, a little shamefacedly. 'Yes, I like,' he replied, his heart still thumping. 'And yes, I scream.'

He waited at the viewing deck for Isla to descend, her legs bent at the knee, her red hair streaming out from beneath the safety helmet, her shrieks even more piercing than his had been. She and Meg had persuaded him to join them on a safari trip, taking in waterfalls, jungle, golden-roofed Buddhist temples, and this, a fifty-mile-an-hour zip line that had been the biggest thrill he'd had for months. 'Why don't you come with us? You can take a day out of your busy schedule, surely?' Isla had said, tongue-in-cheek, that first evening they'd got chatting in the bar. 'Even Jeff Bezos has a *bit* of downtime now and then.'

He'd demurred at first, wanting to give the impression that he didn't have time for tourist frivolities – and also because he wasn't sure he liked her taking the piss out of him. When pushed though, he'd had to admit that no, he hadn't been on any of the jungle safari tours advertised everywhere to holidaymakers. 'And you've been here, what, six months, did you say? You're a slave to the nine-to-five, you. All those tourists to fleece, eh?'

Meg had been somewhat softer in her approach. 'Say yes, come with us,' she'd coaxed. 'You know what they say about all work and no play . . .'

He'd hesitated just long enough for Isla to tease him again. 'Meg, don't badger the lad! Those flip-flops won't sell them-selves!' at which point he'd laughingly admitted defeat. Why shouldn't he have a bit of fun? Besides, there was something about Isla that he found very appealing. She was stunning, for one thing, and he liked her fiery spirit – at least, he did now that she was no longer shouting at him. Born and raised in Stirling, she'd trained as a paramedic and was soon to be moving to Aberdeen with a new job. In the meantime, she was taking a month-long break to have some adventures around Thailand. As for Meg, she was a chef en route to Australia, armed with a year's work visa, in the pursuit of new kitchen experiences and fun. After some beach time in Koh Samui and Koh Phangan, they were planning to head up to Chiang Mai to go trekking, explore Bangkok and then – 'Well, whatever takes our fancy, basically,' Isla had shrugged. 'Before Meg heads down under and I fly home again in February, to sicken the rest of Scotland with my incredible tan.'

'How's that going so far?' he'd teased, with a pointed look at her milk-white skin, to which she'd scowled, pretending affront.

Meg was still thinking about their itinerary. 'Any tips you can give us for travel would be great – any cool places you've been to, or stayed in, anything that's a real must-see,' she'd said that evening in the beach bar. By now they'd decided to order cocktails and Will felt obliged to buy a round, wincing at the marked-up tourist prices as he did so. Oh well, he thought. He'd redouble his beach-selling efforts in the morning.

'Um,' he'd said, busying himself by prodding a juicy slice of orange with the end of his straw. 'Well ... yeah, Chiang Mai is a big tourist spot,' he blustered. 'You can go elephant trekking there, and that.'

'You've been, have you?' asked Isla. 'Where did you stay, can you remember?'

'Um ...' The thing was, he hadn't actually been to Chiang Mai. He hadn't, in fact, been anywhere other than Koh Samui since he'd left the UK, but if he admitted this, they might think he was a bit of a loser. People packed so much into their holidays, didn't they – boat trips, snorkelling, trekking, everything ticked off at an exhausting pace … Will was in no rush. Of course he wanted to go to all of these places – and he would, definitely. He just hadn't got round to it yet. 'I can't remember, sorry,' he replied, then decided to change the subject. 'So you're a chef, that's cool,' he said to Meg. 'Have you got a job arranged in Australia, or are you planning to rock up and see what happens?'

Meg launched into a long story about the gorgeous but snooty hotel she'd been working in in St Andrews, and how strange it was to be out of Scotland this January, and not cooking up Burns Night dinners for pissed hotel guests.

Isla had been quiet throughout this, although Will caught her looking at him quizzically now and then. 'And how about you?' she'd asked.

'What do you mean, how about me?' he replied. 'I'm flip-flop guy, I thought you knew that? I'm Mr Koh Samui beach bum.'

'No, I mean – after this. Other than this. What does British Will get up to? Or does your flip-flop empire stretch all the way around the world?'

British Will … Right. Was it overly dramatic to say that the words struck an instant sensation of dread into his blood-stream? It was like thinking back to someone you'd met a long time ago, barely able to recall their features any more. 'British Will …' He broke off and looked down at himself in his sun-bleached singlet, his board shorts, his sandy grey

Converse with the rip on one toe. It was so long since he'd even dressed as his old self, it was hard to imagine his tanned legs clad once more in jeans, a pair of spotless designer trainers on his feet. 'I used to work in engineering,' he said eventually, aware that this might sound boring to them, compared to their more adventurous lives. 'For a construction company near Swindon.' He gave a self-conscious laugh and spread his hands wide. 'Now it all makes sense, right? Who'd want to go back to that?'

They'd laughed in response, as he'd intended them to, but Isla had given him another of her glances, as if trying to figure him out, and he'd quailed a little beneath her gaze, braced for another personal question. It hadn't come and he was relieved at the time, although afterwards he'd wondered if it was a bad sign, that she hadn't wanted to find out anything else. Because there *was* more to him than his job, he felt like saying. He wasn't just a nerd with a calculator and graph paper; he did have a personality, mates, family, actual interests. Well, before he left them all behind, that was. Not the personality, obviously. He hadn't left his personality behind. Had he?

Back at the zip-wire viewing platform, Isla was taking off her helmet and shaking out her hair as she walked towards him now. 'Wow! That's got my heart pumping all right. I feel as if I could do anything.' She grinned at him, rummaging in a pouch attached round her middle for her phone. 'Come on, let's take a photo while we're still sparkly-eyed and euphoric.'

He liked the way she took the lead, he thought, making his way over. He could just imagine her in a crisp, green paramedic's uniform, issuing firm instructions, calmly taking control of a situation. *You can take control of my situation any time, darling*, he might have said back in the UK if he'd met her in a bar. (*Ugh, cringe, Will*, his sisters piped up in his head, pulling faces as if they were about to throw up.) Something told him Isla was the sort of woman who'd wet herself laughing at such a cheesy line anyway, he thought, standing beside her as she reached out a long freckled arm before them and snapped a few photos.

'There,' she said, showing him a picture of the two of them, heads close together, both looking dazzled and – yes, actually pretty euphoric – in front of the dense green jungle, with Meg just visible in the background, skimming down the cable. 'One for the grandchildren. Well – not *our* grandchildren, obviously . . .' she laughed, as he gave an involuntary jerk of surprise. 'I just meant . . .' Her cheeks had turned rosy pink with a blush; it was the first time she'd seemed wrong-footed since their paths had crossed. Interesting. 'Ach, you know what I meant. Anyway, here's Meg. Meg!'

The moment was over because then Meg was being unclipped and staggering towards them, beaming and hoicking her shorts out of her bum, exclaiming hoarse-voiced how she'd started to think she'd have a wedgie for the rest of her life what with the G-force. Then Isla was replying, 'Ah yes, that well-known medical phenomenon, the G-force wedgie – you wouldn't believe the number of times we paramedics have been called out to deal with this predicament,' and Will laughed alongside them. But he hadn't imagined it, he was sure; that frisson between them, that wordless exchange. That sudden rosy blush on Isla's face as if she maybe liked him too.

He came to his senses soon afterwards as they headed back towards their safari jeep, ready to take their seats for the next leg of the journey. So what if he and Isla liked each other? It wasn't as if anything would happen. She and Meg would be leaving Koh Samui soon for the rest of their adventures, like all the other women he'd met so far. And there had been plenty of other women, let's face it: tipsy and sunburned, in their little sundresses and shorts and bikinis, looking for something to spice up their holiday. He'd been happy to go along with it when they started coming on to him, ending up in their hotel rooms, or on the beach, once even around the back of a bar, the two of them propped against kegs of lager, the air fragrant with the stink of stale alcohol and drains.

None of it had meant anything, for either party. But with Isla … she was different. Funny. Feisty, in the way that Leni had been, he realised, before he could hold back the thought. Damn it. Too late. Now his sister's face had floated up into his head and he was remembering that last phone call – *Can I ask you a favour, Will?* – and his equilibrium was in danger of shattering to pieces. Don't think about that. Don't think at all, in fact.

He pulled his sunglasses over his eyes even though the jeep windows were tinted, and sighed, wondering if he'd ever be able to travel far enough to rid himself of the shadows that dogged him. If he'd ever stop hearing his sister's last request – and if he'd ever forgive himself for what he had said in reply.

Chapter Twelve

Leni McKenzie memorial page

Sorry I'm late to this, I've only just heard the news. I imagine Leni's family and friends must be devastated. I knew Leni as a teenager and into my twenties. She was such a fun person to be around. One of my proudest memories was when she anointed my shoulders with a peacock feather and told me I was an honorary Flying Beauty along with her and Alice. Apparently this was a very exclusive club! Leni, I will do my best to keep flying, but the world is definitely a greyer and less beautiful place without your peacock-bright presence.

Jacob

The post had come in moments after Lou had said that thing in the curry house about Leni sending her something great, and Alice couldn't help but see this as the mother of all signs. Jacob Murray, holy moly: only her sixth-form boyfriend and one-time light of her life for the three happy years they'd spent together, right until he was offered a place to study at

Harvard that he couldn't turn down. The distance between them had proved too much within a few months – she became jealous and insecure, struggling to remember how to study up in York after their gap year travelling together, while he seemed perplexed by her sudden transatlantic neediness. She'd been one for self-sabotage even then and, anticipating that he'd soon move on to some rich, tanned American girl (who *wouldn't* prefer a Harvard super-brain?), she pre-empted the inevitable heartache by ending it that Christmas, telling herself it was a mercy killing that would save a lot of anguish in the long run. Years had gone by since then; they'd both lived their separate lives – the last she'd heard about him, he was living in Gothenburg with his molecular biologist wife and little boy (how come everyone except her seemed to have got their shit together?) – but she'd always felt a residual fondness towards him, not least because, unlike other boyfriends she'd gone on to have, he'd never done her wrong. And now here he was, popping up unexpectedly, just when she needed something good to happen.

A swift foray into Jacob's social media profile revealed that he was no longer in Sweden but living in London. Alice felt herself seized by the compulsion to see him again. Think of the stories he might have about Leni that she had forgotten! She had met up with a couple of her sister's friends now, in order to pass on clothes or other items they had asked for, and been gifted in return with anecdotes and reminiscences about her sister, new knowledge she hadn't been aware of before this time. She still hadn't got to the bottom of Leni's cryptic diary entries, but there had been the occasional throwaway remark – *We used to go to this Greek restaurant together in Soho* or *We always seemed to end up in this one cocktail bar in Farringdon on the espresso martinis* – and she'd found herself making mental notes. She too would go to that particular Greek restaurant, she decided privately. She too would seek out the cocktail bar in Farringdon. She'd even force herself to drink an espresso martini, despite disliking coffee, because it would make her feel closer to her sister. At Leni's funeral, she'd sat there vowing, *I will live for both of us now*, but she hadn't exactly followed through on her promise. Yet. Maybe this could be a way for her to honour Leni and break out of her usual routines though? By visiting Leni's old haunts, maybe even fulfilling things her sister always wanted to do and never had the chance to?

So far she hadn't mentioned such intentions to any of her friends – they were encouraging her to stop immersing herself in the past and instead look ahead, suggesting new restaurants, Pilates sessions (February's fitness challenge), tickets for a film that was getting great reviews. Jacob might understand though, especially as an honorary Flying Beauties member himself. They could chat about old times together – there were sure to be parties, nights out, stupid obsessions the three of them had shared that Alice had forgotten about. If Jacob could shed any light whatsoever on them, so much the better.

Hi! she messaged him on Sunday, unable to fake nonchalance or even try. This was someone who'd held her hair back as she vomited up cider and black at countless teenage parties, after all; someone who'd let her dance on his shoulders to the Flaming Lips at Glastonbury, bellowing along the words to 'Do You Realize??'; someone she'd swum with underwater on the Great Barrier Reef, gleefully pointing out the octopus and colourful fish to one another; the smart, gorgeous boy she'd fallen in love with under the glitterball at the Year 12 Christmas disco. She'd never been cool or nonchalant and he of all people knew that. *Lovely to see your name! Flying Beauties forever etc,* she typed. *And you're in London! Fancy meeting up for a drink and reminiscing?* He didn't reply immediately as she'd hoped, and he still hadn't by the next morning. Her earlier optimism had all but evaporated by the time she arrived at work. She'd probably been too keen, freaked him out. Perhaps his wife had seen the message, got the wrong idea and deleted it without telling him. Maybe he'd only left his original message on the memorial page to be polite and couldn't care less about Alice, still hated her in fact for dumping him on Christmas Eve back in the day.

The maternity cover job she'd taken on largely consisted of administrative duties for the loss adjustment team of a large insurance firm – typing correspondence, processing claims, managing files and looking after the diaries of more important people – and there was always plenty to do, which helped the days speed by at least. Sage and Golding was an old-fashioned, traditional company and although coming in on a temporary basis was exactly what she'd needed, buying herself time while she got her act together, she was already looking forward to working somewhere more creative again. She had the feeling that Sage and Golding traded heavily on their history as one of the oldest insurance providers and seemed to take it for granted that they were safe, snuggled into their strong market position for all eternity. Alice was no expert on the world of insurance, but even she knew there were shiny new companies appearing every year, specifically targeting a younger demographic. It was a mistake for a firm to rely so much on its past performance, surely?

Also, while she was on the subject of dinosaurs, she couldn't help thinking that whoever was running their comms department needed dragging into the twenty-first century. This boring leaflet, that dreary print ad ... it was as if nobody cared enough to put together a proper campaign strategy. As for their social media, it was abysmal – completely unengaging and clearly very low on the company priorities. God, she missed working at ReImagine, she thought for the millionth time, as she began typing another letter. Why hadn't she merely put up and shut up, done her best to ignore Rupert's poor management decisions and carry on, rather than resign on the spot like a massive drama queen?

'Um ... Alison, is it?' came a voice just then, interrupting her thoughts. 'Could you take the minutes for our morning meeting, darling? Ruth's off sick.'

Alice looked up to see Stuart, one of the team leaders, at her desk. He was in his fifties, overweight and apparently so uninterested in anyone below management level that he couldn't be bothered to remember their names. 'It's Alice,' she said, grabbing her notebook and pen. 'And Rosalind, for that matter. Yes, I could take the minutes.'

He wasn't listening, however; he was already walking off down the corridor, his back fat rolling beneath his jacket. 'It's room seven,' he called over his shoulder. 'Starting now.'

Alice saved the file of correspondence she'd been working on, tried to suppress the snarl inside her and rolled her eyes at Tina, one of the PAs who sat nearby.

'I love it when he talks dirty to us,' Tina said, pulling a face in response.

Alice snorted a laugh, grateful for the solidarity, and set off for the meeting, hoping it wouldn't take up too much of her time. She wrinkled her nose, hoping too that she wouldn't be sat anywhere near Stuart, whose sour, sweaty smell lingered pungently in his wake. Then her phone beeped and it was a message from Jacob.

Alice! Great to hear from you, although I'm sorry it's under these circumstances. Would love to reminisce. I'm now working at UCL so anywhere in central London is easy for me. Want to suggest somewhere? Dinner? Pint?

She stopped in the corridor, the opening guitar chords of 'Do You Realize??' strumming in her head, certain that if she didn't reply to Jacob's message before the meeting, she'd be completely unable to think straight for its entirety, let alone take any minutes for sweaty Stuart and his squad.

There's a nice Greek restaurant in Soho, she found herself typing. *Dimitris on Berwick Street? When are you free?*

Then she walked in, only for her smile to vanish abruptly in the next second. Because sitting there at the meeting table, in a smart charcoal suit and gold tie, was the man with close-cropped hair she'd met in the bar after work the week before. Darren, the man she'd taken home and had sex with over her living-room table.

She went hot and cold all over to see him again so

unexpectedly – the perils of drinking in the pub nearest to your office, she realised, stricken – and dropped her pen in a fluster. Taking a seat at the far end of the table, she ducked her head so that her hair swung forward, hoping that he might not recognise her – please God, let him not recognise her. So Darren worked at Sage and Golding too – oh help. Better start praying for the quickest meeting in history, she thought, heart thudding.

Chapter Thirteen

McKenzies Together group

Saturday
Tony: *Happy weekend, all. What have you got planned? Jackie and I are going to a friend's housewarming tonight and then Sunday lunch with her folks tomorrow. How about you guys? Love Dad/ Tony x 08.45*
Will: *Dad, you don't have to sign off at the end of every message – we know it's you [eye-roll emoji]*

Sunday
Alice: *Hi all, here's a pic of Hamish snoozing. Look at those magnificent whiskers! I think we're starting to get the hang of this cohabiting business x 10.22*
Tony: *What a hunk!! Glad for you both. Have a good day, everyone xxx 10.25*

Monday
Tony: *Morning all. Hope you had good weekends. I was going*

*through some old family photos again last night – a few attached
here! – and found myself thinking ahead to Leni's birthday in May
this year. She used to love getting everyone together for the occasion,
didn't she? Should we maybe try and do that this time, in her
honour? Xxx 08.35*

Tony: *PS I know you told me not to sign off, Will, but I like it!
So get used to it, kiddo!! Love Dad xxx 08.36*

Belinda cruised to the side of the pool, put her hand against
the wall, then turned and began tanking slowly in the other
direction, twisting her face away as a fast, splashy front-crawl
swimmer passed in the neighbouring lane, showering her with
water. Ray had suggested they take the morning off and go
to the leisure centre together, then have lunch in town. 'It'll
make you feel great for the rest of the day,' he'd told her over
breakfast that morning, talking her into the idea. 'And it's
good for headspace too.'

He was currently upstairs, taking part in a gruelling-
sounding Body Combat class, while Belinda was having a
much more mellow time of it in the water. This was the pool
where she'd taken her children for lessons all those years before,
and now here she was again, creaking along with her rusty
breaststroke, wondering if this was part of Ray's plan to keep
her off her phone whenever possible. If so, the joke was on
him because, rather than this being an exercise in mindfulness
(and exercise, for that matter), all she could think about was
her phone: namely, Tony's latest post on the McKenzie family
group chat.

It had taken the wind out of Belinda's sails, reading the

message while she buttered her toast that morning. Who did her ex-husband think he was, trying to organise something for Leni's birthday when he hadn't even remembered it last year? And had he forgotten that he'd have a newborn baby by then? Probably. It wasn't until she read it again that she realised he was merely asking, rather than organising, but still. It irked her that he had got in first with the subject, months away as it still was, rather than her. 'Honestly,' she'd tutted, stabbing the knife into the marmalade with such violence Ray had looked over from where he was stirring porridge at the hob. 'It's nothing,' she mumbled, because Ray was estranged from his ex-wife and children and she knew he'd give anything to get messages from them, however irritating.

She still hadn't replied to any of Tony's comments but had noticed Alice and Will both tentatively engaging. Despite her initial annoyance with him for corralling them all in this group, she could see that, yes, okay, it might actually turn into something good; a nice place for them to share. Should she respond? Of course she wanted to do something meaningful for Leni's birthday. But what should she say?

Back in the leisure centre, she had notched up another length and felt as if she was hitting her stride, her body finding a rhythm. Turning and pushing off from the edge, she smiled, seeing a group of mums and toddlers walking towards the baby pool for a swimming lesson. Goodness, look at those tiny little bodies, so wriggly and delicious, with their brightly patterned costumes and trunks, neon armbands and life jackets worn like protective armour. Their high-pitched voices were eager and excited, carrying through the warm, chlorine-smelling air.

The mums, by contrast, looked rather less enthusiastic to be there, with their hair tied up in hasty topknots, sporting the large sober-coloured costumes of motherhood. No doubt their heads were crammed full of lists for the rest of the day – meals to be prepared, other children to pick up, what time the car park ticket would run out, and all the rest of it. If she closed her eyes, she could remember that time as if it were yesterday.

The joy on her children's faces when they won their first swimming badges, when they became confident enough to jump in! Not that Leni ever had any qualms about leaping in, out of her depth – one of Belinda's worst motherhood memories had been here at the pool with the girls, aged about four and two, when Leni, seizing a moment while Belinda was wrestling with a locker, had rushed ahead to the water because she simply couldn't wait. Belinda had snatched up Alice and pelted after her, just in time to see a lifeguard hauling Leni out of the shallow end. He'd given Belinda such a ticking off about the dangers of children falling into water unaccompanied, and how important it was that parents did not take their eyes off their toddlers, not even for a second, that Belinda had burst into hot tears. So had Leni. So had Alice, who never wanted to be left out of anything.

Today though, she had no such responsibilities. Now her children were scattered, with messages pinging through on her phone rather than daily physical contact. *Hold each other tight*, Apolline had urged recently. This had been the day in town when she'd sidled into a coffee shop while waiting for Ray at the bank, only for her precious time to be interrupted by Tony, of all people, waving at her through the window like an idiot. She could have slapped him for it! *Leni wants the four of you to be united, to lean on one another during this time*, Apolline had said after Belinda shooed him away, which was ironic, under the circumstances. There had been no further pointed mentions of 'a man' from Leni, at least, she thought, shuddering as she remembered the unnerving conversation the two of them had had on her eldest daughter's last birthday.

'I had the funniest coincidence yesterday, Mum,' she had said, all smiles. This was after lunch, when things had become a little more relaxed, thank goodness. Will and Molly were telling some long story about a night out they'd had in Swindon, while Ray and Alice were making teas and coffees for everyone. Belinda had asked about Leni's garden and Leni had opened the back door for them both to go out there, and, once she'd admired the roses and alliums and lavender, they'd sat at the small white patio table together. Then Leni dropped her bombshell. 'We had an Ofsted inspection at school this week – you'll never guess who the inspector was!'

No, Belinda hadn't guessed. 'Who, darling?' she'd asked, all innocence.

'Our old neighbour – Mr Fenton!' the answer came and Belinda felt her throat tighten immediately, the Prosecco repeating itself in her mouth, sour and vomit-tinged. Graham Fenton? No.

'Oh,' she managed to say, her heart almost thudding through her ribcage. Shit. Was Leni about to say what she thought? Was this the moment where her world came tumbling down? 'Wow!' she added to fill the silence. She hardly dared look at her daughter's face. What kind of judgement might she find there?

'I know! I never would have recognised him,' Leni went on. Her sunglasses hid her eyes but Belinda could see her own self reflected in the brown lenses: scared-looking. Old. 'I introduced myself and I swear he did this double take. *Coincidence!* he said. *I used to know a Leni McKenzie!*'

Who knew what else might have been revealed, if Alice hadn't come walking towards them in the next moment, coffee mugs in hand? Belinda was all too grateful for the interruption. 'Oh, perfect!' she cried, trying to suppress the hysterical note in her voice. 'Come and join us, Alice, you can share my chair,' she added, shifting over. Surely, if Leni had any truly damning accusations, she wouldn't make them with Alice there, she'd figured, adrenalin racing.

She hadn't. Conversation had turned elsewhere. The subject of Mr Fenton – and what else he might have said – remained unfinished and Belinda, to her shame, had never quite been brave enough to bring it up in subsequent phone calls. What did Leni know? The only way she could ever find out now was through Apolline, and she still wasn't sure if she was ready for that.

Don't think about it, she told herself, kicking hard through the water. It's all in the past; let it stay there.

The mums and toddlers were in the baby pool now, singing 'Five Little Ducks' together, the mums swishing their charges through the water to giggles and shrieks. There was one older lady there too, Belinda noticed, a grandma presumably, and she felt such a surge of envy at the woman, she almost forgot to swim. She thought of the knitted yellow baby jacket, the symbol of all her hopes and dreams, now stuffed into a box of keepsakes at the bottom of her wardrobe, never to be worn. Had things been different, she could have been a grandma herself by now, in a swimming pool somewhere with Leni and Adam's wee one, singing her heart out with a similar group. *Five little ducks went swimming one day, Over the hills and far away. Mother Duck said, 'Quack quack quack quack!' But only four little ducks came back.*

Oh gosh, and now Belinda had tears running down her cheeks at the thought of her eldest little duck never coming back. Of Leni swimming away, and her, poor old Mummy Duck, quacking uselessly into the void.

She reached the edge of the pool, intending to turn and continue swimming, but it was as if a switch had been flicked somewhere inside her, because she couldn't stop crying all of a sudden: the tears pouring, a loud sob issuing from her throat. Embarrassed, she put her hands over her face, leaning against the wall trying to get a grip of herself, but the sadness was too deep, the awfulness too overwhelming. On warbled the singers – three little ducks left now – and her grief only intensified. She had lost so much! So much that she could never get back again. It was as if there was a hole in her, a terrible gnawing hole where Leni had been ripped away. The pain was too much today. She couldn't bear it.

There was a tentative tap on her shoulder. 'Can I help you?'

Gulping as she wrestled to stop the tears, she looked up to see a middle-aged woman in the water beside her, pushing a pair of clear goggles up on to her forehead to reveal kind blue eyes. Oh no, and the pretty, young lifeguard seemed to be coming over too, white trainers squeaking across the wet concrete floor, a concerned look on her face. For heaven's sake, Belinda! Of all the places to have a meltdown. 'I'm sorry,' she hiccuped, dashing the tears away with the backs of her hands. 'I'm fine, really. Just having a moment.'

The lifeguard had reached them now and squatted down, her tanned, hairless thighs right in Belinda's eyeline. (Even in the depths of grief, she was able to envy another woman's legs, apparently.) 'Are you all right?' the lifeguard asked. 'Do you want to get out and sit somewhere quiet for a minute? Can I call anyone to come and get you?'

Lifeguards had become a lot nicer since the one who'd bollocked her all those years ago, at least. She shook her head, feeling foolish. Who on earth got undone by a children's song anyway? How mortifying. 'I'm okay,' she said with a final hiccup. 'Sorry. Thank you, both. I think I'll get out now.'

She could feel them watching her all the way back to the changing room entrance. The walk of shame, she thought to herself with a sigh.

Showering afterwards, she felt her equilibrium returning as she rinsed her hair. She felt lighter, even, as if the wave of crying had been cathartic. Not that she was about to tell Ray what had happened, mind. *Can't take you anywhere*, he'd say, hugging her tightly.

Dressed once more, her hair still damp and faintly chlorine-scented, she waited for him in the reception area, noticing as he appeared that he looked rather wild-eyed. 'Wait till you hear who I've just had a call from,' he said, holding up his phone with a stunned expression on his face. 'Ellis!'

'*Ellis?*' she repeated in surprise. 'Gosh! Is he all right? Are *you* all right?'

Ellis was Ray's mysterious son from his first marriage – mysterious to Belinda, at least, because father and son had been estranged for as long as she'd known Ray. When his ex-wife Nicky had eventually tired of her drug-addicted, gambling, irresponsible husband, there had been a messy evacuation of him from the family home, and then she'd upped sticks and taken herself and the children off to her home town of Crickhowell, for the three of them to begin a new life without him. Ray had made financial contributions since then, but otherwise ties had broken down completely. Once he was sober and clean, he'd tried to start over with his kids, but there was a limit to how much repair work he could do, when they steadfastly refused to have anything to do with him. Belinda knew it had broken his heart, even if these days he rarely talked about Ellis and his sister, Rhiannon. They must be in their twenties now, his son and daughter, and Ray had all but given up hope of reconciliation. Until today.

'He's got a job interview in Abingdon next week,' Ray said, as they headed out to the car park. 'Asked if we could meet for a drink while he's over this way. He wants to meet me, Bel!'

'Oh wow, that's brilliant,' she cried, squeezing his hand. He looked dazzled by the news, his face lit up in a way she couldn't remember seeing in a long time. 'Does he want to stay with us while he's in the area?' she added, because oh, this would mean so much to Ray if he could help his son in a practical way: not only with a drink and a chat, but with a bed for the night too.

'I did offer but . . .' Ray's face dropped a little. 'But maybe that was too much for a first time. I think he probably wants an escape route, in case he decides he still hates me after all these years.'

'He won't hate you,' Belinda said staunchly, as they reached the car and Ray unlocked it. 'Because you are a good man, the very best man, Ray, and as soon as Ellis sees you again, he'll realise that. Gosh, this is big! Did he say anything else?'

'Not a lot. He's going to text me a pub where we can meet later on.' He got into the driver's seat and put a hand to his heart briefly before pulling the seat belt across himself. 'I can't believe it. I'm so happy. My boy . . . Honestly, this has made my day.'

She settled herself in the passenger seat and rubbed his arm affectionately. 'What a lovely bit of news. You deserve this.' It had hurt Ray so much to be cut off from his children, rejected time and again. Who would have thought? It just went to show that life – and people – really were full of surprises. And she couldn't help thinking that if his family, seemingly damaged beyond repair, could see their way to reconciliation, however tentative, then maybe . . . might there be hope yet for hers?

She took her phone out to read through Tony's latest group message once more, noticing that a reply from Alice had arrived in the meantime.

McKenzies Together group

Alice: *We should definitely do something, even if it's just a video call. You know what Leni was like about getting us together — she'd have been pleased to know we were making an effort! It'll be a tough day x 11.13*

Gazing out of the window, half listening as Ray chattered on about Ellis and how he hoped this might be a turning point, Belinda felt torn in two, in regards to her own family situation. If Alice wanted to get together, of course she wouldn't deny her that. She mustn't.

Hello everyone, she typed, then took a deep breath. Life was short, wasn't it? she reminded herself. Too short to waste. *I was going to take some flowers to her headstone that day. Then I think I'll cook her favourite dinner (roast chicken — you're all welcome to come over and join me) and have a very large glass of wine. Raise a toast to her. But yes, it would be lovely to see you, either in person or on a call. X*

She read the words through again, considering adding a few of her beloved emojis for good measure, but deciding against it. There was such a thing as being over-friendly, after all. Then she pressed Send.

Chapter Fourteen

McKenzies Together group

Monday
Alice: *Sounds great, Mum — count me in for roast chicken. Dad? Will? You in for this? X 17.44*
Tony: *That's a lovely idea, Belinda. I would like that very much. Will, might you be back by then? Love Dad/Tony xx 19.33*

Tony was glad that Belinda had finally responded to one of his messages on the group chat (at last!) but he hadn't been able to stop thinking about that strange moment when they'd seen one another in town the week before, her shiftiness in the café when he'd interrupted her phone call. Perhaps she was simply displeased to see him, but instinct told him there was something else afoot. It had troubled him, actually. Was his ex-wife all right?

The encounter might have drifted from his mind if he hadn't bumped into Ray a few days later, on a garage fore-court, of all places, filling up their cars beside each other.

They'd exchanged pleasantries – Tony had always rather got on with Ray, whenever Leni had organised one of her family get-togethers – and then, after a moment's deliberation, Tony found himself saying, 'I saw Belinda last week, actually. Is everything okay? Only ...' He hesitated, trying to find the right words. 'She was having a strange phone call. She seemed to be talking about Leni as if she was still alive. Unless I misheard, maybe ...' But he could tell from Ray's face, the way it sagged with dismay, that the other man knew exactly what he was talking about.

'Bloody Apolline,' Ray muttered, busying himself replacing the petrol nozzle in the holder. 'Belinda's got herself involved with some supposed psychic. It's all a massive scam, of course, but this woman has convinced Bel that she can talk to Leni beyond the grave, and keeps apparently passing on messages.' His eyes were dark, his mouth in a grim line. 'She's the one who told Bel to put the house up for sale in the first place, apparently, and now we seem to be house-hunting with this absolute charlatan having a say in which place we buy. I mean ...'

Tony was finding all of this hard to take in. 'Bloody hell,' he commented, realising too late that the petrol nozzle was clicking in his hand where the tank was full. 'Presumably Belinda's paying through the nose for this, too.'

'I dread to think how much,' Ray replied heavily. 'And once the house has been sold, she'll have a huge amount of capital at her disposal too.' He shook his head. 'I hate seeing her taken advantage of like this, but she's refusing to listen.'

He'd changed the subject then, and that had pretty much

been the end of it, but Tony had been mulling over the situation ever since. Should he say something to the kids? Tackle Belinda himself about it? He didn't want to tread on Ray's toes though, nor did he feel comfortable going behind his ex-wife's back. By the time he met Jackie for their first antenatal class that evening, he still didn't have the answer. He'd have to sleep on it, he decided, putting it out of his mind.

'Well, here we all are – welcome!' said Sallyanne, the course leader, beaming around the group. She was in her mid-forties, at a guess, with short yellow hair and large red-rimmed glasses. To Tony's mind, she had the manner of an infant teacher: smiley and enthusiastic on the outside, but with an authoritative firmness which suggested she'd have no qualms about making you miss playtime with your friends if she caught you being naughty.

'It's lovely to see you, our mummies- and daddies-to-be, plus our small growing passengers along for the ride, of course! Mummies, I hope you're all sitting comfortably. Daddies, I hope you're listening hard and ready to take notes if need be. Let's go around the room and introduce ourselves, shall we? I'll start. I'm Sallyanne, a midwife with eighteen years' experience, and so I've seen pretty much everything in my time. Take it from me, you're in for one incredible journey over the next few months, and I feel very privileged to be guiding you through your first steps of this life-changing time.'

Tony's expression might've been neutral, but inside he was fighting the urge to catch the eye of a fellow 'daddy' and pretend to vomit on to the community centre floor. What was it about some of the people working in baby-related professions that compelled them to infantilise and patronise at any opportunity? He felt fidgety already, and he'd only been in the room a matter of minutes.

As if sensing his discomfort – maybe he'd sighed unacceptably loudly – Jackie swung her head towards him, eyes narrowed. It was the expression of someone approaching the end of their patience and he sensed he'd be in for a series of sharp nudges this evening if he didn't watch himself. 'All I want is to meet a few local mums,' she'd said beforehand, when he started protesting about joining her for the class. 'And I know you've done this whole "having kids" thing before, but I haven't, so humour me, okay? Also, not to be rude, but it's been years since you actually witnessed a birth or changed a nappy, so you could do with brushing up on the knowledge. As well as learning how you're going to make the experience as stress-free as possible for me, obviously.'

With those words ringing in his ears – and the threat of upsetting a hormonal woman – he gave her a nervous smile and tried to concentrate on Sallyanne's summary of the forthcoming sessions. Then the door burst open and everyone turned to see a pink-haired woman rush in, hand in hand with a shyly smiling woman wearing denim maternity dungarees.

'Ah! I was wondering what had happened to you two,' Sallyanne said, with a hint of reprimand as she consulted her list. 'You must be Genevieve and Penelope, welcome. As I was saying—'

'Gen and Pen, that's us,' said the pink-haired woman, ushering her partner to a seat, then sitting beside her and taking her hand. 'I'm Gen, this is Pen. Hi, everyone. Sorry we're late.'

Tony, meanwhile, was having a senior moment where he tried to place the pink-haired woman in his memory. Had he met her through work? Then the woman – Gen – clocked him staring at her and he saw recognition dawn on her face. His own brain caught up in the next second. Yes, of course: the cringe-worthy bereavement group he'd attended, never to return. It wasn't a dissimilar set-up to this evening's do, actually, although the chairs here were more comfortable at least and nobody was weeping. Yet. His heart sank as he smiled weakly back at her. Damn it. Oxford was a big enough city that you could usually get away with anonymity when you needed it, but irritatingly, it was also small enough that paths crossed and recrossed more often than you might choose.

Never mind, he told himself. Hopefully Gen would have enough tact not to mention the group here, or make a thing about it. He focussed back on Sallyanne, who was asking the other couples to introduce themselves. 'If you could give us your names and what you're hoping to get out of the course, that would be a wonderful start,' she said. 'I'm here for each and every one of you, so let me know what you'd like addressing: any concerns, confusion, fears. No question is too silly!'

She gestured at the woman at the far end of the semicircle of chairs to begin. This woman, it transpired, was called Alice, and Tony felt a sparking of warmth inside as he always did when he encountered anyone with the same name as one of his children. After his last conversation with his younger daughter had ended so frostily, he'd been trying to think of ways he could make her like him again, suggesting lunch dates at weekends and then, when she didn't seem to be free on any of the days he offered, wondering to Jackie about turning up at her flat as a surprise. *You need to slow down, back off a bit,* Jackie had advised. *You're her dad, not a stalker. Give her some space.* As for Will, Tony didn't seem to be making much progress there either, bar the very occasional group chat message.

'Our next couple, please?'

He jumped back to the room at the prompt, along with a nudge from Jackie.

'I'm Jackie, forty-two, first baby,' she said. 'Absolutely delighted to have reached this point, although I still can't quite believe it's real.' She put a hand on her bump. 'I had sort of thought that ship had sailed, that it wouldn't happen for me, but . . . Well, here we are.'

Everyone was smiling warmly at Jackie. Now it was Tony's turn. 'I'm Tony and I've been here before – I've got three grown-up children,' he said and then broke off as the reality caught up with him. *Make that two*, he corrected himself unhappily. *Neither of whom seem to like me very much.* 'I . . . um . . .' If in doubt, crack a joke, the chimp part of his brain instructed him. 'Well, it was all a bit different in my day, I've got to say,' he went on, taking refuge in glibness. 'Women just got on with the birth, while us blokes had the easy job of standing in the car park, having a fag.'

He was joking – of course he was joking! – and yet the atmosphere changed in an instant, with the previous air of friendliness taking on a distinct tinge of frost.

'Right,' said Sallyanne primly. Oh shit. He'd misjudged the mood; he'd be ordered to sit on the naughty step in a minute.

'Well, I, for one, think it's *good* that we've moved on from those less progressive days, but . . .'

'So do I! I was only having a laugh,' he tried to say, but she was talking over him now, moving on to the next couple, and his excuse petered out. Jackie rolled her eyes at him, looking exasperated, so he was in the doghouse with her, too. Off to a cracking start, Tony.

The evening proceeded with some graphic talk about labour, what it involved, and the options available to the mothers-to-be. Then a weird one-upmanship kicked off, with several of the women saying, rather piously to Tony's ears, that they wanted drug-free births because that seemed more natural and holistic. Which was all very well, sure – and Tony admired their optimism in the face of what was sure to be extreme pain – but in his opinion, there was nothing holistic about women routinely bleeding to death during childbirth in the Middle Ages, for instance. Belinda had agreed with him, he remembered, feeling a burst of solidarity with his ex. 'Why would anyone in their right mind choose to go through hours of agony if they didn't have to?' she'd asked, flummoxed. *Why indeed,* thought Tony.

Still, after his first attempt at humour had bombed so dismally, he wasn't about to disgrace himself further to the group, even when one woman talked eagerly and at length about hypnobirthing and reiki power, and the uplifting play-lists she was already compiling. What did he know? He was a man. He knew nothing, in other words. Nobody would want to hear his opinion: that despite having a rather hazy idea of what reiki meant, he was pretty sure it would be bog-all help when a ten-pound baby was insistently making its painful, bloody exit.

He was on safe ground with Jackie's birth plan at least, because she'd been very clear before now: caesarean, plenty of drugs, job done, get me home. She'd even said the words, 'Just unzip me and get the kid out already,' when speaking to friends about it. But then Sallyanne, going around the parents in turn, asked for Jackie's thoughts on the matter, and Tony, once again, found himself wrong-footed.

'Well, we were previously thinking of a caesarean—' Jackie began.

'Hashtag "unzip me and get the kid out already",' Tony interjected, grinning around the group in the hope of winning back favour.

'— But I'm coming round to the idea of a natural birth,' she went on, which gave him a start. She was? Since when? His surprise must have shown on his face because then she said, 'Tony, I know you think natural births are for masochists, but—'

You could almost hear a pantomime hiss of disapproval sweeping around the group. Oh God. Why did she have to say that, in front of this lot? 'I don't think I actually used the word "masochist",' he retaliated, accidentally catching Reiki Woman's eye and wishing he hadn't. She was practically clenching her fists now, as if tempted to cross the room and poke him in the eye with an incense stick. 'It's just . . . Look, I've seen it three times over, remember, and—'

'I thought you were in the car park, having a fag?' one of the women muttered sarcastically.

158

'And – that was a joke! I'm just saying, it's not a pretty business. Blood everywhere. Screams of agony . . .'

'I really don't think—' someone put in sharply, but he was going full throttle now and couldn't stop.

'Total carnage, from start to finish. I mean, my ex-wife, Belinda, she was an absolute trooper, but—'

'What, and I'm not?' Jackie asked, rounding on him, sounding hurt. Oh Christ. This was going from bad to worse.

'No! I mean, yes! Of course you are! I'm just saying—'

Sallyanne came to his rescue – if you could call closing him down with steely authority a rescue, anyway. 'Perhaps that's a conversation to have outside the class,' she said. 'And while all the partners here will have opinions about what *they* think should happen, it's my firm belief that a mother's wish is paramount.'

'Absolutely!' Tony cried, desperate to defend himself. 'I agree! So—'

'Moving on,' Sallyanne said sternly. 'Eve and Nathan, what are your intentions regarding your birth?'

Tony sat there with his head down, feeling Jackie's leg move incrementally away from his, while Eve twittered on about pregnancy yoga and homeopathic bullshit. He wasn't quite sure how it had happened, but in the space of two minutes, he'd managed to antagonise every single person in the room, it seemed. Although . . . He risked a glance up to see that pink-haired Gen was giving him an amused look; the only person who didn't hate him, apparently.

Barely able to listen to the other introductions as Sallyanne went around the semicircle, he bristled with the injustice of being misunderstood. They'd all painted him as some oaf now, he reckoned, some chauvinist throwback, when they had no idea how deferential he was to Jackie in the relationship, how much he admired her and marvelled at her. He wished he hadn't blurted out that thing about Belinda though. Jackie was not a fan of Belinda, and he'd almost certainly have to listen to her telling him why this in particular had pissed her off all the way home in the car later.

Once everyone had spoken, Sallyanne announced a tea break – 'And a loo break, obviously – I know *all* about pregnancy bladder issues!' – and everyone started getting up and making conversation with one another. Jackie was immediately grabbed by the reiki woman and a yoga devotee who hustled her away, presumably with intentions of signing her up for natural birth workshops or possibly even staging an intervention to rescue her from her caveman partner. *I know a cry for help when I hear one!* Whatever, thought Tony, getting out his phone and pretending he had an urgent email needing his attention.

'Hi again,' came a voice and he didn't need to look up to know that it was Gen. 'Are you okay?' she asked.

He raised an eyebrow. 'It's a pretty hostile crowd,' he replied drily. 'I'm half expecting to find that a massive bonfire has been built for me in the car park when I try to leave later. Chants of "kill the pig" echoing around the perimeter, pitchforks, that sort of thing.'

She sniggered. 'Bit po-faced, aren't they? Christ! Get a sense of humour, people.' Then she elbowed him. 'Don't worry, the lezzers have got your back. Pen would have come to say hello too but she's queueing for the loo. Says it's her main hobby these days.'

He felt his equilibrium returning a touch with her cheerfulness. 'When is she due?' he inquired politely, because even he knew that this was one of the questions you were meant to ask.

'Star Wars day. May the Fourth be with you? We're hoping for a Wookie.' Then she leaned closer. 'Top tip for you, by the way. Friends of ours went to a class like this in Brighton, and apparently it's one of the ice-breaker things to bond the mums, where they go around and see if the partners have a clue when the due date is. Most of them have no idea and then the mums get to cluck and moan about how hopeless their other halves are. So whatever you do, make sure your due date trips off the tongue, all right? You might even claw back a few brownie points with the mega-mums that way.'

'Blimey, thank you so *much*,' he said, almost dropping his phone in his haste to check his calendar app. This was Premier League information. Absolute gold. 'Ours is April but I have no idea of the day. Let's see . . . ah, the 5th. Got it.' He mimed wiping his brow. 'Thank you, I think you might just have saved my life.'

She grinned at him, then pretended to speak into a walkie-talkie. 'Call off the bonfire. Repeat – call off the bonfire,' and they both laughed, Tony with a slight edge of hysteria. 'Seriously, though, are you okay with this?' she asked. 'I'm finding it a bit of a shocker to get my head around, the whole birth and death thing. You know, what with the bereavement group and all?' She bit her lip. 'That's not me being nosey, I know you didn't want to talk about ... about whoever you were grieving. But you're clearly going through a lot right now. As am I.' Her green eyes glistened momentarily and she looked away.

'Yes,' he agreed. 'It's a lot, like you say.' There was a weighty pause, then he found himself helplessly plunging on into it. 'It was my eldest daughter who died, actually, so ...' His voice trailed away, his eyes suddenly wet.

'Oh God, Tony, I'm sorry,' she said, horror on her face. 'What an absolute headfuck this must be for you. I can't imagine how—'

'Hello, hello,' came a friendly voice just then, and there was Pen, Genevieve's partner, appearing with paper cups of juice for them all. 'Let's pretend these are really full of wine and see if that helps us get through the rest of this sodding evening,' she said. Pen had long hennaed hair and dimples, and spoke in a Yorkshire accent. Tony liked her immediately.

'Thank you,' he said, taking the drink she passed him. 'Cheers to the pair of you – to all three of you, I should say.' He raised his cup to them, grateful that he hadn't been entirely cold-shouldered by the group. 'A lovely glass of crisp, perfectly chilled Sauvignon blanc,' he said after a mouthful of the lukewarm apple juice. 'Delicious.'

'Do you think you'll go back to the other lot, the bereavement massive?' Gen asked, just as they heard the distant foghorn call of Sallyanne requesting that they reconvene for the second half of the meeting.

'I ...' He faltered because he had already scrubbed the so-called other lot from his mind, written off as a bad idea. And yet there was something about Gen that made him reluctant to say no to her. 'I'm not sure.'

'Give it another go,' she urged him. 'Honestly. I was really surprised by how helpful they've been. Going there, talking to other people – it's turned things around for me.'

Tony noticed that Pen had reached down to squeeze Gen's hand, and he felt a pang of envy at their obvious togetherness, especially when he felt he'd only managed to rile his own partner so far. 'Um,' he said, failing to think of an excuse. Damn it. 'Yeah. Sure. I'll give it another go,' he ended up mumbling. Then he glimpsed Jackie approaching, cackling with some new friends she'd made. 'Nice to talk to you both,' he said, as everyone returned to their seats.

In exactly one hour this will be over, he reminded himself. Sixty minutes, and you can get into the car, go home and pour a very large glass of crisp, perfectly chilled Sauvignon blanc for real. In the meantime, he simply needed to smile serenely, agree with everything Jackie said, and reply '5th April' at the right moment. He could manage that, couldn't he?

Chapter Fifteen

Leni McKenzie memorial page

Leni was two doors down from me in the university halls of residence where we both lived during our first year. I was quite shy and homesick, especially in the first term, and watched in envy as she seemed to flit from party to party, drama to drama. Two months in, my grandma died and I was in bits for ages. Leni made a point of knocking on my door to chat, making me cups of tea (and once, memorably, a really terrible tuna fish curry), and she was not afraid of my sadness. Her kindness meant so much to me. It really helped me through a bad time. Thank you, Leni. You were a good person.

Stephen Teale

'Hello, stranger,' said Alice when Will answered the phone, and he felt a little jolt at her voice, sounding impossibly close despite the miles between them. 'How's my favourite brother?'

'Great,' he said automatically, lying on his thin mattress watching a cockroach scuttling across the tiled floor. It was early evening but the heat from the day still filled the room like a solid block, despite the efforts of his ceiling fan to stir up a breeze. 'Living the dream – sun, sea, sand, parties: you know how it is . . .'

He heard her laugh. 'Er, no, actually, you wanker,' she replied. 'That sounds very far from my life of freezing London, tube strikes and office knobheads.'

'Sorry, not sorry,' he told her. 'How are you, other than dealing with all of that?'

'I'm okay. Not an angry mess any more,' she said, with a rueful note in her voice. 'I'm still trying to piece together what Leni was doing on that last night, and the weeks before,' she went on, before launching into details about some address in Shepherd's Bush. He shut his eyes, saying *La la la la la* in his head so that he didn't have to think about Leni's last night.

'Oh yeah, and the weirdest thing,' Alice said. 'Did you see the message from Jacob on the memorial page?'

There was no chance he'd have seen a message on the memorial page because he never looked at it. Why would he torture himself like that? 'Jacob – your ex-boyfriend Jacob?' he asked in surprise.

'Yeah! Total blast from the past. We're going out for dinner next week and—'

'Whoa, whoa – what?' Will had always liked Jacob: the big brother he'd never had. Jacob had compiled playlists in an attempt to give the eleven-year-old Will some musical education, and took him to his first Oxford City match when someone he knew had spare tickets, and let him win at arm-wrestling occasionally, even though Will was the puniest boy in his year back then.

'Not like that! He's married with a kid, it's not a date or anything. Anyway, I've got . . . Well, it's complicated,' she added cryptically. Oh God, don't say she'd hooked up with that bellend Noah again, he thought, not daring to ask. He and Leni had been united in their dislike for the slimy weasel-boy, as they'd privately called him. 'No, with Jacob, I'm just tapping him for his Leni memories,' Alice continued. 'Hoping he's got some anecdotes that I've forgotten, that sort of thing.'

And now they'd come full circle again. Will frowned, unable to understand why his sister was apparently so determined to keep putting herself through this shit. He couldn't see the point when it only seemed to make her feel sad and guilty. 'Right,' he said after a moment. 'Um . . . give him my best. Hope you find out what you want.'

'How about you? What are you up to? Have you fallen in love out there? Tell me the juicy bits, liven up my bleak British winter, it's the least you can do.'

'Well . . .' He made the mistake of hesitating and she immediately pounced.

'Ooh! A mysterious pause. That means gossip, I can tell. Okay, I'm making myself comfortable, let's hear the details.'

He rolled his eyes because, despite everything, he missed his sister. He wished he could transport himself to her London flat for the evening – or afternoon, whatever time it was there – and give her a hug, go out for a pint and catch up properly. But how could he? How could he go back and look her in the eye, after what had happened?

166

'All right. So I met this girl . . .'

'I *knew* it! Amazing. Tell me everything.'

Her enthusiasm was infectious and despite his earlier reticence, Will found himself warming up. 'Yeah, I'm trying, give us a chance!' he laughed.

'From the very beginning.'

'Okay. From the beginning. Well, you could say, we didn't exactly get off on the right foot. That's a joke, by the way, but you won't find out how it's a joke until a bit later. Anyway . . .'

It was nice to talk about Isla. She'd now left Koh Samui, bound for new adventures, and he'd found it hard to stop thinking about her, in part because the last time he'd seen her, everything had gone wrong. He'd blown it.

On the evening in question, he'd been in a funny mood, unexpectedly thrown by two words that had appeared on his phone screen earlier that day: 'roast chicken', part of his mum's debut posting on the family group chat (so she'd cracked at last). The conversation was about how they as a family should get through Leni's birthday in a few months' time, but rather than dwell on the date and its implications, Will's mind had snagged on the tripwire of his mum's roast chicken offer. Suddenly it was all he could think about: the crispy skin of the meat, golden and glistening, with the juicy, succulent flesh beneath. His mum's Sunday dinners were the absolute best: her roast potatoes with the perfect amount of crunch, the gravy in its blue spotted jug, the dishes of vegetables. He remembered how, on childhood Sundays gone by, the smell would drift up through the house until they were all drawn helplessly towards it, sniffing the air like hungry dogs, offering to set the table in the hope it would speed the process along.

Leni's favourite, Belinda had written in her message, but it had always been his favourite too. The dinner that made everything feel a bit better, that eased you towards the upcoming week at school or college with a full, contented stomach. He found himself yearning to be taking a seat at his mum's laden table again, in the cosy, cluttered kitchen, steam on the windows, the radio playing *Sounds of the Seventies*. Thinking about this, and about seeing her again, her cheeks flushed from the heat of the stove, wearing the navy and white striped pinny she'd had for as long as he could remember, made him feel a tearing sensation inside that was almost painful.

'Everything all right, Will? You look miles away.'

He was down at the Elephant Bar at the time, a place he'd taken to frequenting and not simply because it was close to the hotel where Isla and Meg were staying. ('Yeah, yeah, I believe you,' Alice said on hearing this.) Isla had appeared at the table, dumping her bag on the seat beside him as if the two of them were meeting for a date. They weren't, obviously, but he felt a little pinwheel of happiness spin inside him nonetheless, because already the evening had taken a welcome turn for the better.

'Hmm? Oh, hi,' he said, as she sat down. Her hair was in a long plait over one shoulder and she wore a black top that was almost sheer in a certain light, with cut-off jeans and silver low-top Converse. She looked beautiful, in short, and he swallowed, promising himself that he must keep his eyes on her face, rather than getting distracted with the outline beneath her clothes. 'Yeah, I'm fine,' he said, in reply to her question. 'No Meg tonight?'

She waggled an eyebrow. 'Hot date with a guy we met diving earlier. He's an Aussie, from Sydney; he's promised to give her the intel on the restaurant scene out there. Which is kind of a niche chat-up line if you ask me, but it worked for Meg.'

'I see,' he said and then, feeling a stab of envy at the thought of a bunch of handsome blokes chatting them up on this trip, was unable to stop himself from adding, 'There was no one you fancied on the dive, then?'

'Well, it was mostly women, apart from this one particular guy, so ...' That eyebrow again, so expressive in its flexibility. 'So no. Can I get you a drink? Oh –' she hesitated, 'do you mind me sitting with you, by the way? You're not waiting to meet someone, are you? Got one of your business meetings arranged?'

He laughed, if only because she always looked so chuffed with her own wit whenever she teased him about his work. 'Yeah, it's a global conference tonight. All the big guns flying in for this,' he said, before pulling a face at her. 'Or in the real world, no, I'm not waiting for anyone, and I'd love you to sit with me. I'm fine for a drink, thanks.' He indicated the half-bottle of Singha he'd been stringing out for the last twenty minutes. It was lukewarm by now and less refreshing than it had been, but he was trying to be frugal and make it last as long as possible after another unsuccessful day on his rounds. Nobody wanted to buy a fan or a sarong from him, apparently. Zilch on the sunglasses, also. Had he lost his touch or was it that he'd stopped caring enough about winning over his punters? Maybe it was there in his eyes, the certainty that he considered his products to be pretty shit and not worth anyone's money. Whichever, something had changed to jolt him out of his sales groove into this losing streak. He hoped he could find a way back to profit soon.

You could always take a sideways step in my direction, his friend Juno had said the other night, with a meaningful glance. Juno sold weed and pills to holidaymakers and made astronomical profits, but the Thai laws around drug-dealing were so hard-core, Will had always been too intimidated to consider this an option. But if he wanted to stay on the island longer – and he did – then maybe he should think again?

A few minutes later, Isla was back and setting down two hurricane glasses on the table, clinking with ice and some peach-coloured concoction or other. 'Here – I went crazy and got us a cocktail each,' she said when he looked at the glasses, then up at her in surprise. 'I know you said you were okay for a drink, but sod it, it's Monday, everyone needs a drink on Monday, right? And it's my last night here too, so . . . Cheers.'

'Thank you,' he said, touched. 'What is this, by the way? Not some slow poisonous revenge for the mis-sold flip-flop, I take it?'

She laughed. 'If it is, I'm drinking the same, so we'll go down together. It's a Samui Sundowner, apparently. Bottoms up, my friend. Let's get the evening started.'

He asked about the diving trip she'd been on that day and she talked for some time about the turtles, barracuda and stingrays they'd encountered, the incredible visibility. Then she sharpened her gaze and asked in return, 'So go on then, what were you thinking about when I got here? You looked a wee bit sad, you know. Is everything all right?'

He gave her a small smile. 'To be completely honest, I was thinking about my mum's roast chicken,' he confessed.

She laughed. 'Okay! I would not have guessed that.'

'Yeah, bit random,' he agreed, but then faltered, wanting to change the subject before he waded out any further. Since he'd been in Thailand, he hadn't talked to a single person about Leni, about home. It had been a deliberate policy: to detach himself from the mess and sadness by acting like it had never happened. Yet now it was as if home had risen to the surface of his feelings, as if he could no longer put a lid on that night back in June.

'It's a good roast chicken, then, I take it,' she prompted, sipping her drink through a straw, her eyes steady on him.

'It's the best.' He managed another weak smile, desperately wishing they could return to the safer territory of her diving trip because he could feel his usual façade cracking, and he didn't like that at all. 'Anyway, tell me more about—'

'When I first left home for uni, it was my dad's Saturday fried breakfasts I missed the most,' she said at the same time. 'He properly goes for it at the weekend – it's like he's cooking for an army. Eggs, bacon, sausages, beans, mushrooms, piles and piles of toast ... At the start of my first year, I kept waking up on Saturday mornings in my halls of residence with this absolute ache of homesickness. Or maybe an ache of hunger, I don't know. Maybe my stomach was finely tuned to its weekly routine and was like, *Hey, where's my massive fry-up then?*' She laughed, and he noticed the way her eyes crinkled at the edges. She was so pretty. Mesmerisingly so. It was all he could do to stop himself from offering to cook her a fried breakfast right there and then.

'Of course, it wasn't just his fry-ups I missed,' she went on, 'it was him too, but the breakfast was ... I dunno. Symbolic, I guess. Food does that, doesn't it?' She patted her belly with both hands then smiled at him. 'What's your mum like, then? Apart from being a wonder with a roast chicken. You haven't said much about your family.'

The question caught him off guard. 'Oh,' he said. 'She's ...' Then he stopped because the last time he'd seen his mum she'd been crying at the airport and now it was all he could think about. *You will come back, won't you? Please take care of yourself. I can't lose anyone else. Please, I mean it, Will.* 'She's had a rough time,' he blurted out, then felt like kicking himself.

'Sorry to hear that,' Isla said. 'Anything you want to talk about?'

No, definitely not, was his instinct, but there was something about the way she was looking at him, gaze unwavering, chin propped on her palm as if she had all the time in the world to listen, that gave him pause. 'Well—' he said haltingly, because it turned out to be really hard to drag himself away from her periwinkle-blue eyes, impossible to fob her off. 'Actually, my sister died,' he went on before he could help it.

'Oh God!' Her eyebrows signalled how little she'd anticipated such a bombshell. 'Will, I'm so sorry.'

He looked away, already regretting opening his mouth at all. These were words he hadn't said aloud for so long, for months and months. The last person he must have said them to was his boss when he took some time off work, or maybe one of his mates, who knew the family. *My sister died.* They were terrible words to say. Absolutely awful. And then to have Isla gazing at him with such concern, such empathy, only made him feel a hundred times worse. 'Yeah,' he managed to get out. 'So . . .' The rest of the sentence eluded him and he shrugged, trying to throw off the bad feelings churning up his guts. *Can I ask you a favour, Will?* he heard Leni's voice in his head, and emotion surged perilously. 'Let's not talk about it, anyway,' he said, gruffly. 'You're on holiday, it's not exactly holiday chat.'

He sought sanctuary in his drink but could feel her watching him. 'I don't mind,' she said. 'Just because I'm on holiday doesn't mean I've turned into a selfish tosser who doesn't care about anyone else's troubles. It's your call.'

You could tell she was a health professional, he thought, meeting her eyes again. Underneath her tough exterior, she was kind, she was straight with you. 'Tell me about your family,' he said, desperate to switch the spotlight away from himself. 'Do you have brothers and sisters?'

She took the baton and regaled him with tales of her three younger brothers, and soon the atmosphere had lightened once more as he laughed at her stories and felt his turbulent feelings subsiding. Okay. Dodged a bullet. Moving on, he thought, mentally patching up the fractures that had appeared so disconcertingly in his protective shell. Nothing to see here.

They had another round of Sundowners, then ordered plates of noodles and then, because why not, she was on holiday and it was her last night on the island, they ended up in Hush, one of the nightclubs, dancing to old R'n'B under the colourful lights. His body felt loose with alcohol, and the music took hold of him in the best kind of way. How could it be that during the course of a single evening, you could swing from feeling sad to joyful and celebratory? Isla was a good dancer and, in the crush of bodies on the dance floor, he felt alive once more, as if he was in the right place, as if nothing else mattered. What was the point in dwelling on the past? You couldn't change it, however much you'd like to, however hard you wished you could have said to your own sister, *Sure, you can ask me a favour. Yes, I can help.*

Around midnight, Isla professed tiredness and they left, the resort still pumping with music from the surrounding bars and clubs. His senses felt heightened, taking in the distant roar of generators, the Thai boys on their mopeds buzzing through the streets, the smells from the food stalls serving up moonlit curries and satay skewers while stray dogs sniffed around for scraps. Walking along together, he took her hand in his and then, emboldened, pulled her towards him and tried to kiss her, only for her to push him away under a flickering streetlight.

'No,' she said. 'Sorry.'

He felt discomfited, as if he must have misread the signs. 'Oh,' he said. 'That's okay.' Still confused, he added, 'I thought we were getting on?'

'We were,' she said. 'I mean, we are. But—' She shrugged and they went on walking, her face pale in the half darkness.

He had the sinking feeling that he might not want to hear

the rest of that sentence, although a masochistic streak in him prompted her to finish nonetheless. 'But … ?'

She gave him a rueful smile. 'You're a lovely guy, Will. You're gorgeous and funny and good company. But you play your cards so close to your chest, I still don't have any real idea who you are. I get that you've suffered an enormous tragedy and I'm really sorry for you and your family. But—'

'That's got nothing to do with anything,' he said stubbornly.

'It has, because you're like a closed book, sealed all the way shut,' she replied. There was silence for a moment where he didn't know what to say, then she went on, her tone gentle but still devastating. 'If I kissed you – and don't think I wasn't tempted – I wouldn't know who I'd be kissing.'

He felt himself deflate. There was nothing he could say by way of self-defence because she was right and they both knew it. 'Fair enough,' he replied, trying to let the criticism slide right off him. *Let it go, don't think about it.* There was nothing wrong with being a closed book. 'That's cool.'

'Is it, though? You're happy to be like that? This is you now, forever, is it?'

He felt winded by the criticism in her words. 'Wow,' he said. 'Don't hold back, will you? Say what you really think.'

He must have sounded hurt – he *was* hurt – because now she was grimacing. 'Sorry. Ignore me,' she mumbled. 'I've had too much to drink.' They'd reached the building where she and Meg were staying and she gave him an apprehensive smile. 'Thanks for tonight, I had a great time. All the best, yeah? I hope you find what you're looking for.'

She hoped he'd find what he was looking for? What the

hell was that supposed to mean? 'Right, sure,' he said, none the wiser. He wasn't looking for anything, other than a good time. 'Same to you. Have a nice life.'

Her mouth opened as if she wanted to say something else but he didn't give her the chance, turning away, his hand raised in farewell. 'Night, then,' he said, without looking back.

His eyes stung as he walked back towards the main drag; his mouth trembled as if he wanted to cry. It didn't matter, he told himself fiercely. *She* didn't matter. Who was she? Some girl on holiday. Nobody who could hurt him or leave any kind of trace on him, that was for sure. *You're like a closed book*, he heard her repeat in his head. *You're happy to be like that?*

Yes, he replied, hands knotting into fists, telling himself it was the smoke from a nearby noodle stall making his eyes water. Of course he was happy to be like this. Why wouldn't he be?

He didn't tell Alice the full story, obviously. He sprinkled a little glitter over the details, focussed on the chemistry and banter, kept Leni – and the roast chicken – out of it.

'So ... oh.' She sounded disappointed when he got to the (heavily edited) part about them saying goodbye. 'So that's it? She's gone now? But you're going to stay in touch?'

'Probably not,' he admitted. Isla had made it pretty clear that Beach Bum Will wasn't enough for her, and he knew he couldn't open up his closed book and give her Real Will, tarnished and ugly as that version was. He tried to lighten the mood. 'You know me – easy come, easy go. Loads more tourists arriving every single day.'

'But ...' She sounded confused, as if he'd sold her short on the romantic story she'd been expecting. Understandable. He wasn't sure why he'd even told her now.

'Anyway, I'd better go,' he said, grabbing one of his shoes and throwing it across the room at the cockroach. Too slow; it had run for cover beneath the ancient chest of drawers. 'Good to talk to you, Alice. Bye!'

He hung up before she could ask him anything else or start talking about Leni again, and flopped back on the bed, his eyes shut. *Easy come, easy go*, he reminded himself. *Smile – you're in paradise!*

Chapter Sixteen

Alice: So guess who I'm meeting tonight? Jacob Murray!

Belinda: WHAT???!!!! Oh my goodness! Give him my love. Such a lovely boy [heart-eyes emoji, smiling-face emoji, heart emoji]

Alice: Don't get too excited, Mum, we're only having a drink and reminiscing about Leni.

Belinda: Sounds like a date to me!! [red heart emoji, pink heart emoji, red heart emoji]

Alice: It's not a date, he's married with a kid! Friendship only.

Belinda: [sad-face emoji, broken-heart emoji]

Alice: Talking of dates though, did you ever hear Leni mention someone called Josh? Was she seeing anyone last summer, do you know?

Belinda: Josh. Hmmm. That name is ringing a bell but I can't think why. [bell emoji, confused-face emoji] Love you. Have fun tonight! [red heart emoji]

★

It's complicated, Alice had told Will in reference to her love life, although other, juicier words had sprung to mind when she walked into the meeting room at work, only to be greeted by her one-night stand, Darren Not-a-Baron, there at the table. Goodness knows how she managed to take any minutes; it had been practically impossible to concentrate. She would never go drinking alone in any bars near work again if this was what happened, she thought, blushing with mortification. The worst thing – the second worst thing – was that he actually looked pretty hot in his dark suit and snazzy tie, which was not the sort of confusion she needed right now.

He, at least, didn't seem to have noticed her. Maybe he was one of those men who saw a woman in a meeting with a notebook and pen, and instantly dismissed her as having no value, no worth within the discussion. Tosser. From the meeting's agenda, she could see that he was an actuary, so would be based in the legal division up on the ninth floor, with no connection to Alice's usual work. If her colleague Rosalind had been in that day to take notes as usual, chances were Alice could have got away with never seeing him again. Her one crumb of comfort throughout the deeply uncomfortable experience was imagining how Leni would have screamed with mirth on hearing the story later on. *Oh my Godddd! Noooo! This is hilarious. So awkward!*

The meeting finally ended and just as she was thinking she'd successfully remained under his radar, they ended up alongside each other in the bottleneck to leave the room. 'Nice to see you again, Alice,' he'd said in a low voice – aargh, excruciating, she was actually *dying* now – and she responded with a sound that was half yelp, half laugh, before escaping quickly through the door and away. Nightmare, she thought with a full-body shudder. Genuine did-that-just-happen nightmare.

Anyway. It was Friday now, and she'd survived the rest of the week without any further sexy-Darren interactions, thank heavens. Dare she say it, office dramas aside, the week had been pretty good. Hamish was definitely getting used to living with her, even if he was yet to permit any strokes or other affectionate moves. He had stopped scuttling under the bed or behind the sofa whenever she came into a room, for one thing, and had filled out a little, no longer appearing quite so scrawny and unkempt. In a sign that he might have accepted her flat as his new home, he had settled on a few preferred spots around the place too. He particularly enjoyed sitting on the kitchen windowsill for garden surveillance sessions, his beautiful orange tail occasionally flicking with interest whenever a bird flew into view.

The cats' home had advised her to keep him indoors for at least three weeks before allowing him to explore outside, but she could tell already he was desperate to bust out of there. Lou, who was good at such things, had promised to come over at the weekend so that she could fit a cat flap before Freedom Day in a week's time, and also, Alice suspected, so that she could get the full low-down on her forthcoming evening with Jacob.

'Meeting up with your first love, oh wow! This is so exciting!' she'd cried when they had met for lunch yesterday. Lou worked for a drugs charity in Holborn, two tube stops away from the Sage and Golding office, and Alice enjoyed escaping to meet her for a break, especially after an interminably dull morning spent wading through a backlog of claims to be processed. 'You know what they say, don't you? About getting straight back on a horse?'

'I will not be getting on any horses, Lou,' Alice said, wishing everyone would stop jumping to the wrong conclusions about this. 'We're—'

'The sex horse, I mean, before you think I'm making Pony Club references.'

'The sex horse?' Alice found herself giggling at the ridiculous, exaggerated winks her friend was now giving her. 'Stop it,' she gurgled. 'You look like you're having a stroke. And no, I'm not having sex with a horse – not for you, not for anyone. Definitely not for the horse.'

'God, I would,' Lou said dreamily, eyes glinting as she bit into her prawn sandwich. 'Where's your sense of adventure, Alice? Come *on*! With Valentine's Day next week, too.' She gestured towards the counter, where a line of scarlet hearts had been strung across the coffee machines like tinsel. Valentine's Day decorations were a *thing* now? No doubt that had been dreamed up in a marketing meeting somewhere, Alice thought, feeling a brief pang for fun creative meetings where the wildest ideas could be bounced around. Nobody would be festooning the walls with Valentine bunting at Sage and Golding any time soon, that was for sure.

'If the thought of a manufactured, commercialised day of so-called romance doesn't make you feel like throwing caution to the wind, or your knickers to the wind, whatever the

181

phrase is, then I don't know what will,' Lou was saying. 'Get with the program, girlfriend.'

Alice snorted. 'Knickers to the wind, indeed. Are we still on horse sex, by the way? I can't keep up.'

'That's what the horse will say,' Lou had sniggered.

Remembering this now, Alice smiled to herself, pulling her coat around her as she exited the tube at Tottenham Court Road and headed towards Berwick Street. She was due to meet Jacob in Dimitris, the Greek restaurant Leni had loved, according to her friend Rosie. What better place for a meeting of the two remaining Flying Beauties? No doubt this was silly of her, but already Alice was feeling a thimbleful of comfort at the thought of sliding on to a banquette that her sister might have sat on, experiencing the exact same view of the street outside that Leni might have enjoyed, lingering over the menu and wondering which dishes had tempted her tastebuds. *Here I am, living for you* and *me, just like I promised,* she would think, breathing in the ambience, silently raising a glass to her sister's memory.

Dimitris was busy when she arrived, the windows steamed up, the tables set with paper tablecloths, bouzouki music playing from a wall-mounted speaker high up in one corner. An aproned waiter was pouring red wine from a carafe for a couple nearby; elsewhere she could smell herbs and tomatoes and grilled cheese. Then she saw Jacob, sitting at a table in the corner frowning at the menu, and her heart stuttered a little, trying to take in his appearance before he could notice she'd arrived. Stupidly, her first thought was that he was a man now, rather than the skinny teenager she'd dated – he looked broader around the shoulders (was he working out?), his cheekbones no longer quite so angular (to be fair, whose were, post-thirty?), and he sported a short, tidy beard that suited him. His dark brown hair was a bit longer than when they'd been together, sitting maybe an inch above his collar now, and he wore a pair of black-framed glasses (since when did he need glasses?). He also had on a rather crumpled grey shirt, the sort that she knew would be soft between her fingers, and she blushed all of a sudden, imagining touching it, before reminding herself, semi-hysterically, how inappropriate that would be. Look at him though, all grown-up and good-looking. It was doing strange things to her.

'Alice McKenzie, oh my God,' he said, getting to his feet when he saw her. There was his lovely wide smile again, the one in all the photos she'd found herself poring over the night before. 'Wow, look at you. Time flies!'

She had wondered beforehand how they might greet one another – a polite kiss on the cheek or just a smile? – but he didn't seem to have any qualms about grabbing her for a hug, and in the next minute she was pressed against his (disarmingly beefy) shoulder with his arms around her. He had always been a good hugger, she thought fleetingly, a montage playing in her head of other embraces – when her gran had died, A-level results day, the night they had to sleep in a train station in India, when she'd never been so grateful for another person's bodily warmth. 'Hello,' she said, suddenly shy as she sat opposite him. 'Thank you so much for this,' she went on, wanting to set the agenda from the start. 'I was so pleased to see your message on the memorial page. Do you know, I'd forgotten that we even made you an honorary Flying Beauty?'

'Forgotten? How dare you,' he joked. 'You can't rewrite history that easily, mate.' Then he looked awkward, as if remembering what this was all about. 'I was so sorry when my mum told me the news. You know she and my dad have moved out of Oxford now? They're down in Paignton, both retired; they love it there. Mum got together with some old friends after Christmas and one of them mentioned Leni.' His gaze was sincere and direct. 'It's just . . . You must be devastated. I'm so sorry, Alice. How are you doing? If that's not too inane a question.'

'I'm okay,' she said, because that seemed the safest reply, and because she didn't want to frighten him with confessions of her rock-bottom times. 'Yeah,' she added, more rallyingly. 'So this was one of Leni's favourite restaurants, apparently. I thought it might be nice to come here, in the hope that I'd feel close to her again.'

He nodded, still meeting her gaze. His eyebrows had grown bushier in the last decade, she noted, but his eyes were just how she remembered them – coffee-bean brown and expressive. He had cried that Christmas when they split up, the first time she'd ever seen him like that; his hands curling and uncurling by his sides as if he didn't know what to do with them. 'Sounds a good idea,' he said now and she felt a rush of relief. She knew he'd get it.

They ordered food and launched into nostalgic stories over the bread and dips that the waiter brought, clinking their bottles of Mythos together by way of a toast. Alice had always known Jacob was smart – he had aced his A levels, he'd been awarded that incredible scholarship, he'd gone on to study for a master's and then a doctorate – but she became increasingly grateful for his pin-sharp memory that had captured all sorts of events she'd forgotten. The day in December many years earlier, for instance, when the two of them plus Leni had gone into town together. The trip was ostensibly to do some Christmas shopping, but they'd become cosily ensconced in the Turf Tavern drinking pint after pint (the joys of fake ID). Some time later they re-emerged, ending up drunkenly singing carols alongside the Salvation Army in front of the Mound, before being asked by a French-horn player, pretty forcefully, to sod off. 'Oh my God. Yes! And we ended up giving them all our change because we felt so bad,' Alice cried, helpless with laughter.

'Didn't Leni get the phone number of some guy on the bassoon too?' Jacob asked.

'Sounds about right,' Alice said, shaking her head. Then she caught his eye and felt a swell of happiness inside, remembering them being carefree teenagers together. They'd had so many good times.

They smiled at one another, the memory hanging in the air between them. 'So what are you up to these days?' he asked. 'If that isn't too much of a screeching handbrake turn back from drunken carol-singing.'

Still deep in times gone by, she misunderstood the question. 'Well, I'm sorting through Leni's belongings and catching up with some of her friends to return various bits and bobs,' she replied. 'And I'm trying to make a point of going to places that were important to her. Doing things that she loved. It kind of haunts me that I don't know much about the night she died – how she was feeling, or where she was even going – so I've been trying to piece together what she was doing then, and in the weeks leading up to that day, so that ...' Jacob was looking at her as if he didn't quite follow and she momentarily lost her thread. 'So that I feel connected to her. It's why I was so keen to meet up with you,' she went on. 'To hear all of your stories. I feel as if I'm collating this mental scrapbook – I want to fill it with everyone's memories, all the snippets of her life.' She could feel tears in her eyes suddenly – oh gosh, she'd got embarrassingly earnest on him now, she hoped he could handle it. Thankfully the waiter arrived to take their empty plates away and the mood was broken.

'Thank you, that was delicious,' Jacob said, and Alice blinked, realising that she'd barely noticed her food again. They'd shared all sorts of little dishes – prawn skewers, calamari, spinach pie – but she'd been so engrossed in Leni stories, it had been as if Leni was there at the table, and she'd felt too happy to care about dinner. Never mind. 'Back to what we were talking about,' Jacob went on, once the table was clear. 'When I asked what were you up to, I meant *you, Alice* – you know, for yourself. Where do you work, for instance? Not that I'm not interested in what you're doing for Leni, I mean ...' he added, perhaps because her face had fallen.

'Oh.' It was as if she'd been jolted out of the warm bubble of nostalgia back into the real world, where Leni was no longer present. Couldn't they have stayed longer in the past? 'Um. I'm just temping at the moment. A maternity cover. I left my old job just before Christmas. Let's not talk about that though,' she said quickly, seeing his eyebrows rise. 'Oh!' she exclaimed as something occurred to her. 'I know what I was going to ask you – do you remember that barbecue at my mum's house the summer after our A levels? Remember those boys who fancied Leni gatecrashed and the shed ended up catching fire?'

He hesitated, like he wanted to say something else, his eyes flicking sideways for a second, but maybe she'd imagined it, because in the next moment she felt his focus full on her again, and he was smiling and leaning back in his chair. 'Remind me,' he said.

Chapter Seventeen

Leni McKenzie memorial page

I had never believed in love at first sight until I had to go to a speed awareness driving course, walked in and saw this woman arguing with the teacher that there was no one, absolutely no one, who didn't break the speed limit now and then. I thought — she sounds kind of feisty. And then she turned around and I saw her properly and I swear that the world sort of juddered a bit because I thought, bloody hell, she's gorgeous too. I was smitten, there and then.

We hit it off — over a shared hatred for speed awareness courses initially, but then over a shared love of beach holidays, classic sitcoms, Spurs (all right … maybe that was just me), tennis and curry. So many other things. Our marriage didn't work out in the end, but I'm so happy we were together at all, that I knew her and loved her. The privilege was all mine.

Leni, I can't believe you're no longer in the world. Rest in peace, princess.

Adam

★

Up in Oxford, Belinda was quite glad to be in the house alone. Ever since her public breakdown in the swimming baths, she'd felt fragile; an egg liable to be broken by the smallest upset. Tonight, Ray had gone to meet his long-lost son, and she was able to lower herself into her favourite corner of the sofa, a massive glass of wine within reach, and exhale. Sometimes keeping up appearances was bloody exhausting.

She'd always been a cheerful person. You had to be when you worked in social services – it was no place for pessimists – but it was more than that: she loved life, she loved people, she loved being busy. 'You're the most fun I've ever had,' Ray had laughed to her soon after they got together, when they'd been swept up with passion and excitement, off on a new adventure every other week, or so it seemed. And then, of course, life had walloped a curveball at her, right when she least expected it.

Those early weeks of hell, where she'd woken up each morning still living the nightmare, made her shudder to think about now. It hadn't been simply the shock and pain of her own bereavement, it was having to deal with the ripples that kept on coming, the messy business of mopping up after a life lost. Belinda was named as Leni's next of kin and for a while her phone kept ringing with one person or company after another saying apologetically that they'd been unable to get hold of Leni and were contacting Belinda now because this, because that. It had felt like some kind of torture, having to explain the circumstances each time. *She's dead. She's gone. She won't be coming to any more appointments. Yes, you can send me a form to fill in for your wretched system if you must.*

Belinda had dragged herself through it again and again. She'd handled the calls, dealt with the emails, she'd told herself she was coping – *fake it till you make it* had always served her well – right up until the moment when she wasn't coping any more, when faking it was no longer an option, when she had a worried lifeguard squatting in front of her and she couldn't stop crying. Ever since then, it was as if something had cracked inside her, something she couldn't quite fix. She kept experiencing irrational bursts of anger – at the manufacturer of Leni's bike, which had turned out to have a dodgy steering column, at Graham Fenton for popping up again when she'd all but forgotten him, at her own self for failing to be entirely honest about the part he'd played in her life. She'd even sat down and written a heated, blame-throwing letter to Adam, her former son-in-law, telling him that if he'd only been faithful to Leni, if he'd only loved her more, then Leni would probably still be alive. It was all his fault!

She hadn't posted the letter, needless to say. She'd written everything she wanted to say and then she'd burned it over the kitchen sink and washed the black remnants down the plughole. It had felt pretty satisfying getting the anger off her chest, mind you.

Sipping her wine – delicious – she wondered how Alice was getting on, presumably having dinner with Jacob right now (Jacob Murray!! Belinda had adored that boy). Then she remembered her daughter's question about this Josh person, and wished she could think why the name was still ringing a faint bell in her head. *Josh.* Someone had definitely mentioned a Josh to her, but who?

It was the wrong time of day to speak to Will, so she wrote him a long gossipy email instead, full of news about the people who'd come round to look at the house that day (a very nice family, fingers crossed) and how she'd bumped into Will's friend Hattie in town earlier, who sent her love. Then it was time to check in with her eldest daughter, and she topped up her wine in readiness before picking up her phone to call Apolline.

Wait, though – the phone was buzzing in her hand with a new message, and in the next moment, she saw Tony's name on the screen. This time it wasn't a message to the group chat, but one just for her.

Hi Bel. How are you doing? With a new one on the way and antenatal classes and appointments, I keep finding myself remembering moments with our children when they were tiny – their births, Leni's first word, first Christmases, those exhausting first holidays we somehow made it through. We had some good times, didn't we? Sometimes I look back and think those were the best days of my life. And for many of them – particularly when Leni was a baby – you're the only other person who was there too. I know we've had our differences, I know things didn't work out, but if you ever want to chat about old times, either messaging or in person, I'd love to get together and do that. No agenda! Just for the sake of family ties. Love Tony x

Belinda nearly choked on her wine. Heavens above. What was she supposed to do with that?

Apolline would know, of course. Her friend had the answer to everything. Although Belinda should probably make it a quick chat this time – her card had been declined in the supermarket earlier that day, which had been mortifying, and when she rang the bank to find out what was going on, the young man who answered said they'd been trying to get in touch with her to authorise a number of recent, large payments. The system had flagged them as suspicious, he said, reading the payment details back to her. They were for Apolline's hotline, needless to say, and she found herself wincing about how much she had spent lately, until remembering that contact with Leni was priceless. Besides, it was nobody else's business.

Some hours later, still comfortably ensconced on the sofa and deep in conversation, with Friday night telly muted in the background, she heard Ray's car outside. 'I'd better go,' she said into the phone, because she and Ray hadn't spoken about Apolline since their last argument on the subject and she didn't want to dredge that up again. She was also keen to find out how he'd got on with Ellis. Ray had bought himself a new shirt for the occasion and got his hair cut, and he'd even jotted down a few topics of conversation so that he wouldn't run out of things to say.

'You've got years to catch up on, you'll be dying to know all about him and his sister,' Belinda had assured him, because she could tell he was getting in a flap. 'You just be yourself, because that is plenty good enough. Show him your hang-gliding photos if you want to impress him.'

She hurried through to the hall at the sound of Ray's key in the front door. 'How did it go? How was he?' she asked as the door opened. Then her eyes widened as she realised that Ray was not alone.

'Here we are, come on in,' he said, walking into the hall, with a tall, mop-haired young man trailing behind.

Ray looked overjoyed, Belinda thought, feeling thrilled for him. 'Hello,' she said warmly to them both. 'You must be Ellis, it's lovely to meet you. I'm Belinda.'

'Gosh, sorry, yes,' Ray gabbled, looking flustered. 'Ellis – Belinda. Belinda – Ellis. You're both so important to me, this feels pretty momentous,' he added, blinking.

Ellis had the same brown eyes as his dad, and a similar smile, albeit a wary, watchful version tonight. He held himself with a rigid stillness as if on his guard within what might yet turn out to be enemy territory. 'Hi,' he said, looming near the door.

'You're very welcome here,' Belinda told him, unable to resist putting a hand on his arm, as if needing to check he was actually real. 'Now – have you two eaten? Can I get either of you a drink? Ellis, there's a loo just along the hall here if you need it and – you're staying the night, I take it?' she interrupted herself.

He was carrying a scuffed blue sports bag and glanced down at it as if uncertain where it had come from. 'Er ... yeah?' he replied, eyeing Ray and then Belinda. 'If you're sure that's okay? It's only for tonight and he – Dad – did say ...'

'Of course it's okay! Absolutely,' Belinda assured him. 'I'll go and make a bed up. Ray, are you sorting out drinks?'

Ray took the cue, and ushered his son down into the kitchen without offering to take his coat first. Never mind. After so long apart, this would not be a deal-breaker, she consoled herself, hurrying upstairs. Her heart thumped with excitement at their unexpected visitor; she wanted everything to be perfect, for him to feel welcome and relaxed while he stayed. She'd win him over with home comforts alone, she vowed, switching on the radiator in Will's old room and stripping the bed linen even though it was clean. Fresh sheets in place, plus a couple of towels; she made sure the bulb in the bedside lamp worked, then left a good thriller she'd just enjoyed on the little table there, in case he, like Belinda, was in the habit of reading a chapter of something before he fell asleep. What else? Would he need pyjamas? A toothbrush? Presumably he had those in that blue sports bag, but she made a note to double-check later. Would it be over the top to put a vase of something on the chest of drawers? Yes, she decided. Plus it was dark outside, and if she went out into the garden and started snipping narcissi and twigs of winter jasmine by torchlight, he'd think his dad had shacked up with a total weirdo.

Okay. Stop fussing. Go down and give that boy some attention and make sure Ray is looking after him properly, she told herself, thudding back downstairs.

'It's just like the old days,' she said, ten minutes later, frying bacon and eggs and a couple of leftover boiled potatoes, now chopped into pieces and sizzling in the pan. 'My son Will would often turn up with a load of friends in tow, who'd want feeding at the drop of a hat – I'd always get the bacon out for them. This takes me right back.' Gosh, she'd forgotten how much she'd loved it when they all bundled in after football, or if they'd been drinking in the park and felt hungry. How important she'd felt, bustling about, providing hot food and a bit of mothering for these lanky, graceless teenage boys with their loud laughs and constant wind-ups. How she had drunk in the compliments like a thirsty plant receiving water. And they'd eaten so much! *You boys, I don't know where you put it!* she'd always marvelled as they tore through loaves of bread in one sitting, as they made short work of a twelve-box of eggs.

Ellis had installed himself at the table, although he hadn't yet let go of the tension about his shoulders. 'Smells great,' he said politely. Then, as the toaster popped up two browned slices, 'Should I butter those?'

So he was well-mannered *and* thoughtful – a good start. Belinda twinkled her eyes at him. 'Yes, please,' she said. 'Thank you, darling. Tell me about yourself, anyway – you're in the area for a job interview, is that right? How did it go?'

Ellis seemed delightful, what with his Welsh twang (Belinda did love a Welsh accent) and his slight shyness, warming up gradually as he tucked into a plateful of food. There was, admittedly, something of a strain to be detected between the two men – Ellis keeping his distance, apparently unwilling to reveal too much too soon, while Ray was perhaps trying a little too hard. Ellis had applied for a trainee management position at a retail park nearby, it transpired, and Belinda tried to flash Ray glances that said *Tone it down* whenever he got over-enthusiastic about his son's prospects. She had to widen her eyes quite warningly at him when he began jotting down the names of a couple of local estate agents for when (if) Ellis needed to find somewhere to live. 'Although, it goes without saying, you're welcome to stay here,' he gushed. 'Right, Bel? For as long as you like.'

'Of course you are,' Belinda told him. 'Absolutely.'

'Thanks, but you're moving, aren't you?' Ellis asked, swishing a square of toast through the puddle of egg yolk on his plate. 'Selling up?'

'Ah. Yes. Not immediately,' Ray assured him. 'I've sold my old flat now and this place is on the market, and we're looking to buy a place together further out of town. Become bumpkins in our old age.'

'Become the owners of a successful B. & B., you mean,' Belinda corrected him, with a wink at Ellis. 'Your dad might be heading for bumpkin-hood, but I'm not ready for that just yet.'

He smiled, but he seemed preoccupied with something. Subdued, even, she thought. Was he worried he'd mucked up the interview, maybe? Having second thoughts about coming here? 'Must be nice,' was all he said.

'If there's anything else I can do that would help, you only have to say,' Ray assured him in the next breath. 'Like – you know, if you want to borrow my car or something, to get around to this job or other interviews. Maybe I could treat you to a really sharp suit that makes you feel extra confident about yourself.' His eyes were pleading, Belinda registered with a twist of empathy. *Let me help,* his face said. *Please, son. Whatever you need, I want to give it to you.* It reminded her of how Tony used to get every now and then, when he realised he'd neglected his kids for the latest woman he'd been after.

'Same goes for Rhiannon,' Ray went on, hands open in front of him as if offering up invisible goods. 'I know I messed up. I know I let you two down, and your mum too. But if there are ways I can start putting that right somehow ...'

Ellis had finished eating and set down his cutlery. 'We're

fine, thanks,' he said, then feigned a yawn. 'This has been really nice, but if it's okay with you, I might just call it a night.'

Ray slumped in his seat as if the air had gone out of him, and Belinda felt an ache of sympathy. Okay, so he had gone off the rails as a young father, he'd said as much himself, but he had turned his life around since then. And he *was* Ellis and Rhiannon's dad, at the end of the day. People could change, couldn't they? Look how Tony had surprised her with his recent efforts.

Leni thinks you should meet him, Apolline had said when Belinda had talked through the message she'd received from her ex-husband earlier on, and if it was all right by Leni, then it was all right by Belinda, she'd decided. Besides, Tony was right about there being certain moments that no one else knew about. Presumably he didn't mean the bad ones though.

'Of course,' she said quickly to Ellis now, seeing as Ray still hadn't responded. She glanced up at the clock to see that it was only nine thirty, surely far earlier than anyone in their twenties usually went to bed. 'You must be tired, you've had a long day,' she went on kindly, as much as a reminder to Ray as anything else. *Give him some space. Back off a bit.* The lad did look pale, even after a large plateful of food, and this was a strange, intense situation for him; it was hardly surprising he wanted to retreat. 'Can I run you a bath, or get you anything else? Glass of water to take up with you?'

The chair squawked as he stood up, shaking his head. 'No, thanks. Um ...'

'Let me show you where you're sleeping,' Ray said, hurrying around the table to lead the way.

'See you in the morning,' Belinda said. 'Lovely to meet you, Ellis.'

'You too,' he said. 'Thanks again.'

Well! She couldn't stop smiling as the door closed behind them. Having Ellis here was not only great for Ray, it made her feel as if she had a purpose again, someone new to look after. And she had missed fussing about over a guest! Will was so far away and Alice didn't come home much any more. But now here was Ellis to bring Ray some optimism for a new father-son relationship. There was so much to discover about him and his sister, so many stories she wanted to coax out. *Death has taken much from you but life will continue to give,* Apolline had said to her that very evening, and she'd been spot on, as ever.

She could hear the tread of footsteps above her head, the low rumble of male voices, and experienced a small charge of happiness inside. Hope, even, about what might yet come to pass. She had almost forgotten what it felt like but there it was, flickering away, a flame that hadn't ever quite died out. 'Thank you,' she whispered into the bright kitchen, grateful for the unexpected gift she'd been handed. 'Thank you for this.'

Chapter Eighteen

Leni McKenzie memorial page

We lived next door to the McKenzies when I was a little kid and one Easter, I must have been about 4, Leni (a few years older than me) convinced me that Easter eggs were made out of dog poo and if I ate mine, the dogs on the street would know and come and get me in the middle of the night. I totally freaked out and started to cry at this information!! She kindly (or so I thought) offered to take the Easter egg off my hands and I was all too happy to pass it over the fence. We moved away and I forgot all about it until years later I bumped into her in The Old Bookbinders. I said, 'Oi, you owe me an Easter egg' but we had a laugh about it. She bought me a pint so I forgave her.

Liam

'Tonight,' Sallyanne told the antenatal group, 'we'll be trying a few breathing exercises, and I'll show you mummies some birthing positions that will make the whole beautiful experience more comfortable.'

Seated amidst the enthusiastic parents-to-be, Tony had to clamp his mouth shut so that he didn't let out a snort at the words 'beautiful experience' and 'comfortable'. He was determined to avoid getting himself in trouble this time, not least because he was already in Jackie's bad books. Was it really *that* big a deal that he'd forgotten it was Valentine's Day? Apparently so. Over breakfast that morning, realising his error, he'd tried to make amends, searching online for a restaurant that had spare tables for dinner that evening. This only made her huffier than ever, for overlooking the fact that it was their wretched antenatal class then. According to Jackie, this was yet another sign that he was not as committed to their child as she was. 'I bet you never forgot Valentine's Day for *Belinda*,' she'd muttered, slamming out of the house moments later.

He *had* forgotten, obviously, plenty of times, but that didn't seem to be an argument-clincher. Sometimes you couldn't win, he'd figured, ordering a lavish bouquet of flowers to be sent to her office that morning and almost choking on his toast at the exorbitant cost.

As the group split off into pairs and began the breathing exercises, Jackie didn't seem in a forgiving mood though. Sallyanne had advised the partners that they should encourage the mothers-to-be by breathing along with them but Tony couldn't even get that right – he was too loud, too fast, too annoying, according to his stroppy partner. 'I've got to be a *bit* loud so that you can hear me and tune in with what I'm doing,' he pointed out, wishing they had gone for a Valentine's dinner instead. He tried not to think about the very good

Hereford rib-eye steak he could be tucking into right now; the perfectly cooked chips. A glass of robust red wine to wash it all down.

'I don't *want* to tune in with what you're doing, I can breathe perfectly well without you,' she retorted crossly.

His stomach gurgled, thinking of Béarnaise sauce spooned over his steak; it was an effort to stay focussed. 'Yes, but when you're in the throes of agony, you might appreciate some help, that's the whole point,' he reasoned.

This was met by an irritated exhalation. 'I don't think that telling me I'm going to be in the "throes of agony" is very helpful, actually, Tony,' Jackie snapped, with enough vehemence that a couple of people nearby exchanged looks.

'Seriously? We're trying to be positive over here!' one woman called out, her expression so judgey you'd think he'd just told them that they were all going to die.

'Yes, come on, encouraging words only, please, people,' Sallyanne put in primly.

Tony's teeth were clenched so hard together, he would be grinding down his own jawbone in a minute. Why was it that nobody in this group had the faintest sense of humour? He was starting to wish they *were* all about to die, he thought savagely. From across the room, Gen wrinkled her nose at him sympathetically and he gave her a rueful smile in return, grateful for her comradeship. Yesterday evening, he'd braved it back to the bereavement group, where not only had he managed to say a few words about his own situation, but Gen had talked movingly about losing her brother too, and how difficult his girlfriend was finding it, being left alone with a small, energetic three-year-old who couldn't understand where his dad had gone. She at least understood that life could come at you fast; the world could change in the blink of an eye.

'Shall we try again?' he asked Jackie now, mining his reserves for extra patience. 'Or have you had enough breathing for one evening?'

He jinked his eyebrow comically, but she didn't smile at his feeble quip. 'I'm fine with breathing, it's you I've had enough of,' she replied. Was she joking? It was hard to tell.

He had a fair idea what had provoked her prickliness; they'd had a difficult few days, with the Valentine's Day argument the cherry on the cake. Maybe he shouldn't have confided in her his worries about his ex-wife after all. Had he been insensitive? He'd run out of options though. He'd tried calling Alice a few times after the strange conversation with Ray regarding Belinda's psychic hotline addiction, but she always seemed to be on her way out somewhere, or unable to talk. At a loss for what else to do, he'd messaged Belinda himself about having a chat, although goodness knows if he'd have the balls to say anything to her face. Would Jackie have any suggestions? he'd wondered. Well, nothing ventured ...

'Can I talk to you about something?' he'd asked her last night. 'It's to do with Belinda.'

'Oh.' Her face immediately became pinched-looking and her hands stole to her belly as if protecting their unborn child from the other woman's presence. 'What is it?'

He'd gone on to describe the peculiar half conversation he'd heard in the café, and then what Ray had said about

Apolline, the so-called psychic charging Belinda an astronomical amount for a pack of lies. 'It's clearly a crutch, but not a very healthy one,' he'd said. 'I just don't know what to do, if anything.' He'd spread his hands helplessly. 'Any thoughts?'

'Hmm,' she'd replied, typing quickly at her laptop. 'This is her, I guess. The psychic.' They'd peered at a lurid web page with a list of phone numbers plus the face of a dark-haired woman, her hand on a crystal ball, gazing out from the screen.

Tony pulled a face. 'Christ,' he said. 'It's so ... tacky.' The thought of vivacious, dynamic Belinda being sucked in by this rubbish made him feel sad. Angry too. How could anyone set themselves up to deliberately deceive other people that way?

'Good work, everyone!' Sallyanne said at that moment, and Tony snapped back to the room, blinking away his concerns. In hindsight, he probably *had* pissed Jackie off by talking to her about it. She'd muttered that thing about Belinda and Valentine's Day at breakfast too; it had clearly been on her mind. Why did everything have to be so complicated?

'Now, before we take a break, I'd like us to have a group discussion about managing birth expectations,' Sallyanne went on. 'So if we could all – yes, Ruth?'

'Sallyanne, I don't want to point the finger, but there seem to be some very negative attitudes in the class, and I'm finding it unhelpful,' said Ruth piously. Tony had to try extremely hard not to groan aloud. This was a dig at him, presumably. Well, boo-fucking-hoo, Ruth. Get over it!

'I feel *exactly* the same,' put in Reiki Woman, whose name Tony couldn't remember. She flashed him a glare just so that everyone could be quite sure who the villain was. 'It's like ... can't we have some solidarity? Group positivity?'

Jackie snorted. 'Tell me about it,' she muttered. 'You don't have to live with him!'

Tony stared at her, hurt that she could side with these self-righteous strangers. 'Jac!' he protested. 'Steady on.'

'Well, what do you expect, Tony, when you keep banging on about your ex-wife all the time? Even though I'm right here, carrying our baby!'

There was a hiss of sucked-in breaths, an audible cluck of tutting tongues. Was he being paranoid or was the hostility rising? The atmosphere in the room seemed medieval to him suddenly, as if he were a bear being poked with sticks. He could almost hear the crackle of flaming torches and wondered how much more of this he could stand. But then came a different voice.

'Can we give Tony a break, here? You all seem to have made your minds up about him, but most of you don't know that he's a grieving parent. He's lost a child, for heaven's sake!' It was Genevieve, eyes blazing as she glared at every single person there in turn. 'Jackie – I can see you're scared about having a baby –' *Christ*, thought Tony in alarm, 'scared' was pretty much the most inflammatory adjective anybody could ever throw at his partner – 'but please – Tony's scared too. Even I can see that. Wouldn't you be, if you'd already suffered the worst grief a parent can undergo? Wouldn't any of us be terrified?'

She swung her arm around to encompass the entire group

and, one by one, faces fell and their antagonism swiftly turned to guilt. Jackie looked furious but said nothing. Tony too was unable to speak for a moment, partly in horror that Gen had just outed him to the room so bluntly (so much for any bereavement group code of silence) but also because she had come between him and his partner in a way that was undeniably damning for Jackie.

'Tony, I'm extremely sorry to hear that you've experienced something so painful,' Sallyanne said after a moment, eyes glistening with a new compassion behind her glasses.

Her words were echoed by a murmured chorus of similar sentiment. They were sorry, so sorry, their awkward faces said. No, they couldn't imagine how it must feel. Yes, they did all feel quite shit about themselves now. (Okay, so nobody actually said this last thought out loud but he could tell a fair few of them were thinking it. Even Ruth was hanging her head, looking uncomfortable. Good.)

Tony put up his hands wordlessly because there was nothing much to say. He couldn't come back with an easy 'That's okay' or 'It doesn't matter', for instance, because frankly, it wasn't okay and it did matter. Also, if he was honest, because he was rather enjoying knowing that the haters were now absolutely squirming.

'I think we've all learned a lesson today when it comes to not making assumptions about other parents,' Sallyanne went on solemnly. There was always a teaching moment to be found, as Belinda would have said, rolling her eyes. 'Let's all respect one another and acknowledge the fact that it's impossible to know what a person has been through, or might be feeling, based on first impressions alone. Okay! Moving on. This might be a good moment for a break, actually – let's take ten minutes, shall we, to get refreshments or use the loo. And when we come back, we can look at some complications that may arise during the birthing experience – and how you're all going to react calmly and competently in those circumstances.'

Well done, Sallyanne, safely steering them past the car crash and back on track, Tony thought, still avoiding anyone's gaze. There was a subdued feeling in the air as the group broke up, any previous jollity now seemingly on hold following their collective scolding. Tony eyed Jackie, who looked as if she was trying very hard to keep it together. 'You okay?' he asked quietly.

'Sorry,' she muttered, reaching for his hand. 'That was a bit out of order.'

He wasn't completely sure whether she meant she had been out of order, or if she thought Gen had been, for wading in, but then she made a little hiccupping sound and he knew it was the former. 'Hey,' he said, putting an arm around her. 'It's okay. Storm in a teacup.'

She leaned against him. 'I think . . . I think I *am* a bit scared,' she confessed into his shoulder, so low he had to strain to hear her. 'It *is* really fucking scary, all of this.' Her voice was becoming smaller with every word. 'I don't even know if I can do it, let alone if you . . . Well, if you leave me too.'

Ouch. Was that what this was really about? 'I am not about to leave you,' he said. 'It is the biggest regret of my life, not being a better father for my children. I am in this one hundred per cent with you, and with our child. I don't need Valentine's Day to prove how committed I am to the pair of you—' He broke off, registering too late the fact that her insecurities indicated she *did* need this sort of thing. 'Although I'm hearing loud and clear that I need to do better to show you that commitment,' he added in the next breath. 'And I promise I will.'

Over her shoulder he noticed that Genevieve appeared to be getting an ear-bashing from her other half, Penelope, and that they both kept shooting apologetic glances over in his direction. He attempted a *We're okay* face in response before returning to the business in hand, the pep talk he needed to nail.

'As for whether or not you can do this ...' He shook his head, because she was the most competent woman he'd ever met and he had no doubts about her abilities himself. 'Jackie Global Director Parker, of *course* you can bloody well do it,' he said, encircling her with both arms now. 'You'll be such a great mum,' he assured her. 'Fun. Energetic. Loving. The best possible role model. And I'm going to be with you every step of the way, I promise.' He rubbed her back bracingly then released her. 'Now – do you want me to get you a special Valentine's cup of peppermint tea? A romantic glass of water?'

She smiled weakly, still leaning against him. 'Sorry, Tony. I felt a bit weirded out, talking about Belinda last night, to be honest,' she confessed, stroking his arm. 'Also, I'm starving. I must have been mad, turning down dinner out tonight. That'll teach me to be pig-headed.'

He kissed the top of her head. 'I'm with *you* now, not Belinda,' he told her. 'And all our favourite restaurants will still be there tomorrow. But in the meantime, let's get a massive takeaway on the way home, yeah?'

Chapter Nineteen

It was confusing, but ever since she'd met up with Jacob the week before, Alice hadn't been able to stop thinking about him. Having previously filed him in a part of her brain labelled 'History', it had been an unexpected thrill to have her life bump tangentially against his again, dislodging all sorts of memories in the process. She'd found herself remembering what it was to be that young, hopeful Alice, carefree and open to anything. More disturbingly, she'd dreamed one night that she was a teenager again, kissing Jacob amidst the chaos of a house party, only to catch her reflection and discover that she was actually in her thirties and so was he. She'd woken up in an absolute puddle of guilt – he was married! Off limits! – but the dream must have poked a little tendril into her, nevertheless, because when her phone pinged mid-morning and it was a message from him – *Up for Flying Beauties reunion number 2?* – a heady thrill spread through her entire body.

According to Leni's diary, exactly a year ago to this day she'd been in Kiki's, a cocktail bar in Farringdon; a quick search online provided Alice with pictures of her on social media from the night itself. Off-duty Leni, with her hair piled up in a loose chignon, holding an espresso martini with a glint in her eye. Perfect, thought Alice, suggesting it to Jacob. Now here she was, retracing her sister's footsteps as she walked into a dimly lit bar with fairy lights strung from the rafters. There were candles flickering in jars on the tables, a long mustard-yellow banquette running the length of the room, and an old Fleetwood Mac song playing from the speakers. Outside it was raining, the icy sort of rain that was almost sleet, but stepping through the doors of Kiki's was like entering a magical fairy grotto, warm and cosy, spangled with soft lights. *Check it out, Leni*, she thought, spotting Jacob on a high stool at the bar and waving to him. *Look – we're both here, your fellow Flying Beauties. Doing just what you were doing this time last year.*

She and Jacob said hello and had an awkward little hug, and she felt so pleased to see him again, real and solid and smiling, that she was overwhelmed for a second. Who would have thought it, the two of them all grown-up and friends again? 'So,' she went on, glancing up at the cocktail list, chalked above the bar. 'A year ago today, Leni was right here with friends, drinking espresso martinis, so that's what I'm going to have. Can I tempt you?'

'I'm enjoying a very good whisky sour here, but thanks,' he replied, indicating the glass beside him before smiling in what looked like surprise. 'So you're a coffee drinker these days, are you? I remember you hating it back when we were young. In fact, I remember once kissing you after

I'd had a cup and you being disgusted by the taste. Scarred me for life.'

'Oh God, did it really?' she asked, blushing because she'd forgotten this particular moment and it made her feel kind of gauche to have it recounted. Also, having him reference them kissing so soon after her dream felt worryingly as if he could see directly into her head, and knew exactly what her pervy subconscious had been up to.

'Well, years of extensive therapy later, I'm just about over the trauma …' he teased, eyebrow raised. 'I'm kidding, no need to look so horrified.'

'Ha ha,' she said, defensively. 'And yes, I'm going for it on the drink. Coffee is still the devil's work, but I'm doing it in honour of Leni. One espresso martini, please,' she said as the ginger-goateed bartender appeared in front of her. 'Do you want another of those?' she asked Jacob, who gave her a thumbs up. 'And a whisky sour as well. Thanks.'

They found an empty corner and sat down with their drinks. Alice had painted her nails specially for the occasion – something else that made her think of Leni – and waggled them contentedly under the lights. 'It's so nice to imagine her here,' she said, her voice thick as she mentally conjured up her sister beside them, wearing her favourite blue geometric-print shirt, a big necklace, jeans and army boots. She sipped her drink, only to recoil immediately. Ugh. Coffee.

Jacob must have noticed because he looked as if he was trying not to smirk. 'That good, eh?'

'It's fine!' she said brightly, taking another sip. Yuck. How had Leni drunk this stuff? She set the glass down. 'I wonder how she discovered this place,' she mused. 'I mean, she lived in Acton, and worked at a primary school in Hanwell, so it's not as if she was in the area on a daily basis.'

'I didn't know she was a teacher,' Jacob said. 'Huh. I can see her doing that, actually, but I always figured she'd end up with a more artistic career, like fashion design or . . . I dunno.' He drank his whisky, reflecting. 'How about you, anyway? We spent so long talking about the old days last week, I don't think I know where you're working now.'

'Oh.' She waved a hand dismissively because the thought of letting the dreary details of her nine-to-five at Sage and Golding infiltrate this spangled evening was the last thing she wanted. Although not everything about it was dull, she supposed. She had spent all week hoping to avoid Darren, only to get stuck in the lift with him that morning. Damn it, he still looked sexy even in the too-bright light there, a rain-spattered mac over his crisp suit, his aftershave clean-smelling. He'd smiled at her, cool and composed, while she underwent an agony of awkwardness. 'All right?' he'd said.

'Yep,' she replied, jabbing at the button for her floor and then the Close Doors button, in the hope of speeding things up.

'Fancy going out some other time?' he asked conversationally. 'Maybe even tonight?'

She shook her head, a rigid smile on her face. 'Sorry, I'm busy,' she said, then stared down at her feet. The rest of the journey to her floor had been spent in excruciating silence.

'Nothing very exciting, to be honest,' she said to Jacob, glossing over the subject. 'But going back to Leni, you're right, she did want to be a fashion designer, but it never quite panned out. She had a stall in Spitalfields for a while after she graduated, selling these gorgeous tweedy scarves she made – there was a little piece in *Vogue* about them, can you believe – but it was hard work, slogging over the sewing machine all week, then sitting there on a freezing market stall at the weekend, having to be nice to hipsters who'd try to haggle her prices down ...' She'd run out of breath and picked up her drink to refresh herself, only remembering too late that she didn't like it. 'Christ, that's horrible,' she admitted, unable to stop herself pulling a face at the bitter aftertaste.

He burst out laughing at her. 'I'm going to get you another drink, something you actually like,' he said, getting to his feet. 'No arguments. Nostalgia has its limits, Alice, and forcing down a cocktail you actively hate is a step too far.'

She blushed again, unable to argue the case. 'I'll have a Dorset Horn then, please,' she said meekly after a quick glance at the menu. She wouldn't tell him that this too was a tribute to her sister, what with Dorset being the birthplace of the Flying Beauties and all.

He returned with a fresh drink for them both and she found herself telling him about Leni's next job, as a delivery driver, but how she'd got the sack after getting points for speeding – only then, silver lining, she had to go on a speed awareness course and that was where she'd met Adam, who ended up becoming her husband for five years.

'Cupid works in mysterious ways,' he said with a smile. 'How about you, are you married?'

'No,' she said, wrinkling her nose, unable to avoid Leni's words of accusation spiking through the moment. *When are you going to grow up though? What do you know about adult life? Nothing, because you're still acting like a teenager, passively letting stuff happen to you; you've never had the bottle to commit to anything. Lucky you!* The Dorset Horn must have gone to her head because then she blurted out, 'I was dating this guy Noah for a while, but we split up last year after I got into some trouble with the police and ...' For some reason she couldn't stop herself – 'Well, he thought I'd lost it, basically, although in retrospect, I pretty much had, so ...' Now Jacob was staring at her in alarm and she cursed her own big mouth. Shut! Up! Moron! 'Anyway, that's another story,' she said. She briefly considered mentioning Darren before deciding that was an even worse idea. 'So yeah, Leni and Adam had this whirlwind romance and—'

'That sounded pretty bad,' he interrupted. 'Rewind a minute. What happened with the police? Is everything okay? Are *you* okay?'

She stirred her drink vigorously with the straw so that she didn't have to look at his concerned face. Any minute now he would make an excuse and get out of there, then block her number, deciding he didn't have space for a madwoman in his life. When would she learn to rein herself in? 'Oh yeah, I'm fine. It was a fuss about nothing. Not worth repeating.'

He said nothing in response but she could feel the weight of his gaze on her, watchful and concerned. Lana del Rey was singing about summertime sadness in the background, and Alice's face burned as she searched around for a change

214

of subject. 'Anyway!' she said again, with new brightness. 'Where was I?'

'Alice,' he said gently. 'What's going on here? I'm finding this all a bit ... strange.'

She blinked. 'What ... What do you mean?'

'I mean ... Last week we met up for the first time in, what, ten, eleven years and we talked extensively about your sister. Which is fine!' he added quickly as her face changed. 'I can see you need to talk about her and I get that. Totally. But ...' He spread his hands, taking his time to find the next words. 'But I'm not sure I've got anything else to contribute here. I was hoping we could talk more about ourselves tonight, but you keep dodging every personal question I ask you. And dodging them really badly, I have to say. Sorry,' he said, as her face fell.

She hung her head, her face hot. 'Was it that obvious?' she mumbled.

'Well ... yes,' he told her. 'Look, I realise we don't really know each other any more, but you *can* talk to me. It's still me. You don't have to give me the Instagram version of your life, the same as I hope I don't have to pretend that everything's amazing in mine.'

His words stabbed tiny needles of shame into her because she realised in the next moment that she hadn't asked him a single thing about his life, either tonight or the time before. That was rude, wasn't it? She had been on dates like that, when the man had bored on about himself all the time, completely uninterested in her. Had she become this sort of person herself? 'Right,' she said stiffly, before self-defence kicked in. 'I did say it would be nice to meet up and talk about Leni,' she replied. 'I was under the impression you wanted that as well.'

'Yes, but we can do that *and* talk about other stuff too, can't we?' he countered. There was a pause which felt almost as interminable as the lift journey with Darren, and similarly mortifying. 'Or are you not interested in me as a person? Only my memories of Leni?'

She bowed her head, stricken. 'Sorry,' she mumbled, because everything he'd said was on the nail. She couldn't deny a single word of it. 'Sorry, you're right.' She pressed her cold glass against her cheek because her face was so hot. 'I *am* interested in you, of course I am,' she added for good measure. 'I know you're working at UCL and you're married, and have a little boy.'

'That all used to be true,' he said, then put his hands out in front of her. She stared at them, not following, until he said, 'Not married any more,' and she realised he wasn't wearing a ring.

'Oh,' she said, gazing dumbly from his bare fingers up to his face. To think she'd felt a momentary gaucheness earlier – now she was fully appalled at her own bad manners, for not asking him the most basic of questions. For not showing any interest in him at all, in fact. 'Sorry to hear that,' she said, humble with contrition. 'Was it recent? Is she in the UK too?' She sighed, shaking her head. 'Jacob, I've been a really rubbish companion, haven't I? Both last time and tonight. I'm embarrassed. You might not even want to talk about your marriage, but if you do, I'm absolutely going to listen.'

'Don't worry about it,' he said after a moment. 'No harm done. It was a couple of years ago, pretty amicable in the end. Yes, she's in London too, working at King's.'

'She's an academic as well?'

'Yeah. We met at a conference in Zurich eight years ago. She's very smart. We moved to Sweden because she was asked to head up the department at Gothenburg university – we had some very happy years there together.'

'You sound proud of her,' she commented, sipping her drink. He'd had this whole life full of adult things, she marvelled. Marriage. Life in another country. Career glory. A kid. In comparison, she was getting blind drunk and shagging a randomer from work and stuck in a dreary temp job, emotionally stunted; her biggest commitment being a cat who didn't even like her. Leni had been right about her passively letting life just happen to her, she thought dismally. Why was she like this?

'I am,' he said and she imagined him thinking how relieved he was to have managed a proper relationship with an amazing woman after dating car-crash Alice.

'What about your son?' she asked, swallowing the lump in her throat. 'How old is he? Have you got any pictures?'

'Of course,' he said, picking up his phone, and scrolling. There was a small private smile on his face, she noticed; a smile of love for this boy, a smile of gladness that he was a father and had a son. 'Here – this is Max. He's four.'

Max had white-blond hair that fell into his eyes and, with a look of utmost glee, was brandishing a massive stick in a forest. He was wearing a blue coat, unzipped, with mud all over his trousers and a pair of wellies striped yellow and black like a bee. 'Cute,' said Alice, smiling too as she took him in. 'He looks fun.'

'He is *so* much fun,' Jacob replied, taking back the phone. His eyes were soft with fondness, and Alice – ridiculously – felt shut out. Unimportant. She stared down into her drink, wondering if maybe she should have said yes to going out with Darren tonight instead, after all. It would have been a very different evening, conducted on far shallower levels, but at least she'd have felt that they were equals. And maybe that was all she could handle right now?

Later on, coming home and feeding Hamish, Alice knelt beside the cat as he ate, chancing a stroke along his soft, striped back. Embarrassment still tingled through her about how the evening had unfolded, and she cringed as she remembered the moment Jacob had called her out on her unintentional rudeness. The tube journey home had cast a new filter on the evening though, defensiveness increasingly spiking through her with every new station along the line. It wasn't that she wasn't *interested* in him, she argued in her head, it was more the case that her priority was Leni. So sue her!

Conversation had resumed, with her talking about how she had been dragged, kicking and screaming, to a Pilates class with Lou and Celeste the day before – 'I'm surprised they let you in if you were kicking and screaming,' he'd said, mouth twitching in amusement – and then she asked him lots more questions about his life, while successfully deflecting his attempts to go into further detail about her own work. 'Honestly, it's just a temp job and it's deadly dull, there's nothing to say,' she told him, holding up her hand like a stop sign.

'That surprises me,' he'd said. 'I don't want to sound patronising but I always thought you, out of everyone in our sixth form, would go on and do extraordinary things.'

Ugh. Sod off, she thought. Not everyone could get high-flying academic jobs around the world with brilliant brainy spouses. It was on the tip of her tongue to retaliate with tales of previous career glories – great campaigns, promotions, award nominations – but the thought of trying to prove herself in this way seemed demeaning. And what if she told him all of that and he still looked unimpressed? 'That *is* quite patronising,' she retorted instead. 'I feel like I'm one of your students, being badgered about a late essay or something. Any minute now you're going to tell me you're very disappointed in me, in a horribly serious voice.' *Don't you dare*, she thought, her whole body stiffening at the prospect.

'I'm not!' Now it was his turn to hold his hands up. 'I'm absolutely not, Alice. It was meant to be a compliment, although yeah, I'm sorry, it definitely didn't come out how I intended. Anyway, for all I know, you're a secret agent, working undercover and this is all an incredible double bluff.'

'Yeah, you got me,' she said blandly, although soon afterwards, she found herself necking her drink and making an excuse that she needed to go, because the whole conversation about her shortcomings was making her feel uncomfortable. Pissed off, in fact. 'I need to get back to MI5, give them my

findings,' she deadpanned. 'Finish that dossier I've been compiling on you.'

She sighed again now, still unsure what to make of his words.
I thought you'd go on and do extraordinary things, indeed. Did that
mean he'd found her a massive downgrade in expectations?
He'd even seemed dismayed when he asked if she still made
her amazing birthday cakes for people and she'd had to confess
no, not since last summer.

Her phone rang and it was Lou, calling for an update on
how the evening had gone. 'Badly,' Alice summed up, leaning
against the kitchen cupboard, her legs stretched out before
her on the lino. 'I think he's actually a bit of a knob.'

'Oh no! What happened?'

Her body felt heavy as she sat there, the floor cold beneath
her bottom. 'He just ... It wasn't what I was hoping.'

There was a small pause. 'Which was ... ? Enlighten me.'

'Well, I wanted to reminisce about Leni – that was the reason
I suggested meeting up! – but he kept asking me questions
about me, instead.'

'Rude bastard,' said Lou. 'How dare he?'

Alice gave a feeble laugh. 'And then when I did talk a bit
about me, he seemed really disappointed, like he thought I'd
done nothing with my life.'

Lou whistled. '*What?* Did he say that?'

Alice replayed the conversation in her head for the hundredth time. 'Not exactly, I suppose,' she conceded grudgingly,
'but that was the impression I got. I could tell he thought I
was a massive loser.'

'Well, take it from me: you are not,' Lou said heatedly. Then there was a pause. 'Or is this a case of you being hard on yourself?' she asked. 'Because I'm willing to bet he didn't think that at all. Unless he's a total idiot, in which case, forget him.'

'He's not an idiot, worst luck,' Alice replied with a sigh. 'He's the brainiest person I know.'

'He sounds pretty bloody dumb to me.' You couldn't fault Lou on her loyalty, that was for sure. 'Or possibly just emotionally clueless. Maybe he's never had to deal with grief himself, he doesn't know what it looks like. And he was fully expecting you to be the Alice he once knew – go-getting and ambitious and optimistic.'

'As opposed to the miserable version of now,' Alice said, trying not to take offence that her best friend clearly thought she was none of those things any more. 'The version who's stuck in the past and apparently can't move on.'

'Hey, nobody's saying "miserable",' Lou corrected her, although Alice noticed she didn't argue with the bit about her being stuck in the past. 'You're just in a dip, that's all. And if he's too thick to realise that, then that's his lookout.'

Alice took this in, still sitting there on the floor even though Hamish had finished his dinner and long since stalked away. 'I was pretty rude to him,' she confessed. 'The worst conversationalist ever, pretty much.'

'Sounds like he got what he deserved, then,' Lou said. 'Forget him, Alice. It doesn't matter what he thinks. You just do you. There are plenty of us Alice fans still out there in the meantime. Anyway – you *are* moving on. You're doing that pottery thing at the weekend, right?'

'Saturday, yeah,' Alice said, although Lou seemed to have

forgotten that she had booked the *kintsugi* workshop in order to mend Leni's plates. Did it still count as moving on in that case? Probably not. Would she ever move on? Probably not.

'And we're doing Pilates on Tuesday again, yeah? That's another new thing. So you're doing brilliantly, all right? Hang in there.'

Chapter Twenty

McKenzies Together group

Tony: *Did we all have a lovely Valentine's Day, then? Jackie and I celebrated with . . . an antenatal class. Who said romance is dead?? This weekend we're off to Blenheim to stay in a posh hotel though, while we still can. Hope you all have nice plans ahead. Will, did you see the Liverpool game? Incredible goals! Love Dad/Tony xx 09.33*

Alice: *Romance definitely dead in my life!! All good though. X 11.34*

Belinda: *We've had an offer on the house from a lovely family – probably going to accept. If any of you want to come back for a bit of nostalgia in the next few weeks, please do, it might be your last chance. You too, Tony 14.06*

Tony: *I'd really like that, Bel. Thank you. Maybe sometime next week? Love Tony x 16.52*

Belinda: *How about you, Will, do you think you might be back any time soon? Would be so nice to see you [heart emoji] xxx 17.45*

★

Will read the messages, screwing up his face. *Doubtful,* he typed. *Got quite a lot of work on right now. And – no offence – but Oxford in February vs Thailand in February? Only one winner for me.* Just for good measure, he sent them a beach photo: the sea a sparkling sapphire ribbon splitting the golden sand from the vast, cloudless sky.

He wasn't even lying about the work. He'd moved on recently, having had a serious word with himself: time to get his act together, sharpen up the old sales patter. He'd made an effort socially too, and had been to some brilliant parties up in the hills, dancing until dawn with some of the ex-pats he knew. And then, dazzled with amphetamines and optimism, he'd come to the conclusion that Juno was right, selling flip-flops was a mug's game; it was time to take her up on her suggestion of dealing in more profitable goods. He was on his way to meet her now, having scraped together the last of his savings so that he could pick up a decent stash of weed and pills with which to begin his new career.

His phone buzzed in his pocket and he grimaced, hoping it wasn't Juno, getting in touch to change the arrangements, now that he'd plucked up the courage to go ahead. To his surprise though, he saw a message from an old school friend, Hattie.

Will! How are you? Hope you're having a good time out there (but also hope you'll be back for September – you know Gaz is getting married, right?? He's been trying to pin you down for his stag – check your DMs!!) Just a quick one to say Sam and I have booked a holiday – to Thailand! Impulse trip – we'll be there at the beginning of March. Still working out an itinerary but would love to see you if possible. Love Hats xxx

Walking along the street reading this, he stopped dead at the thought of his two worlds colliding, at the idea of Hattie being here. He was almost mown down by a woman pushing a trolley full of water bottles towards a restaurant and had to dodge out of her way.

'Sorry,' he mumbled, but barely heard her annoyed exclamation, the slap of her plastic sandals as she shook her head and marched past, because he was thinking of sweet, lovely Hattie, who he'd known since primary school. She'd been so thoughtful after Leni died, turning up at the funeral to support him, even though she hadn't really known his sister. Lots of people had seemed unsure how to act around him; lots of people, in fact, said nothing at all, because the news was so big, so terrible, where did you begin? Even Molly, the girl he'd been dating, started seeing someone else – 'I didn't think we were exclusive!' she claimed. Hattie had been different – she'd made a concerted effort to be there for him, sending sympathetic messages for days and weeks after Leni's death, making sure he was still invited to everything. Even now, she was trying to include him in Gaz's wedding preparations where he'd cut himself off.

What would she think of him here, with his flat full of fake designer sunglasses, with a stash of pills to sell to hedonistic holidaymakers?

Don't think about that, he told himself, walking a little quicker. This was not the time for an existential crisis; he had a job to do.

Juno's apartment was in an area of town he didn't know too well, and as he followed the map on his phone, he found himself becoming disoriented in the heat. These streets were off the tourist trail, quieter and narrow, with blocks of housing three storeys high either side, ropes of washing strung in colourful zigzags above his head. A couple of elderly Thai men playing backgammon watched him from a doorstep; the sound of a baby crying floated down from an upstairs window. He'd brought a backpack with him in which to carry his purchases, currently empty apart from the cash he'd got together, and queasily imagined himself walking back this way with hundreds of pounds' worth of drugs in his possession. It would be all right, wouldn't it? Other people did this. Other people made an absolute ton of money doing it, more to the point.

With an increasing sense of trepidation, he approached her apartment block, noticing too late the two enormous blokes sitting on the wall outside who rose to their feet on seeing him. A sixth sense told him to run, his skin prickling with the premonition of trouble. Both men were squat and muscular, their black T-shirts stretching over their beefy chests; total football-hooligan vibes. 'All right?' Will said, trying to sound casual although his voice became a squeak as they walked towards him, swift and purposeful. 'Er ... I'm here to see Juno?' Did she have bodyguards now? he thought in alarm. Were they about to pat him down for weapons, check him over before letting him in?

Not exactly. In two strides they were either side of him, smelling of sweat and danger, and Will's life flashed before his eyes in a moment of extreme terror. 'Phone,' demanded meathead number one, flicking open a knife and pointing the blade at him, his tone one of menacing intent. The other guy was already tearing at his backpack, almost wrenching Will's arms out of their sockets in an attempt to rip it from his body. 'Hey!' he yelled, stupidly trying to hang on to it – all his money! – but they overpowered him embarrassingly easily, the first guy snatching Will's phone from his puny, clutching fingers for good measure.

Meathead two gave Will a shove that knocked him to the ground and then they both ran, their footsteps thudding as they vanished around the corner. Will's heart pounded, adrenalin pumped uselessly; his wrist and hip throbbed where they'd smashed to the ground. 'Juno!' he called up to the building, dragging himself upright, checking himself for damage. He'd gashed his elbow, he realised dimly. His head felt woozy, his body flooded with shock and hurt. *That's not fair!* They had taken everything from him, he realised. He had his door key in his pocket but that was all he had left. 'Juno!' he yelled again, his voice echoing off the walls around him. He staggered to her door and pressed the buzzer, once and then again. Where was she? 'JUNO!' he shouted for the third time.

A young Thai woman was watching him from the neighbouring building, arms folded. She was wearing a mango-coloured vest top and cut-off blue trousers, her dark hair tied back from her face. 'She gone,' she told him, making walking motions in the air with her fingers. 'Lady gone.'

'Lady gone?' he repeated, confused, because even then he still believed, like the innocent he was; even then he thought he'd been the victim of bad luck, nothing more. He pointed at the door. 'Lady here – gone?'

The woman nodded and shrugged. 'She gone.'

Shell-shocked from the mugging and the heat, his brain struggling to make sense of what had just happened, he ended up getting completely lost on the way home, without his phone to guide him. It made sense, he supposed dazedly. He'd lost everything else, after all: why not his sense of direction too? Then, stumbling round a corner, he blinked to see before him a large red-stone temple with a red and gold triangular-stepped roof, and a row of arched columns decorated with gold paint. Saffron-robed monks sat cross-legged behind the columns, chanting and banging drums, while in a courtyard area at the front of the temple, an ornate white casket was being towed around an unlit pyre on a gleaming gilded cart. It was a funeral, he realised with a jolt, noticing a group of mourners, dressed in black and white, some chanting, some with their heads silently bowed. The mourners all held the same long piece of rope attached to the back of the cart, and followed it in procession.

Will felt unable to turn away, thinking inevitably of Leni's funeral: a day he could hardly remember because he'd been so drunk from start to finish. It was hard to forget the shock on everyone's faces though; the stunned atmosphere of *Is this really happening?* that permeated each row of the crematorium. His mum had been weeping so noisily she'd had to lean on Ray for bodily support when they stood for the hymns. His dad was ashen-faced in a black suit. Alice had given a reading from *Winnie-the-Pooh* – or rather, she'd tried to, but had broken down in sobs, with her friend Lou eventually coming to stand with her at the lectern to help her through the remainder. And then there had been the moment when the crematorium curtains jerkily opened – one lagging behind the other as if it had temporarily become stuck – then the conveyor belt began rolling with an unoiled squeaking, and the coffin trundled backstage into the secret area that nobody wanted to think about. It had all been so neat and tidy, in hindsight. So British. Cover it up, don't think about it, done.

Afterwards, they'd gone to a pub in Headington and he'd got so hammered he ended up falling over in the gents and getting piss all over his smart trousers. He'd had to walk back to his mum's at the end of the night because none of the taxis would take him.

Meanwhile, at this funeral, there were no juddering curtains or squeaky conveyor belt. The casket was being loaded on to the pyre – a tower of wooden pallets – and the mourners were posting flowers and what he guessed were offerings between the slats before putting their hands together in prayer. Stupidly, he felt a shiver of repulsion on realising that they were actually going to light the pyre right there in the open and burn the casket, rather than tucking the scene away behind closed doors. It seemed so medieval somehow, so basic – but then, this was the reality of a cremation, of course. This was what happened behind the curtains.

Feeling as if he were intruding on a private moment, he moved on, searching for landmarks that might help him find his way back to the flat. He really wanted to get home to

tend to the throbbing wound on his elbow and work out
what the hell he was going to do now that he'd lost all his
savings. He still couldn't quite believe that Juno had stitched
him up like that. What an idiot he was. What a gullible fool.
She'd seen him coming, all right.

He must have been walking blindly around in a circle,
because after what felt like ages, he found himself back at the
temple again and groaned in dismay. It was like being in a
bad dream where he was forced to repeatedly confront death
and his own ineptitude. At the funeral, a fire was now alight,
flames crackling up through the dry wooden tower. Candles
burned at the base of the columns, while floral tributes had
been laid on the shallow steps leading up to the main door
of the temple, along with large gilt-framed pictures of a man
in a suit, presumably the deceased. The mourners sang and
prayed; he could smell incense as well as burning wood, and
all of a sudden, he felt so overcome by everything that had
happened, he found himself raising a hand and clutching one
of the painted railings that enclosed the temple courtyard, then
leaning his head against it.

Leni's gone, he thought wretchedly, as a new drumbeat
started up, slow and sonorous. Leni's really gone and she's
not coming back. Not ever. He'd always known that, obviously, but it was as if he'd disguised the truth from himself,
shoved it behind a pair of creaking crematorium curtains,
conveniently out of sight. He had stepped on to the plane
at Heathrow and crossed into a different, self-constructed
realm where the pain and reality of death could not touch
him. But death was impossible to avoid now as the flames

took hold of the pyre, as the singing and drumming grew louder, as the smoke curled and twisted in grey ribbons up against the dense white sky.

In the next moment, it felt as if something was breaking within him. Tears spilled down his face, emotions swelled inside his chest; his own skin suddenly felt too thin to contain his inner self. Everything he had suppressed for so long, everything he had refused to look at, now forced its way seismically to the surface.

'Are you okay?' came an Australian voice from nearby and he turned to see a tall bespectacled woman astride a bike. She was in her late forties, at a guess, with short grey hair, and she had a kindness about her, a mellow art-teacher vibe. Her gaze flicked to the funeral scene behind him. 'Have you lost someone too?' she asked.

'My sister,' he said, gulping a breath. He clenched his fists, trying to control himself. 'Leni. It was last year, nothing to do with this funeral, but ...'

'But you're remembering her now,' she said gently. 'And it hurts. Of course it hurts.'

'The thing is, it ... it was my fault she died,' he blurted out. His darkest secret, bursting from him before he could stop it. He knuckled the tears from his eyes, shoulders shaking. 'It was my fault!'

He half expected lightning to strike him for his confession, thunderclouds to boom overhead now that he'd said the words aloud. But instead the woman put a hand on his back and just left it there in solidarity while he wept, unable to control himself any more. 'Sorry,' he said, eventually pulling himself together. 'I'm ... It's been ...' None of the words seemed right, or enough any more. 'I'm having a really bad day,' he said eventually, and almost wanted to laugh at such a pathetic understatement.

The woman patted his back then reached into a battered wicker basket attached to the front of her bike to retrieve a dented silver water bottle. 'Home-made lemonade,' she told him. 'Try some.'

He accepted gratefully and took a long, cool swig. It was sweet and sharp, insanely refreshing. 'Thank you,' he mumbled, wiping his eyes on his forearm.

'I don't know what happened to your sister, but I can see you're very sorry,' the woman told him kindly. 'And it's especially hard to lose someone when they're young.'

'Yes,' he managed to say.

'In some ways, I think Buddhists have the right idea about death,' she went on, gesturing at the scene before them. 'They see the funeral almost as a staging post before the deceased moves on to a better place. I rather like that, don't you? It's soothing to think the person we love hasn't gone forever; that they still exist in some form or other. Comforting to those of us still here, trying to carry on without them.'

'Yes,' he said again, thankful for her slow, mellifluous voice which felt like a balm to his troubled soul. 'I like that too.' He pushed away the last of his tears, wondering what form Leni might have taken if she had returned. A bird of paradise, maybe, colourful and exotic. A peacock, even – she loved those. Or, of course, a baby, a whole new person, starting the cycle again. He wasn't sure he believed in this theory – he was a scientist, he liked evidence and facts – but the woman was right: the thought itself was consoling regardless.

'Whatever the case, it's good to honour those who go before us,' she said, putting her hands together in prayer and making a neat, respectful bow towards the funeral scene. 'And to allow the grief to flood out when it needs to. At the end of the day, it's another form of love, isn't it? Our tears say: you were important to me, I remember you, I loved you.' She patted him on the arm. 'There's no need to be afraid of your grief. You loved your sister.'

'Thank you,' he stammered, moved beyond words. *You were important to me, I remember you, I loved you.* Yes – that was it exactly. This kind stranger had managed to articulate, within a few clear sentences, the enormity of feeling he had experienced, emotions he hadn't known how to handle. 'And thank you for the lemonade,' he added, giving her back the bottle.

The woman was able to give him directions back to his street and then they said goodbye. His body ached where he'd been knocked to the ground, his throat hurt from the smoke of the funeral pyre, but as he began walking, he felt a new clarity settling on him like quiet flakes of snow. He'd been hiding from everything out here; he'd buried himself on this island far from home in the hope of forgetting his pain and guilt, but it was still there, beating away like an infected wound inside him, wasn't it? And if he ever wanted to scissor it out again, he knew, deep down, that he would have to go home and confront the truth. Look his family in the eye and tell them.

Oh Christ. It was terrifying. But now that he'd lost all his money, now that his life had crashed down around him, he no longer had the luxury of choices. He just had to hope he'd still have a family left once they knew what he'd done.

Chapter Twenty-One

Tony: If you're sure it's all right for me to come round to the house one last time, how does next Tuesday suit you? I could be there for four o'clock? X 10.25

Belinda: Sounds good to me. See you then. 11.41

Belinda's life had suddenly taken a turn for the busier. In the last week she had accepted a good offer on the house from a couple who seemed to genuinely love the property. The thought of leaving the place where her children had grown up was a wrench, but it was for the best, she told herself. Because this was also the house where her marriage had broken down, where the kids had moved out, where she'd had the shattering news about Leni. Buildings could retain echoes of sadness as well as happiness, she'd always thought; as if the very walls were papered with good and bad memories.

Still. Along with the inevitable melancholy of moving on, there had also come an unexpected buffer of solace; that her old home would be loved anew by a different family, that the rooms would once again ring with the sound of children's laughter and songs and play. Far better this, than for it to be purchased by a nameless developer, say. The offer and its acceptance now meant an avalanche of paperwork and solicitor dealings, plus extra impetus in the search for a new home.

Out with the old, in with the … well, maybe the even older, she thought, when she and Ray returned to see the crumbling doer-upper for a second viewing. Having stormed out on their previous visit, telling the estate agent they weren't interested, she had nonetheless found herself thinking about the house ever since, particularly whenever they had viewed more sensible, ordinary properties. Had she been too hasty, too emotional in her dismissal, she had wondered aloud to Ray, who immediately talked her into a return trip. It turned out he'd been hankering after the place too, and was all too keen to give it another look.

This time, she planned to keep a cooler head, not least because Ellis was back in town and accompanying them for the viewing. A few days ago, he'd got in touch with Ray again to say that he'd been offered the trainee management position, and they had invited him to stay while he looked for a flat to rent. Ellis's job wasn't due to start for another week so he had time on his hands – but despite Ray hoping this might be the launch of a new father-son bonhomie, it hadn't quite worked out that way so far. There was something very guarded about Ellis – watchful, even. You could talk to him for a whole evening and realise that you didn't know him any better; he would deflect and side-step and swerve with all the deftness of a professional footballer. At first Belinda had put it down to shyness, but now she was wondering if the lad was hiding something. Or up to something?

Ray had soft-soaped him today, saying that they'd love his opinion on the house, and so here they were, the three of them roaming the dusty, echoing rooms. The second viewing, Belinda knew, was all about being cold-eyed and realistic, peering into corners, asking the big practical questions – and she indeed felt able to see the place more clearly, knowing that Apolline had assured her of Leni's approval of the property. Unfortunately, rather than being hard-headed and detail-focussed, she was experiencing what could only be described as a rising tide of infatuation for the place, before which any issues regarding damp, wiring or insulation seemed trivial. It would occur to her, for instance, walking through the high-ceilinged hall, that heating costs would be an absolute shocker. (Yes, but the big windows, once cleaned, would let in so much light! replied her inner optimist.) The roof too would surely be a money pit, seeing as it needed a complete overhaul, no doubt running to tens of thousands of pounds. (Yes, but the garden, once they'd pruned and planted and loved it, would be the most wonderful sanctuary on sunny days. They could have chickens! And a vegetable plot! And beautiful statues in unexpected places!)

'So what are you planning, four double rooms for paying guests, is it?' Ellis said, as they tramped around upstairs. For all his reticence about his own affairs, he was certainly taking a great deal of interest in theirs, Belinda couldn't help thinking. 'Have you actually broken down the figures, potential income against expenses, Dad, or is this still a bit of a wish and a promise at the moment?'

Seeming pleased that his son was engaging with the matter, Ray hurried to assure him that yes, they had drawn up a business plan with an accountant friend, before taking him through the details. His whole face lit up whenever he and Ellis spoke, Belinda had noticed, and she felt a pang of envy, wishing that she too could have a lost child returned to her, that she too could be granted a second chance. Ray was such a nice, natural, easy-going dad; whatever demons he'd been in the grip of years earlier had left him now, and the reappearance of his son had given him a new lightness she hadn't seen before.

But, she kept wondering, how did Ellis feel in return? She'd tried to draw him out of himself a few times, but he gave little away. 'Plenty of room for you to stay any time,' she said now, spotting a chance to winkle out some personal information. 'If you wanted to bring a girlfriend, or ... Did you say you had a girlfriend, Ellis? Or someone special?'

He only shrugged and went to peer through the window, as if that was classified information. It had been a perfectly reasonable question though, Belinda thought to herself with renewed suspicion. Why couldn't he answer like any normal person?

They wandered into a bathroom where the ceiling had collapsed into the bath, Belinda's mind still whirring. She didn't want to make presumptions, but couldn't help worrying that Ellis's reasons for being back in Ray's life were ... well, not entirely honourable? Earlier, she'd heard him ask Ray if he could borrow the money for a deposit on a flat, plus a month's rent, and Belinda fervently hoped he could be trusted.

Not that she could articulate this to Ray though, when he had shown nothing but complete faith in his son's intentions from day one. He'd even seemed upset when he noticed her moving her handbag from its usual position in the hall up to their bedroom at night. Just in case.

'What are you . . . ? He's not going to steal your credit cards, if that's what you think,' he'd said, spots of indignant colour appearing on his cheeks.

'It's not that,' she'd protested. What Ray seemed to forget sometimes was that she had been a social worker for her entire working life; she had seen a lot of unpleasant behaviour between family members. People could be weak, however much you wanted to see only good there, and that was the unfortunate truth, like it or not. 'But Ray . . . at the end of the day, we don't know him, do we?'

'*I* do,' he'd retorted, turning away but not before she'd seen his hurt expression. 'He's my son, and he's not a thief.'

Ellis almost certainly *wasn't* a thief, and it wasn't as if Belinda had much that was worth nicking in the first place, but all the same, this was what she did when there was anyone she didn't know well in the house: plumbers or builders or the meter reader. 'It was habit more than anything personal,' she'd fretted to Apolline that morning, recounting the exchange. 'The lad seems nice, I've got nothing against him, of course, but . . .'

'But he's a cuckoo in the nest,' Apolline put in. 'You know nothing of his motives.'

'Well . . .'

'And Leni doesn't like him being there,' Apolline went on, which cut Belinda to the quick.

'She doesn't? What did she say?'

'She says not to trust the mouse. She says this will mean something to you.'

'Not to trust the *mouse*?' Belinda tried to transpose Ellis's rather long, lugubrious face with that of a mouse but the image didn't quite work. If you were to call him an animal, he'd be a horse, she found herself thinking, before racking her brain to interpret this mouse business. When she was a child, there had been mice in their family home for a while, that occasionally gnawed through the wires in the cellar, plunging the house into sudden darkness at unexpected moments. She remembered the shock of it, how she and her sister Carolyn would shriek and clutch each other, like something from a horror film. Was Ellis planning to bring darkness into their lives?

She was still musing on this as she wandered into the large, light kitchen that once must have been the heart of the house, with its big stone hearth and windows looking out on to the garden. She wanted to trust Ray's son, but...

'So,' Ray said, appearing behind her just then. 'What are we thinking today?'

For a moment Belinda felt hot with embarrassment, as if he'd been able to see *exactly* what she'd been thinking, until she oriented herself – flagstone floor, dripping tap, dusty windows – and realised that he meant, of course, what was she thinking about the house. This gorgeous, expensive, crumbling wreck that would require plenty of hard work but also offered the bonus of tranquillity, she realised. The space to exhale. She could begin again, in a place where she wouldn't be bumping up against ghosts and memories every moment of every day. They could all come here for Christmas, she thought – Alice and Will, and their partners-yet-to-meet, and maybe one day these corridors would patter with the footsteps of grand-children (yes, she still held out hope), their voices high and excited as they played hide and seek, or came rushing into this same kitchen to bake scones with Grandma. It could be a place of healing for them as a family.

'Well,' she said, as Ray slotted his arm around her and she leaned comfortably against him. 'That is the question.' They stood there for a moment together, considering the grimy old cabinets (oak perhaps, beneath the dirt), along with the broken blinds hanging at drunken angles along the top of the windows (she could make new ones in the space of an after-noon, no problem) and the view through to the walled herb garden beyond (it would be such a suntrap on summer days, she was sure of it). She returned her focus to the kitchen and gestured to the ageing range cooker. 'I bet this would be lovely and cosy on winter days,' she said, her head nestling into the soft space beside his shoulder. 'I'm imagining us cooking in here, getting a stew in the oven or an apple crumble. Friends coming over for raucous dinners, the smell of cakes baking on a Sunday afternoon, a proper larder of food and drink.'

'Not to mention all those bacon and egg breakfasts we'll be frying up for our guests,' he joked, and they both laughed at the image of themselves fussing about in aprons here, making up pots of tea and coffee, cutting toast slices into triangles and wedging them into white china racks. It almost felt as if they would be playing a game, pretending to be hosts; the idea tickled her. Then she forced herself to get a grip on her daydreams.

'We'd have to gut the place, you know that, don't you, if we actually want to reach any health and safety standards,' she said with deliberate sternness. 'New floors, new wiring; I bet the plumbing's ancient. Everything's going to need replacing.' She paused for breath, then her phone chirped with a text from Alice, commenting on the photos she'd sent her. *Wow! Mum, it's incredible. You'd be Lady of the Manor!* Belinda read, and felt herself buoyed by her daughter's words. 'Alice thinks it looks incredible though,' she said, holding the screen in front of him so that he could see.

'How about you?' he prompted, squeezing her gently. 'What do you think?'

He was too kind to remind her of the last time they'd been there, with her flouncing out, saying they didn't want the place. She loved that about him. You could bet your life that if she'd still been married to Tony, he wouldn't have let her histrionics pass without teasing her about them at least twenty times a day.

'I think it's pretty incredible too,' she replied to Ray now. 'And I can't help thinking that once we've knocked it into shape, it will have far more appeal and wow factor to anyone searching online for an Oxfordshire B. & B., won't it?' She'd already sized up the competition on her laptop – a stream of perfectly nice houses on the outskirts of the city, but none as visually appealing as this place. 'I mean, faced with this, or some bland semi on the Woodstock Road, you're always going to pick the gorgeous one, aren't you? We could make it a proper destination for people. Who wouldn't want to stay in a house like this?'

'Well, idiots, that's who,' he said. 'Idiots who we don't want here anyway. So sod 'em!'

'Exactly! And luckily neither of us are scared of hard work, are we?' she went on.

'Like I'd be with you if I was,' he joked.

'Oi!' she cried, elbowing him indignantly, but she knew he didn't mean it. They'd been such a good team in recent weeks, the pair of them decluttering and painting their current home in readiness for selling up. A montage played in her head, of them here together in matching white overalls: up ladders with paint trays, pulling up ancient carpets amidst clouds of dust, cleaning windows simultaneously – one inside, one out, like two characters in a sitcom. Or maybe Laurel and Hardy, she thought, although hopefully a less accident-prone version. 'I'm trying my best to be businesslike and not to fall too hard for this place but ...' She turned her head to smile at him. 'Sod it, I'm in. I love it.'

'Me too,' he said happily. 'And I love you. The two of us, living here ... I think our best days could still be ahead of us, Bel, I really do. Besides, there's nobody with whom I'd rather share the honour of a gargantuan new financial commitment.'

Belinda spluttered with laughter. 'Aww, shucks. You old sweet-talker, you.'

They heard footsteps just then, and turned to see Ellis walking into the room. 'What do you think, son?' Ray asked.

'I mean ... it's a lot of money,' Ellis said dubiously, hands tucked into the pockets of his slouchy grey hoodie. 'Do you really want to be taking on another mortgage at your age? No offence,' he added, more to Belinda than to his dad. 'I mean . . .' He trailed away, apparently unsure how to dig himself out of the implicit insult.

'We really like it,' Ray said, immune to his son's doubts. 'No doubt the survey will throw up all kinds of woes, but hopefully that means we can bargain the price down. The mortgage we're looking at it is a short-term one anyway.'

Belinda eyed Ellis's impassive face. Was his nose out of joint because he was comparing their potential new home to the crummy flats he'd been viewing? He wasn't about to argue that a larger share of Ray's cash should be funnelled into his own living arrangements, was he? 'Anyway, it *is* a lot of money, but we've worked hard for it,' she heard herself saying defensively, but her words must have come out with a sharper edge than intended because Ray's arm tightened around her momentarily and then he was speaking over her.

'I don't think Ellis is implying that we *didn't* work hard for it, love, but—'

'I know! I wasn't saying that,' Belinda interrupted as the boy scuffed at the uneven flooring with a grubby trainer, his expression mulish. Somehow a shadow had fallen across their beautiful moment, the fizz of excitement she'd felt about living here evaporating into the air. 'I just meant—'

'Well, it's none of my business anyway,' Ellis said before she could finish the sentence. His shoulders lifted with a shrug, then he sloped out of the back door without further comment.

Ray went after him and Belinda sighed into the empty room. What had just happened there? She could feel the undercurrents between their triangular dynamic but couldn't quite identify them. Had something changed for Ellis, now that he knew precisely how big a property she and his dad could afford?

Walking over towards the sink, she peered out to see the two men standing on the overgrown patio with their backs to her, heads bowed in conversation, Ray with his arm around his son's shoulders where it had been on Belinda's moments before. Her feelings of mistrust surged like a breaker against a harbour wall and she had to look away, biting her lip. 'What do I do?' she asked the house. 'Why has he come back all of a sudden?'

The house, of course, said nothing, but she put a hand to its scarred worktop nonetheless, seeking reassurance from its stillness. *I've got my eye on you*, she thought, with one final glance through the window.

Chapter Twenty-Two

Will: *Are you around this weekend? I've decided to head back to the UK and I've got a ticket on the next flight out. It gets in Saturday evening your time, was wondering if I could crash at yours for a bit? X*

Alice: *OMG YES YES YES of course! For as long as you want! Xxx*

Having woken up to the surprise message from her brother on a different number (had he splashed out on a new phone? Talk about living the high life), Alice was now in a large pottery studio in Hackney, tying apron strings around her middle and exchanging shy smiles with the seven other people who'd signed up for the *kintsugi* workshop. They were all seated on high stools at intervals around a central U-shaped workbench with a potter's wheel in one corner and shelves behind them that ran the length of the walls, filled with stacked bowls, plates and pots, presumably made by students. Sunshine poured through the high windows and Alice felt buoyed by it, and by the cardboard box at her feet too, containing the colourful shards of Leni's broken plates. Here she was, about to enact a great big metaphor by transforming the shattered pieces into something new, mended and beautiful. If only it were so easy for people.

Two days had gone by since her second evening out with Jacob, and she still felt disconcerted about the way he'd looked at her, the way he'd talked to her, as if, in his view, she was as damaged as Leni's crockery. She'd mentioned that she was booked in for today's workshop and had explained about *kintsugi*, how it was the centuries-old Japanese art of restoring broken ceramics with a mixture of gold pigment and lacquer. The point was not to hide the imperfections of a piece, but to draw attention to them and beautify them. He'd seemed really interested, until she went on to say that she was hoping to mend some of Leni's plates that way, at which point you could see the light dim in his eyes, his engagement wane. *I always thought you'd go on to do something extraordinary*, she heard him comment again and stiffened at the memory. Get stuffed, Jacob. What right did he have to judge her?

She hadn't wanted to talk about her job because it was nothing to boast about, because she knew he'd glaze over with boredom, all right? Just like she did herself most days, Darren dodges aside. (She hadn't seen him since the lift trauma and wasn't entirely sure whether to be relieved or disappointed.) With four months left on her contract at Sage and Golding, the days passed by with treacly slowness compared to the buzz of working at ReImagine. Just yesterday, she'd noticed that the same line had been used across the company's social media eight days in a row. *Looking for great insurance? Ask your grandad — he knows!*

As a slogan, this would have been laughed out of the door at ReImagine within a millisecond. Was this seriously their attempt at drawing in younger customers, by telling them to ask their grandparents which insurance company they used? On which planet would this ever happen? In Alice's opinion, it would only have an adverse effect: young people didn't like being patronised or advised to consult an older person, and they certainly didn't appreciate sexist old tropes where the grandma didn't get so much as a mention.

'Everything all right over there, Alice?' Tina, her colleague, had asked her yesterday. 'You keep sighing so much, I was starting to think the air conditioning had been turned up.'

Alice had responded with a sheepish smile. 'Sorry. I was just ... Tina, I don't suppose you know who writes the company's social media, do you?'

'The company's social media? What, like Facebook and that?' Tina pursed her lips thoughtfully. She was in her sixties, with neatly shingled salt-and-pepper hair and a penchant for pastel-coloured blouses. Today's was a soft lavender, yesterday's a cool pistachio.

'It would be someone in the comms department,' Alice said. 'Communications,' she added when Tina still looked blank. 'Or marketing?'

'I don't think there *is* a communications department,' Tina replied. *This explained a lot,* thought Alice. 'But marketing's on the fourth floor. Dawn Ellery is the department PA, she's ever so nice. Do you want her number?'

248

'No thanks,' said Alice, feeling spontaneous. *Maybe I'm not so passive after all*, she thought. *Watch this Flying Beauty go, Leni.* 'I'll pop up there in person.'

Her pulse had quickened as she checked her reflection in the ladies' loos a few moments later, running possible lines of introduction through her head. She would be taking something of a risk by rocking up unannounced to the marketing department, especially when her reason for doing so was that she thought their output was pretty poor and that she could do better. But of course she wouldn't present it to them in those terms. She would smile and be charming and subtle. Plus, given the chance, she might be able to sniff out further information and make a cheeky move. And then, the next time anyone new asked her what she did, she could say, *Well, I was temping at this boring insurance company but then used my initiative and . . .*

Not that it mattered what opinion anyone else had about her life anyway, she'd thought crossly, dismissing Jacob from her mind.

'Good morning, everyone!' said the workshop teacher just then, a young woman called Ichika, whose long black hair was tied in a sleek ponytail down her back. Alice snapped back to attention as Ichika began the session with an introduction to *kintsugi*. Its rise, she told them, could be dated back to the sixteenth and seventeenth centuries, when there was a great tradition of tea-drinking from fashionable tea bowls. Broken bowls would be mended by Japanese lacquer masters using a particular lacquer called *urushi,* made from tree sap. Once the bowls had been stuck back together, the lacquer could take weeks to harden, and then the piece would have to be carefully sanded until the surfaces were perfectly flush. Only then would the lacquer master paint over the seams with gold.

'That is the way a true artisan works,' she smiled to the group, 'but as we only have a three-hour workshop together, we will take some shortcuts so that you can at least finish something today.'

Alice glanced down at the stack of plates she'd brought with her. Ah. Maybe she'd been a tad optimistic, thinking she'd be walking out of the workshop with a fully gilded crockery set and a loving-sister task mentally ticked off. But even one mended plate would be a start, she supposed. She imagined herself proudly showing it to Will when he arrived at her flat. God, she couldn't wait to see him. Her brother, home at last. A piece of the family, a piece of her, about to be fitted back in place. He'd be getting on the plane soon, she calculated, feeling jittery at the thought. She hoped she could keep her envy in check when he told her about all his adventures.

Ichika had brought some broken white saucers for everyone to practise on – 'Nice clean breaks, very straightforward' – and demonstrated how to mix epoxy glue and putty with gold powder as a quicker-drying modern version of the ancient lacquer technique. She went around the tables, distributing the saucers, and when she reached Alice's workstation, Alice hopped off her stool to show her the broken plates she'd brought along. 'I was hoping to work on these,' she said. 'They were my sister's. Would that be okay?'

There was a wobble in Alice's voice which must have been audible, because Ichika's face softened as she glanced down at the bright, shattered crockery pieces, within their newspaper and bubblewrap outerwear. 'Ah,' she said apologetically. 'We do advise on the booking form that it's best not to bring your own materials, as time is so limited in the class, unfortunately.'

'So ... could I make a start on one of these or ... ?' Alice could feel her earlier buoyancy slipping away. She really hadn't thought this through properly.

Ichika picked up a couple of the shards, examining them beneath the light. 'They're really beautiful, aren't they?' she said kindly. 'I can see why you'd want to restore them, rather than throw them away. But I'm afraid it would take even a professional many hours of work to put them back together. Maybe for now you could try with the saucer I have for you and see how you get on? We do hire spaces in the studio if you love *kintsugi* and decide you want to spend the time working on your own crockery – or I could put you in touch with a couple of experts who might be able to help?'

The other woman was doing her best, but Alice felt crushed with disappointment all the same. She knew already she wouldn't be hiring a space in the studio – how could she, when she worked full-time, and had bills to pay? She almost certainly wouldn't be commissioning a professional to repair Leni's crockery either, if it was going to be such a huge job. 'It's fine,' she managed to say. 'I'll use the saucer. Thank you.'

And it *was* fine, in terms of carrying out a calming, mindful activity: mixing her own gold glue and carefully sticking the saucer pieces back together. Piano music tinkled in the background, the group was friendly and chatty, Ichika made them all cups of green tea and produced a plate of dainty little shortbread biscuits decorated with Sakura cherry blossoms. In fact, Alice was surprised to realise towards the end of the workshop that, even though this hadn't been a Leni-centred activity after all, she'd enjoyed herself. It had been deeply relaxing, working with her hands, a chance to let her mind drift. She'd replayed, several times over, the satisfying encounter she'd had with Dawn the marketing PA yesterday, for instance. How, having lavished on her a number of compliments about her jacket and bracelet, Alice had been able to glean that the department had an intern running the social media campaigns – and just between the two of them, Dawn thought he was a bit of a spoiled brat who thought he was a cut above everyone else because he'd been to a posh university. 'I could probably do a better job of it than him,' she'd said, rolling her eyes conspiratorially.

'Well,' Alice had said, taking a deep breath. 'Actually, that's why I'm here …'

The workshop flew by, with everyone exclaiming their surprise – and disappointment too – when their time was up. The mended saucers needed to be left to dry for forty-eight hours and so Ichika asked everyone to write their names and addresses on stickers that she would use to package and send on the completed pieces. Then, as the class began to disperse, she approached Alice with a smile.

'Have you got a minute?' she asked. 'I've had an idea.'

Chapter Twenty-Three

Will's plane landed on Saturday night, and as he peered out at the dark runway, the pilot announcing that it was seven forty British time, and two degrees outside, he didn't know whether to laugh or cry. Or whether he should stow away and get himself on the first flight back out of there again, for that matter. Shit. Could he really do this?

Inside the terminal, everyone around him was hurrying towards the baggage reclaim area, but Will lagged behind, in no hurry to be reunited with his battered rucksack and scant possessions, and in even less of a hurry to be reunited with his old life in the UK. He still didn't have a clue what he was going to do with himself now that he was back, how he could start over here. Then his phone beeped and it was a message from Alice. *Thought I'd pick you up! Here in Arrivals waiting for you. Welcome home!*

The bubble he'd formed around himself, the protective shell of foreign distractions, of distance and denial, had been stretching thinner and thinner ever since he'd made his decision to leave Thailand. Alice's cheery message all but undid him. She was here, somewhere in this building, waiting to meet him; it was almost over. Was he ready for this? But in the next moment, he felt a rush of gratitude also – she'd done that for him? He hadn't expected that. He'd envisaged being ejected alone into the melee of Arrivals, having to navigate the journey across London to her flat by himself, tired and broken. The thought of her presence nearby was like a lantern in the darkness.

'Hey! Oh my God! Look at you! Look at your *tan*! Oh, Will, it's really you!' Fifteen minutes later, he was being crushed by her embrace, and he found himself overwhelmed by how unfamiliar and yet exactly the same it felt to have his arms around her, his own sister, once again. He'd noticed her as soon as he emerged through the Arrivals doors, standing a little apart from everyone else, self-contained and watchful in her dark blue coat, a little thinner than he remembered but unmistakably her, his one remaining sibling. Someone who'd known him from the very first day he'd been alive. Was that what it meant to be part of a family, that instant recognition of a person amidst the crowd, knowledge of them imprinted within you like indelible ink?

'Hi,' he said, jet-lagged and emotional, choking on the word as he breathed in the smell of her hair. He'd been so alone, he realised. For months and months, he'd been so lonely, existing in his own safe sphere, cut off from his family and life as he'd once known it. 'It's so good to see you,' he said thickly. 'How are you? Thank you for being here – you didn't have to—'

'Like I was *not* going to meet you, fart-brain,' she said as they finally drew apart. She reached up to ruffle his hair, just as she'd always done when he was a pipsqueak little boy and she was a big cool teenager. 'I couldn't believe it when I got your message. And Mum is absolutely hyped too. Hang on—' She stretched out her arm and took a photo of them both. 'Let me just send this to her ... Okay. My phone will now explode under the weight of all her incoming emojis, you wait. Shall we go?'

It was strange to be back in Alice's car, seeing the familiar British road signs rush by, the rain falling heavily against the windscreen as she drove them across London to her flat. Already he could feel his island life, with all its vivid colours and smells, beginning to recede into the back of his mind, like a mirage once seen. She told him about a pottery workshop she'd been to that day and about her cat, and he in response told her safe things about his life too: a diving trip he'd been on, the party scene, the food. He didn't tell her about the mugging, his failed careers in both drug-dealing and flip-flop selling. He didn't describe the indignity of having to return all the many boxes of unsold goods back to the wholesaler for a last handful of notes so that he could buy his cheap new phone and pay for an airport transfer.

Neither of them mentioned Leni on the journey either, but if he'd thought he could keep this up for long, he'd been kidding himself. As soon as he walked into Alice's flat, it was like stepping into a museum starring their sister, and it was impossible to avoid her. There was Leni's cat, glaring at him and hurrying from the room. Bags of her clothes in one corner. The broken plates Will recognised from her birthday lunch there on the table, along with a pile of paperwork and what looked like a six-week timeline of events pinned up on the wall. Oh God. Was Alice actually all right in the head? he wondered uncertainly as she set about making some pasta and popping open a couple of beers.

'Mind if I have a shower?' he asked, feeling sweat break out on his neck, despite the tepid temperature of her flat. The walls seemed to be closing in; everywhere he turned he was confronted by one picture of Leni or another. He felt as if he had been forced into Guilt Central against his will, with no way out. *Welcome home, sucker. Time to confess your sins!*

'Of course! There are clean towels in the cupboard, help yourself to anything,' she said, handing him a beer. 'Food will be ready in fifteen minutes or so, take your time.'

He escaped into the bathroom, took a massive gulp of cold lager and stared at his crumpled, bloodshot-eyed reflection with what felt increasingly like panic. Fuck. He had the growing conviction that coming back had been a really bad idea. Maybe even his worst yet.

Chapter Twenty-Four

Alice: Hi Mum. Look who I bumped into at the airport!

Belinda: [red heart emoji, gold heart emoji, blue heart emoji, green heart emoji, smiling-face emoji, blowing-kiss emoji, heart-eyes emoji] LOOK AT YOU TWO!!!! I just screamed out loud at the picture, nearly gave Ray a heart attack [laughing emoji] I LOVE YOU BOTH!!! XXX

'Come in,' said Belinda on the doorstep, and Tony almost wanted to pinch himself because he couldn't quite believe he was there, back at the old house all these years later. Of course he'd stood outside many times, dropping the children off after weekends and what have you, but it had been a long time since he'd been welcomed over the threshold. *Come over for a last look at the place*, Belinda had suggested, and it had seemed like a good idea at the time, but now that he was stepping inside his former home, a place that held so many memories, good and bad, he was no longer quite so sure.

'Gosh,' he heard himself saying politely, 'it's immaculate. Last time I was here, there were children's paintings all the way up and down the hall and toys crunching under foot. You've done a great job.'

'Amazing how having loads of prospective buyers trooping through your house focusses the mind,' she said drily, leading him through to the kitchen. 'It's just us in, Ray's gone to look at a flat with his son. Coffee?'

'Please.' They were both being very civil and grown-up, he thought, following her into the large sunny room. He had to blink and transpose it over his memories of this space, from the chaos he'd known back then, of there being dolls and games everywhere, school uniforms draped over the radiator to dry, lunchboxes needing to be filled or emptied, half-completed jigsaws on the table, children's party invitations stuck to the fridge with colourful magnets. 'Gosh,' he said again, a lump in his throat that he had once lived within that life, been a part of this house's routines. All the times he'd had breakfast in here before work, the scorched smell as Belinda ironed a shirt for him, the girls squabbling over some toy or other – gone. And yet he still knew exactly how the back door handle would feel in his hand, how the sun sent a shaft of light across the room every morning; the memories contained within this room, this house, were an intrinsic part of him, like woodgrain.

'Two sugars still?' Belinda asked, fussing about with mugs.

'No sugar any more,' he said, smiling a little at her surprise. He wouldn't tell her that he'd given it up when he'd married Tanya, wife number three, he decided. Belinda had liked clean-living, verging-on-pious Tanya possibly least out of all his wives and girlfriends. In hindsight, she'd had a point.

He wandered over to the window to peer into the garden,

only to catch a glimpse of someone in the neighbouring garden, at which point he froze. Old habits died hard, he thought, turning back round. Come on. Those days are gone.

'So how are things? I take it you've spoken to Will?' Belinda's face lit up at his name. 'I can't believe he's back. I'm hoping to get to London in a day or two to see him, how about you?' She put their drinks on the table and went on before he could reply. 'Have a seat. Or would you rather wander round first?'

'I'll sit,' he said, doing just that. Same chairs, he noticed. Same table. He put his hand on its scored pine surface, appreciating how quietly reliable a piece of furniture could be. 'Yes, I'm glad he's back,' he added. 'I can't wait to see him again.' He really was determined to put in some legwork with Will before the baby came along. The two of them had got off to such a difficult start when Will was born – before then, even – and Tony knew he'd never really filled the father space in his son's life afterwards either. It wasn't that he hadn't loved him, more that the relationship had always been ... well, it was complicated.

'Things are okay,' he went on, in answer to Belinda's original question. 'We're into the last six weeks or so before the baby's due, and Jackie's ...' He hesitated, not wanting to betray a confidence. 'Jackie's fine. I've got to say though, Bel, it's all changed since our day. There's this whole new industry around childbirth, you wouldn't believe it. Baby showers and 3D scans and ... and reiki.' He wrinkled his nose, still not entirely sure what reiki actually was. 'I keep thinking of our three being born, how we didn't have any of that business, but how you didn't need it.' He moistened his lips. 'How magnificent you were.'

'Oh, Tony,' she scoffed but he could tell she was pleased by his words. 'I don't know about that.'

There was a pause when he geared up for raising the subject of this psychic hotline – *Someone needs to say something*, Jackie had encouraged him – but Belinda got in first. 'Tony,' she said, looking uncharacteristically nervous, 'I need to ask you a question. On Leni's birthday last year, she mentioned that she'd seen ... um ... Graham. Graham Fenton.'

The name was like a whip-crack in the air; Tony recoiled as if he'd been hit. 'Graham, as in ... ?'

'Yes. He did the Ofsted inspection at her school, recognised her name,' Belinda said. She looked as if she were about to be sick all of a sudden. 'And then when Alice and I were sorting through Leni's things, I found his name and number there on a bit of paper.' She swallowed, staring down at her mug before raising her gaze to him once more. 'Tony, I need to ask you this – did she ever talk to you about him? Did she ... know?'

'So how was Memory Lane?' Alice asked when Tony called her later that evening. He'd already had a full update on Will's return – how his son was uber-tanned, jet-lagged, currently out with mates – and now Alice was handing the conversation baton back to him. 'Did you enjoy your trip back to the old place?'

'Yes, on the whole,' he told her as breezily as he knew how. He was sitting in a room Jackie called 'the snug', a cosy space kitted out with his favourite reclining armchair and a wood-burning stove. She was elsewhere with a friend, so he'd treated himself to a whisky and had lit the fire, the flames leaping mesmerisingly between the logs. 'Funny how your brain can distort things though,' he went on. 'The bedrooms upstairs seemed so much smaller than how I'd remembered them. It all looked so clean – and that posh shower they've put in! Much better than the hold-it-yourself job we had when I was still living there.'

'And things with Mum?' Alice prompted. 'She was nice to you? Didn't give you too much shit about ... well, you know. Everything?'

'She was nice,' he confirmed, trying to push from his mind the conversation he'd had with his ex; how complex and emotional it had become. *Did she know?* Belinda had asked him and he'd sighed and said no, nobody knew, he'd kept his promise. She had become tearful and upset, unable to look him in the eye momentarily as she apologised to him all over again. And he had felt ... Well, he had felt unhappy himself to be thrust back into that difficult time, a time he had tried very hard not to think about ever since. He had assured her it was water under the bridge now though, that what was done was done, because he knew she was desperate for him to say those words. Even if he wasn't sure he meant them.

Afterwards, he couldn't face broaching the subject of the phone psychic; he'd try again on another day when things weren't so fraught, he'd decided. Changing the subject now, he asked his daughter about her job, which was met by a noise of frustration and then a full-blown rant about what a bunch of stiffs they were at this insurance place.

261

'So ... can you do anything to shake them up a bit? Give them some of your expert advice?' he suggested. One of the logs gave a loud crack with the heat of the fire; it took him back to scout camps as a boy, the smell of smoke on the night air. There was something so primitively satisfying about watching something burn, he thought.

'Funny you should say that,' she replied, before telling him that she'd wangled herself a meeting with the marketing department the following week, and that she was hoping she could persuade them to let her draw up a plan for their social media strategy on a trial basis. 'But you know, small steps. Making any kind of change in that place would be like trying to turn around a cruise ship with a single piece of bungee cord.'

'Yeah, but you're trying, at least. That's the main thing. Trying to make a difference. And do you know what? They're lucky to have you giving them a kick up the arse. And ...' He hesitated, wondering if she would accept a compliment from him yet, or if she'd throw it back in his face. Sod it, he had to give it a go. 'And I'm proud of you, Ali-cat. Really proud.'

'Oh, Dad!' She sounded so pleased, it absolutely warmed his cockles through. 'Thank you. I'll keep you posted.'

It had been an effort, a sustained campaign of effort for him with his middle daughter, especially as he knew at first he had a lot of ground to make up, but he was starting to think that the two of them were forming a new bond together, their own proper relationship at last. Even getting to use his old nickname for her felt like a win. The strain he'd previously noticed in her voice when they spoke now seemed to have gone; she was starting to confide in him in a way she hadn't done since she was a small girl and worried about Bad Things under the bed. Of course, he was biased, but he really thought she was great: funny, talented, thoughtful. He loved talking to her! He loved hearing about her life – the cat, her friends, the new Pilates class (*Actually quite relaxing, you should try it, Dad*). In return, he told her about the antenatal group, funny stories from his working day, the new restaurant in Broad Street he and Jackie had been to.

Did Alice feel similarly about him? He thought she might. She was taking the piss out of him in a way that seemed affectionate rather than bitter these days; they were laughing and joking more. That had to mean something, right? He hoped so. Their relationship had brought a new layer, new texture to his life. He wasn't only proud of her, he cherished her. Far too much to let her go again, that was for sure.

Chapter Twenty-Five

'Belinda McKenzie, well I never,' said Graham Fenton after she'd opened the call with a stuttering reintroduction. 'I'd have known your voice anywhere. How are you?'

Belinda swallowed hard, her fingers shaking on the phone. It was strange the way a week could be made up of such completely different elements. Yesterday she'd stepped off the train in Paddington to see Will waiting for her in the concourse, both of them with the biggest smiles on their faces. Joy had filled her from head to foot as she flung her arms around him, not entirely certain she'd ever be able to let him go again. Today, here she was, back at the Park and Ride, the wind buffeting the car with such force that she half expected to find herself spinning up into the air, like Dorothy in *The Wizard of Oz*. (Oh my, Toto!) 'Hello,' she managed to croak.

Ever since the day she and Alice had begun sorting through Leni's possessions, the piece of paper with Graham Fenton's number on it had been squatting at the bottom of Belinda's handbag like an unexploded bomb ominously ticking down to zero. She had waited on tenterhooks for Leni's wrath to come via Apolline, angry accusations of hypocrisy – *how could you, Mum?* – until the suspense had turned her into a nervous wreck. Then she'd made the mistake of asking Tony if he knew anything about Leni's encounter with Graham, only to feel as if she'd uncovered an old wound that still hurt him – and her – all these years later. There was only one thing left to do. Call the number and find out the truth for herself.

'I've got something to ask you,' she said now, cringing in the driver's seat. No turning back.

Graham Fenton had been a naughty little secret at first, a bit of fun. He was the sexy dark-haired man who moved in next door and set Belinda's pulse racing. What a cliché she was! Developing a crush on the good-looking neighbour as a distraction from her mundane life: the juggle of two little girls, housework and a tough job in social work, along with a husband who was frequently away, both emotionally and physically. Not that it was Tony's fault, by any means – he was working all hours as the main breadwinner, as well as dealing with the loss of his parents, one after the other, and trying to sort out the sale of the old family home with his brothers. Nevertheless, she had been lonely. So where was the harm, she'd asked herself, in indulging in some light flirtation over the fence with handsome Graham, as a little pick-me-up at the end of the day? Until he upped the ante considerably, by appearing one evening on her doorstep with a bottle of wine and a suggestively raised eyebrow. Both proved equally hard to resist. And so the affair began.

Caught up in passion, Belinda lost her head. She and Graham became more daring, more reckless, kissing in secluded spots in the garden when the girls were in bed and Tony was glued to the cricketing highlights on TV. Graham kept popping round, supposedly to do odd jobs – creosoting the fence, fixing the guttering on the back wall, digging over a flowerbed – but always ending up in Belinda's bed afterwards. She started wearing perfume for the first time in years, singing in the car, feeling good about her body. Then she found out she was pregnant again, and – the shame of it – had no idea whose baby she might be carrying.

Oh, Belinda. Now you've gone and done it, she'd said to herself, her hand shaking with horror as she did three pregnancy tests in a row, just to be sure, only to find them all coming up unmistakably positive. Shit.

'I'm just going to come out and say it,' she began now, trying not to think about how she'd looked at herself in the bathroom mirror back then, wide-eyed with dismay, heart pounding so hard you could almost see it through her dress. Her heart was thudding pretty decisively with this phone conversation, for that matter, she thought, putting a hand to her chest to try and steady herself. 'I know you saw Leni, my daughter, last May. Did you ... tell her anything?'

She had absolutely no idea how he was going to respond, she realised, watching an empty blue-and-white-striped carrier bag swirl up in a mini tornado, its plastic body ballooning like a pregnant belly before suddenly becoming limp as the wind flung it away out of sight. Graham had been impetuous and hot-headed, with a sexy dynamism lacking in her husband. At the time of their affair, he was a headteacher and, on being offered a prestigious new job in Birmingham, his first thought had been to take Belinda with him. 'How about it?' he'd said. 'We could make a new start together, me and you.'

It was the 'me and you' that had brought Belinda up short. Because obviously there was no 'her', singular; she came as a package along with her two daughters. Plus, of course, this surprise new baby, whose existence was still a complete secret, other than to her and the doctor. Graham's question had changed everything.

'I couldn't believe it when I heard her name,' he said now, sounding amused, and images crashed into Belinda's head, of how he'd looked naked in the bed, the weight of his body against hers. He was so dark and hairy after Tony, so musky-smelling; she would always fling the window open afterwards and change the sheets to try and drive out his scent. It was a wonder the washing machine didn't stage a protest and die, with all the extra laundry she stuffed into it during that time. 'Leni McKenzie, blimey. She looks like you, doesn't she?'

The present tense pressed like a bruise. *Looked, actually, Graham*, she thought, but didn't correct him. One awkward conversation at a time.

'Yes,' she said tightly. 'So – did you? Tell her anything? Only I found your name and number in her things, and . . .' *And I've been tying myself in knots wondering ever since if my daughter went to her grave thinking me a liar.*

It had been so awful, when Tony found out. After all their sneaking around, all Belinda's care to keep the secret, the subterfuge was undone by his discovery of a rogue pair of Graham's pants at the end of the bed. The one time she hadn't whipped off the sheets and covered up the evidence!

Afterwards she'd even wondered if Graham had left them there deliberately, trying to provoke a decision out of her. He certainly provoked something, namely the mother of all arguments between Belinda and Tony as the affair exploded into their marriage, culminating in Tony marching next door and punching Graham in the face. (There was dynamism for you, Belinda had been left thinking, but not the sort she'd hankered after.) Graham had moved to Birmingham alone soon afterwards, never knowing about the pregnancy, but she couldn't hide it forever. And of course, when Tony discovered she was expecting, there was only one question uppermost in his mind. 'So whose baby even is it?' he'd asked, devastated.

Oh, Tony. She had done him so wrong, all in all.

'Let me think ... Yeah, she rang me about a week after I'd met her,' Graham said now. 'She left a message saying ... What was it? She'd got my number from the school secretary because she'd mentioned my name to you, and that you'd looked completely freaked out. Something like that. She wondered if I knew of any reason why.'

Belinda swallowed again. She had the worst poker face ever; of course Leni must have been suspicious back then on her birthday. 'And you said ... ?' she prompted, not remotely sure she wanted to hear his reply.

'I didn't ring her back,' he said. 'I just ... Why are you asking now, anyway? This all happened months ago, right? Last summer!'

'So she didn't know,' Belinda said, as much to soothe herself as to him. First Tony, now Graham; neither of them had let slip her worst secret. Tears rushed into her eyes with sheer relief. 'She didn't know about us.'

'Why are you saying "didn't" like that?' he asked, sounding confused. 'Belinda, I don't understand, what—?'

'Sorry, I've got to go,' she said before he could finish his question. 'Thanks, Graham. Goodbye.'

She cut him off, blocked the number and deleted it, then chucked the phone into the passenger seat. Sitting there with her head in her hands, she relived all the guilt and shame she'd felt from that time. How she'd hurt Tony. How she'd damaged their marriage so badly, it had never been able to recover. How she'd gone through her pregnancy feeling sick with doubt the entire time, Tony detached and dispassionate where he'd previously been joyful and excited about her other two. They'd managed to work as a team while Will was unwell as a baby, but it had been very much on practical terms, with none of the shared love and affection from before. And then when they'd split up, when he'd admitted defeat and bowed out of the relationship, she had begged him not to tell the children what she'd done. 'Promise me?' she'd pleaded, practically on her knees. But—

There was a knock at her car window and she jerked back to the present decade, only to be startled almost out of her skin when she saw who was standing there. *'Ray?'* she cried, in astonishment. She opened the car door and began getting out before realising she still had her seat belt on and having to wrestle her way out of it. 'What are you doing here?'

He looked so stern, her brain spun feverishly. 'Are you all right?' she asked. Why had he tracked her down like this? Something must be wrong. 'Is it Ellis? Has something happened?'

'I thought you were going to the dump,' he said, arms folded across his chest. It was still blowing a gale and a tuft of his grey hair flopped up and down comically, although his words were enough to wipe any comic thoughts from Belinda's mind in an instant. 'You told me you were going to the dump.'

'I—'

'I knew you weren't. I knew you were lying. I followed you here and I've been sitting watching you on the phone again. To her, I'm guessing. That bloody woman. Belinda, this has got to stop!'

She opened her mouth to contradict him – *No, actually, Ray!* – only to snap it shut again almost immediately. How could she tell him the truth, that she'd contacted the man with whom she'd had such a shameful affair?

Chapter Twenty-Six

Alice felt as if change might be in the air at last. Thanks to Dawn, her new contact at work, a meeting had been arranged for her to speak to a couple of marketing people, and she was determined to throw everything at the opportunity. Her gut feeling was that there was a huge area of the market the company simply wasn't looking at, and she hoped to show them, as quickly as possible, how to tempt in this untapped swathe of customers. Humour, she'd decided, was the key. Humour plus the lure of exclusivity. Now she had to prove to them what she could do.

Having set up a social media handle, @GuessWho? with a biography that merely read *Insurance? We've got that covered*, deliberately coined to intrigue, she launched herself into the digital waters and hoped she could make a splash – or, at the very least, a few ripples. And if the whole thing bombed, she reminded herself, nobody ever need know about it.

But it wouldn't bomb! Because she was determined, and she had a plan. Back in her old job at ReImagine, she'd headed up the social media team; she knew her stuff. Of course, in those days, she would have brainstormed extensively with her colleagues before launching a campaign; they'd have dug deep into company research; they'd have run focus groups and consumer panels; they'd have drawn up a list of aspirations, targets to hit. This, by contrast, felt like taking a test flight all alone, without knowing if she could steer the plane, let alone land it any place. Even so, surely she could do a better job than the current intern employed to punt out dreary messages to the brand's few followers?

In her tea break that morning, she pored over what was trending on Twitter, then pounced on a news story about a senior government minister visiting a local primary school who, when trying to show off his sack race skills during PE, had fallen over and cracked his glasses. Alice retweeted a picture of the unfortunate minister, broken specs in hand, and added a caption – *Let's hope you're covered by . . . Guess Who?*, adding the minister's name and hashtag #DontGetTheSack so that it would show up in any searches.

She pursued this approach over the next few days, working with any gossipy news stories that she could bend to the vague theme of insurance. A Premier League footballer, famed for his success at penalty-taking, pranged his expensive sports car on a bollard, prompting a slew of memes and jokes about hitting the wrong target – perfect for Alice's Guess Who? caption purposes. A soap star whose Newfoundland puppy had knocked over (and smashed) her new TV – thank you very much. By now, she'd picked up a modicum of traction, a number of likes and retweets, plus a few follows, although it did feel, at times, as if she were shouting down a well. That was only to be expected though, she reminded herself, and there was nothing wrong with a slow-grow campaign, especially one that kept people guessing. If she could work up enough momentum between now and her meeting with the company marketing team, she could talk to them about building the teasers to a big reveal, with the campaign stretching across all social media networks to maximise reach. Then brainstorm strategies to keep new younger followers on board. It felt so exciting to be working within this sort of creative realm again, as if the synapses in her brain were constantly lighting up with new ideas. If only her sister could be there to cheer her on. Or even admit she'd been wrong about Alice in the first place.

'You know, I've kind of been haunted by this argument I had with Leni on her birthday,' she said to Will on Friday night, having suggested they go out for dinner at a Mexican street food place near her flat. It was an uplifting venue, with cheery mariachi music playing, light bulbs dangling from long cords above red Formica tables and, behind a steel counter, chefs flipping great pans of sizzling peppers for fajitas.

Will's face stiffened a little – *Oh God, here we go*, she saw in his eyes. 'Yeah?' he said, without much enthusiasm.

'Yeah – it was pretty horrible. She laid into me about not growing up, not committing to anything – like, never settling down with a proper boyfriend, all this kind of thing. Letting stuff happen to me passively rather than going out and working for it.' She picked up one of the cheesy nachos from their sharing plate and dug it hungrily into the guacamole, her nose wrinkling as she replayed the scene: Leni's accusing

273

face, her own shocked hurt, how she'd all but run out of the flat to avoid hearing any more of her sister's unkind words. 'And ... well, I'm not saying anything's all *that* different. In fact, Leni might think I've acted even more like a kid, giving up my job, and the whole thing with Dar—' She stopped herself just in time, coughing loudly over the rest of his name. 'But I do feel a bit of a sea change inside, you know. Like – if I can make a go of it as a freelancer, say, then that would be awesome. That would be me standing on my own two feet, properly putting myself out there. And I think ...' She broke off, suddenly awkward, before deciding to say it anyway. 'Yeah, I think she'd be proud of me for it.'

The idea was enough to bring tears to her eyes. For all that Leni had hit her – and hurt her – with that fistful of home truths last year, Alice could admit now that her sister had had a point. Alice had always lived safely, never really sticking out her neck to achieve very much or try something bold. She'd had one not-very-good boyfriend after another because it had been easy to go along with them, as if she didn't deserve better. She'd got an internship at ReImagine straight out of uni and hadn't thought to look anywhere else for work from that moment. Life *had* happened to her, until she'd been forced to start rebuilding things herself. But she was getting there now, wasn't she? How she wished she could tell Leni she was getting there!

She made the mistake of glancing at Will for his reaction, hoping that he might be smiling at her and saying he was proud too. He wasn't. He was staring morosely into his plate of food.

'You don't like me talking about her, do you?' she asked with a sigh.

'Not really,' he mumbled.

She knew this already, of course. He had been awkward around the mention of their sister from the moment he'd arrived in her flat. 'Why've you got all this stuff?' he'd asked on the first night, gesturing to the paperwork and clothes she hadn't yet got around to sorting through. He'd picked up one of Leni's broken plates and looked from it to Alice. 'Wouldn't it be better to chuck these out now?'

'Well, no, actually,' she'd replied, telling him how the *kintsugi* teacher had suggested commissioning a mosaic artist to turn the shattered pieces into a beautiful new piece of art, rather than trying to mend them all individually. (Alice was thrilled by this idea! She was already looking into local creatives who might be able to help her.) Will only shrugged in response though, and she could tell he didn't get it. Maybe he was still jet-lagged, she'd told herself at the time, but in the days that followed, he continued to appear unwilling to engage with the subject of Leni's whereabouts at the end of her life.

'Does it change anything though?' he'd said more than once. 'Like ... this mysterious "A" in her diary. Whatever the "T" was every Tuesday night. Does it matter? Shouldn't we just accept that we can't know everything and get on with our lives?'

'I think you can do both,' she'd countered. 'Try to find out as much as possible *and* get on with our lives.'

Even that morning over breakfast, he'd wanted to deflect

the subject. Alice was still having the same dream where she was searching for Leni in a maze, calling her name, the high green hedges preventing her from seeing further than the next few desperate steps. Once again she'd woken up, frustrated and melancholy. 'I don't think we need Dr Freud to tell us what *that* dream means,' she commented glumly to Will as she made coffee, having recounted the details.

'Mmm,' was all he had to say.

Alice couldn't get her head around this approach. 'I think it's good to bring her into the conversation though,' she argued now. 'I never want to *not* be talking about her.' He said nothing, still not looking in her direction, and her earlier feelings of buoyancy deserted her. 'Will – I think it's important to *try*,' she went on after a moment. 'To remember her out loud as a means of . . . you know, processing everything. Honouring her. It doesn't have to be sad stuff – if you look on her memorial page, there are heaps of funny stories that—'

'I don't want to look on her memorial page,' he said, sounding as if his teeth were gritted. 'I don't *want* to remember her out loud! I just want to—'

He broke off without finishing, his mouth closed up so tight she was reminded of him being a little boy and refusing to eat his vegetables. 'What?' she prompted when he didn't elaborate. 'You want to *forget* her?'

'No! Of course not.' His voice cracked. 'I just wish she was still here.'

'Oh, Will, we all wish that,' she said, reaching over and putting her hand on his arm. He felt stiff and unresponsive beneath her touch; he was holding himself rigidly in the seat, she noticed. 'Every single day, I wish I could ring her up or meet her for a drink or ... you know. *Anything*. Some days I still forget that she's gone and grab my phone to message her before I remember all over again.'

He wasn't listening, she could tell. Her words were bouncing off him without hitting the mark. 'No, but Alice, the thing is ...' He looked up at her at last and his expression was one of such intense unhappiness, she almost reared back from him. He swallowed, his Adam's apple jerking in his throat. 'The reason I try not to think about her is that ...' His voice had sunk almost to a whisper. 'It was my fault she died.'

'What? No, it wasn't,' she argued in surprise. 'It was Ferguson. Callum Ferguson.' She heard the soft *crump* of an egg hitting the window, pictured its slow viscous slide down the glass.

Will shook his head, his expression grim. 'The night she died,' he said, and Alice could tell he was really having to force the words out. 'The night she died, she rang me.'

'She rang me too,' Alice put in eagerly, forgetting his anguished face momentarily because this was news to her. 'Oh God, I wish I'd answered. What did she say?'

'She asked me ...' She had never seen him so distraught, she registered with a lurch. 'If I could look at her bike for her. If we could FaceTime so that I could walk her through tightening up the steering column.'

Alice could hardly breathe for a moment because she was remembering the grainy CCTV footage from the coroner's court, the image of her sister weaving wildly across the busy road, apparently losing control of her bike. Her heart thumped as she took in what her brother was saying to her. What he was confessing. 'And you . . .' She faltered, her stomach turning at the look on his face. 'And you said . . . ?'

'I said no.'

Chapter Twenty-Seven

'Can I ask you a favour, Will?' Leni had asked, and he'd felt irritated by the question because it had seemed like one favour after another in recent months – borrowing money, helping her move into her flat, could he fix this, could he do that? Plus he was still a bit annoyed after her weird birthday lunch when she'd been rude and unfriendly to Molly – *I don't think your sister likes me, babe*, she'd pouted – before freaking out over her broken plates, screaming at them all that they were a shit family. So no, he hadn't been in the maddest of rushes to help her out.

'What?' he'd asked grudgingly.

'There's something wrong with my bike, I think it's the steering column. Would you mind having a look at it?' she'd said.

He had rolled his eyes. Here we go, he'd thought. 'Can you not just take it to your nearest bike shop, get them to sort it out?' he'd asked, exasperated. Everyone else managed to look after themselves and their belongings in this way, after all. Plus – newsflash – he lived out in Swindon, not next door to her. He didn't come to her whining about his stuff, did he? She was eight years older than him and he'd never asked her for a thing, even though he had his own problems: an intimidating landlord and a girlfriend he wasn't entirely sure about, for starters, as well as the growing conviction that he might have thrown away his university place prematurely, and still hadn't found his feet in the world. But did he whinge on to Leni about this? No.

'Yeah, but . . . can't you do it?' she'd wheedled. 'I wanted to go out on it tonight. What if we video call and I show you, and you can give me your advice?'

'No!' he'd said, the word exploding out of him with more force than he'd anticipated. 'I'm busy – I'm meant to be going out in twenty minutes.' It wasn't a complete lie, but the only place he was intending to go was the fried chicken place on the corner and then straight back to his sofa. She didn't have to know that though.

'What, you've finally made some friends there, have you? Thank God!' she responded and he had no idea whether she was being sarcastic or joking – or even if she'd seen through his excuse and was taunting him for it.

Whatever the case, he felt prickly, as if she'd been unkind, so he'd said, 'Oh, sod off,' and hung up on her.

'And that was the last time we spoke,' he told Alice now, staring down at the table. 'My final words to her – *Oh, sod off.* Which makes me feel totally shit.' He couldn't lift his gaze, the weight of shame pressing him down. *Why,* he asked himself for the hundredth time, *couldn't he just have said yes?* He was an engineer, he was good with mechanics, it would have taken him two minutes on a video call to explain what to do. Why couldn't he have given her two minutes?

'Oh, Will,' Alice said wretchedly. 'You should have told me.'

'Why? So you can hate me as much as I hate myself? So you can blame me for her dying too?' He ran a hand wildly through his hair, feeling as if he was falling apart right there and then to the warbling accompaniment of a mariachi band. He thought of the way Belinda had gazed at him in Paddington station the other day, the love shining from her eyes, and imagined how the truth would destroy her if she ever knew; the worst possible slap in the face.

'We all did things we regret, we all said things we wish we hadn't,' Alice replied. 'But—'

'Is everything all right with your food, guys? Do you need anything?' came a voice just then and Will turned to see a smiling dark-haired waiter at their table, wearing an embroidered Mexican-style waistcoat and bootlace tie.

'We're fine, thanks,' he said dutifully.

'Delicious,' echoed Alice in the next breath, because at the end of the day they were still their parents' children, they were still McKenzies with manners, even in the throes of an ultimate confessional breakdown.

'Cool. Enjoy!' the waiter told them, making for the next table.

Their eyes met, and even in the maelstrom of his revelation, they felt the black comedy of the moment cut through – *Cool. Enjoy!* – and pulled wry faces at each other.

'So …' Alice began tentatively.

'Yeah,' he put in. 'You're going to tell me what a wanker I

am, right? And that you hate me and never want to see me again.' He was exaggerating for effect, but all the same, there was a part of him that fully expected her to say *yes, how could you?*

'Oh, Will, of course I'm not,' she said, shaking her head. A moment passed where he saw a whole parade of emotions flash across her face – sadness, regret, resignation – before she returned to him with a new fierceness, as if she'd settled on how to respond. 'You're my *brother*, I don't hate or blame you at all. Not at *all*. That must have been horrible, living with such a massive weight on you for so long.'

He nodded, unable to speak. She didn't blame him? Had he heard that right?

'You must have replayed that conversation a million times, just like I have with all the things I wish I hadn't said or done,' she went on. 'But you didn't force her to go out on the bike, did you? That was her choice, even though she knew it wasn't working properly. You fucking idiot, Leni,' she added, suddenly exasperated. 'Why didn't she just look on YouTube like a normal person? Or get a bloody bus?'

He still wasn't able to say anything. He could hardly breathe with the fact that they were actually talking about this, discussing his secret, after it had been toxic and radioactive inside him for so long.

'Plus,' Alice went on, draining her beer bottle, 'she did ask a *lot* of favours. Loads of favours. She was a nightmare for it sometimes, when she couldn't be bothered to do a thing herself.' She was trying to joke but her mouth was unsteady, her eyes a little too bright. 'And I bet before that night you'd done hundreds of things for her. To be fair, like she did hundreds of things for us in return.'

'Yeah.'

There was a round of cheers at the table behind them as the waiter approached with trays of sizzling fajitas but Alice carried on, caught up in her fervour. 'It's not your fault that the one time you said no to her, this had to happen,' she said. 'I mean it, Will. I'm exonerating you here. Absolutely not your fault. It was just really bad luck. Bad timing. Bad all round. And there's no way I'm going to sit here and blame *you*. Who knows, she might have been ringing to ask *me* how to fix her bike and I didn't even answer the bloody phone. I'm just as responsible!'

Will smiled weakly because Alice was the most impractical member of the family, whom nobody would ever dream of consulting about bike maintenance, and they both knew it. But he appreciated the solidarity. Her sisterliness. 'Thank you,' he said. He put a hand to his chest, aware of the adrenalin still pumping around his body post-confession, giving him a light-headedness, a sense of unreality. Was that really . . . it? After all those months carrying his burden of guilt, was it actually over? 'God, Alice,' he said, suddenly overcome. 'Thank you. I've been so worried about telling you. This has been weighing on me for so long.' He pressed his lips together, emotion getting the better of him. 'I'm glad I've got you.'

'Oh, Will, you big baby,' she scoffed affectionately, an old childhood put-down recast as something entirely more loving. 'You don't ever need to keep secrets from me again, all right? You can always tell me stuff. We've got to stick together, us two, right? Come here.' She reached across the table and hugged him. They held one another and it was as if the rest of the world shrank quite away from them, as if they were the only two people left in the restaurant, the city, the universe. Eventually they parted but he could still feel her warmth against him, still felt imprinted by her love for him.

'Okay,' he said rather shakily, still reeling. Her little speech of togetherness had made all the difference though, he registered, remembering to breathe. His shoulders felt lighter, the world a shade brighter. Already he was a different man to the one who'd walked into this restaurant earlier. 'That's enough about me for a while anyway,' he went on, trying to take it all in. 'How about you? How are things going with Heart-throb Jacob?'

He'd assumed he was on safe ground to tease her when, last he'd heard, she'd been so excited about meeting him. But to his surprise, she pulled a face in response, saying she probably wouldn't see him again.

'How come? Not even as friends?' he replied. Back when he'd first heard Jacob had reappeared in his sister's life, Will had looked him up on social media, messaged him to say hi. 'He said how good it was to catch up with you again,' he added, perhaps unwisely, because Alice's face immediately darkened.

'Well … good for *him*, maybe,' she muttered.

Will didn't get it. 'What went wrong? I'll go out with him if you don't want to,' he joked, although she didn't smile. 'I thought he was, like, the nicest man in the world. Wasn't he?'

Alice started detailing how Jacob had made her feel bad about herself, but the whole time she was recounting the things he'd said, Will could only hear Jacob being clumsy, rather than unkind. And yet Alice seemed determined to think the worst of him. Sometimes Will wondered if he would ever understand the way women's brains worked. 'Playing devil's advocate here,' he ventured, 'but is it that much of a deal-breaker? I hear you – he hurt your feelings, but you can still be friends, can't you?'

She didn't look convinced. 'I've got enough friends.'

'Yeah, but it's *Jacob*.' He was disappointed for himself, he realised. He'd been looking forward to seeing his substitute big brother again. 'Don't you think life's too short to miss out on a friendship with someone really good?'

'What, like you and that Scottish woman, you mean?' she retaliated, raising an eyebrow as she crammed a loaded nacho into her mouth.

Touché. He was in no place to lecture anyone, he remembered. A moment of understanding passed between them, a moment that said *We're the same*, and he found it surprisingly comforting. 'Okay, you got me,' he admitted, putting his hands up. 'The McKenzie crap-relationship curse strikes again.'

'Fuck the McKenzie crap-relationship curse,' she said grandly. 'Now, do you know what I'm thinking?' she went on. 'I'm thinking Leni would want us to have dessert *and* maybe a cocktail for good measure, don't you? We haven't been able to do this for a long while, after all. Are you in?'

He drained his glass, feeling a rush of love for her and then one for Leni too, who'd never needed an excuse to indulge. 'Too bloody right, I'm in.'

★

Over the weekend, Will found himself at something of a loose end. Alice was tied up with various plans – going to meet a mosaic artist in Walthamstow on the Saturday, catching up with her girlfriends that same evening, and then heading off to Crouch End on Sunday for brunch with Edie, a former colleague. He tried calling his mum but her line was permanently engaged. Even the cat was busy, now that it had the freedom of the newly installed cat flap, and kept barrelling in and out, triumphant with its own agency.

Will had been back in the country a week now and, Leni-confession aside, he'd so far enjoyed a wave of being the new guy in town, the prodigal son returned to his mother, a novelty act with tales of adventure amidst his old friends. But you couldn't inhabit that role forever, he knew. The wave would eventually crash to shore. At some point, he'd have to make a few choices again. How was he going to spend the rest of his life?

Hi Will, his dad had messaged rather plaintively a few days ago. *Would love to see you now you're back. Can we meet up for a pint? Dinner? A walk?* Will was yet to reply. He and his dad had never had much of a relationship, and although he could tell Tony was trying hard to rebuild family bridges – Alice certainly seemed to think so – something was stopping Will from falling in with his matey suggestions. Maybe when he'd got his life in order, he might feel more confident about accepting his dad's offers, he told himself.

'You're welcome to stay with us as long as you like, you know that, don't you?' his mum had said the other day, eyes shining, as they had lunch in a Soho diner. She'd put her hand on his arm frequently throughout the meal as if unable to stop checking he was really there, in the flesh. Or maybe she was worried about him taking flight again, and planned to grab him and hold on tight if he tried escaping. 'The new house is going to need a lot of elbow grease, you'd be doing us a favour if you stayed to help.'

'Thanks,' he'd replied, appreciating that she was trying to frame this as him being useful, rather than merely sponging off her. That said, he knew full well that it would feel like a backward step, being under his mum's roof, after living independently for so long.

As he roamed Alice's small flat now, his eye fell on the stack of Leni's paperwork that he'd so far studiously avoided looking at too closely, and he found himself remembering how she'd pivoted in her career, from wannabe artist with her own market stall to primary school teacher; how rewarding she'd found retraining, a new way to work. 'Another year as a student, what's not to love?' she'd said cheerfully. He'd been in sixth form at the time, applying for university places himself, and the link must have occurred to her too because then she was saying, 'Hey, we'll both be at uni together, Will – student buddies!' and high-fiving him.

Only his time up north hadn't quite worked out as he'd thought, after all that. His mum had been so proud when he got into Durham University, but he'd felt out of place from the first moment. Everyone else in his halls seemed to know of each other's expensive, exclusive schools, having competed in the same rugby tournaments and public-speaking competitions, moving in similar circles. Whenever anyone asked him which school he'd gone to and he'd replied with the name of his Oxford comprehensive, you could see their eyes glaze over with disinterest; they seemed to detach from him almost at once, as if decoupling from a train that was heading nowhere. It baffled him until a gobby Mancunian girl on his course decoded the situation. 'It's because they're hoping to meet people who can give them a leg up later on,' she'd said, pulling a face. 'Making connections, networking. Rich-kid bollocks.'

He'd bailed out early; went home for Christmas and never returned. 'Don't let a few posh idiots put you off,' Alice had said sympathetically, but it was too late, he'd already changed his mind about the whole idea and applied for an apprenticeship instead.

Now he wondered if he should have stuck it out rather than quit at the first chance. Or if, like Leni, he could maybe try again, return to university as a mature student, someone who'd be less intimidated by the rich-kid bollocks, as the Mancunian girl had put it. The thought was like a mental thunderclap and he found himself sitting very still, recalibrating, as the idea settled fully into his mind and took shape. He could do that, couldn't he? He pictured himself being back in a physics lab, undertaking some knotty piece of research, and the vision was ... actually pretty tempting. Exciting. Why not?

Okay. So there was one option already, he thought, inspired. And wouldn't his teacher sister have loved 'education' as an answer? 'Thank you,' he said, putting his hands together in a prayer, like the woman at the Buddhist temple had done. See – this was what happened when he took his head out of the sand, when he dared to look at what he'd lost.

He remembered Alice chiding him for not having spent time on their sister's memorial page, and in a burst of resolution, he opened his laptop. Having found the page, he scrolled right up to the top, vowing to read everything. Once and for all, he would face up to Leni's loss. No more pretending and looking away.

To his surprise, the experience proved cathartic. He found himself savouring every story and memory, however small, reading through them slowly and affectionately. He broke off for lunch and coffee at intervals but went back and kept on reading. No longer did it seem a chore or a punishment. With so many different voices on the page, so many fragments of Leni's bright, colourful life sparkling back at him, it felt really bloody lovely, as if he was seeing her again, reconnecting after months of deliberate silence. He was letting her back in.

And then, seeing the small grey diary Alice was obsessed with nearby, something occurred to him, a cog clicking in his brain. *I think where she keeps marking her Tuesday nights T 7.30, it's a therapist appointment*, she'd said to Will, but no, he now believed she was wrong. If he wasn't mistaken, it referred to something else altogether.

Back he scrolled through the comments and messages and anecdotes. Back, back, back, until . . .

He read the entry again. Yes. It must be. He picked up his phone and called her immediately. 'Alice,' he said when she answered. 'Have you got a minute? I think I've found something.'

Chapter Twenty-Eight

Belinda was walking towards the Westgate Centre, hoping to pick up a few last bits and pieces for Ray's birthday, when her phone rang with an unknown mobile number. She hesitated – it was probably some crook trying to sell her insurance or similar, let's face it – but then a sixth sense made her pick up.

'Belinda? It's Jackie,' she heard, to her surprise. To her dismay, too – damn it, she should have blocked the call, after all. She wasn't keen on her ex-husband's latest partner – too full of herself by half – although in the next moment, she wondered if everything was all right with Tony. Why else would Jackie be calling? 'I don't suppose you're free to meet for a coffee this morning, are you?'

Belinda hesitated, trying to think of a polite way to say no. 'Er . . .'

'I'll cut to the chase – I've got pre-eclampsia, I'll almost certainly have to go into hospital soon, I'm trying to get everything ticked off my list before I'm plunged into motherhood. Would eleven o'clock suit you?'

It was very hard to argue with a woman using words like pre-eclampsia and hospital as leverage, Belinda thought, grimacing. 'It'll have to be quick,' she replied, rather ungraciously, wondering how on earth she fitted into Jackie's 'list'. Did the other woman want a bitching session about Tony, maybe?

'I can do quick,' Jackie assured her. 'Eleven o'clock at the Art Café – I'll see you there.'

With the prickly, bad-tempered feeling she always got when someone was ordering her around, Belinda reluctantly agreed, and proceeded with her shopping. She was planning to buy Ray a couple of shirts, some of that posh coffee he loved, and the new biography of the rugby star he idolised; apparently Blackwells had signed copies in. Since he'd confronted her in the car park a few days earlier and torn a strip off her for – as he thought – calling Apolline again, there had been an awkwardness between them, a certain coolness. She would make an effort with his birthday presents, and hope it went some way to diminishing her guilty feelings.

At eleven o'clock, she approached the café to see Jackie already sitting outside, frowning at her phone. Her huge bump meant that she was at a slight remove from the table, and she wore a dark grey trouser suit and lilac blouse, her thick glossy hair piled up in a chignon, with make-up so immaculate Belinda wished she'd bothered a bit more with her own that morning.

'Don't get up,' she said as she approached, remembering the indignity of hauling one's body around unnecessarily in the late stages of pregnancy. Perhaps Jackie, like Belinda, didn't take to being told what to do though, because she rose to her feet regardless in order to kiss Belinda politely on the cheek, her spicy perfume making Belinda's nostrils tingle.

They both sat down, then spoke at the same time. 'So,' Jackie began in a businesslike way, just as Belinda said, 'Sorry to hear about the pre-eclampsia. Are you all right?'

Jackie waved a hand. 'One of those things,' she said. 'But yes, I'm fine. And Tony is too, if you were wondering. Although he's worried about you. Which is why I called, because he's been pussyfooting about the subject this whole time, and I thought you'd probably rather just know.'

'Know what?' Belinda asked, taken aback by the abruptness of this opening. The other woman hadn't been exaggerating when she said she could 'do quick'. 'What do you mean, Tony's worried about me?'

'He told me about the psychic hotline you've been ringing,' Jackie went on, so casually it was as if she was chatting about the price of milk.

Belinda's face blazed with the embarrassment of having her precious secret tossed into the open like this, without warning, when until now it had been her private salvation. Embarrassment was swiftly followed by fury. How did *Tony* know? And how dare he gossip about her?

'He's been trying to work up the courage to broach the subject,' Jackie ploughed on, apparently unaware of Belinda's fuming discomfort, 'but . . .'

'It's none of his business,' Belinda interrupted hotly. It was all she could do not to leap up from her chair and march away from this horrible conversation. 'Nor is it yours, for that matter.' A group of people at the next table burst out laughing suddenly and she flinched, imagining they were laughing at her. Did everyone know? she thought wildly, hating the idea of Jackie and Tony talking about her behind her back.

'I found the website and asked one of our legal guys at work to do some digging,' Jackie went on, as if Belinda hadn't spoken. Then her voice softened. 'Look, I'll be straight with you, the findings weren't great. The whole thing is essentially a scam, preying on vulnerable people. The person behind the company is a convicted fraudster; there are links to money laundering and trafficking. It's a really nasty business, Belinda.'

Blood thrummed beneath Belinda's skin as the words attacked her, one by one. The situation felt surreal, as if it couldn't possibly be happening. Like Jackie knew anything about Apolline! 'I trust her,' she said coldly, her chin in the air. *Bore off, Jackie. Take your legal guys and shove them.* 'I believe her. And I—' She was about to say *I need her*, but a ponytailed waitress came over to take their drink orders just then and she had to break off, the words unsaid.

She did need her, Belinda thought, staring doggedly past Jackie to the group of homeless men clustered around the war memorial with cans of extra-strong cider, and the pigeons waddling about, their chest feathers gleaming iridescent pink and green. Without Apolline, how could she go on? It was like an obsession. A compulsion she couldn't ignore.

'Okay, so that's a flat white, a peppermint tea and an apple cake. Is that everything, ladies? I'll be right back,' the waitress said, before bustling away again. Silence fell at the table. A busker outside Marks and Spencer was playing 'Cheek to

Cheek' on the electric guitar and the tune made Belinda remember dancing around the kitchen with Will when he was a toddler, his soft face against hers as she sang to him and whirled him about. *I'm in heaven . . .*

'I'm not trying to be a smart-arse here,' Jackie said after a moment. 'I promise I didn't come here to upset you or make you feel bad.'

Oh really. Like she wasn't absolutely loving rubbing Belinda's nose in it, Belinda thought, humiliation rising. 'You and Tony have had a good old laugh at me, I bet,' she said, her throat tight. 'How did he even know about Apolline anyway?'

'Ray told him. They bumped into each other,' Jackie replied. 'And no one's been laughing at you, I swear. Honestly.'

Belinda chanced a look at the other woman, half expecting to see a crowing contempt on her face, but was brought up short by how sincere Jackie's brown eyes were instead. Compassionate, even. Her head swam, no longer sure what to think, who to believe. Wishing she didn't have to think about this at all. Why couldn't everyone just leave her alone?

'I haven't told Tony what the guys at work uncovered,' Jackie went on. 'This is me talking to you, woman to woman. Nobody else has to be involved. I just thought it was important that . . . well, that *you* knew.'

The waitress reappeared with their drinks and cake, clattering them down on the table. After she'd gone, another weighty silence swelled between them, a silence Belinda didn't know how to fill. She fiddled about adding sweetener to her coffee, stirring so briskly it slopped over the edge of the mug. Jackie, meanwhile, cut the cake in two and put the plate between them. 'Help yourself,' she said. 'I'm meant to be watching my sugar intake but I couldn't resist.'

'Thank you,' Belinda mumbled, taking a piece and nibbling it. Not as good as Alice's, she thought, remembering the spiced apple and walnut Alice had made for her birthday once, the most delicious thing she'd ever tasted. Unfortunately, the family's best baker seemed to have fallen out of love with the whole business; there had been no cakes baked for anyone for almost a year now. *Sorry, I just don't feel like it*, she'd said when Belinda had tentatively put in a request for her last birthday, back in November. Neither of them had mentioned a cake for Ray; Belinda would buy one rather than ask again, she'd decided.

'You've had a horrible time,' Jackie said quietly after several moments had passed. 'The worst. I'm not judging you for anything, I swear I'm not. I can see how ... how comforting it must have felt for you to speak to this woman.' She dabbed up a stray cake crumb with her finger, her gaze lowered. 'I had a couple of miscarriages with my ex-husband,' she went on in a rush. 'And I felt so low for a while afterwards, I could totally imagine myself having done the same as you. Wanting to feel that it wasn't the end.'

Belinda nodded, the words piercing her with their insight. Wasn't that the nub of it, after all, that she just couldn't face it being the end, for her and Leni? 'Sorry to hear about your miscarriages,' she mumbled after another pause.

'And I'm sorry if I've upset you, being too forthright,' Jackie replied. 'You're right, it *is* none of my business, but I hate the thought of anyone being manipulated. Preyed upon.'

A moment passed. Jackie's words about money laundering and trafficking were belatedly making themselves heard in Belinda's brain and she felt a sense of resignation steal over her, as if her last defences were being knocked down. She didn't like the thought of anyone being manipulated either. Not least her own self.

She bowed her head and sighed. 'Okay,' she admitted grudgingly. 'Yes.' It was all she could manage for a second, the acknowledgement like a stone in her throat. 'I ... I kind of knew,' she muttered when Jackie didn't respond. 'If I'm honest, I kind of did know that it wasn't real. That I was kidding myself.' She exhaled heavily, feeling thoroughly wretched. *There. Happy now, Jackie? Satisfied?* 'But I didn't care because anything from my daughter – even if it wasn't true – felt better than nothing.' She swallowed, the words painful to say. 'It's so hard to accept that there really is nothing left of her. I can't bring myself to believe it. I don't *want* to believe it.' Her heart splintered at the idea that now she would have to forgo this last lifeline of hers, the precious connection she'd valued above all others. But how could she carry on with her phone calls after Jackie had laid out the truth so starkly? She couldn't. It was impossible.

She had a little cry to herself after Jackie had gone, retreating to the Westgate Centre loos, feeling as if she was losing Leni all over again. Feeling stupid and embarrassed too, that it had been Tony's partner of all people who had given her the facts like that. Typical! Sometimes it was as if the whole world was queueing up to poke a stick at you.

But then she blew her nose and pulled her shoulders back,

attempting to rally herself. It was lucky, then, that Belinda McKenzie was made of strong stuff, wasn't it? She would delete Apolline's number, she would move on, she vowed. And – looking on the bright side – hadn't she been hoping to give Ray a great birthday present? Telling him she was giving up the calls would definitely do the job, she supposed, pulling a face at her reflection. Silver lining, Belinda! Even if it didn't feel like much of one right now.

Walking towards the bus stop a few minutes later, no longer in the mood to shop, she was jolted from her thoughts by the surprise sight of Ellis walking quickly ahead of her, his slouchy lope unmistakable. She shouted after him but he didn't hear her and her eyes narrowed with renewed suspicion as she watched him disappear into the crowd. What was Ellis doing here in Oxford? His new job was in Abingdon, eight miles away, and it was still only eleven forty-five, too early for him to have popped over for lunch. This was his second day working there too – surely he shouldn't be wandering around town? Unless he was here for a meeting?

Unless he's lying to us, she thought in the next moment, unease churning low in her stomach. *Unless he's playing me and Ray for fools*. Had she been right not to trust him all along?

Back home, after a quick lunch, Belinda had to go over to Summertown with Ray to meet with their solicitor and sign some papers relating to the house sale. Not wanting to ignite another argument, she'd decided not to mention seeing Ellis, but then, when Ray idly commented that he was thinking of giving his son the money for a car so he could get to and from work more easily, Belinda found it impossible to hold back her concerns. 'Is he really working, though?' she blurted out. They were walking up the high street at the time, and he stared at her, so startled by the question that he almost stumbled over a blackboard A-sign outside one of the bakeries.

'What? What do you mean?'

'This job he says he's doing in Abingdon – do you actually have proof of it?' she persisted, quailing a little before his look and hoping she was doing the right thing. Jackie's words echoed in her head – *I thought you'd probably rather just know* – and she forced herself on. 'Only I saw him in town this morning and . . . well, it made me wonder, that's all.'

'Made you wonder what?' Ray asked, then went on before she could reply. 'Of course he's working in Abingdon! Why would he lie about that? You must have been mistaken; it must have been someone who looked like him. Didn't you say you'd been meaning to book an optician's appointment?'

Thankfully, they arrived at the solicitor's office at that moment, and Belinda didn't have to answer him. With their attention now taken up with the documents they needed to sign, that might have been the end of the Ellis-in-Oxford mystery. But then, on leaving the building again, Ray checked his phone and made a sudden noise of surprise.

'Everything all right?' Belinda asked warily.

'It's Nicky,' he said, a frown creasing his forehead.

Nicky? His ex-wife never contacted him. Belinda was surprised they even had each other's number. 'Saying what?' she asked.

'That's strange.' Ray passed a hand over his head, still staring at the phone before reading the message aloud. "'We're trying to get hold of Ellis – he hasn't been at home for nearly two weeks. Said he was going to stay with a friend but have just found out that's not true. Have you heard anything from him? Let me know if you do.'"

They looked at each other, Belinda's stomach turning slowly over. Something fishy was definitely afoot. *Leni says not to trust the mouse*, she heard Apolline repeat in her head, alarm bells ringing louder than ever, before remembering with a sharp pang that she was not supposed to be caring what Apolline said any more. 'What's that all about, do you think?' she managed to ask.

'Let's find out,' he said grimly, pressing Call and holding the phone to his ear. 'Hi Nicky,' he said. 'It's me. Ellis is here in Oxford. He's okay. I thought you knew?'

Chapter Twenty-Nine

Leni McKenzie memorial page

One of my happiest memories of Leni was the fuss she made of me for my eighteenth birthday. She sent me a bottle of vodka and some engraved shot glasses on the day, then invited me to stay with her in London, and took me 'out on the town', as she put it, to a really cool Camden bar and then an even cooler Camden club. I was so dazzled by the experience, and felt so grown-up, it was the best gift she could have given me. At the time I remember thinking that it was the best day of my life! When she shone her light in your direction like that, it was always impossible to resist the heady glow it cast around you. I definitely felt a better person in her reflected light, no question.

Thanks for being my big sister, Leni. Even though you once tickled me until I wet myself.

Love Will x

That afternoon, Tony had just closed the sale on a top-of-the-range Audi – still got it, he told himself, filing the paperwork with satisfaction – when his phone rang: Jackie's number. 'They're keeping me in,' she said glumly, without preamble. 'Blood pressure through the roof. A ticking off from the midwife for overdoing it.'

'Overdoing it? I thought you were taking things easy today!' he exclaimed in alarm. She'd assured him that very morning – promised him, in fact – that she was taking a duvet day to rest before her antenatal check-up. How could anyone overdo a duvet day?

'Well ... as it happened, I had some stuff to sort out. But it's done now.'

She sounded flat and his heart went out to her, knowing how hard she'd found the new restraints of pregnancy, along with its accompanying handmaidens of tiredness and anxiety. 'But the baby's all right? The tests are okay?' His voice rose with worry and he turned away, but not before he noticed his boss, Annabeth, glancing across from her desk in concern.

'We're both fine,' she said. 'There's no immediate worry, you don't have to drop everything and come over. I'm just a bit apprehensive, I guess. I don't think I could bear it if anything went wrong now, Tony. I don't think I could cope if—'

'Nothing's going to go wrong,' he assured her before she had time to finish the sentence. 'Do you hear me? You're in the best place, you'll be well looked after. I'll come over and keep you company after work, and we'll make a plan, okay? We've got this.'

He hung up and sat with his head in his hands for a moment. 'Everything all right, Tone?' Annabeth asked.

'Just going to get some fresh air,' he muttered, striding

across the showroom before she could say anything else. He was remembering the days before Will was born, the stress he had felt as he wondered whose baby his wife was carrying, how dreadfully the question had weighed upon his shoulders in the months spent waiting to find out. In hindsight, he had detached himself there and then from his poor unborn son in an unconscious act of self-protection, dreading seeing Graham fucking Fenton leering back at him from the infant's features. And then Will was born – darling, tiny Will – and he had been so visibly Tony's son with his unmistakable McKenzie nose and long legs, Tony had buckled with relief, right there in the maternity ward. *Oh look, he's overcome*, the midwives had said, smiling. They didn't know the half of it.

It seemed the damage was already done though, an oily mark of doubt staining what should have been a bright and joyful new relationship. He had held his little boy, kissed his small pink face, he had fed and comforted him, he had hung in there for all the months of illness and worry that ensued when Will caught one bug after another, and ping-ponged between home and hospital with exhausting regularity. But still something was missing, the love refusing to simply pour forth for his son the way it had with his daughters. He couldn't forgive Belinda for betraying him, for what she'd put him through. Even after Fenton moved away, whenever Tony glanced through the kitchen window, he still half expected to see the other man lurking in the next-door garden, hoping for a secret tryst with his wife. He had turned away from her and, by association, from his children too. He told himself his exit was for the best, but as a result, his relationship with the children had suffered. Worse, he had taken his eye off the ball, allowed that to happen.

Outside the showroom, he walked across the car park, the wind snatching at his hair and causing him to shiver in his shirtsleeves. He thought about Jackie and the new baby, and then he thought again about Belinda, Graham Fenton and Will, the unholy trinity he had pushed from his mind for all of these years. How could he have let his anger poison the relationship with his own children? The other day when they spoke, Belinda had said she blamed herself for their split, but the only person to blame for Tony's subsequent letting down of their kids was him. He should have done better for them all, particularly for Will, the boy he'd found so hard to love.

The wind blew into his face, causing tears to leak from his eyes. And now here he was, on the verge of it all happening again. Before he became a father for the fourth time, it was imperative that he make amends with Will. If losing Leni had taught him anything, it was that life could be heartbreakingly fragile. More – it had taught him that having a family was too precious a gift to squander.

On impulse, he called his son's number. Why wait a moment longer? 'Will, it's Dad,' he said. 'I'd love to see you. When can I see you?'

Collapsing gratefully into bed that night, Tony could hardly keep his eyes open long enough to turn off the bedside lamp. He'd gone to see his pregnant partner in hospital, loaded up with books, extra pyjamas and her favourite toiletries – she might be there for six weeks, according to the doctors – and he'd finally managed a proper conversation with his son too, where he'd laid his cards on the table. 'I haven't been a great dad and I'm sorry,' he'd said, coming straight to the point. 'But I'm determined to make a better fist of it from now on, if you'll give me another chance.' All being well with Jackie and the baby, Will was going to come and stay that weekend, and Tony was already thinking up a list of father–son activities for them. Nothing would stop him this time.

He was so deeply asleep that he didn't hear his phone at first. He was dreaming that he'd returned to the children's old primary school and found Leni there, a little girl again, her hair in bunches. 'Is it really you?' he asked, astonished with joy. Her face split into a giant smile on seeing him and she jumped up with a shout of 'Daddy!' Then he realised someone was saying his name.

'Tony. *Tony!*'

'Mmm,' he mumbled because he'd been about to scoop Leni up into his arms, his beautiful little girl, and he didn't want this to be taken away from him.

'Tony. *Tony!*' It was his phone, with the ringtone of Jackie's voice that she'd recorded to alert him to her calls. A joke of hers, but he had been too embarrassed to admit he didn't know how to change it back, and now he was stuck with it. 'Tony. *Tony!*' He rolled over, suddenly more alert, and scrabbled to answer the call.

'Hello?' Three thirty in the morning, he registered with a lurch of panic. Was there ever good news at three thirty in the morning?

'It's starting,' his partner said, without so much as a *Good morning.* Fair enough, actually. 'The baby's coming. Oh, Tony, it's too early. I'm so scared!'

'I'm on my way,' he said, already out of bed and heaving on a pair of trousers one-handed. 'I'll be with you as soon as possible, okay? Text me if you think of anything I can bring. It's going to be all right, Jac.'

Fuck. *Would* it be all right though? he thought, blindly throwing on a shirt, finding some socks, almost falling down the stairs in his haste to get going. Last night, they'd been told that the baby would be induced a few weeks earlier than normal, but not this early. 'Premature baby, thirty-four weeks, what is the survival rate, please?' he asked his phone as he started the car engine. His voice caught on the word 'survival' and he squeezed his eyes shut briefly, remembering how blasé he'd been about his older children's births; cavalier, almost. He knew nothing then, obviously. He had no idea that things could go catastrophically wrong.

'Preterm babies born between thirty-one and thirty-four weeks' gestation have a ninety-five per cent chance of survival,' the automated voice told him.

'Thank you,' he said, releasing the handbrake and reversing out of the drive. The road was silent, the night velvety black apart from the dull orange balls of light from the lamp posts. Ninety-five per cent chance of survival – that was good, wasn't it? Good odds. 'Please God, please let them both be okay,' he muttered, voice low.

'I'm sorry, I didn't understand that,' the automated voice replied politely, making him jump.

'Don't worry about it,' he muttered, scrabbling to turn off the app. Then he reached the empty ring road and hit the accelerator. 'I'm coming, Jackie,' he said into the night. 'Hang in there, both of you.'

Three forty in the morning and Belinda was wide awake, fretting. Beside her, Ray snored gently, occasionally making smacking sounds with his lips and, not for the first time, Belinda marvelled at his ability to sleep, even in the most extreme situations. She, meanwhile, couldn't prevent her brain from looping around earlier conversations on repeat.

It had not been the most pleasant of days, overall. After Ray had seen the message from Nicky, he'd called her at once, right there in the street, his face becoming more ashen with every passing moment. According to his ex-wife, there were a number of important details Ellis hadn't thought to share with his dad. Like the fact that his girlfriend back home, Paloma, was pregnant with their child, which had come as a shock to them both – an unwelcome one, by the sound of things. Also that Ellis had walked out on his old job without a word to anyone, apparently vanishing overnight. He seemed to have gone to ground, Nicky said, anguished – except, of course, he hadn't. The blow to Ray's heart was written all over his face as he explained to his ex that Ellis had appeared in Oxford and, in hindsight, might have taken advantage of his father's eagerness for them to be reunited by coming up with stories about a job interview and the subsequent offer. Yes, Ray had been all too quick to believe him. No, of course he hadn't thought to ask many probing questions.

'So you're telling me he's been with you this whole time?' Nicky cried, loud enough for Belinda to hear the snap in her voice. It was the sound of a woman at the end of her tether with worry. 'And you didn't think to *say* anything?'

'I didn't realise he was missing!' Ray replied miserably, his body sagging as if the stuffing had been knocked out of him. Belinda felt her heart break for his crushed face, the realisation that his new-found father–son relationship wasn't actually as good – certainly not as honest – as he'd hoped. 'What do you want me to do when he gets in later?'

'Tell him he needs to ring Paloma, and then ring me, in that order,' came the reply. 'And to come back here and sort his life out, for heaven's sake!'

Ray's hand was trembling on the phone as the call ended. 'You probably heard all that, didn't you?' he said, downcast.

Belinda took Ray's arm and steered him along the pavement. 'I caught most of it,' she replied. 'I'm sorry, Ray. It sounds a bit of a mess.'

'My own son, and he lied to me,' he said, devastated. 'He's lied about everything and I just gobbled it all up like an idiot. Why couldn't he tell me the truth from the start, confide in me? I would have heard him out, I wouldn't have judged him, not for a second. It's not like I've gone through life myself getting everything right, after all.'

Belinda was still holding on to him because he didn't seem all that steady on his feet. 'You mustn't blame yourself,' she said. 'We believe what we want to believe when it comes to our children, because we want to think the best of them. And we want them to love us in return.'

'Yes, but . . .' Ray shook his head. 'What's he been doing all day, when he told us he was at work? Why go through such an elaborate charade?'

Well, Belinda felt like saying, *he was in Oxford this morning like I told you*, but she didn't want to rub his nose in it. 'He's obviously troubled,' she said tactfully instead.

'I'll say,' Ray snorted as they started walking again. 'So the night he rang and said he was in the area – that must have been when he heard his girlfriend was pregnant. Nicky said he vanished for a night – sounds like he panicked and just got out of town. Then he went back to Crickhowell, apparently with some story about getting drunk and stopping over at a friend's. But he must have decided all over again that he couldn't cope, which was when he got in touch with me a second time to say he'd got the job. The job he made up, like you suspected.'

There was such anguish in his voice. How Belinda wished she'd been wrong. 'Look, he's completely freaked out, poor lad, at the thought he's going to be a father – which is under-standable, if it was unplanned. But let's be grateful he came to you at all, rather than being on his own, yeah? He turned to you not once but twice, in fact. Even if he wasn't truthful, that's no reflection on you: more that he's been so confused. He saw you as a port in a storm – that's a positive you can take from this. And you didn't let him down, did you? You were there for him.' She squeezed his hand encouragingly. 'We'll talk to him later when he gets home, sort everything out then.'

'This is all my fault,' Ray had groaned. 'If I'd been a better role model in the first place, he wouldn't be so terrified at the prospect of fatherhood; he'd have had the confidence to deal with it.' He turned even paler as something else occurred to him. 'Christ, and this would make me a *grandad*. A grandad, Bel! I'm not that old, surely?'

A thrill passed through Belinda immediately at these words. In all the drama, she hadn't yet put two and two together, but oh heavens, she would definitely be claiming step-grandma rights if Ellis and his girlfriend went ahead and had the baby, just try and stop her. 'I think it would be absolutely lovely!' she cried. Already her mind was racing ahead to how they could turn the box room in their new house into a tiny nursery. Would it be over the top for her to start buying some sweet little baby vests and keeping an eye out for second-hand cots in the nearby charity shops? 'But we can cross that bridge when we come to it,' she added, possibly more to herself than Ray.

That evening when Ellis came home, it all kicked off. Barely had he walked through the door when Ray lost his cool, demanding to know how long his son would have carried on his pretence, and why he hadn't simply been honest. Ellis blanched then leaped straight on the defensive. 'Yeah, you got me,' he said, putting his hands up sarcastically, avoiding eye contact with either of them. 'Turns out I'm a loser, just like you, Dad.' And then he'd stormed out of the house again, slamming the door behind him.

Belinda had rushed after him down the road, still in her socks, begging him to come back and talk the whole thing through properly. It didn't matter, she assured him, they could help in any way he needed. He'd snapped at her to get off his case with such viciousness, though, that she'd come to a forlorn halt there in the street, the freezing pavement numbing the soles of her feet.

He strode off round the corner and out of sight, while she was forced to slink back home, despondent. There she found Ray motionless on the sofa, head in his hands, proving himself to be impervious to all Belinda's words of encouragement as the evening wore on. 'He'll come back, he's just embarrassed and wrong-footed, that's all,' she told him at intervals, but Ray merely shook his head.

'I've lost him again, haven't I?' he kept saying. 'I've blown it now. You heard what he said – he thinks I'm a loser. And he's right. I am.'

'You're not,' she told him staunchly. 'You listen to me now, Ray: you're a good man, and you've been a good dad to him while he's been here. He knows that. He'll be back soon, you wait, and then you can both clear the air and move on.'

But it was the early hours now, and Ellis still wasn't back. *Would* he come back? Was he already well on his way to a new place to hide out and lick his wounds? The wind howled in the chimney and she hoped he was someplace warm, at least.

She stiffened as a new sound reached her ears. A scratching noise – a key in the lock? – followed by the small familiar judder of the front door being opened, where it was swollen and always caught on the floor. Then a muffled thud, which she recognised as the door being closed by someone trying to be quiet. Her handbag was down in the hall but she didn't care. She knew it wasn't a thief. She nudged Ray, who gave a sudden snort as he woke up. 'He's back,' she hissed to him urgently. 'Ellis. He's downstairs. Go and talk to him. Give him a hug, tell him you love him.'

Ray's eyes opened and he blinked a few times, so she said it all over again. He sat up, then reached over and patted her duvet-covered shoulder. 'Thank you,' he murmured, then went and put on his dressing gown, leaving her alone in the bed.

The door creaked behind him and she listened for a little while, ears straining in the darkness, but there were no raised voices to be heard. No shouts, no accusations. She thought she might have detected the hiss of the kettle being boiled but perhaps that was her imagination.

Tiredness crept over her at last and she closed her eyes, meaning merely to rest them for a while until Ray came back to bed, but then her body became heavier, her mind finally slowed and she was out.

Chapter Thirty

Leni McKenzie memorial page

I only met Leni recently – at a trampolining class! – but she was really fun company and super friendly, suggesting we go for a drink afterwards and taking a genuine interest in everyone. She said she loved trampolining – it made her feel as if she was flying. Leni, you were a beautiful person. Fly free, my friend.

    Shanice

Alice had just emerged from the tube station at St Paul's when she realised her phone was ringing in her bag. *Dad*, she saw on the screen and frowned a little as she swiped to answer it. Calling for a chat at eight forty-five in the morning? This was not his usual style. 'Hi,' she said, walking quickly along the street, the phone pressed to her ear. Up ahead you could see the cathedral, although give it another few weeks and the leaves on the plane trees would be fully out, transforming the view. 'Everything all right?'

She couldn't make out what he was saying at first, partly

because of a bus roaring by in the vicinity but also because he sounded so garbled – was he *crying*? Then she caught a few key phrases: *four pounds, intensive care* – and her brain caught up instantly. 'Jackie's had the baby?'

'A little girl. A beautiful little girl. She's tiny but she's a fighter.' His voice shook again – he *was* crying – then he went on. 'Jackie was amazing. They're both amazing. She – the baby – is in intensive care, she'll need help breathing for a while – but she's got long legs and the McKenzie nose, just like you, Will and Leni.'

'Oh, Dad, congratulations,' she said. A new sister, she thought, feeling a strange twist inside. A tiny new long-legged sister. 'Are *you* all right? Was the labour okay?'

He launched into a lengthy description of what sounded like one stressful complication after another, ending in an emergency C-section for Jackie. He sounded so raw and emotional as he unpacked the story; Alice could hardly bear to hear his vulnerability, especially when she was so many miles away. For the first time in years, she found herself wishing she could give him a hug. 'Sounds like you both did great, Dad,' she assured him. 'So, what are you going to call her, then? My little sister?'

My little sister. Words she'd never said before. Words that gave her goosebumps as soon as she heard them aloud. She'd assumed she'd only ever have one sister in her life. Even though she'd known about the baby for months, the idea of an extra sibling had felt more of an abstract concept than reality, the latest nonsense her dad had got himself into. She'd been almost unable to believe in it – in her – until now. But as of this morning, there was a brand new and extremely real person in the world, her baby sister, small, pink and breathing in an incubator, completely unaware that she had marked herself an extra branch on Alice's family tree.

'We're not sure yet,' he said. 'Jackie's a bit out of it at the moment – it's been one hell of a night – but we'll talk properly later. I'll keep you posted.' He cleared his throat and she pictured him there in a hospital corridor, presumably a mixture of adrenalin and emotional exhaustion. 'I'd better go, I need to ring Jackie's sisters and parents, but I'll talk to you again soon, okay?'

'Congratulations, Dad. I'm sending all my love to the three of you. And yeah, whenever it's a good time for a chat, I'm always pleased to hear from you,' she told him.

'Thank you, darling. Love you. Take care.'

'Love you, Dad.' The words rang around her head. *Love you.* Wow. That was nice, wasn't it? Being able to tell your own dad you loved him and to mean it. To hear him say the words himself, moreover, and know that they were sincere. *Did you hear that too, Len?* she thought, bemused, putting her phone away. *I didn't imagine it, did I?*

Feeling dazzled by such intense and unexpected news, she headed towards the office, glancing back at the shopping mall she'd just walked past, wondering if any of the shops there sold baby clothes, already mentally fast-forwarding to her lunch break when she could mooch around the displays, searching for the tiniest of tiny outfits for a very little sister. Her new, hours-old sister, she marvelled again. She wondered, too, how differently she might have felt had Leni still been around. The two of them would probably have expressed to one another the grossness of their ageing dad becoming a father again; there might even have been a certain lacing of resentment in their reaction to the birth announcement, a slight curling of the lip. *Nothing to do with me.*

Instead, the new baby felt totemic to Alice, a chance to start again; it felt like the quiet (or perhaps noisy) turning of a corner into a reshaped family set-up. She even found herself thinking differently towards Jackie – fondly! Gratefully! – for giving her another sibling. An image of *kintsugi* pottery came to mind once more, the broken pieces held together by golden cement, and thereby transcending the original to become something altered but equally beautiful. Beautiful in a new way; she could celebrate that. Maybe all families were *kintsugi* pots at the end of the day. Hers certainly seemed to be piecing itself back together, what with Will's return, and the conviction that they were all trying hard to reconnect.

Moreover, now that Will had unburdened himself of his secret, he seemed less stressed, more willing to talk to her about Leni. Having finally read through her memorial page (and even added to it), he had also solved the puzzle of the Tuesday 'T 7.30' entries, spotting an entry by a woman called Shanice referencing a Tuesday trampolining class Leni had attended. (Hadn't Leni always wanted to fly? Alice loved the image of her bouncing high in the air.) As the moderator of the memorial page, Alice was able to contact Shanice, asking if they could meet. 'Tell me *everything*,' she imagined herself saying the moment this happened.

The street was full of office workers, moving like a tide

along the pavement together, and in the crowd ahead Alice recognised the back of a man's head, the colour of his raincoat. Her heart played a little chord of surprise. Darren? Yes, she thought, as he glanced sideways and she saw his handsome profile. It was him! *Will you just go for it with Baron Darren already?* she imagined Leni encouraging her, and Alice smiled, figuring there might never be a luckier day for her than this, the day when her new baby sister had arrived in the world. Why not? She could just ask him for a drink, couldn't she? Let's face it, he'd asked *her* for a drink a few weeks ago, it wasn't as if he didn't fancy her back. And wasn't she trying to be less passive in her life, to make things happen for herself? They could have a drink, maybe something nice to eat; they could start over. This time she wouldn't become so drunk she couldn't remember getting home, either.

They were nearly at her building now and she decided to make her move, nab him before they went inside. 'Darren!' she called, but a bus wheezed past at that second and she didn't think he'd heard her.

'Darren!' she said again, trying to catch him up. But then, reaching the steps up to the building moments after he did, she realised he wasn't alone. He was holding hands with a woman in a stylish grey coat and then – oh shit – they were embracing and kissing each other, and Alice didn't know where to look.

'Will you be back for dinner, do you think?' she heard the woman asking. 'Only Becca said she might pop round, and—'

The rest of the woman's evening plans were lost in the hoot of a taxi sailing by, but it didn't matter. Alice had heard enough to have already created a whole picture in her head. They were together, Darren and this woman, a couple who lived together, who shared dinner plans and a bed and – well, their lives, basically. Although presumably he hadn't shared the fact that he was partial to one-night stands, and asking out other women in the office lift.

Alice felt a twinge inside – why did people have to be such bullshitters? It was so disappointing! She walked past them, deliberately catching Darren with her elbow as she went by. 'Wanker,' she said for good measure, striding straight ahead. Not before she heard his girlfriend (wife?) ask, 'Did that woman just call you a wanker? Why did she call you a wanker, Daz?'

Sorry, sister, she thought, swiping her company pass on the electronic gates and ducking into a lift, exhaling as the doors slid closed. But take it from me, that's the right word for him. Going up!

You win some, you lose some, she was telling herself by the time she was due at the fourth floor for her meeting in the marketing department. Darren was no real loss to her, at the end of the day, because her emotional balance sheet was far ahead in credit after the earlier bulletin from her father. She felt pretty good as she walked towards the meeting room, optimism swelling inside her. Yes, the universe could trip you up and take from you, but it could reward you too, if you hung on in there and kept trying. She would give this meeting her best shot and cross her fingers that Fate was feeling generous. *Of course you can do this*, she heard her former colleague Edie say in her head. They had met up for brunch the previous weekend, so that Alice could run some of her ideas past her, and she'd received an affectionate, confidence-boosting pep talk into the bargain. *You're good, Alice. We've missed you. So many clients have been asking after you!*

There were three of them waiting for her in the room – two men, one woman, and all of them a good decade her senior. Her heart started pounding as the introductions were made and she set up her PowerPoint presentation. Now that she was here, the implications of what a stepping stone this could be resounded within her. *Do not fuck this up*, she ordered herself.

'I asked to meet with you because I have had over ten years' marketing experience, specialising in social media strategies,' she began. 'And although the company does a brilliant job of serving its loyal, older consumer base, I believe some of your products could be repackaged and sold to a younger demographic in addition.' She was gabbling, her nerves on show, she realised. It was so long since she'd had to do anything like this without a full team backing her up, without having fully chewed over every tiny detail together. Practising in front of her brother plus a disinterested ginger cat was really not the same. Now here she was flying solo, and even though, beforehand, she'd been telling herself how exhilarated she felt, the truth was, she was actually plain old bricking it.

She cleared her throat, forced herself to breathe slower. She thought about Leni, who'd be cheering her on if she could; she thought about her tiny new sister, the raw pink newborn face in the photo her dad had sent. *Come on, you can do this.* 'Until last year, I was heading up the socials team at

ReImagine, an award-winning branding and communications agency,' she went on, 'but as of January, I've been working here, in the claims department, on a maternity cover. Long story,' she added quickly, when she saw the woman's eyebrows rise. It wasn't the moment for all of that. 'I'm passionate about social media, and the rocket boosters it can give to a campaign, so I've been thinking about how I could increase interaction for Sage and Golding's output.'

One of the men was glancing down at his watch; she seemed to be losing him already. Shit. Time to cut to the chase. 'For example, over the last week, I've embarked on a guerrilla campaign in my spare time,' she said. 'Not mentioning the company by name, just trying to build up some interest out there by being nimble, witty and engaged. Creating a bit of mystery. I've started a digital identity called Guess Who? to stir up interest, with the idea being that I – or an interested company – would eventually reveal all with a big fanfare. But as it stands, you don't have to go along with any of this; it's packaged so that any insurance firm could run with it if they chose to.' She paused, hoping her subtext would sink in: *if you don't like it, I can take my followers elsewhere.*

She clicked on the first slide, and the three of them sat forward in their seats as she explained the thinking behind the name and her simple teasing strategy. Then she took them through her progress so far, showing them a bar chart she'd drawn up, which tracked the rise of engagement throughout the days. There were small increases in numbers but nothing to write home about, and she caught the woman narrowing her eyes as if to say, *Is that it? I gave up half an hour of my day for this?*

'Then,' Alice went on, 'I got a lucky break. Or rather,' she corrected herself, 'the lucky break that comes after you've put yourself in the right place at the right time. I became part of the story.'

It had happened two days ago, when she'd ended up in (digital) conversation with a game-show-winning singer, Liam Frost. Usually famous people ignored advertisers who tried to engage with them, let alone mystery advertisers with hardly any followers, but Frost was something of a maverick, known for occasionally chatting with a fan or follower for no reason other than that he was a bit bored (or, let's face it, a bit pissed). She happened to be scrolling through a list of famous accounts she'd set up Guess Who? to follow when she noticed that he'd recently posted an image of himself with a faceful of make-up, as a promo for his upcoming tour: ruby-red lips, massive false eyelashes, the works. *My oh my!*, she'd written in reply. *Please tell us those gorge eyelashes are fully insured? Because they should be!*

It was only an off-the-cuff remark, a small piece of bread dangled before a very big fish, but to her great surprise, he'd bitten. He replied with a laughing-face emoji. *Eyelash insurance! I knew there was something I'd forgotten to put on my list!*

Babe, she wrote back, heart thudding with her own daring, *you wouldn't believe some of the things we have to cover ... If only I could tell you more!* She'd signed off with the hashtags #GuessWho and #GuessWhat and then, to her immense shock and even bigger joy, he retweeted her comment.

'He retweeted my comment!' she told the marketing panel. 'To his 62,000 followers, with the quote tweet – *Here's a fun guessing game for you all.* And as a result, hundreds of them responded – I'm still getting responses even now – and there was a knock-on effect of a huge spike of new followers for the Guess Who? account.'

She brought up the slide showing Liam's tweet, along with the 5,000 likes and the 600 comments, and the man she'd previously seen glancing at his watch sat up straighter in his seat. 'Gosh!' he said.

'*Would* we insure a person's eyelashes, though?' the other man asked, looking perplexed.

'These are your people,' she went on, clicking the next slide to show a bar chart illustrating the acceleration in interaction. She'd already decided not to show them the actual comments, most of which were decidedly on the smutty side. 'These are your customers, the very consumers it would be good to reach. And this is where I would go from here, if you were interested in working with me.'

She ended with a summing-up of two different approaches available: first, that they could build on the initial success of her Guess Who? account with a full strategy she could draw up for them; or second, that she would dream up an entirely new approach within their existing social media channels that would broaden their output and appeal. 'Either way, there's a huge market out there we could bring into the fold,' she said. 'A huge market that's currently looking elsewhere. I know where they are, and I'd love to help you connect with them.'

She could hear the passion ringing through her voice and hoped it was audible to them too, because she wanted this, so much, and she knew she could deliver on her promises. They went on to ask her a few questions – firstly about how this might dovetail (or not) with her current maternity cover role, and then some light grilling about her experience and previous campaigns she'd worked on. Before she knew it, her time was up, and she was shaking hands with them all, dishing out her newly made business cards and thanking them for their time. Done.

Leaving the room again, she felt light-headed, wondering what they might be saying about her: whether they had genuinely liked her ideas or whether they'd merely been polite. She kept thinking ruefully about the man who'd mused, '*Would we insure a person's eyelashes, though?*', seemingly missing the entire point of what she'd done. Well, she'd tried her best, and if it wasn't their thing, she could keep working up the Guess Who? concept and present it to a different insurance company. Why not? She believed in her own idea; she backed herself as a winner. This was definitely a good outcome.

Once outside, she took her phone off Do Not Disturb and saw that a couple of texts had come in – from her dad and from Lou, both wishing her luck. Also, to her great surprise, there was a message from Jacob.

Hello Alice, she read and then she put her hand to her chest as the word 'sorry' leaped out at her. She forced herself to take a deep breath and then read it all the way through properly.

Hello Alice, hope you're doing okay. I've been thinking about you since our last night out – and thinking too that I didn't exactly behave like a friend should. I'm sorry if I inadvertently trampled on your grief. I don't know why I thought badgering you into hurrying on with your life was a good decision – I could see on your face that it wasn't. Anyway, I'm sorry. No excuses, just sorry. And if you want another Flying Beauties nostalgia trip out, I've thought of the perfect place. Let me know if you're interested. Love Jacob x

She could feel her heart pounding beneath her fingers but she was smiling too, feeling good. Good about herself. Good about him. Good about the fact that as soon as it was lunch-time, she was going to hit the shops and hunt out the cutest outfit and hat she could find for her new baby sister. Maybe splurge on a bunch of brightly coloured anemones for herself too, just because she had a feeling her luck might be turning at last, that she might finally be clawing her way upwards once more. Sod cheating Darren. He was nothing to her.

I'm intrigued! she typed in reply. *Tell me more!*

Chapter Thirty-One

Alice: Tell me you haven't been playing Cupid and egging on Jacob to message me?? You didn't, did you? Because he has. And I think I'm going to meet him. Unless I find out you've put him up to it, in which case I might change my mind!

Will: Like I've got time to try and sort out YOUR life when I'm trying to get my head round my own?? Don't flatter yourself! PS Definitely meet him

DM Will to Jacob: By the way, if Alice asks, I didn't message you about her, all right?

As Belinda had predicted, the fall-out between Ray and his son had all 'come out in the wash', to coin a phrase from her mum, God rest her soul. Down there in the kitchen, in the wee small hours, Ellis had unburdened himself of the whole story to his dad, truthfully this time, before apologising for his deceit. Ray, in turn, merely hugged him hard and said he understood, and that he was here to listen and help Ellis however he could.

'You were right,' he said to Belinda when he brought her a coffee in bed that morning and got back under the covers beside her. 'Of course I wanted to think he had sought me out for the right reasons, that he wanted to get to know me again.' He pleated the duvet cover between his fingers, before turning back towards her looking tired. 'But I do think he's a good lad at heart, Bel. I do.'

'Oh, without a doubt he is,' she replied. 'He's smashing. A really nice kid.'

'And, you know, nobody's perfect, are they? Especially at that age. Everyone makes mistakes.'

'They do,' said Belinda, suddenly finding she needed to stare into her coffee, hoping he wouldn't notice how pink in the cheeks she'd become. She knew about making mistakes, after all. About how you could learn from them, too. Since Jackie had hit her so bluntly with the truth about Apolline, she hadn't made a single call to the hotline. Like Ray had suggested, maybe there were other people she could talk to instead, professionals trained to help a bereaved mother who was finding it hard to accept a loss. Her fingers itched constantly to pick up her phone, but instead she went back to her crochet hook and wool each time to keep them occupied. She had decided to make herself a long and beautiful scarf for the autumn, and every stitch, every row, felt like a tiny symbol of her progress.

She'd made mistakes with Tony, too, of course, but the two of them had had a long, frank conversation when he'd dropped in at the house that day, and she felt as if they'd each been left with a better understanding of the other. It had been decent of him, for instance, not to tell the children about her affair in all the years since, allowing them to carry on thinking the best of her. Belinda wasn't entirely sure, truth be told, that she'd have managed to be quite so self-sacrificing, had the tables been turned. 'Thank you,' she'd said stiffly, eyes down, at which point he'd put his hand on hers and thanked her in turn for having done the lion's share of the child-raising. She was surprised how much she appreciated him acknowledging this, how deeply sorry he appeared. 'I'll never forgive myself for not giving the kids my full attention when we broke up,' he told her, shamefaced. 'I owe you a lot, Bel.' So they'd both got things right and wrong, in other words. But didn't every parent, at the end of the day?

Ellis went home to Wales that morning, a thorny conversation with his pregnant girlfriend awaiting him. Also on the agenda would be some grovelling to his boss, in the hope that he might still have a job. It turned out he didn't even work in retail, he worked for a young people's charity, sorting out counselling and practical help for those who needed it. 'Sounds wonderful, I bet you're brilliant at that,' Belinda had told him warmly, hugging him goodbye at the train station. In the next moment, though, she'd felt a memory glimmering at the back of her mind, a tiny but important connection that wanted to be made. What was it? There was no time to think because then the train was coming in, and Ellis was thanking her and Ray for their generosity, promising to visit again soon and repeating his offer of help with their house move in ten days' time.

'I'm glad we're part of the same family,' he told Belinda before boarding the train. 'Thanks for being there for Dad.'

'I'm glad too,' she assured him as Ray gave him one last bear hug.

'We both are,' Ray echoed, clapping him on the back.

Once back from the station, Belinda went up to the bedroom to continue packing, in preparation for the big move. She had turned her attention to the more personal items kept at the bottom of her wardrobe, things she treasured, and as she lifted out Leni's laptop in its bright pink case, the flag at the back of her mind started waving again, alerting her to the connection she hadn't quite been able to make before. Something about youth work. Leni's laptop. This Josh that Alice had mentioned before, was he relevant too? She shut her eyes, frowning, trying to piece it all together. Then her phone rang and the sound proved to be the final piece of the puzzle.

'Hi Mum, I'm just calling to pass on Dad's news,' Alice said, only for Belinda to squeak as the laptop slithered off her knees and on to the floor. 'Mum? Everything all right?'

'Sorry! I just . . . Josh, wasn't it, you were asking me about the other week?' Her thoughts whirring, she tucked the phone between her shoulder and ear so that she could unzip the laptop case and switch it on.

Alice seemed confused by the zigzags this conversation was taking. 'What? Oh – Josh? Yes. His name was in Leni's diary. Why, have you remembered something?'

'I think so. It was you ringing that did it. And Ellis talking about youth work.' The laptop seemed to be taking forever to boot up and she jabbed at the mouse pad impatiently. 'Hold on. I'm just ...'

'Mum, I'm not following. What are you—?'

'He was a kid Leni was mentoring. A teenage boy she'd started meeting through a charity. They rang me, back in the summer, wondering why she wasn't returning their calls, but—' She paused to punch in the laptop's PIN; thankfully Leni had been a 1234 girl for all of her passcodes. 'But I had so many calls to deal with back then, so many people and companies I had to tell what had happened, they blurred together after a while. I knew I'd heard the name Josh somewhere though. Here we go,' she said, clicking open the emails. 'Let me check.' She scanned through the list and found one where the charity had arranged the initial meeting between Leni and the boy.

'A teenage boy,' Alice repeated. 'Oh, Leni. Of course he was. Of course she was doing that.'

'Josh, fifteen years old,' Belinda read from the email. 'Excluded from school. Really smart but bored and unmoti-vated. They thought he and Leni would be a perfect match, apparently.'

'I bet she was great at talking to him,' Alice said wistfully. 'And what a shame that ... Well. That we all lost her, but that he did too. I hope he's all right. I wonder if we could do anything for him?'

They talked about it some more, with Belinda promising to forward Alice details of the charity so that she could contact them herself. Then – 'God! I can't believe it's taken me this long,' Alice said in a rush. 'Jackie's had the baby! A little girl. Tiny and premature but they're both doing okay, Dad said.'

Heavens, the rush of emotions that went through Belinda in that moment! The heady gush of motherly feeling at the thought of a new baby in the world, a burst of affection for Tony and his partner. Love, even. 'A baby girl,' she said, choking up as she remembered, so vividly, hearing those exact words herself, twice over, on the labour ward, and how she'd cried tears of real joy to meet her daughters each time.

And so, having said goodbye to Alice, and returned to her packing, when it happened that the very next thing she took from her box of precious things was the small yellow jacket she'd knitted for the baby Leni didn't have, fresh tears came rolling down her face. Who knew that it was possible to cry because you were sad *and* because you were happy, all at the same time?

She dried her eyes, then put the tiny, soft jacket to her cheek one last time, remembering how she'd poured such hope into its making. Then she set it aside, planning to wrap it carefully in tissue paper as a gift for Tony and Jackie's tiny new daughter. It didn't cost anything to be nice to someone, did it? She was happy for them, besides. 'See how magnanimous I'm getting in my old age, Leni!' she said aloud with a watery smile.

Tony's finger was trembling as he put a hand into the incubator to stroke his baby's soft fragile head. Her skin was rosy pink and downy like a peach. Her eyes were tightly shut. She was four pounds three ounces and had the tiniest fingernails he'd ever seen, plus the most delicate shell-like ears, newly minted. He could hardly breathe as his finger brushed her rounded cheek and her nose twitched in her sleep. She was *beautiful*.

She had passed all of the doctors' medical checks, although babies born this prematurely needed help to breathe and feed, and so she'd have to stay in the NICU for a few weeks, they'd been told. Jackie was on the ward, dozing off the combined assault of surgery, blood loss and a ton of painkillers, and so Tony was tiptoeing between his two sleeping beauties, whispering encouragement at their bedsides until one of them needed him.

'My little girl,' he said now, his voice cracking on the words. He thought back to himself in the babycare shop, dismissive and bored, and that man seemed a world away from this new version of himself, broken open like an egg, emotions spilling everywhere, love swelling above all. 'I'm here,' he told her. 'I'm right here. I'm never going to leave you.' He was already imagining golden, dappled-sunshine days with her in the years ahead: the two of them paddling at the seaside, cycling through woodland, snuggled up with a bedtime story. He could hardly wait for it all to start.

Chapter Thirty-Two

McKenzies Together group

Tony: *Morning all. Picture of Amelia Helena McKenzie here – isn't she beautiful? I am besotted. She'll be in intensive care for a little while yet but doing well. Love Dad/Tony xxx 11.33*

Belinda: *Gosh, Tony, what a little sweetheart she is! [red heart emoji, baby emoji, baby-bottle emoji, hatching-chick emoji, sunshine emoji] Sending the three of you so much love. I've popped a little parcel in the post but please shout if there's anything I can do that would be a practical help [red heart emoji, pink heart emoji, heart-eyes emoji] xxx 12.15*

Alice: *Dad, she is so gorgeous!!!! Lots of love to you and Jackie. And I LOVE that you have given her 'Helena' as a middle name. Perfect. On my way out for the afternoon now but let's catch up later. Love to you all xxx 13.08*

Will: *Congrats again, Dad! Can't wait to see you all x 13.27*

★

In a new spirit of McKenzie togetherness, Will had come to Oxford to stay with his dad. It wasn't the greatest timing, days after the very early birth of Amelia, and Will had braced himself for a Tony McKenzie U-turn, the inevitable let-down change of plan, until the very second he was due to board the train. 'Of course you can still come,' his dad had surprised him by saying though. 'I've been looking forward to it.'

His mum had surprised him too when he mentioned the visit. Throughout his entire childhood, his parents hadn't exactly got on well, to the point where Will was left feeling disloyal towards his mum whenever he'd been to stay with his dad. But something seemed to have changed. 'I'm so glad you two are getting together!' she'd said down the phone. 'You are?' he'd replied, taken aback.

Tony picked him up from the station looking as if he hadn't slept much; his eyes bloodshot, his chin stubbled. He'd had an emotional few days, by the sound of it – his voice wobbling as he described the birth, the baby, Jackie – and Will could see he was struggling to keep himself together. But Tony insisted on them going out to Wolvercote together for a lakeside walk, to 'blow away the cobwebs' as he put it.

It was a crisp, cold day but there were signs of spring every-where – leaf buds on the trees, pale primroses nestling below their trunks, the blue sky reflected in the still water of the lakes. Will remembered being dragged here for walks with his sisters on the weekends they'd stayed with their dad, and them moaning about being bored, tired, wanting to go home, but today he appreciated the tranquillity. He'd missed the English seasons when he'd been out in Thailand, the change in the air as the year turned.

There was something about walking together that felt companionable too. He'd been apprehensive about how the two of them would get on after so long, but it was surprisingly easy to talk when you were side by side, intermittently pointing out birds of prey or weirdly shaped tree stumps. Will told his dad about how he'd been looking into trying again at university, and it turned out Tony had recently sold a car to a woman who worked at the local further education college who, he claimed, was sure to know all about the university admission process. Will was about to reply that he was pretty confident he'd be able to figure it out for himself, until he realised how chuffed his dad was looking at this opportunity to be helpful. 'That would be great, Dad. Thanks,' he said instead.

Jackie rang at one point and Will could hear the tenderness in his dad's voice as he spoke to her. He thought about the wives that had popped up after his mum – bolshy Isabelle and prissy Tanya; how fake he'd always found them both, how they'd come between the McKenzie kids and their dad like beautiful, cold interruptions. He didn't know Jackie at all but remembered she'd tried to be kind at the funeral, and recognised, moreover, that his dad was speaking to her lovingly now, asking fussy questions about what she might want him to bring her later, checking in on the latest from the doctors.

'You really like her, don't you?' he said when the call was over. It seemed an odd comment to make about his dad's partner, especially when they'd just had a new baby together, but he and Tony had never discussed women or relationships as adult men together. Besides, he too wanted to make the effort, he admitted.

'Jackie? Yeah, she's brilliant,' came the reply. 'I honestly thought I was done with relationships. After me and your mum . . . after our divorce, I made a few mistakes with women. It was all a bit shallow. Ooh – buzzard,' he said suddenly, pointing out the large bird above, gliding on a thermal current. 'But with Jackie – she gives as good as she gets. I've met my match. I think she's absolutely fantastic, to be honest. I love her.'

Will, who'd been expecting broader brushstrokes from him, maybe even something glib, was taken aback by such sincerity. 'Blimey, Dad, I've never heard you talk like that,' he commented, with a sideways glance.

'Yeah, well, when you know, you know,' Tony said. 'And with her . . . well, I just know. I do often wonder what she sees in me, but I'm grateful there's something.' His expression was bashful – for at least two seconds, anyway, before switching the focus away. 'How about you, son? Anyone special on your mind at the moment?'

If you'd told Will when he boarded the Oxford train that morning that he'd end up confiding in his dad about his love life, he'd have laughed his head off. *Yeah, and back on this planet . . .* he'd have scoffed disbelievingly. And yet, in the next minute, he found himself telling his dad about Isla, who he kept thinking of even now.

'So how come you're not up there in Aberdeen, knocking on her door, telling *her* all this?' Tony asked at the end. 'You can pontificate all you like, but sometimes you have to take direct action, do you know what I mean? Especially while you've still got your tan and all. Handsome so-and-so like you, she'd be mad to turn you down.'

'She thinks I'm a closed book, remember,' Will felt compelled to point out. 'She's already turned me down once. And I had a better tan then as well,' he added for good measure.

'Well, then,' his dad said. 'You need to open this closed book, don't you? Show her what you've got. Not like—' He mimed opening a flasher mac and they both laughed. 'Just ... let her in. Be honest with her.' He clapped Will on the back. 'It's not easy, I get it. At the end of the day, nobody likes feeling vulnerable, putting yourself out there, not knowing what response you're going to get. But you have to be ... real. Yourself. Honest. That's what I've learned, after three failed marriages; that's my best bit of fatherly wisdom for you, son. Otherwise, what's the point?'

Chapter Thirty-Three

Alice: How's it going? Have you seen our new sister yet? Are things okay between you and Big Daddy?

Will: New sister alarmingly tiny, luckily for her doesn't look too much like Dad. Things are good – Jackie's house is insanely posh, like luxury hotel. Keep worrying I'm going to break stuff. As for me and Dad . . . we're getting on okay. I see what you mean about him having changed. I'm actually enjoying spending time with him. WHO KNEW???!!!

Alice smiled at her brother's message as she took a seat on the west-bound tube the following day. It had been such a year of reckoning for the McKenzies, she thought. Such a period of readjustment. Without Leni, they'd each had to shuffle into new positions, work out different dynamics between themselves. She felt as if they were all starting again in their own ways, taking steps to reshape their lives accordingly.

She arrived at Holland Park half an hour later, intrigued but also apprehensive. She had no idea what Jacob was planning – all he'd said was that he'd meet her here, Sunday afternoon, and she would find out more in due course. She hoped it wouldn't be weird between them after the last time they'd met.

He was waiting outside the station and she felt a surge of gladness to see him again. Will had been right; he *was* important to her. Too important to let slip away again. 'Hello and welcome to today's Flying Beauties experience: tribute number three,' he said after a brief hug. 'Follow me.'

'This is very mysterious,' she commented as she fell into step beside him. Having previously met up on dark winter evenings, in the Greek restaurant and the cocktail bar, it felt rather nice to be walking along a quiet street with him on an overcast March day, the years vanishing as he smiled down at her. He was wearing a black waterproof coat and jeans, and she remembered the photo he'd shown her of his little boy, wondering if this was his sensible-dad coat, worn for outdoor excursions. The pockets looked as if they might be secretly full of pine cones and small round stones and other interesting finds from his son.

'Well, I'm a very mysterious man, if you hadn't already noticed,' he replied.

'Oh, really?'

'No. Absolutely not. Transparent as a piece of cling film. But I *am* an apologetic man, if not a mysterious one,' he said, glancing over at her, his brown eyes suddenly serious. They paused at the traffic lights and she wondered again where he was taking her. Was this where he lived? she thought, before registering the earnest note in his voice and looking back at him. 'I really am sorry for last time, me trying to browbeat you into conversations you didn't want to have,' he went on.

'Misguidedly trying to push you forward into the future when that wasn't what you needed at the time. I'll go with you to all the Leni-places you want, Alice, if it helps you deal with losing her.'

'Thank you,' she said with a small smile. They crossed the road and walked past some large, elegant houses, set back from the pavement. 'Although, to be fair, you probably had a point. I spoke to some friends about it – I was all indignant, like, "He made out I was stuck in the past!" and they were like, "Um, yep" – which pulled me up a bit. I think I actually *have* been living in the past, quite a lot lately, to be fair. Not really engaging with the rest of my life. But funnily enough, that's all changed this week.'

He gestured up a street on their right. 'This way,' he said. 'So what happened this week then? If you want to talk about it?'

She smiled at him. 'I've had a good few days at work,' she replied, before going on to elaborate with the backstory about Sage and Golding, the meeting she'd requested, and the brilliant news she'd received on Friday. 'The upshot is, the marketing people I spoke to – Emma, Sanjay and Phil – have met with HR, and between them, they've arranged it so that I'll continue the maternity cover for four days a week and then, on Fridays from next week, I'll be working on a free-lance basis, as a social media consultant for their department.'

'Alice! That's brilliant news! We're going in here, by the way. Into the park.'

It really was brilliant news, she thought proudly as they left the street behind and entered the park. Emma, in particular, had been quick to tell her how much they'd loved her ideas and approach for a new digital campaign, and had asked her to work up a full strategy. She'd also indicated that, were things to go well, come the end of Alice's temporary contract, there would almost certainly be the prospect of ongoing freelance work. *The thing about Sage and Golding*, she said, *is that once you're in, you're in. People joke about never leaving but that's because, if they like you, this company are extremely keen to hang on to you.*

'Your business empire starts here,' he said warmly. 'Have you got a name for your new company yet? McKenzie and Associates? Alice McKenzie International?'

'You make me sound like an airport,' she laughed. 'Let me at least have Oxford bus station named after me first.' They were walking around the park, with its mature trees and broad pathways, joggers panting along in Lycra, parents and children, an elderly couple holding hands. 'It's lovely here,' she commented. 'Very peaceful.'

'Yes,' he said. 'And I've taken a bit of gamble today because I'm hoping we'll see something, but we might not. I came here the other day on a recce and saw one, but I gather it's not always guaranteed.'

'You saw one what?' she repeated, intrigued. 'A recce? What are you talking about?'

'It's a surprise,' came his cryptic reply. 'Or rather I hope it will be. Worst comes to the worst, we'll have a walk and then I'll shout you a cup of tea to get over the crushing disappointment of a non-event. But let's head for the Kyoto Garden and keep our fingers crossed in the meantime.'

'The suspense is killing me!' she groaned. 'My brain is absolutely spinning here, trying to work out what you've planned.

I can't cope!' She elbowed him affectionately. 'But thank you for this magical mystery tour anyway, I'm enjoying it so far.'

She remembered to ask him about his week, like a normal person, and he recounted some funny stories about his little boy and told her about the modules he was teaching this year. She responded with news about Will having come to stay with her – 'He sends his love,' she passed on – and how he'd forced her to re-evaluate her approach to Leni. Not only by helping with her investigation of Leni's last few weeks, she explained, but by pointing out what was written at the very end of the diary, details Alice had skimmed over before now.

'Look,' she said, stopping momentarily to retrieve it from her bag. 'I brought it to show you.' She flipped to the last page of the little book, where Leni had written 'NEXT YEAR' at the top of the page, with a list of plans below. *Fall in love,* they both read, heads close together as they leaned in over it. *Have adventures. Girls' holiday! Family get-together. Make a new friend (maybe even two!!) Start an evening class (flamenco??) Get cool haircut. Paint!!! Go to Barcelona on my own. (Or Venice? Both?!) Book theatre tickets. Swim in the sea. Dorset trip with Alice!*

'Wow,' Jacob said. 'She was a dynamo. I can almost hear her saying all of those things with that pure Leni McKenzie *joie de vivre.*'

'Same! Exactly! But do you know what my favourite thing of all is?' Alice asked, pointing to the top of the page. After originally writing 'NEXT YEAR' in black pen, Leni had later added in blue the words '. . . will be amazing!!' 'Isn't that brilliant? *Next year will be amazing.* She was the most optimistic person ever. Even when she'd been through the toughest time of her life.' She put the diary carefully back in her bag. 'Don't laugh at me, because I know this will sound cheesy, but I'm going to try to channel that Leni-spirit from now on. To think – next year will be amazing – and to believe it, too. Because who knows?'

'I love that,' he said. 'And it's not cheesy. Everyone should live with those words in mind. I'm going to try as well. Optimise the optimism! The best days of our lives are yet to come!'

Alice smiled at him. 'I'm absolutely going to get "Optimise the Optimism" put on a T-shirt and I'm going to force you to wear it,' she laughed, glad to have shared Leni's precious words with him, and glad too that he had immediately got on board with the sentiment. More than anything, she was glad to be here at all with him, after Will had made her rethink their friendship.

By now they had reached the Kyoto Garden in the centre of the park, which was very picturesque with a large pond and waterfall, and Japanese planting. She told him about her mum uncovering the mysteries of 'Josh' and how Alice had since contacted the mentoring charity and spoken to someone there. 'They couldn't give me too many details because of confidentiality, but apparently Josh, the boy she was mentoring, is doing well these days. I know Leni would be so pleased about that,' she said, a lump in her throat. 'They also told me that Josh had really liked her.' She broke off, suddenly emotional. 'I felt so ... so proud of her.'

'What a lovely thing to do,' Jacob agreed. 'And what a lovely person she was.'

'I know, right? Will and I were talking about it, saying we

both felt inspired to do something similar in her memory. Passing on that generous spirit of hers, if you know what I mean.'

'That would be amazing. I bet she'd have loved that,' he said. Then he nudged her. 'Aha,' he said, a new note of excitement in his voice as he pointed. 'There. See it?'

She had just noticed a small stone pagoda-like ornament and thought at first he was referring to that, but then she lifted her gaze and saw ... 'Oh my God,' she said, clapping a hand to her mouth. She almost wanted to rub her eyes and check she was seeing properly. 'No way. Is that ... real?'

There ahead of them was a *peacock*, an actual peacock strutting slowly across the path. Its blue and green colours gleamed iridescent in the sun, its tiny head bobbling on a long curved neck as its astonishing many-eyed tail feathers swept the ground behind like the train of a wedding dress. 'It's real,' he assured her, and, as if demonstrating that yes, it certainly *was* real, thank you very much, the peacock chose that moment to fan its tail in an exhilarating plumage display. Other people in the vicinity had stopped to see too; you could hear children's voices, high and excited – *Look! Look!* – and Alice found herself joining them from inside her head. *Look, Leni!* she marvelled silently, unable to take her eyes off the extraordinary creature. *Look!*

'Wow,' she breathed, standing motionless as the peacock continued its stately procession across the grass away from them. She briefly considered taking a photo but knew there was no need, because she would remember this moment forever. 'I feel as if I'm in a dream,' she said, a laugh in her voice. 'An incredible dream. Now you're about to tell me you arranged all that, aren't you?'

'To the very last detail,' he replied, pretending to salute the departing bird. 'Cheers, mate. Perfect timing. Oh, and look, he's showing off to his lady friend over there. Must be mating season, I guess.'

He pointed out a peahen almost hidden within the undergrowth towards which the peacock was strutting, its tail wobbling a little with each step. Alice had a visceral memory of pressing the peacock feathers of her 'wings' against her face, feeling how soft and delicate each one was. Then she was remembering the rush of leaping off a bunk bed with her sister. *I think I really did fly a bit just then.* 'Flying Beauties forever,' she said in a shaky voice.

'Flying Beauties forever,' he echoed, putting an arm around her briefly and squeezing her shoulders.

'Thank you,' she said, as the birds vanished into the undergrowth. They continued walking, the vivid scene still replaying in her mind. 'That was the most amazing, wonderful idea. The best thing you could have thought of. I didn't even know there were any peacocks in London, let alone wandering freely around Holland Park like this. I assumed they were all in zoos or on rich people's estates.' She shook her head, still a bit dazed. 'I feel like I'm in some kind of enchanted land, a fairy tale. I don't actually think I've ever seen a real one before now. I wonder if Leni ever did?'

'Well, you've done it for the both of you now, if not,' he replied.

'I have, haven't I?' she marvelled, smiling at him. 'Thank

you, Jay. Honestly. That means so much to me. You've made my week.'

'I think you made your own week, when you sorted out that great bit of work for yourself,' he reminded her. 'But I'm happy to share the credit. And I'll still shout you a cup of tea to toast your success when we get to the café.' They smiled at one another. 'Changing the subject, how come you were working for the insurance company in the first place, if you don't mind me asking? You said something about resigning before Christmas – what happened?'

She would have batted away the question a few weeks ago but was feeling so euphoric from the peacock sighting that she told him the truth: about losing her temper when Nicholas Pearce tried it on, and about the bad old days of her incandescent anger; taking her revenge out on Callum Ferguson, getting escorted home by the police and all the rest of it. She'd become ashamed of her own actions, so ashamed that she'd preferred to bury them away out of sight, but here, in the calm surroundings of the Kyoto Garden where peacocks could appear like magic, she felt a new distance from those dark stormy rages, as if the cool spring breeze had blown them clean away.

He shot her a sympathetic look. 'You've been through such a trauma,' he said. 'A really hard, painful time.'

'Yeah,' she agreed. 'But I'm definitely on the up now. Coming out the other side. Next year will be amazing, and all that. It might even be true.'

'Too right,' he said. 'Do you know, I was listening to a podcast the other day on my way to work,' he went on.

'About rebuilding your life after a traumatic event. And the interviewer referenced an old experiment done with – I can't remember if it was moths or butterflies, actually. Let's say butterflies. Anyway, in the experiment, the butterflies' chrysalises were cut open with a scalpel prematurely, before they were ready to emerge themselves. And each time the butterfly inside would be perfectly formed, with nothing anatomically wrong, except they were completely unable to fly. Every single time. The scientists came to the conclusion that normally a butterfly would push and push and push against the side of the chrysalis in order to break through – and that it was this struggle and this repeated pushing that built up their muscles and ultimately meant they could fly.'

Alice frowned. 'So you're saying—'

'I'm saying, possibly in a heavy-handed way, that sometimes the act of getting through a trauma can give you a strength you didn't have before.'

'The strength to fly,' she said, voice wavering, because yes, she wanted so much to believe in this; hadn't she and Leni always tried so hard to take flight? She gave a little sob and immediately felt embarrassed. 'Oh gosh. That's actually really beautiful. And sort of upsetting at the same time.'

'I'm sorry,' he said. 'I didn't mean—'

'No, it's fine. It's lovely. I'm upset, but in a good way, because . . .' She tried to smile but knew her mouth was going wonky with the emotions she was experiencing. 'Because I feel like I have been bashing against this . . . well, chrysalis, if you like, for so bloody long, and I'm so ready to burst through it, put it behind me, and yet it seems to be going

345

on forever. But I do really want to ...' It was hard to get the word out because it was suddenly loaded with such meaning. 'I do want to fly.'

They had stopped walking and he put his arms around her. 'Oh, Alice,' he said, holding her. 'You will. I know you will.' She shut her eyes because it was so nice to stand there within his embrace, to feel the fabric of his jacket beneath her cheek, to know that he was holding her tight. 'It's going to happen,' he said, his breath warm on her ear. 'I promise you.'

Chapter Thirty-Four

The time had almost come: this was to be the last week Belinda would ever live in her house, and before Friday, she and Ray had to finish packing and tackle an intimidatingly long list of jobs, big and small. A stressful few days, in other words, which was why Belinda made the executive decision to start Monday with the best stress-buster she knew: swimming. This might be the last chance she had to snatch an hour to herself and she planned to make the most of it.

Once there and changed, she stuffed her shoes and clothes into a locker, smiling indulgently at a little boy wearing Paw Patrol trunks who was capering around his mother's legs while chattering non-stop. *They grow up so fast*, she thought, with a pang for the days when her children had been that size.

Approaching the pool, she eyed up which lane looked emptiest (she did so hate the men who pointedly overtook you with their pathetic competitive zeal) and headed towards the end furthest away, where she could see a single woman in a flowered rubber bathing cap slowly tanking up and down in a relaxed backstroke. Perfect. Even better, today's lifeguard was a beefy bloke rather than the pretty blonde who'd been unfortunate enough to witness Belinda's previous meltdown. But then, as she was nearing the steps, she heard a scuttle of little footsteps behind her, a mischievous high-pitched giggle and a splash.

She almost didn't look round because there were always splashes at this time of day if kids were having lessons, or were here on an inset day. But something urged her to turn – and as she did, she was just in time to catch a glimpse of the little boy with the Paw Patrol trunks disappearing beneath the surface of the water. His mum was nowhere to be seen. The lifeguard's whistle shrieked through the air and he leaped from his chair, and for a millisecond, Belinda thought she was having a flashback to when Leni was a tiny girl and had thrown herself similarly into this very pool. Then her instincts took over.

She jumped in after the boy, whose small flailing body was already sinking towards the tiled bottom, dimly aware of a scream of 'CALEB!' – the poor mum rushing towards them. Hands in a prayer position, Belinda surface-dived down to the child, grabbing a tight hold of his narrow shoulders and hauling him up and out, water raining from his little limbs. He seemed limp, she thought in a panic as the lifeguard appeared at the edge of the pool, followed by the mum, her mouth open in a wail. It must only have been half a second – the longest half second of Belinda's life, it seemed – but then the boy coughed, water spraying from his mouth and nose, and he promptly let out a cry.

'He's okay,' Belinda said, shock pounding through her.

Shock, and relief too, that she had caught him, scooped up into the air like a rebirth. 'You're okay, aren't you, darling?'

She relinquished him to the distraught crouching woman who enfolded him immediately in her arms, her bright pink hair falling over his small bare shoulders. 'Oh, Caleb!' she gasped.

'Are you all right, buddy?' the lifeguard asked the little boy, kneeling on the wet, dimpled concrete tiles. 'Did you bang your head?'

'I just wanted to jump in,' the boy said, pressing himself against the woman.

'And you did, didn't you? While Aunty Gen was still sorting out the locker!' she said, eyes hollow. Goodness, so he wasn't even her son, Belinda thought with a stab of sympathy. Nightmare. 'Thank you,' the woman went on to her, still clutching the child as if she'd never let him go. 'I'm sorry,' she said to the lifeguard. 'I've just had a bit of bad news, I lost my focus.'

Luckily this lifeguard was a lot more understanding than the one who'd yelled at Belinda so many years earlier. 'These things happen,' he said. 'No harm done. And you won't do it again, will you, mate?' he asked Caleb. 'When you're a really good swimmer like me, you can jump in all by yourself, okay? But not before. Understand?'

The boy nodded. Then, shyly lifting his head, he looked at the lifeguard there in his Aertex polo shirt and shorts. 'You've got very big arms,' he said.

'I have, haven't I? Big and strong, so that I can swim really well,' the man said, winking at the two women in a self-deprecating way and flexing his bicep at the boy. He couldn't have been much more than twenty-five, Belinda thought, but there was something really kind about him.

'Sorry,' the pink-haired woman – Aunty Gen – mumbled as the boy reached forward to pat the lifeguard's bicep admiringly. 'He lost his dad last year – my brother. We get this quite a lot with men your age. I hope you don't mind.'

'Not at all,' the lifeguard said, tousling Caleb's hair and rising to his feet. 'Take care of yourself, okay? Remember what I said about learning to be a good swimmer!'

He loped back to his lifeguard chair like a superhero and Belinda rubbed her own, considerably less toned arms self-consciously. 'Sorry to hear about your brother,' she said, because Gen still looked a bit tearful. 'Are you all right?'

The stress of the last few minutes seemed to catch up with the other woman, who shook her head, lips pressed together. 'Not really,' she said. 'We'd just got here and I had a text message from my partner saying she's started bleeding. She's six months pregnant. The midwife said for her to go to hospital and … I didn't know what to do. It's my morning to look after this one – I'm trying to help out his mum – but I'm worried about Pen – Penelope, my other half, so …'

Belinda was battling to keep up as the words spilled out, on and on. She thought about all the times she'd had to struggle on her own with the kids, lurching from one drama to another – how she'd wished, frequently, that someone would just come to her rescue for once. She could go swimming any time, she figured. They had packers coming in on Wednesday, and both Will and Ellis had offered to muck in too; the work would get done. 'Let me help,' she said, clambering out of the pool.

'I've got my car. I could take you to the hospital, and even sit with little one here, if you need an extra pair of hands. It would be no problem.'

Gen looked as if she might cry with relief. 'Oh my God, really? Are you sure?'

Belinda batted aside thoughts of bubble-wrapping the kitchen crockery and taking cuttings from the garden, as had been her plans for the rest of the day. She would rather put some goodness out into the world, help a stranger whose path had collided so splashily with hers. Wasn't this what living was about, really? Trying to be a good person in society, taking pride in her own actions? 'I'm absolutely sure,' she replied.

Chapter Thirty-Five

Two months later

Dear Leni,

Happy birthday, my darling! I wish we could be celebrating together today, I know you always loved a family occasion. We will do our best without you but you'll be very much on our minds.

You would have been thirty-six today. Thirty-six years, and yet I remember your birth as if it were yesterday, the hot rush of love bursting through me when I saw your beautiful face for the first time. I thought, yes, here she is, as if I already knew you. But lucky me, I still had so much to find out, not least what a wonderful, funny, kind daughter you turned out to be. A piece of my heart.

So! What's been happening since the last time I wrote? Well, the house is coming along in leaps and bounds — we've moved properly into our bedroom now, curtains and all, and I love it so much. A load of Ray's friends came over last weekend and we got heaps more work done between us — Will and Ellis have been back and forth helping out too. I think we're going to be really happy here, you know. We're beginning work on the first couple of guest bedrooms next week so that we can actually – yikes! – start getting bookings for the summer. Alice and Ray keep teasing me, calling me 'Lady of the Manor', but I have to say, I quite like my new title. There are worse nicknames, right?

This is just a quick one as I need to get the roast chicken on, but we'll all be thinking about you today and I'll write again soon to let you know how it all went. And if there's any gossip, obviously!!

Love you so much. Miss you every day. Thank you for being a light in my life for thirty-five years, my gorgeous, precious birthday girl.

Mum xx

It was mid-May, and Oxford was bursting into bloom: the trees along the river in full leaf, the stately old college buildings pale yellow in the sunshine, boat races up and down the river cheered on by students and passers-by alike. Two weeks ago, the bells had rung from the Magdalen College tower to see in the month, the choristers serenading the city from the rooftop, and Morris dancers had paraded their jingling way through to Radcliffe Square. Now everyone had settled into the late spring warmth with an eye on summer just around the corner.

Out in her Oxfordshire home – newly rewired, with working plumbing and a kitchen so recently decorated you could still smell the paint – Belinda was basting a roast chicken. She was looking forward to having the whole family under her roof for the day, together again for the first time since Leni's funeral. Today would have been Leni's thirty-sixth birthday – seven short words that added up to one of the saddest sentences she could think of – but the McKenzies were coming together to mark the occasion, to hold each other up through the day. *Leni's death has left you in great pain, but it's important that you allow yourself to feel it*, her new counsellor Rachel had told her during one of their sessions. *Over time, the pain will lessen, your wounds will heal, and life will reshape itself around the loss of your daughter, like a stream flowing around a rock. Be gentle with yourself in the meantime.*

What on earth had she done before Rachel? Kind, wise, non-judgemental Rachel, who listened to Belinda with great empathy, passed her tissues whenever she needed them (frequently) and who seemed to be holding a lantern for her to follow through the darkness, as she stumbled towards acceptance. It had been Rachel's idea for Belinda to write letters to Leni whenever she wanted to say something, and it had proved both comforting and cathartic. Rachel had also put her in touch with a support group of other bereaved parents who met every fortnight in a neighbouring village to reminisce and encourage and commiserate. How wonderful it was to meet people who understood what you were going through, who indulged you with compassion while you showed them your favourite photos, then squeezed your arm if you started tearing up. Apolline was in Belinda's past now, where she belonged – although it had made her feel gratifyingly less of an idiot, hearing that a couple of other grieving parents within the group had taken similar paths themselves while in the depths of heartbroken denial. 'And who can blame us?' one of the women had said. 'Wouldn't we all give anything for one more conversation with them? One more day?'

All in all, Belinda felt as if she was starting to live again. The house move had been a huge distraction, keeping her busy for many weeks, but it was a positive busyness; she loved being in their new space, painting and unpacking, making curtains and flinging open the windows so that the spring sunshine and fresh air could pour in. Day by day, unpacked box by unpacked box, she and Ray were turning the old neglected building into their home, with August earmarked as the B. & B.'s grand opening. And yes, although she hadn't dared say as much, you bet she had secretly earmarked a small upstairs room for a grandchild's bedroom. You bet she had already spent some time planning a soft cream colour palette with rosebud-print curtains. Or maybe a sweet farm-animal print, or ... Well, whatever, she'd make it gorgeous and cosy by the time Ellis and Paloma had their little one in October, that was for sure. Was it terrible to admit that she was very much hoping for a Christmas visit from them? She and Ray had gone over to Crickhowell a fortnight ago for a weekend break, and Paloma seemed a sweet girl, with Ellis much happier and more relaxed now that he was home. Ellis turned out to be something of an adrenalin junkie like his dad, suggesting he and Ray go off for a gliding session in the Black Mountains, which they both seemed to love. Best of all for Ray was the fact that Rhiannon, his estranged daughter, had consented to see him for the first time in years as well, and after an initial slow burn, they were getting on like the proverbial house on fire.

'My children! And a new little mouse to look forward to!' Ray had said the other evening when they'd been looking over some photos Ellis had sent.

Sitting on the sofa, Belinda had jerked in surprise. The word 'mouse' was ringing a bell in her head and she couldn't think why. 'A new little mouse?' she repeated, looking at him quizzically.

'Oh! It was what we used to call Ellis when he was born, Mouse. Mouseling, sometimes.' He had the fond smile of one remembering a happy time. 'I'm getting used to the idea of being a grandad. Having a tiny new mouseling to look after and love.'

Mouse. Ellis. There was definitely something there, the bell in her head continuing to jangle, but Belinda couldn't think, for the life of her, of the connection. It would come to her, she assured herself, smiling back.

In the meantime, it was a privilege to be party to his happiness, and to get to know these fine young people, and to feel that her own life was a touch richer, a touch warmer, for them being in it. And today she was thankful for her own two children, yes, and her ex-husband as well, who would be joining her and Ray here today. She couldn't wait for them all to be around her table, in the hope that any happiness they could share, any reminiscences, would be something to celebrate.

Tony was yet to see the new house – he had his hands full, with Jackie and the baby only recently out of hospital, and a few extra grey hairs to show for the stressful time they'd all had – but Alice and Will had both come over several times already. In fact, Will, bless him, had not only helped on the day of the move but had stayed for a few days afterwards too, heaving furniture around with Ray, cleaning and unpacking. It had been so nice to see him and Ellis get to know one another, the two of them really hitting it off. She and the boys had rather ganged up on Ray, joking that any unlabelled boxes must be more of Ray's 'extensive wardrobe' – the punchline being, of course, that Ray only had about four T-shirts and two pairs of jeans to his name. You could tell Ray absolutely loved the ribbing though. What was a family, after all, if they couldn't take the mick out of one another at all times?

As she was smiling to herself about this, the fashionista himself came in from the garden, where he'd mown the lawn, set up the patio table and chairs, and hung bunting between the ancient apple trees that had surprised them both by flowering with the most exquisite blossom. 'Can I do anything?' he asked. 'What are you smiling about?' he added suspiciously, noticing her expression.

'Just thinking how much I love you,' she said, sliding the bronzed chicken back into the oven, then walking over to hug him. By now, she'd come clean about the whole Graham Fenton business and, to her relief, he'd told her it made absolutely no difference to the way he felt about her. *You think that's bad? I'm glad you didn't see me in my youth, put it like that,* he'd told her, holding her tightly. *We all make mistakes, right?*

Just then the doorbell rang and her heart swelled with joyful anticipation. 'Ah!' she said, disentangling herself from him. 'Who's first, I wonder?'

★

357

Tony stood on the doorstep, a bunch of white roses in his arms, as well as a bottle of fizz and a somewhat belated New Home card for his ex-wife and Ray. He glanced down at himself, checking for baby-sick patches on his shirt (nope) and also to make sure his flies were done up (thankfully yes). Ever since Jackie and baby Amelia had been allowed home, he hadn't been getting very much sleep. Small, previously mundane things – doing up his trousers properly, brushing his teeth regularly, managing to wear matching socks, getting dressed before midday – had been far more difficult to keep on top of lately. He had got in the car the other day, and stared blankly in front of him, wondering what had happened to the steering wheel, before realising he was actually sitting in the passenger seat. Then he'd wondered if perhaps he was too tired to even consider driving at all.

But they had made it this far, he kept telling himself. After a fairly nail-biting start to life, Amelia – or Mimi, as they'd soon switched to calling her – had thrived in the intensive care unit, quickly putting on weight and gradually becoming more animated and alert. 'The doctors are hopeful she'll have no serious health repercussions as a result of her prematurity,' he'd been able to update friends and family, faint with relief every time.

Jackie, however, had been less fortunate. She'd somehow picked up an infection after the birth that had developed, frighteningly fast, into full-blown sepsis, leaving her very ill for almost a month. There had been a few dark times when it seemed Tony was staring right into the abyss, with no glimmer of light on the horizon: times when he thought he might fall apart. Except then he'd go to see his tiny girl in her incubator and he'd feel such strength of will, it gave him the fuel to keep going each time. Will stayed on for moral support, and Tony was grateful to have him there. Alice too had been a godsend, popping back and forth between London and Oxford whenever she could manage it. She'd had tears in her eyes the first time she met Amelia, and Tony had found himself welling up too, so emotionally charged had the moment been. Seeing Alice hold her new sister, stroke her tiny round cheek, tell her about all the fun the two of them were going to have together ... Tony felt love waterfall into him at the sight; the most soothing balm against old scars. It was no magical cure-all to give his daughter a new sister when she was still grieving the loss of Leni, but he could see that there was a comfort to be had, the consolation of tiny Amelia, nestled in the crook of her arms. A brand new love unfolding before his eyes.

Outside the two spheres of home and hospital, normality was suspended meanwhile. His boss, Annabeth, herself the doting aunty of twins born prematurely, was understanding, rearranging his workload to reduce pressure, reminding him to take care of himself. Friends of theirs had offered help and advice. The antenatal group rallied with support and small kindnesses (Reiki Woman of all people turned out to make a cracking vegetable lasagne, as he discovered when she dropped round with it one evening). And the bereavement group were there for him too, listening and helping with practical suggestions. Gen insisted on taking him for a pint and chat after their last session, not least because she and Pen were now the proud parents of hefty ten-pounder Otto. In the run-up to his birth, Pen had suffered a couple of worrying bleeds, but she'd carried Otto to term, and both she and Gen were besotted with their boy. Tony was glad. Who would have thought, a year ago, he'd have a confidante like Gen? He was grateful for her, and all the other good people in his life.

And now Jackie and Amelia were home at last, the three of them trying out family life for size. Jackie was understandably still shaky and traumatised by her experience, worried that she had lost out on precious bonding time with their daughter and upset that she'd missed her chance to breastfeed. But she was alive and recovering a little more every day. Tony had taken a month's paternity leave, starting from when Amelia had been allowed home, and had thrown himself into fatherhood and caring; doing everything for them all, badly at first, admittedly, but he was learning on the hoof. He took care of the laundry; he washed, fed and changed Amelia; he organised supermarket deliveries, dealt with household bills and cleaned everything, so thoroughly and energetically that their existing cleaner clucked at him, complaining he was doing her out of a job. That was fine, though, because it meant he was on top of things; he was pulling his weight. Wasn't this proof that he was a committed partner, a proper dad?

It was all good, in other words, although, God, it was exhausting too. He had somehow overlooked the sheer fatigue of living with a tiny baby, however delightful, who needed feeding and winding and washing and wiping at frequent intervals. Now that he was no longer pumped so full of adrenalin, he could feel tiredness filling him like insulation foam from an aerosol can, expanding into every corner. He had known nothing of what Belinda had gone through with their children together, he'd realised. Absolutely nothing. But all of the slog was worth it now, to have his new daughter in the world. Every single bit.

It had been with a strange mixture of feelings that he'd left Jackie and Amelia behind half an hour ago, to travel around the ring road to Belinda and Ray's new place. They'd been invited too, but Jackie sensed that this might be better as a McKenzies-only day, and wanted to give them space to reminisce. 'I'll come along next time,' she'd said, hugging him goodbye. 'Give everyone my love.' She was probably right, but as he parked in Belinda's posh new driveway and tried to get himself together in readiness for what was sure to be an intensely moving reunion, he found himself unsure if he could manage this alone. Leni's birthday, and she wasn't alive to be with them. How could it be anything other than awful?

'Tony,' said Belinda as she opened the door and saw him standing there looking emotional. 'Are you all right?'

He looked back at her, momentarily overcome, because of course he didn't have to manage this alone. Here was Belinda, a woman he'd once loved more than anyone, the woman who'd given him three wonderful children. She was so important to him, after everything, and it had taken a tragedy to make him appreciate her. Instinctively, he stepped forward and put his arms around her, slightly crushing the bouquet he'd brought, but never mind. 'Thanks, Bel,' he said, his throat tight with sentiment. What a strange, beautiful, wild day it had been, when Leni came into the world and changed their lives forever by making them parents. 'Thanks for everything,' he said. 'With all my heart.'

She embraced him, then stepped back with an air of puzzled concern before her eyes narrowed. 'You haven't slept, have you?' she said knowingly. 'And you're mad with tiredness, aren't you? I can tell. Come in. Lunch will be another half an hour, why don't you have a quick kip upstairs before the others get here?'

He staggered as he crossed the threshold; the past few months catching up on him in a single moment, overwhelming him body and soul. 'That,' he managed to say, choking back his gratitude, 'is the best offer I've had all year.'

Chapter Thirty-Six

Will shoved his bag up on to the luggage rack, then slid into the window seat, waiting for the train to depart. He'd flown down from Aberdeen to Bristol the day before, spending the night with an old friend who'd lived there since university, then today he'd set off for Oxford. Now he was on the last leg of the journey, on the small stopping train headed to the village station nearest his mum's new place.

It would have been Leni's birthday today, he typed into the memorial page. Ever since Alice had encouraged him to be a part of it, he had found real solace in adding to it frequently. *One of my earliest memories was a birthday party of hers – her twelfth, possibly, which would make me nearly four. The house was full of these enormous loud girls wearing shiny clothes, dancing to music in the living room, balloons bobbing everywhere. I remember being transfixed by the sight of my sisters with Leni's friends, as if they were briefly transformed into princesses or goddesses who had taken over the house. That, and the fact that they all screamed 'A boy! A boy!' whenever I tried to join in the games. (In hindsight, this explained a lot about my love life in later years.)*

Another memory is of her coming back really pissed on her six-teenth birthday, where she'd gone out to the park with friends, taking with her a buttercream-iced cake that Mum had slaved and sworn over, but also, it later emerged, with several dodgy-looking bottles of alcohol nicked from Mum's collection. I was fast asleep in bed but got woken by the front door banging when she crashed in after dark, followed by unmissable, prolonged vomiting in the downstairs toilet. When I crept on to the landing to peer down through the banisters, there was Leni staggering around the hall with what looked like handfuls of buttercream in her hair, being held up by an extremely cross-looking Mum. Cross, because Leni had had a cake fight after all Mum's hard work, I guessed as an innocent seven-year-old, thrilled at such naughtiness, but the next morning at breakfast, Mum made a few tart remarks about Leni's hangover and yes, she did have to go to school, actually, and I had to think again.

Happy birthday, Leni, you buttercream-haired legend and total party animal. Definitely going to raise a glass or two in your honour later (but might hold back on the cake fights). Will

He posted the message only to see a reply from Alice appear almost immediately.

Oh my God, yes, I'd forgotten that!! She was in SO MUCH TROUBLE! I absolutely loved it!!!

He smiled, and then again as a message appeared from Belinda. *The work I put into that cake!!! Ungrateful little minx. I've only JUST forgiven you, Leni, love Mum xxx*

'Have you thought about doing something positive to honour her memory, like a legacy?' Isla had asked one time when the subject of Leni came up during his stay. Will had booked the cheapest room of the cheapest hotel when he went up to Aberdeen, but a mere two hours into their first evening out together – that truly wonderful, fun, joyful first evening – she'd cocked her head at him and said, 'Why don't you come back to mine tonight?' Which was where he'd stayed the entire fortnight, as things turned out. (There was a distinct possibility that it had been the greatest fortnight of his life, truth be told.)

'Actually, I've found this charity that teaches people how to mend and care for their bikes up and down the country,' he had replied, turning pink with sudden self-consciousness. 'I was thinking I might volunteer for them, just so that …' He couldn't get the words out. 'You know. So that other people like Leni could learn that sort of stuff.'

Isla got it immediately, of course. 'That's such a good idea,' she'd said, folding her slender fingers around his hand. By then he'd abandoned the closed-book approach and told her all about his secret guilt around his sister, and now they were draped cosily along her sofa together, music playing, both of them full after a takeaway curry. Her red hair smelled like jasmine flowers and he felt a moment of supreme happiness that he was there at all; certain that he had done the right thing in facing up to both his past and his future. *I've changed,* he'd messaged her on Facebook when he first got back in touch, his dad's words about being honest ringing in his ears. *I've thought about what you said and you were right. I was massively in denial. But I'm back in the UK and I'm dealing with everything, and trying to put a new life together for myself. Would you like to meet up?*

Thank God she'd said yes. She'd been thinking about him

too. She'd come to pick him up from Aberdeen airport and they'd had a moment of recognition – attraction, definitely – and then she'd thrown her arms around him. 'It's good to see you, Will,' she said huskily in his ear and he'd almost exploded with lust, right there in the Arrivals area.

He felt, at last, as if he had something to offer her, as if there was some substance to him, other than light-hearted charm. He'd made the decision to reapply to university and, to his surprise, the woman at the FE college his dad had put him in touch with proved to be fantastically helpful when it came to making that happen. With her assistance, he'd been able to organise meetings with a couple of different universities, Glasgow and Birmingham, both of whom had ended up offering him a place on their Physics courses for September. 'Come on, it's got to be Glasgow, surely?' Isla said on hearing about this, just as he'd hoped she would. 'We're going to give this a shot, right?'

His heart had stuttered a little with joy at her question. 'I would love to give me and you a shot,' he replied.

In the months before he moved up to Scotland, he had a few things to be getting on with. He'd have to return to his old textbooks, for one, in order to swot up on some of the content he'd forgotten over time, but he was looking forward to reimmersing himself in the subject. He also needed to earn some money over the summer to buffer himself through the penny-pinching student years. He had a meeting lined up next week with the bike-repair charity, plus he'd looked into the mentoring charity Leni had worked for, contacting their Glasgow office to say he'd love to get involved with the programme if possible. Life was shaping up pretty well, all in all.

'We are now approaching Pearbridge,' the automated voice announced at that moment. 'Pearbridge will be your next station stop in approximately two minutes.'

The hedgerows outside were full of flowers as the train rattled past them, the fields lush and verdant. Will stood up and heaved down his bag, feeling ready for the next chapter in his life.

Chapter Thirty-Seven

Later on, after the roast chicken had been polished off, Alice produced her contribution: a chocolate cake with three layers and white chocolate icing. It had been the first time she'd baked anything for over a year and she found herself holding her breath as her mum plunged the knife in, to *Oohs* and *Aahs*. Before now, she'd always taken pride in baking birthday cakes for family and friends, but she'd felt so terrible, not making the effort for Leni last May, she'd fallen out of love with the idea for a while. This was her way of redeeming herself for the supermarket brownies the year before. She just wished her sister could have had a slice too.

'Amazing, Alice,' her mum said warmly, licking chocolate off her fingers.

'That is *good*,' agreed Will, going in for a second piece.

'A triumph,' Tony declared, scraping up the last crumbs with his fork.

The four of them were out in the garden, drinking champagne and swapping old memories. Ray had made a tactful exit, claiming he needed to sort out some paperwork, but really, Alice knew it was so that the McKenzies could fully abandon themselves to the retelling of old family tales, with all the in-jokes, bad impressions and other shortcuts enjoyed by people who'd been there.

Alice had been dreading this day, there were no two ways about it. She'd woken that morning, tried (and failed) to interest Hamish in a loving embrace – he was still having none of it – before leafing through an album of Leni photos, smiling one moment and feeling like bursting into tears the next. 'I wish you were here,' she murmured to different versions of her sister – in a gold bikini and aviator shades on a beach in Ibiza; looking effortlessly glamorous in front of the Eiffel Tower in a trench coat and red lipstick; laughing her head off at someone's house party in a glittering silver dress with a short-lived bleached-hair experiment. 'I bloody wish you were here, mate.'

Her phone had been pinging away – her dad and Will, saying they were looking forward to seeing her later. Belinda, sounding frazzled, asking her to bring various bits and bobs – a tablecloth, some champagne glasses – because hers were still packed up in boxes somewhere, as well as a further message about driving carefully and checking her tyres (old habits died hard). There had also been a couple of messages from her friends – Celeste saying, *Hope it all goes well today. Thinking of you*, and Lou saying, *Have a good day. Let's have a pint after dance class next week and you can tell us all about it*. She'd added a second message: *Just like real dancers do, I bet*, with several pint glass emojis and a laughing face.

Alice smiled because, despite her earlier doubts, she had

come to enjoy her friends' monthly challenges. After some drizzly netball sessions in March, they'd tried aqua aerobics in April (hilarious) and now they were learning street dance at a studio in King's Cross. It was so hard! And made her feel so uncoordinated and unfit! But thankfully Lou was even more uncoordinated than she was, and so far, every week they'd ended up limp with breathless giggles at the back of the class. The three of them were off to Palma for a long weekend at the end of the month and Lou was already suggesting they bust out their new moves in the clubs there. Alice knew for a fact it would take *mucha cerveza* for her to be persuaded to join in, but stranger things had happened, after all. Sometimes you had to say yes and sod the consequences, right?

As she lay in bed, not sure she quite wanted the day to start yet, Alice's eye fell on the mosaic now taking pride of place on the wall opposite. Last Saturday, she had returned to Walthamstow to pick up the piece she'd commissioned, an image of a peacock (what else?), made from the broken shards of Leni's crockery set. The plates were unrecognisable in their new form: teal and green and purple pieces nestling alongside one another to create the bird's gleaming body, its tail, its crown, all held in place with cement. Alice had hugged the mosaic artist, in awe of what she'd created. 'It's perfect,' she said, gently stroking the dazzling surface. 'Absolutely perfect.'

It had made what was always going to be a tough week more bearable, the spur to get her out of bed that morning, showered, dressed and eventually on to the motorway, putting on the radio and smiling to hear an old Pixies song playing, one of Leni's favourite bands. Having arrived at her mum's, she'd found the others already there: Belinda chopping mint from the garden to sprinkle over the buttered new potatoes. Her dad, dazed and a little crumpled-looking where he'd just had an impromptu nap. Will, full of tales from his Scottish trip and walking tall. 'Will's in *lurrrvvve*,' Alice teased him, because embarrassing your little brother was never not fun.

To her surprise, their get-together had so far been a thoroughly jolly occasion. For long periods of the lunch, Leni barely got a look-in as they caught up on each other's news. Tony proudly showed everyone the latest pictures of Amelia (did he realise that he'd forgotten to shave that morning though, Alice wondered, hiding a smile), while Ray provided cheerful updates on how things were going with his son and daughter (swimmingly, in a word). Will talked enthusiastically about his university plans ('Finally!' cried Belinda) and what a great time he'd had in Aberdeen with Isla ('Finally!' echoed Alice with a grin). As for Alice herself, she had plenty of her own good news to share.

The first thing was that she already felt as if she had proved her worth in her new extracurricular role at Sage and Golding. Having officially taken over responsibility for the company's social media output, she had suggested a strategy based around the slogan *We get you. We've got you,* cleverly showing how the company both understood and looked after a broad range of people. The accompanying visuals were humorous and deliberately diverse, carefully avoiding stereotypes. The focus groups had loved them and now that the campaign was under way, there had been a noticeable uptick in engagement online, with the stats showing that enquiries from new customers had similarly risen. *We get you, we've got you – you've got this!* Emma had emailed her jokily. *We're all delighted, Alice.*

With her maternity cover contract due to end in another six weeks, she'd been busily networking with other possible clients, as well as contacting a few familiar faces at companies she knew from her ReImagine days. She had a number of meetings in the pipeline thanks to further intel from her friend Edie, too. 'I don't want to tempt fate,' she said now, swiftly touching the wooden table as she spoke, 'but it's going pretty well. I'm excited!'

Things were going pretty well with Jacob, too, she thought, her eye falling on a cabbage-white butterfly touring her mum's garden, its papery wings translucent in the sun. Since the peacock day in Holland Park, they'd gone on to spend more and more time together, ostensibly for Flying Beauties nostalgia and chat, until it dawned on her, one Saturday lunchtime in a Brick Lane café, that they hadn't so much as mentioned Leni's name, and that, actually, this had become something more than a mere nostalgia trip. They'd gone out for dinner in all of Leni's favourite places by now, and made a few new favourites of their own. He'd taken her to the climbing centre he went to (exhilarating!); they'd hired a boat on the Serpentine one sunny April afternoon; they'd taken a one-day wine-tasting course together and got hilariously sozzled. Best of all, they'd talked and talked, about the big stuff and the small stuff: life, friends, dreams, love, the latest trashy TV show they were both obsessed with.

She loved seeing him, she loved having him back in her life. Her mum was totally right: he'd always been number one in terms of the best boyfriend she'd ever had, and he'd grown up into this lovely, funny, clever, kind man. A little bit uncool with his dad coat and crumpled shirts, but after all the shallow, vain boys she'd dated since him, this could only be a good thing. *Transparent as a piece of cling film*, he'd joked to her on the way to Holland Park, but thank goodness for that, after years of faking and posturing in other relationships. She'd take Sincere over Cool, any day.

All of these feelings had rushed up inside her that day in Brick Lane, as they ate lunch in an outdoor café. 'Jacob,' she said, interrupting him because she couldn't wait a second longer, not even for him to finish his sentence. She was done with passivity, after all. 'Are you feeling this too? Me and you, I mean. I'm not imagining it, am I? We ...' Then she broke off, unsure how to say the words. All she could think about was his lovely expressive mouth and how much she wanted to kiss him. So then she gave up on words entirely and, instead, impulsively leaned forward to do just that.

'Oh,' he mumbled in surprise as her lips landed on his. Then they drew apart, looked at one another wordlessly and mutually went in for another. *'Oh,'* he repeated afterwards. 'Where did that come from? Was the anecdote about my boss *that* erotic, or ...?'

'Sorry,' she said, giddy at her own daring. She had forgotten what a good kisser he was. How they had kissed for hours on end as teenagers, until their lips became swollen. 'I suddenly felt like I couldn't contain myself any more. I felt compelled to pounce on you. Was that – is that – okay?'

He moved a tomato-shaped ketchup bottle out of the way

so that he could take her hand across the table. 'Is it *okay*?' he repeated. 'I've wanted that to happen since approximately Christmas Eve twelve years ago when you dumped me. Yes, it's okay, Alice. It's better than okay. It's . . .' He looked overcome for a moment. 'It's good.'

'What do you mean, you've wanted that to happen? You didn't have to wait!' She laughed. 'Newsflash: you could have done something about it yourself.'

He gave her the side-eye. 'Yeah, like that's not the ultimate dick move: take advantage of a grieving woman,' he scoffed. 'Although . . .' He screwed up his face. 'Well, okay, there were times when I nearly *did* do that, if I'm honest,' he admitted with a laugh. 'It's been killing me, Alice. Getting to know you second time around . . . hand on my heart, I've been quietly falling in love with you all over again. Maybe even more than before. Seeing you is always the best bit of my week. I just . . . love being with you. In fact, I knew, right from the sixth-form Christmas disco, that you were something special.' He smiled at her, eyes soulful. 'Can we give it another go, do you think? You and me, the star-crossed lovers beneath the glitterball?'

'Oh, Jay,' she said, overwhelmed by his words. *Something special.* She had spent so many months last year feeling as if life had lost its gloss, and as if she had too; free-falling through the darkness all alone. For someone as good and true as he was to be saying these things, to see her as special, made her glow inside with such unalloyed pleasure. 'I love being with you too. And even though we don't have a glitterball right now, I'm saying a million per cent yes, let's absolutely give it another go.' It was almost impossible to manage her feelings any more;

they were swelling inside her, overflowing. She couldn't stop smiling. 'I never thought I'd feel happy again,' she blurted out. Losing Leni had been like having all the light blotted out from her life, as if the sun would never shine again. Somehow her friends and family – and Jacob – had brought her out of the shadows. 'But you make me happy,' she told him.

They kissed some more, their lunches growing colder by the second, and she felt her whole body quickening towards him, the enchanted princess waking from a spell. She leaned her head against his shoulder, then smiled to herself. 'Hey, you know who's going to be really delighted about this, don't you?'

'Well, *I'm* feeling pretty delighted . . .'

'My mum! Because you've always been the OG boyfriend, according to her; the greatest of all time. She will be *buzzing* when I tell her.'

He laughed. 'Oh God, mine too. She was so excited about us getting back in touch. Every time I've spoken to her on the phone since February, it's been her first question – *And how's that lovely Alice doing?* – like it's some kind of soap opera she's following.'

'We should send them selfies of us snogging, it'll blow their minds,' Alice giggled. And then they were grinning at one another and kissing again, lunches stone cold and congealing by now, but who cared? She was here with her first love, the best of all men, certain that he was the real deal. 'Oh wow,' she said, as something occurred to her. 'Does this mean I get to meet your little boy?'

'Of course!' he said. 'You'll love him. And if you swot up on your dinosaur knowledge beforehand, there's a strong chance it'll be mutual.' He quirked an eyebrow. 'The big question is, do I get to meet Hamish?'

She burst out laughing. 'I'm afraid you'll have to lower your expectations on a warm welcome, but yes, you definitely get to meet him. It's meeting my friends you *really* have to worry about. Spoiler alert: they're already pumped and dying to grill you.'

Since then, Alice had met Max (adorable) and managed to win him over, drawing him a comic strip featuring his dinosaurs ('My daddy can't draw *anything*,' he'd said, impressed), and both she and Jacob had met each other's friends. 'Oh my days, what an absolute doll,' Lou had swooned to Alice in the pub loos during a grilling break. 'And you *dumped* him?' Celeste put in, sounding appalled. 'Jesus, Alice. Imagine if you'd never found him again!'

Jacob had also become a frequent visitor to her flat and, miracle of all miracles, Hamish had not only allowed Jacob to stroke him but had also produced a rusty old purr, the first Alice had heard from him. 'Oh, right, like that, is it? Prefer him to me, do you, Hamish, you traitor?' she'd complained, rolling her eyes. Secretly she was delighted though. Surely this, above anything, was a stamp of approval – proof that Jacob was the right one?

He had certainly put some kind of spell on her, as well as on her cat, she figured now as the butterfly twirled and spun through the sweet-smelling apple blossom. Because not only was she feeling happier, as if there were spots of warmth and brightness spangled liberally through her life again, but she'd also gained a little perspective on the past year. Sorted out some unfinished business at long last. It had been Jacob who'd persuaded her that getting in touch with Callum Ferguson might be a kind of closure for her, a means of turning the page on a difficult period in her life. 'And say what?' she'd asked, initially panicked at the suggestion. 'Don't ask me to say "I forgive you" to him, because I just can't.'

He'd shrugged, replying that it was up to her, and that he wasn't going to try and put words in her mouth. 'It's only a thought,' he said, before changing the subject.

She'd mulled it over afterwards and decided that it wouldn't be any skin off her nose to say sorry for the way she'd gone after him. Imagine how shit you'd feel, accidentally knocking a woman off her bike and killing her. Imagine how it would haunt you. And then, for the woman's sister to track you down and come to your house, incoherent with distress and hell-bent on punishing you for what had happened ... She felt sorry for him, if anything. The anger had quietly trickled away and now she felt pity. It wasn't his fault. He'd suffered too.

It had taken her a while to find the right words but eventually she'd managed to compose a short letter, apologising for her behaviour. *I realise this must have been awful for you as well*, she wrote. *I'm sorry that I made it worse. I hope you're doing okay.*

She wasn't expecting to hear back from him – she was half dreading a visit from his antagonistic son, if anything *(What part of 'leave him alone' don't you understand?)* – but a week later, a response came.

Thank you, Alice, for your kind letter. I appreciate it more than I can say. I don't blame you for being angry, I would have felt exactly the same way. I'm so sorry for what happened and will have to live with it for the rest of my life. Whenever I dream about that night, I manage to swerve away just in time and she cycles on down the road. I wish with all my heart that this is what had happened.

His words had been more eloquent and moving than she could ever have anticipated. She found it comforting, the thought of Leni cycling on down the road in Callum Ferguson's dreams. Carrying on to her audition, singing the words under her breath as she pedalled ... Alice sat a little straighter in her chair, remembering that this was something she'd meant to tell the others. It had felt too big a deal to drop into a phone conversation; she'd deliberately waited until they were here together. This was the moment. 'Oh! By the way,' she said to them. 'I found out where Leni was going the night she died.'

She explained how Will had made the connection with the mysterious 'T' in Leni's diary being her trampolining class, when it had been there in plain sight on the memorial page the whole time.

'And so I messaged this Shanice woman and asked if I could meet her, because it was the first I'd heard of any trampolining – did you know Leni had enrolled on a course?' Her parents shook their heads blankly. 'Anyway, Shanice said, sure, come over.'

Shanice was a nurse in her late thirties with two young girls, and she'd immediately invited Alice round on hearing who she was. Making Alice tea in a small colourful kitchen adorned with childish drawings and paintings, she confessed she'd taken up a trampolining class because she'd loved bouncing with her daughters in their local trampoline park, and wanted to learn some skills to keep up with them.

'I felt a bit shy at first – it's ages since I've done anything like that, with people I don't know, but your sister was really lovely to me from the start, saying hello and chatting away. She said she'd been in the doldrums lately – split up with her husband or something? – but was trying to throw herself into the world again.' Shanice smiled sadly, pouring boiling water into mugs. 'That was her exact phrase – throw myself into the world again.'

The words made Alice smile in return, although she had mixed feelings to hear this second-hand, from a woman her sister had barely known. 'This is all news to me,' she admitted, her mouth twisting. 'We'd had an argument at the time. We weren't speaking much.' She accepted the mug of tea, warming her hands around it. 'I'm glad she was feeling on the up though.'

'Oh, she was. And she loved trampolining, so much. She used to say, *I've always wanted to fly and this is the closest I've ever got to it* – with this big smile on her face. Real euphoria, you know.'

Alice did know. She could easily imagine her sister leaping for joy on the trampoline, just as she'd leaped off their grandma's old bunk bed all those years before, her face alight with the thrill. *I think I really did fly a bit just then. Did you see?*

'Was there anything else? Was she planning other ways to "throw herself back into the world"?' she asked, suddenly greedy for every one of this woman's memories, however banal. Her mind jumped to the list of ideas Leni had written

in the back of her diary. *Paint! Fall in love! Make a new friend!*
She'd done the last one, at least, Alice thought to herself.

Shanice's face fell. 'Well ... Yes. There was something,'
she said. 'I mentioned singing in a choir and she was really
interested – said how happy singing made her and what a
lovely thing to do. So I suggested she audition to join us.'
Now it was her turn to drop her gaze. 'Alice ... I hate to
say this, but I think that she died coming to the audition
that night. Because I'd arranged to see her there and she
never showed up.'

The air seemed to leave Alice's lungs for a second. 'She
died ... on her way to the audition, you think?' And then she
remembered the Cherry House listing, how there had been a
Thursday evening choir. A for Audition – of course. 'Was this
at Cherry House, by any chance?'

Shanice nodded miserably. 'Yes. The choir leader said she'd
hear Leni and a couple of other try-outs before the main session, only Leni never came.' Her eyes clouded. 'We'd chatted
the day before – she said she'd been practising her audition
song all week. She'd picked the song from *La La Land* – it's
actually called "Audition", the one Emma Stone sings at the
end? And that evening, she texted me saying she was excited
about seeing me later, only ...' Her words trailed away. 'Afterwards, when I saw the news on Facebook, I couldn't help
feeling it was my fault. I shouldn't have suggested—'

'No!' said Alice immediately. 'No, Shanice. You mustn't
think that. Not for a minute.'

'She would have been alive if it wasn't for me though,
wouldn't she? She would still be coming trampolining every

week, and getting on with being your sister and everyone's friend, and—'

'You weren't to know! How could you possibly have known?' Alice could see how distraught the other woman looked; clearly this had been preying on her mind. She seized Shanice's hands. 'Please. Please don't feel bad, at all. You did a really nice thing, inviting her along. A lovely thing. And actually—' Her mind filled with an image of Leni cycling along, no doubt mentally giving it her best Emma Stone in her head, chords rising, blissfully unaware of the traffic around her. 'It's still awful but I'm glad at least that she was singing.' Emotions rose inside her. 'That she was happy.'

'She was so happy and excited,' Shanice said. There was a pause and then she added, 'I thought you must know about this, otherwise I'd have got in touch before. She said she was going to call you that night, you see. She said, *my sister's like Dutch courage in human form.* I remember thinking how lucky the two of you were to have each other.'

Alice had to swallow down the lump in her throat. 'She did call me. I never answered,' she replied, her voice barely more than a croak. How she loved that Leni had said that about her – *Dutch courage in human form* – but oh, how she wished she could have picked up the call, so that Leni could have excitedly told her about the audition. Knowing her sister, she'd have asked if she could practise her song down the phone for good measure. What Alice would give to go back in time and answer the phone, to hear her sing! 'I didn't give her any Dutch courage,' she added, feeling hollow inside.

Now it was Shanice who was squeezing Alice's hands. 'She

loved you,' she said simply. 'Focus on that. She loved you, she was happy, she was singing. And the end, when it came, would have been fast. She wouldn't have felt a moment's pain.'

'Oh my goodness,' Belinda said, putting a hand to her chest as Alice finished telling them. 'I like to think she was happy that day. I can't believe how nice that is to hear.'

They all had a wobbly few moments thinking about Leni singing on her bike and had to hug each other and blow their noses. Alice, for her part, had found peace in knowing, at last, Leni's last moments and her frame of mind, and since finding this out from Shanice, she'd stopped dreaming about chasing through the maze after her sister. Well, almost. She'd dreamed about the maze a few nights ago, actually, and it had started out like all of the other dreams, with Alice running and running, desperate for a glimpse of Leni, trying her best to catch her up. Until she'd rounded a corner of the maze in her dream and there she was, standing waiting, with a huge smile on her face.

Leni! Alice had cried, overjoyed. *You're here!*

I've been here all along, you dozy fart, Leni laughed, then came over and hugged Alice so tightly, Alice thought she might combust with sheer happiness. She could smell her sister's perfume, feel the solid warmth of her body, their faces pressed against each other.

I love you, she said. *I've missed you so much.*

I love you too, Leni said. *But I'm okay, you know. I'm actually really busy. And I'm happy!*

In her dream, Alice had burst out laughing – she might even have laughed out loud for real because suddenly she was awake, lying there in the darkness, and she was all alone. 'Did I just dream you?' she whispered aloud. 'Or were we together for real?' In some ways it didn't matter, because she'd had that moment regardless; she'd felt their togetherness. And it was so very Leni to be busying around in the afterlife, wasn't it? Knowing her, she'd probably already drawn up a new *Next year will be amazing!* plan for herself and was going about ticking it off, Alice had thought, smiling as she fell back to sleep.

Belinda got up now and started stacking the empty cake plates together. 'If I open another bottle of fizz, will anyone help me drink it?' she asked, and everyone agreed that it would be a good idea, even Tony, who was driving and not drinking. Alice and Will were going to stay over for the night and, as the family's collective sadness receded once more, a conviction took hold inside Alice that they were in for a really memorable evening together. It seemed that Belinda thought the same.

'This feels truly special,' she said, lifting her glass in a little salute once she'd poured everyone new drinks. 'I'm so glad you're all here. I've just been talking to Ray in the kitchen – he's going to come out and join us again in a bit – and we would like to have an ongoing family open house, on the first Sunday of every month, for a roast lunch and a get-together. You're all welcome – partners and babies too, of course,' she said, twinkling her eyes at Tony, and then at the other two. 'And Ray's family as well. Because it's important, this, isn't it? Us being together. It's so precious to me, spending time with you all. I know Leni thought so too.'

'Mum, I love that idea,' Alice said warmly. 'Thank you.'

'Obviously I'm hoping Jacob will come with you,' she said at once. 'And Will, I'm desperate to meet Isla—'

'Here we go, I knew there was an ulterior motive,' he groaned, but you could tell he was pleased all the same.

'And it goes without saying, I can't wait to get my hands on little Amelia – and to get to know Jackie properly too,' Belinda went on, which had Alice and Will exchanging surprised looks. A new matiness seemed to have sprung up between their mum and Jackie in recent weeks, and neither of them quite knew where it had come from. But some mysteries could be appreciated without being fully understood, Alice figured. 'We can be this evolving, organic family, can't we?' Belinda continued. 'McKenzies United – and the ones we love too.'

'McKenzies United,' Tony echoed, clinking his glass against hers. 'The very best team.'

'Hear hear,' Alice said, a new lump forming in her throat at the sight of her parents so amicable with one another. It felt so nice, she thought, smiling at them both and then Will. Then she reached down to the bag she'd brought with her, pulling it on to her lap. 'And in that spirit of family togetherness, I've got something for you all here. You know the memorial page up on Facebook? So many people have left lovely stories and memories of Leni there, I wanted to make a permanent record of them, for us to keep. So . . .' She dipped a hand into the bag and pulled out four white-covered books. 'I had these printed up, one each,' she said, passing them around.

It had been a labour of love, collating and typesetting the many stories, arranged in roughly biographical order, so that they began with recollections of Leni as a little girl, through teenage shenanigans, university life and onwards. Alice hadn't been able to read it all the way through herself yet without choking up – or cracking up – at one story or another, and she already knew it would be a precious object for her, for the rest of her life: a kaleidoscope featuring over a hundred bright, funny, memorable slices of her sister's life, recaptured by a host of different voices. They had known her. They had loved her. They remembered her.

Peace fell for a moment as everyone leafed through the pages, before Belinda punctured the silence with a snort.

'Oh goodness.' She had her hand to her mouth. 'I've just read the Easter egg story. I'd forgotten all about that.'

'Oh, from Liam-next-door?' Alice sniggered. 'I love that one.'

Tony and Will were also flicking through their copies. 'The driving test story, Christ, how come this is the first I've heard about it?' Tony said, looking appalled. 'How did she get away with that? She could have been arrested!'

Belinda had gone misty-eyed again. 'She was a one-off, wasn't she?'

'Some might think that's a good thing,' Will said, raising both eyebrows at the page he'd just read. 'Like that poor bloke in the ice cream van, here.' He'd seen the story before, of course, but it still brought a smile to his face. 'I mean, what the hell?'

Alice laughed because she knew exactly which driving test and which ice cream van they were referring to. A delicious giddy feeling began to unfurl in her, the pleasure of being here, with these people, on this warm May afternoon. 'What a privilege to have known her,' she said, raising her glass in the air. A second white butterfly had joined the first – sisters? she wondered tipsily – then she clinked glasses with her mum, her dad and her brother. 'How lucky we are to have had her in our lives.'

There was so much love in the garden in that moment as they chorused Leni's name and raised their glasses. Sadness and heartache and regret, yes, of course, but a great force of love too, as pure and golden as the beams of sunlight shining down on them. *We are broken crockery, glued back together*, Alice thought, her mouth full of cold, bubbling champagne. *Different and still broken, weakened and yet strong. We're together and we're all going to live happily ever after, with the best yet to come.* She, for one, was ready to break through, take a leap ... and fly.

Acknowledgements

A book is a true team effort and I'm lucky enough to have a really great team behind this one. Huge thanks to the Quercus superstars, in particular Cassie Browne, editor extraordinaire, for enthusiasm, creativity and precision red-penning – it's so brilliant to work with you! This book is a hundred times better for your input. Thanks also to Milly Reid, Kat Burdon, Bethan Ferguson, Ellie Nightingale, Dave Murphy and the entire sales team. Take a bow, Micaela Alcaino, for your artistic cover wizardry and thanks to everyone in design and production for turning my pages of words into another truly beautiful book. Sharona Selby deserves a medal for pin-sharp proofreading and attention to detail.

Many thanks as ever to the David Higham dream team – first and foremost Lizzy Kremer, the best in the business, plus Kay Begum, Maddalena Cavaciuti, Emma Jamison, Margaux Vialleron, Alice Howe, Johanna Clarke, Sam Norman, Ilaria Albani and Imogen Bovill. Thanks also to my foreign publishers around the world for all your fantastic work.

I'm immensely grateful to Amy Stobie and Emilie Hawes

from Agency UK in Bath – thank you both so much for brainstorming ideas with me around Alice's storyline and for giving me your time, imagination and marketing expertise. I loved talking to you both and hope I've done your advice justice (obviously any mistakes are entirely mine).

Lots of love to my author friends, for always brightening up my day with your humour, kindness and generosity – especially Ronnie, Milly, Harriet, Cally, Mimi, Jo, Rachel, Emma and Jill. Thanks also to Hayley, Kate, Fran, Cath and Cath for friendship and awesomeness.

Thank you to the booksellers and festivals who have supported me this year, and the readers who have got in touch with kind messages about my books or left lovely reviews. Your words always give me such a boost and are very much appreciated (even if I am hopeless at replying promptly – apologies).

Finally, last but never least, my wonderful family – Martin, Hannah, Tom and Holly, as well as my mum and dad, Phil, Ellie, Fiona, Ian and Julian. I am so very lucky to have you all.

Discover more from *Sunday Times* bestselling author

Lucy Diamond

Visit www.lucydiamond.co.uk for:

About Lucy

★

FAQs for Aspiring Writers

★

And to contact Lucy

To sign up to Lucy's newsletter, scan the QR code here:

Follow Lucy on social media:

@LDiamondAuthor

@LucyDiamondAuthor

@lucydiamondwrites